PRAIRIE PREACHER SERIES

www.PJHoge.com

BUCK FIFTY

Thirteenth in the Prairie Preacher series

P J HOGE

iUniverse, Inc.
Bloomington

Buck Fifty
Thirteenth in the Prairie Preacher series

iUniverse books may be ordered through booksellers or by contacting:

iUniverse
1663 Liberty Drive
Bloomington, IN 47403
www.iuniverse.com
1-800-Authors (1-800-288-4677)

ISBN: 978-1-4759-7598-7 (sc)
ISBN: 978-1-4759-7597-0 (ebk)

Library of Congress Control Number: 2013902503

Printed in the United States of America

iUniverse rev. date: 02/11/2013

For Jered and Cade

Special thanks to Mike H.
Thanks also to Michael, Randi and Tado

September 1963

Spaulding, California—

Thursday evening, after receiving reports from several citizens that a large gathering of bikers had converged on a local bar, the police arrested twenty-three members of Satan's Horde Motorcycle Club in an incident outside the small town of Spaulding.

They were drunk and disorderly, breaking up most of the barroom. The police swept in when some of the bikers abducted an employee, pulling her out the back door. There, several members assaulted, raped and beat her to death.

Charges of murder and rape are considered against five men. However, all of the men were charged with crimes varying from aiding and abetting, disorderly conduct, possession of controlled substances, and resisting arrest to assault, rape and murder. Many have previous felony arrests. Arraignments are pending and court dates will be set. Meanwhile, all men are detained in the county jail.

State Police are assisting the local police due to concerns of the presence of four hundred members in affiliated chapters of the outlaw group in the area.

The victim remains unidentified at this time, pending notification of the family.

- 1 -

APRIL, 1971

The seven-year old boy frowned as he put his hand under the hen and felt around for some eggs. Even after another check, he found none. His frown deepened as he moved the hen out of the nest, stood on his tiptoes and studied the nest. "What did you do with the eggs?"

He checked the nest to see if there were broken ones in it. There was no sign of any eggs. He usually got about eight to ten eggs from each nest. The others were just like normal, but this one was completely empty. He narrowed his eyes at the hen, that was now trying to get back into the nest, and said, "Are you being a nest hog? I'm gonna talk to Mister about this."

He finished feeding the chickens and while doing so, checked the coop and the fence around it. Everything seemed okay. There were no holes dug under the fence or signs of an owl swooping in from top. The little guy took his basket of eggs back to the barn where the rest of the family was finishing the milking.

CJ Grey Hawk had only been promoted to Chicken Man a few months earlier. In January, his parents died in a car accident not far from his South Dakota home, leaving him and his siblings orphaned. They had an older stepbrother, Jackson Fielding, who was living with a family in North Dakota while recuperating from his war injuries. Jackson was staying with the Schroeder family because he and Andy Schroeder had become best friends in Vietnam. When Jackson's mother and CJ's father were killed, Jackson felt responsible for his 'Steps', as he called his step-father's children.

The Schroeders took Jackson down to Pine Ridge Sioux Reservation for the funeral and brought all five of the Grey Hawk children home with them as their foster children. Now they all lived on a big farm near Merton, in central North Dakota.

CJ met a neighbor kid, the minister's son, Charlie Ellison, and they became best buddies. Charlie had been Elton Schroeder's Chicken Man, but when Elton also ordered turkey chicks this year, Charlie was promoted to Turkey Man. CJ was trained to be the Chicken Man. He would care for the two hundred laying hens and three hundred baby chicks.

CJ was very worried now because he hadn't been Chicken Man very long. He made $1.50 a month for his work as Chicken Man. He and Charlie were saving up for a real airplane, but if he lost his job . . . well, he might not get his plane. He heard they cost a lot of money.

Besides, he wanted to show Mister and Missus (the names the kids called Elton and Nora Schroeder) that he was that R-word. It was something about being careful. These folks talked different from his mom and dad. They had rules all over the place, but they were fun, too. Mostly though, things were good. They always had enough food to eat and the house was warm. Since he had been there those four months, the Schroeders had never traded away his clothes. CJ missed his parents, but he thought this was a pretty good family.

On the way back to the barn, CJ remembered that he also needed a buck-fifty for the rabbits. The Schroeder's grown son, Kevin, lived nearby and came over to help milk twice a day. He had promised Charlie and him they would go into the rabbit business together. He would help them because they didn't know anything about rabbits. Kevin read them books about breeding rabbits and building the cages. They got an old shed and fixed it up to put the cages inside to protect them. The boys helped Kevin order them and they were supposed to come the next week. Each boy was to put in $1.50 to help pay for them. CJ had counted on his Chicken Man money for that.

He and Charlie also worked across the road for Mr. Kincaid, taking care of his three hundred ducks. Kincaid paid them each $1.50 a month for that. His duck money had to go for savings, which the Schroeders insisted on, for church (or helping someone) and for his fun money.

His bottom lip was hanging down to his shoe tops by the time he got back to the barn. Elton came up behind him from feeding the pigs, "What's troubling you, CJ? Need to talk?"

"Mister, I have a chicken problem." CJ worried. "You said I should talk to you and we could put our heads together, but I don't want you to be mad."

Elton set down the pails he was carrying and squatted down by the boy, "Don't see why I'd be mad. You came to me as soon as there was a problem, right? That is very responsible."

"That's the word!" CJ grinned, "I knew it was an R-word."

"So, let me set the pails inside and we can find a place to sit on the wood pile and hash it over, okay?"

"I'll put the eggs inside, too."

"Good thinking."

A few minutes later the young boy and the sixty-five year old man were sitting on the wood pile. "Okay, what's the problem?"

"When I gathered the eggs today, one nest was all empty. Not a single egg in it! There are always about six or ten eggs in each nest. I don't know if one hen was a nest hog, or if a skunk stole the eggs. I looked all over and couldn't find broken shells, tracks or nothing."

"Hm," Elton rubbed his chin, "Was the gate and door closed soundly?"

"I don't know if it made noise, but they were shut like always."

Elton's blue eyes twinkled, "Soundly means safely."

"Yup, they were shut good and safe."

"Were there more eggs in the other nests?"

"No, sir."

"Did it smell like skunk or weasel?"

"Nope."

"Did you look in the nest to see if there was anything strange?"

"Yup. It looked the same."

"Were there chickens missing, or were they all churned up?"

"No, just like always."

"Well," he put his arm around the boy, "I don't think it was anything you did. If there was no sign of animals or the door wasn't open, it could have been just a weird thing that happened. Why don't you go clean out the nest and put new straw in it? That way if there was something peculiar in the straw, it will be changed. Okay? Keep an eye on it. We'll figure out what's going on. It seems to be a real mystery."

"Mister, are you going to fire me?"

"No. Things happen even if you do a good job. Let me know if there is anything amiss. That's all I can think of."

CJ hugged the slight man with salt and pepper hair, "You're a pretty good guy."

Elton chuckled, "You aren't so bad yourself! Should we go help those lunkheads clean the barn?"

CJ giggled, "I guess we better."

Inside, the group let the animals out and then cleaned the barn. Clarissa, CJ's five-year old sister, was all wound up. "I can't wait to go to the big airport today, Mister! I get to see Diane and give Matt a big hug. I'm so glad we didn't have to put Mr. Matt in the ground."

"Me, too," Elton grinned. "I'm glad the doctors were able to get him well."

"That was nasty business out there. I have to admit, I used to wonder how bad Diane's mom could be. Guess we all found out, almost too well!" twenty-seven year old Kevin said. "So, we're taking two cars to pick them up?"

"Darrell is taking his car and Clarence is riding with him. I've missed our Clarence, but it was good he was off on Easter break to help Darrell with the calving while Matt was gone."

"Okay, I'll take my car, too. If all the kids come, we'll need a car for the kids!"

"I know," Elton nodded, "But they've never met anyone at the airport before."

"Are they all coming?"

"I am, Mister!" Clarissa patted her chest. "I just gotta because Diane and I are the most like sisters of everybody! She said she is bringing me the mostest, bestest surprise ever! I know she just wants to see me first thing!"

The auburn-haired man chuckled, "Yes, Clarissa. We know!"

The little girl quit pitching hay and stared at the tall, lanky fellow. She almost frowned, but it was sort of a pout. Kevin knelt down by her, "What's the problem, honey?"

"I don't know if you were making fun at me."

"I'm sorry, Clarissa," Kevin put his arm around her. "I didn't mean to hurt your feelings. I was only teasing. I love you just the bubbly way you are!"

"I don't have bubbles!"

"Not real ones, but you bubble happiness. I love that."

CJ crossed his eyes, "Clarissa, don't be a sooky calf! Kevin likes you good enough; but if you don't put clean straw in that gutter, I'll whack you."

"No," Elton intervened, "We don't whack each other."

CJ grimaced, "I'm sorry."

"Don't tell me you're sorry. Tell Clarissa."

"I'm sorry Clarissa, but you still better get done with the straw because Missus was making blueberry pancakes for breakfast and I'm hungry."

By noon, the family was loading into the cars. Kevin asked who wanted to ride with him and CJ grabbed his hand immediately. "I want to talk about our rabbits."

Clarissa frowned, "I was going to ride with him because I'm over being mad about him funning me. Now I won't get to."

"You still can," Kevin said, "I have room for both of you, but you have to behave. No squabbling! Hear?"

"Yes, sir," they answered, and raced out to his car.

Elton shrugged to Nora, "Guess I know where I stand! Nobody's riding with me."

Then they heard a whimper and looked down. There was three-year old Claudia Grey Hawk, nicknamed Kitten, watching the whole thing. She had pulled her coat down and was dragging it along the floor. Nearly deaf, Kitten hardly talked. She was just getting used to wearing hearing aids and beginning to develop verbal skills.

Elton smiled and held his hands out to her, "You want to come with me?"

Kitten held her arms up, "Me, too."

"Of course," Elton hugged her. "Let's get your arms in the coat though and then we can go get Matt and Diane."

"Bye, bye."

Nora made a pretend sad face, "Now, I'm alone."

Kitten gave her a dead serious expression, "Pockets."

Nora hugged her and smiled, "That's right. I'll be here with High Pockets."

High Pockets, Clancy, was the youngest of the Grey Hawks. He was twenty-months old and might have loved the airport, but not the hour ride each way.

-2-

In Kevin's car, the kids discussed the pending arrival of the rabbits and the mystery of the missing eggs for at least twenty minutes. Suddenly, Clarissa started clapping her hands and squealing. "I know! I know! I puzzled out the egg mystery! I am the smartest girl in the whole wide world!"

"When you squealed like that I darned near drove off the road! Chill out." Kevin chuckled, "Tell us how you solved the mystery."

The little girl calmed down, according to Clarissa standards. "See, I was thinking about the Easter bunny. He came to our house, remember? He left those pretty eggs all over the place? I thinked—bunnies don't lay eggs, so I couldn't figure out where he got them. I know! He took them from CJ's chickens!"

"Oh," Kevin nodded. "I guess that could happen, but the eggs weren't missing before last night. Easter was over by then."

Clarissa looked at him as if he was the stupidest person on the planet, "You know, Kevin, he has to get them early so he has time to paint them, make letters on them and stuff! That takes a lot of time if you don't have hands."

Kevin laughed, "You have a point there. It would be hard to hold a paintbrush."

"He uses his tail. Don't you know nothin'?" She rolled her eyes.

"I guess not."

"How did he get the coop door open?" CJ scowled at her incredulously, "It wasn't him."

"He just hopped right over it! You forgot, he's magic," Clarissa folded her arms. "You're just huffy because I thinked of the mystery first."

"Yah, that must be it," CJ crossed his eyes at her.

"Kevin," Clarissa whined. "Could you whop him for me? He is being all mean about it."

"No, I have to drive. I can't be whopping anyone."

"Okay, I'll do it for you," Clarissa readily volunteered.

"No. He doesn't need whopping. Let's talk about something else. Okay?"

Her eyes enlarged with expectation, "What're we going to talk about?"

"Oh, I don't know," Kevin mumbled, beginning to feel a great pressure in his chest. "So, are you kids ready for the baptism on Sunday?"

"Missus said that baby Holly is getting backertised the same day, huh?" Clarissa asked. "She said that your big brother is going to be her Godguy."

"Yes, my brother Keith and his wife, Darlene. You know them. They live in Bismarck. Zach stays at their house when he is on call."

"Yah," CJ nodded. "Keith is our big stepbrother too, right?"

"I knew he is Mr. Kevin's brother. That's why!" Clarissa stated. "So I knowed about it before you did."

"Did not!"

"That he is." Kev smiled. "Do you guys argue about everything?"

CJ shook his head no, "Only the stuff we talk about."

Kevin laughed. "You guys kill me!"

"No, but somebody almost killed Mr. Matt and then we would've had to put him in the ground. We don't like that," Clarissa said.

"No, we don't," CJ agreed.

"Wow! You guys finally agree on something."

"That's because Clarence and I had to explain it to her," CJ stated.

"Did not!" Clarissa snapped. "I knew about it since I was a borned baby!"

"Okay, you two! Knock it off," Kevin groaned.

A little later, they were all at the airport. Clarence and Darrell had arrived just as Elton and Kitten were walking in. Darrell, their longtime friend and neighbor, held the door open for them as they entered the airport.

On the runway side of the building were huge windows. The kids found places to stand in front of them. They were full of questions about everything they saw. At one point, Kev asked his Dad, "Do all little kids ask so many questions?"

Elton grinned, "Yup. Just wait until Holly starts talking! She is only four months old now, so she'll have stored up a pile of questions before she can talk."

"Yea gads," Kev said. "There is more to this kid business than I thought."

Elton clapped him on the back, "You ain't seen nothing yet!"

The plane landed with great cheers from the Grey Hawk kids and they were all excited, even Clarence who never reacted much. He was eight and looked the spitting image of CJ, except he was always serious and worried. CJ decided to leave him to it. He was too busy having fun.

When the passengers began descending the steps, the excitement was almost too much for Claudia who had started clapping when the plane made its approach and continued until she saw Ian and Ruthie deplane. Then she put her arms around Elton's neck and whimpered until they all came in the terminal.

There were hugs all around and everyone was talking at once. It was great to have them home again. Then they gathered their bags and headed out of town for Merton. Ian, known also as Harrington, and his wife, Ruthie, rode with Darrell and Clarence. Clarence was anxious to hear about the big fish Harrington caught on the ocean. Mo and Carl Kincaid rode back with Elton and Claudia. Claudia sat in the backseat with Mo and fell asleep before they left the Bismarck city limits.

"What did you do to this little one?" Mo asked as the little girl curled up on Mo's lap.

"She was so excited and clapped for fifteen minutes solid. I think she wore herself out." Elton smiled. "Besides, it is her naptime. I hope you had some good times on your trip. It was a bearcat what happened to Matt. Sounds like a bad scene."

"That old barracuda," Mo snapped. "She wanted to get rid of her children's fiancées!"

Carl turned to Elton, "Loretta did herself no good service this time."

Elton shook his head incredulously, "What possessed her?"

Mo answered, "All the demons ever created!"

"Now Mo, settle down." Carl said, "The rest of us had our hands full trying to keep our Mighty Mo under wraps. She was eating the grapes off the wallpaper, I tell you!"

"Nobody tries to kill one of my kids," Maureen Harrington Kincaid pronounced, "Without having to deal with me!"

Elton smiled at her through the rearview mirror, "I don't blame you. She really intended to kill him, huh?"

The retired FBI agent nodded, "She admitted it. She was upset because the doctors were able to save him! She's a piece of work. I have to admit, I wondered sometimes if Diane wasn't exaggerating about her mom. Now

I wonder how she survived her childhood at all! People aren't very nice sometimes."

"No, they sure aren't."

"So, any gossip in the neighborhood since we've been gone?" Carl asked.

"Not much you don't know about. Of course, Jeff took Sister Abigail out to Montana because her mother was dying. They should be back Friday. She saw her before she passed away. She told Father Vicaro it was worthwhile trip. I guess she and Jeff got along real well."

"Jeff is a good kid. I can't imagine what that Bishop in Boston was thinking when he pushed Jeff and Matt to leave the priesthood."

"Me either," Elton agreed. "Darrell got that plowing done you wanted in front of the house. What are you going to plant in there? Certainly that isn't your garden, is it?"

"No," Carl laughed. "And there's no need for you to be nosy about it. You'll find out soon enough."

"Sometimes you scare me half to death." Elton chuckled. "So, other than that, the kids have no school all week. Guess the teachers go back tomorrow, huh?"

"Yah, meetings or something." Carl explained. "I see there is still a bit of snow around."

"Every time it thaws off, it snows a little just to let us know that winter isn't finished with us yet. This is good. It gets some moisture in the ground but not too fast. The farmers can get in the fields without getting stuck." Elton said. "And let's see, Suzy's pregnancy is coming along fine. Even though Zach is a pediatrician, he is as uptight about their baby as any other father."

"Guess it makes a difference if it's your own." Carl agreed. "I was more objective about attempted murder while with the FBI than when it was our Matt."

"Yah, huh? Unbelievable that woman would do that."

"Talking about family, you and Byron taking the veterans for their checkups in Fargo this week?"

"Yes. We leave tomorrow morning. Hopefully, the VA can get to work on Jackson's artificial foot. He has come a long ways since Pine Ridge and is definitely ready."

"Getting that infection healed up really made a difference. All those little Grey Hawks are doing well, don't you think?"

"It makes me feel so good. Those kids are developing their own personalities. I love to see it. Only thing I'm not too crazy about is High Pocket's wolf howl. I sure wish he would go for something quieter." Then Elton laughed, "So, when are you seeding your front patch?"

"It's just killing you not knowing, isn't it?" Carl laughed with glee, "Have you got all your farming plans set for this year?"

"Almost. I need more pasture. I rented that section of pasture to the southeast of our place. The Effan family owned it for years. They had moved to California about fifteen years ago and I rented his pasture all this time. Gus Effan died last year. I guess their family is splintered. So, the court was trying to settle everything. They had two girls and one boy. Anyway, when I contacted the attorney this winter, he said that the girls inherited the properties in California and the boy got the farmland up here. He said he'd see what he wanted to do with it. That was in November and I still haven't heard."

"Hm. Maybe he is going to farm it."

"Not likely. There are only a few ramshackle buildings barely standing and the rest of the section is pasture. They only had a small patch the size of my garden that ever saw a plow. Regardless, it looks like I have to find another pasture. I'm going to do that next week when I get back from Fargo."

"Have you ever thought about slowing down, Magpie?" Carl asked. "You know you're in your mid-sixties!"

Elton chuckled, "Oh no, Coot! You aren't going to swindle me into telling you how old I am. Nice try! I'm not the guy that plowed up half a section for a mystery field between his house and the road! Not to mention that orchard you got going. I think you are daft."

-3-

That afternoon, CJ was anxious to check the chickens. He was relieved no more eggs were missing and decided that old hen must have just been a nest hog after all. He talked it over with his comrade, Charlie. They decided to lay a trap, just in case.

First, they checked the chicken fence. It would be hard for anything to crawl under the fence because Elton had buried the wire a foot and a half below the ground. However, they worried that whatever it was would climb over the top. The two seven-year olds contemplated the situation with great gravity.

Charlie was going to be over at his Grandma and Grandpa Jessups for the rest of the week because his cousins from Texas were visiting. They were fun enough, but Charlie was much more interested in the mystery of the missing eggs. He extracted a promise from CJ to keep him informed.

The boys hit on an idea. They loosened the wires holding the fence to the top of the posts for the first foot down. They figured that if a skunk crawled up there, its weight would bend the wire down and he couldn't get over it. They would worry about other things later. They only had time to loosen the wire on the south side of the pen before Charlie had to go home. Even though it wasn't the best idea, they figured it was a start. In their hurry, they forgot to put the stepladder away. CJ made an oath that he would stay awake all night to watch and then call Charlie if they caught anything.

That night while milking cows, Diane and Clarissa noticed that Snowflake and Buttermilk hardly gave any milk. Both gave some milk, but nowhere near what they usually did. Elton and Kevin exchanged a worried glance, but never said anything to the rest of them.

On the way back to the house, CJ was walking between them. Kevin asked quietly, "What do you think, Dad? Eggs, milk? A poacher?"

"Don't know. I just can't imagine. Most folks around here know if they needed something, all they have to do is ask. Just keep an eye out. It could be nothing."

"What's a poacher?" CJ asked, taking Mister's hand.

"That is someone who steals your eggs, milks your cows, steals a chicken, pig or stuff from your garden."

"Isn't that being a crook? When we catch them, do we hang them?"

Kevin almost choked, "No. There are laws against hanging someone!"

"I saw that on the TV. This man took the other man's cows and they hanged him!" CJ pointed out.

Elton answered, "Yah, that was on TV. In real life, we call the sheriff."

"Oh." CJ walked in deep thought, "Do the poachers steal pets or kids?"

Kev reassured him, "No, they don't. Gee, Dad, why didn't the dogs bark?"

Elton raised his eyebrows, "These two? Good grief, if someone came in to steal from the gas tank; they'd probably show him the pump switch! Anyway, let's not borrow trouble. Just keep watch. We need to keep things put away, like a certain stepladder that is over by the chicken coop. What were you and Charlie doing?"

"Checking for poachers." CJ said, "I'll put it away now. Okay?"

"Good idea, son."

CJ ran about five feet and then stopped. He turned around and ran back, "Did you call me your kid?"

"Yes, I did."

"Why?"

"Cause you are."

The boy beamed and said, "Good idea, Dad."

That night, Matt was over to visit his fiancée, Diane. The talk turned to the possibility of a poacher. Matt frowned, "Have you ever had one before?"

"We woke up missing an acre of corn on the cob one year." Elton laughed. "Whoever it was must have worked like the devil to pick it all before daybreak."

"What did you do?"

"Told Sheriff Bernard about it. He said that a guy up north had the same problem with a big patch of melons. Nothing was ever found. I guess it just happens. About six years ago, Andersons had someone milk their cows one night."

"How do you milk someone's cow?" Matt asked. "I mean out in a pasture?"

"Some cows wouldn't stand still for you, but some of the older, gentle cows will. It would be nothing to get Snowflake and Buttermilk to stand still for you."

Matt grinned. "Guess being a city slicker, I would've just thought I had to steal milk from a grocery store!"

"Yea gads," Elton laughed. "I'm going to bed. We're leaving about four tomorrow morning. Jackson's appointment is at eleven."

"It will be a whirlwind around here for a while," Nora smiled as she poured some more coffee. "This weekend is all the birthdays and the barn dance! The boys will be playing."

"You mean your Uncle Bill and his band?" twenty-seven year old Diane asked.

"Yes, but don't forget, Uncle Bill said the kids could play one song. They're driving me bananas!"

"I know and I'm sorry," Diane laughed. "As their music teacher, I should've stayed to help them practice!"

"Uncle Bill came down every afternoon last week. He got them all lined up. Believe me, it is something to hear! And those boys! They wanted Katie to make shirts with their band name on them, but they couldn't decide on the name of their band!"

"Who all is in this band?" Matt asked.

"Charlie, CJ, Little Bill, Clark and Junior. Did you hear the latest?" Nora's eyes were sparkling. "It was a nightmare, but they finally worked it out! They're having two singers!"

"Really, who?"

Both Diane and Matt were curious, but Nora said she was sworn to secrecy. "The boys are still trying to think of a way to squirm out of it. Problem is Uncle Bill thought it was a good idea. You really missed something. Grandma Katherine and I were about ready to pack our suitcases and check our passports!"

"Somehow, I believe it." Matt laughed. "Did they decide on their band name?"

"Not the last I heard, and please don't ask. Katie refuses to talk to them anymore!"

Diane shook her head, "Katie has the patience of Job! Only those guys could drive her to that point."

Since Clarence was staying over at Darrell's to help with calving and kidding (when the goats had their babies), CJ didn't have to worry about keeping his brother awake all night. In his room, he took his flashlight and leaned up on the windowsill to keep a watchful eye on the farmstead. The beam of his flashlight didn't brighten the yard, but it made him feel like he was doing something official.

In the morning, he was asleep on the floor in front of the window and his flashlight battery had gone dead. Nora woke him up, "CJ. It's morning. Did you get any sleep last night?'

"I don't know. I was going to watch out for chicken poachers, but I couldn't keep awake. I really don't want to lose my Chicken Man job. I need the buck fifty to pay Kevin for the rabbits." Then his eyes filled with horror, "Missus, do poachers take baby rabbits? Will they steal our bunnies? I need a better flashlight!"

Nora hugged him, "CJ, don't worry. I'll give you another battery for your flashlight. You can talk to Kevin about the buck fifty. I'm certain that things will work out. Okay? He is going to be here soon to do chores. Run and get dressed. You can take a nap later today. I think you're still tired."

Nora had explained the situation to Kevin before CJ got downstairs. CJ was very quiet on the way to the barn, but Clarissa had not missed any sleep and was jabbering non-stop. CJ looked at Kevin in exasperation, and Kevin just patted him on the back. This morning, all the cows gave their full amount of milk. CJ helped Kevin feed the pigs while Diane and Clarissa fed the calves. On their way back to the barn, Kevin asked CJ to sit with him a minute on the woodpile.

"CJ, I don't want you to worry about losing your Chicken Man job. Mom said you were worried that something might happen to the rabbits. Don't. We'll take every precaution. Okay?"

"What's that caution thing?"

"It means we'll be very, very careful. I promise."

"Thank you, Kevin. I was so worried. I don't want somebody to cook our baby bunnies."

Kev frowned, "Neither would I. Now, since Dad is gone to Fargo, if something comes up that worries you, call me at the shop. Okay? Either Harrington or I will be here, right away! No problem. Got it?"

"Got it."

"So, what are your plans for today?"

"Clarence and Charlie are both gone so I am the Chicken Man, Turkey Man and Duck Man! Then I am going to feed Bruno, Marty's puppy. I have a lot of stuff to do. The rest of the time, I want to go exploring."

"Where are you going to explore?"

"I don't know." CJ shrugged, "Can I take care of the chickens after breakfast this morning, so I can help you clean out the barn. The chickens won't care, will they?"

"No, not if it's right after breakfast."

"I want to check the coop in the daylight."

"Good idea."

After breakfast, he went out to the chicken pen and unhooked the latch. When he gathered eggs, one nest was empty again! He ran outside to check the five-foot tall fence. Sure enough, the wire was bent down on the backside. It looked like something big had fallen on the outside. There were marks in the snow and broken eggshells.

His heart was beating a hundred miles an hour as he ran to the house. He set the egg basket on the table. Grandpa Lloyd and Clancy were sleeping in the big rocking chair. He heard the ladies cleaning upstairs, so he'd have to take off his boots to go upstairs. He didn't think he had time to do that and follow the trail! He didn't know Charlie's grandparents phone number. Everyone else was at work. He was so excited he forgot what Kevin had told him. What could he do? He went back outside.

The Chicken Man decided to follow the tracks like that Tonto guy did on TV. He went back over to the coop and started to follow the tracks through the patches of snow on the ground. The dogs, Elmer and Rags, were running all around him and messing up the tracks, so he took them back to the barn. He'd never be able to follow the tracks with them. Then he quickly finished taking care of the baby chicks and turkeys.

He went to the house and wrote a note for Missus. "I Xploor. CJ".

Then he put a sandwich in his pocket, because he never went too far without food. He put on his stocking cap and went back to the coop. He looked it over again and found a small piece of red material stuck on one of the twists of wire poking out. He figured it was from the poacher's shirt. He put his ear on the ground like Tonto did on television, but he didn't hear any footsteps. All that happened was that he got a cold ear. CJ decided Tonto didn't live where there was snow.

15

It only took him a minute to find the trail again. He followed it down by the fence between the Schroeder place and Zach's house. The footprints followed the fence on Schroeder's side. The dead brush between the barn and the fence down by the creek made it very easy to follow the tracks. CJ crossed the creek and headed out into Mister's big pasture. After CJ got out of the ravine by the creek, most of the snow had melted making it very hard to find tracks. He was lucky though, because they followed the fence.

When he got over half a mile from the house, he found four eggs thrown in a pile. He couldn't figure out why someone would poach eggs and then throw them away! A little way further, there was someone's butt prints in the snow. Apparently, the poacher sat down to rest.

CJ decided he was a real good tracker.

By this time, CJ was out of sight of the farm, but he knew he was still in Mister's pasture. He had gone out this far to bring the cows up for milking several times and besides, he didn't cross any fences. Before long, he came to the fence on the section line to the pasture that Mister rented. He had never gone that far before, but the gate was open all the time, so he wasn't afraid.

He walked along, finding fewer tracks. Off to the east, he noticed another fence. Hanging on a fence post was a rope. He went over to it to see what was there. When he got closer, he saw a rope and a three-legged milking stool leaning against the fence post. He figured it was the poacher's for milking cows.

CJ stood there for a while deciding what to do. Should he go back and tell someone, or should he just keep going? He sure hated to walk this far for nothing. He took a deep breath and climbed through the fence. He could see tracks on the other side of the fence that headed east. CJ knew the road was not too far over that way, so he could make his way back home without getting lost.

He went over a couple small rises and came upon an old run-down farm surrounded by untrimmed trees and overgrown weeds. Nobody would be in the nearly-collapsed barn. There was an outhouse and a shed, all caving in. The roof of the house was in severe disrepair with a gaping hole in one end. There was no smoke from a fire. The paint was peeling or worn off all the dilapidated buildings. He decided it must just be an empty place. He would eat his sandwich there, before going back home. He still had to feed the ducks and Marty's dog.

He came down the slope and into the trees. There he could see that weeds and brush covered the road, so no car had driven in lately. He saw the windmill over an open well and that flowed into a rusty cattle trough. There was a little water in it, but it could have been from the snow. He wandered by the barn, but it looked too rickety to trust going inside. Then he went to the house. The little boy was about to go up the wobbly steps when he thought he heard something rummaging around inside. He froze with fear. Suddenly, he could envision himself tied up and rotating slowly over the hot fire of a barbeque pit!

He backed down the steps and went to the side of the house. He was about to take off over the slope, when curiosity got the best of him. 'Maybe it was just a gopher or something. I don't want to be a scaredy cat.'

He went around to the side window of the house and brushed through the tall Russian Thistles and weeds. He tried to peek over the decaying windowsill. It was too high for him, so he looked around for something to stand on. He moved a big rock that was near the propane tank over to the window and then stood on it to look through the filthy window.

Inside the derelict old house, he could only see one room. The door was closed to the other room; the one CJ figured was where the hole was in the roof. There was a small cot with a blanket that looked new. Next to it, on the floor was a backpack. On the table was a plate with three unbroken eggs, a bucket and half a glass of milk. The old cook stove was not lit and everything else was covered in a layer of dust, dirt and cobwebs. Then he noticed that on the table was a First Aid kit and a revolver! He had found the poacher's hideout! CJ swallowed very hard.

He hadn't thought this far ahead! Now what should he do? He couldn't knock and ask a stealer guy to please quit taking the eggs and milk. He knew it was not good to be sneaking around. The poacher could be little kid murderer.

Nobody at his farm knew where he was. They could never find him. He was a goner, for sure. His breakfast was coming back up his throat and he thought about the whistle that Mr. Kincaid had given him to whistle if there was ever trouble. First of all, nobody would hear it way out here except the bad guy and besides, he didn't have any air left. He decided to get out of there as quickly as he could.

That's when he felt a man's hand squeezing his shoulder. His eyes opened as big as full moons and his mouth came open, but nothing came out.

A man's deep voice asked gruffly, "Whatcha doin', kid?"

-4-

CJ took off as if the devil was after him. He let out a scream that would wake the dead and ran as fast as his legs could carry him. He went about fifteen yards before he fell in an old rut and twisted his ankle. He tried not to cry because Sioux Indians were very brave, but he did anyway. It hurt. Any smart Indian would cry if he twisted his ankle and was going to be shot by a poacher! He just knew it! As he tried to get up, the man came over to him. "Sit!" he ordered with his deep baritone voice.

CJ didn't know why, but he did. His ankle was already beginning to swell.

"I broke my damn arm. Grab my good one. I'll pull you up," the acerbic man demanded.

CJ wondered why this skinny, stinky man didn't just shoot him right there. The poacher wore all black leather clothes except for his torn red shirt. He had dark sunglasses, a black beard, and scraggly hair. He looked like he was sick or something, but CJ took his hand to get up.

Together, they walked into the old house. CJ didn't know if the man had that gun with him or not, but he was taking no chances. Inside, the man pointed to the chair. CJ sat. The guy felt his ankle with one hand, "Not broken. Take this and wrap your foot."

The churlish man pushed a soiled Ace bandage across the table toward him. CJ reached for it and noticed the revolver laying there. The man saw that the boy noticed the gun and grabbed it immediately. Then he stepped behind CJ, so the boy didn't know what the man did with it.

The frightened little kid took off his shoe and sock. Then he took the very old Ace bandage and tried to find the end of it. The man growled at him from the cot where he was now sitting, "Shouldn't go poking around folks' places where you aren't invited. You should be damned glad I didn't whip you."

"I am," CJ answered, trying to hold back his tears.

"Wrap your foot and get the hell out of here! Don't come back and sure as hell, keep your mouth shut I'm here!"

Then the man started to cough, a lot. At first, CJ thought it served him right for being a poacher, but the man didn't look very good. CJ started to get worried. "You okay, Mister?"

"Hell no! I broke my damned arm!"

CJ turned to look at the man, "You need a doctor."

"Get out of here!"

"I'm not done wrapping my foot."

"Hurry up and . . ." then the man fell onto the floor.

CJ stared at him, thinking the guy might be dead! He didn't know if he should stay or run away. Mister said people should help each other. Even when the man was mad at CJ, he gave him a bandage for his foot. The young boy bent down over the guy, "Mister! Mister! Wake up!"

The man groaned and CJ quickly finished wrapping his foot and put his boot back on. The man was still groaning and CJ sat down on the floor beside him. "Can you sit up, Mister? Do you want some water?"

"No water!" he almost yelled. "Milk."

CJ held the glass of room temperature milk from the table up to his lips and the guy took a swallow. He looked at CJ and almost smiled. Then he fell asleep or died. CJ didn't know which.

The little boy sure wished he had stayed home that morning. What should he do now? They probably didn't even miss him yet. CJ was about ready to leave and go home as fast as he could, when the man groaned again.

CJ picked up the poacher's head and asked in exasperated desperation, "What should I do, Mister?"

The bearded man turned to him, "Don't know."

"You hungry? Do you want my sandwich? It's in my back pocket!"

The man looked at him with sunken eyes, "Yah."

CJ tore off a bit of the squashed peanut butter sandwich and stuck it in the man's mouth. The guy chewed it. "More?"

"Yah."

It took a while, and more of the old, souring milk, but CJ helped him eat the whole sandwich. When he was done, the man said. "Good."

Then he fell asleep. CJ knew he was sleeping this time, because he could hear him breathing. The man's skin felt hot and the boy tried to make him comfortable on the floor. He rolled up the blanket and put it under his head.

CJ tried walking on his foot, but he couldn't go very far. It hurt too bad. He certainly wouldn't make it all the way back to the farm. He sat on the floor next to the man and figured he would just have to die there. That would be it. Charlie would never know that he had found the poacher and Mister would never be proud of him that he saved the farm from stealers. He cried a little bit and before long, fell asleep next to the grungy man on the floor.

CJ didn't know what time it was when he woke up, but it was still daylight. He heard voices calling in the distance. He went out onto the dilapidated porch and took out his whistle. He blew it for all he was worth. He was the happiest kid alive when he heard a whistle back. He knew that someone was coming to save him. He was so excited, he forgot about the man on the floor. The man yelled, "Get out of here! Run!"

The skinny man tried to get up but only managed to get to his cot. He plunked down on it sideways and it toppled over on top of him. He screamed in agony when the edge of the cot landed on his broken arm. He passed out again.

CJ moved the cot off his arm and never left the man's side. Scared to death that whoever was looking for him might not find him, he kept blowing that whistle for all he was worth.

The door burst open and there was Kevin. CJ ran to him and jumped into his arms. A couple minutes later, Harrington came in and then CJ heard the pickup. It was Carl. He had taken the old pickup out through the pasture to look for CJ, following Kevin and Harrington, who were on foot.

CJ told them what happened, but they didn't say much. They loaded the man into the pickup and returned to the farm. CJ held on to Kevin for dear life while they sat in the pickup bed with the bad guy.

When they got to the farmhouse, Nora called their closest neighbor right away. Zach Jeffries was a doctor and came right over to look at the man. The rest of them sat in the kitchen, waiting for him to say what they should do.

Carl Kincaid, who lived across the road, was the first one to say anything to CJ, "Glad you used the whistle, but why didn't you come get me right off? I'd have gone with you this morning."

"I never thought," CJ said. Then he started to cry, "I didn't think so pretty good."

Harrington shook his head, "No Little Man, you sure didn't. You could've been killed. Don't ever take off like that again."

"I won't. I promise." CJ said, "I followed his tracks like Tonto on TV did. I just didn't think what to do when I found him."

"I called and called for you after I found your note. I was worried that you'd do this. That's why I called everyone to come help me find you." Nora hugged him, "Carl found the chicken fence broke down, so we guessed the rest. Don't do that again! I should tan your hide!"

"Yes, Ma'am. I really figured I was a goner." Then he looked toward the guest room where the man was, "Is he going to die? He had a gun, but he didn't shoot me. He gave me a bandage for my ankle and told me to get lost."

"You were darned lucky," Harrington said. "He looks to be in worse shape than you. I think he broke his arm when he fell over the chicken fence."

"Yah," Carl agreed, "But he is sick, too. There is something wrong with him. Something is making him real sick."

"Should Kevin and I go back over to check out his place?" Harrington asked. He had been a detective in Boston, and his skills were resurfacing.

"Not until we hear from Zach. Lucky he was home this afternoon," Kevin said.

Zach came out to the kitchen. He took the cup of coffee that Nora handed him, "Our visitor has major problems. He has a broken arm and wrist. He has to go in the hospital for X rays and get them set. I can't do that here. I gave him something for pain, but I can tell you, he is a doper. I gave him enough drugs to wipe out this whole room before I could get it to help him with the pain. But he has something else underlying all that. It looks to me like he might have some sort of intestinal infection. What was he eating, CJ?"

"All the food I saw was eggs and a pail of milk on the table. I asked him if he wanted water, and he said 'no water' kinda loud. I don't think he likes it." CJ answered. "I gave him my peanut butter sandwich."

"I'm going to take him in to the hospital. Can someone come with me? I don't want him to bail out on me while I'm driving down the highway. He is very opposed to going to the doctor."

Carl raised his eyebrows, "He could be running from something. I'll go in with you, but let me call Sheriff Bernard first. Okay?"

After talking to the Sheriff, Carl said, "I'll go with Zach. Bernard would like you guys and CJ to meet him at that farm house."

They loaded the man in the station wagon and Coot and Zach headed off to Bismarck. The other three drove over to the abandoned farmhouse to meet with Sheriff Bernard.

CJ told the Sheriff everything that happened. He was very patient and asked several questions. Then he said, "Next time you get a hair-brained idea like this, call me first! You were trespassing. Know that? That's against the law!"

"But he stole our eggs and milk!"

"I know, but two wrongs don't make a right. If there is a problem, you call me! That's my job."

At the old farm, they found the man's motorcycle in the shed. It was a 1969 XLCH Harley Davidson Sportster with California plates. Bernard asked Kevin if they could take it back to keep it for a few days. No one wanted it stolen, since it was obvious the owner wouldn't be back for a day or so. It was a nice, new bike. Kevin said they would store it in Elton's garage.

Bernard went through the man's backpack. There was a copy of August Effan's will and identification, discharge papers from the Marines, and release papers from a prison in California in the name of Harold Effan. Bernard said, "Gather all this up and we will hold on to it until I check with California. His wallet says he is Harold Effan, in which case, he has every right to be here."

"Yah, the Effans that lived here had a kid named Harold. I remember him from school." Kevin asked, "Is there something around here that's clean enough to catch water in?"

"There were a couple fairly clean canning jars in that cupboard. They are dusty on the top but were stored upside down. One of them work?" Harrington asked.

"Yes. I want to get a water sample and send it in to the State Lab. That could be what made him so sick. It's an open well that hasn't been used in years."

Back at the house, Bernard called California before he called the hospital. When he hung up, he said, "Here's the deal. I called that attorney whose name was on his stuff. Guess Effan was released from prison a few weeks ago. He told his attorney that he wanted to get away from some biker gang. His attorney thought he might be in trouble with them about something that happened in prison. When this Effan guy heard he had inherited this farm, he told his attorney he wanted it, but made it clear that he didn't anyone to know where he was going."

"What was he in prison for?" Kevin asked. "If I'm not being nosy."

"He was involved in an incident where a woman was raped and beaten to death by about twenty plus of these Satan's Horde thugs. He was arrested for minor, peripheral charges; but it was a felony because he was with those who did it."

"Yikes, that's not fooling around!" Kevin made a face as the harsh realization set in, "He might have . . . I mean . . . CJ, don't ever do this again!"

CJ's eyes got big, "I'm sorry. I promise I won't."

"I'm going to call Zach and then head to Bismarck. Don't say too much about this, okay? If there are others from the gang up here looking for him, I'd rather that no one knows you have any connection with him. I also don't want the whole neighborhood turning vigilante. I'll take that water sample in, if you like. I have to talk to this biker."

"Sure, here it is." Kevin handed him the jar. "We'll only tell those who need to know. Okay?"

"Okay. Thanks. See you later and CJ, fine work. Next time, just don't do it!"

"I give you my word, sir."

As the Sheriff drove out, the schoolteachers drove in. Matt, Diane and Jeannie got out of the car, "Was that Sheriff Bernard?"

"Yes, come in. We have to keep this under wraps, but you guys need to know." The men explained the situation as they knew it and everyone agreed the fewer who knew about it, the better. "We will keep an eye out for any unsavory characters around here."

There were many phone calls late that afternoon. After much consternation on Nora's part, the decision was made that Harold Effan would come to Schroeder's to recuperate. He refused to stay in the hospital. Since he had no health insurance, the hospital didn't argue. Zach paid the bill for getting his arm set. The patient was unable to care for himself at his old farm. Zach had the lab run some tests on the water. It was deemed not fit for human consumption by the lab. It contained decaying rodent parts and several interesting bacteria, the cause of his severe intestinal problems. The well would need chemical treatment before the water was drinkable. With good care, the biker could be back on his feet in about ten days. His broken arm and wrist would not heal in ten days; but if his stomach problems were resolved, he could take care of himself.

The Sheriff talked to the warden from the California prison. He assured him that Effan was a decent prisoner and attempted to make an effort to turn his life around. Effan wasn't having much luck, since many of Satan's Horde were in the same prison. When there was a fight in prison involving one of Satan's Horde, Effan did not come to the man's aid. That brought down the wrath of the entire gang on him. According to the Club's code, every member stood up for every other member, no matter what. For Effan's own protection, he was placed in isolation most of the last while he was in prison. The warden didn't think that Satan's Horde would travel all the way out of state to make an example of someone; but common sense had little to do with anything they did.

That evening, Zach and Carl came back from the hospital with their passenger. Nora was not very happy when they helped the biker into the house. Matt, Ian, and Kevin had set up the hospital bed in the guest room again.

"Good grief," the normally gentle Nora grumbled to Katherine. "We have someone using this bed all the time! I guess I should be grateful that we have it. We have certainly used it a lot over the years."

Diminutive Grandma Katherine put her arm around Nora, "I know, but tell me again, which one of those folks are you sorry you helped?"

"I know, Katherine, but this time I'm concerned. Maybe our luck is running out."

"It has never been about luck, Nora." Grandma said firmly. "Maybe you don't like the sound of this guy compared to the others. Is it that you don't think his credentials aren't as good?"

Nora turned as if she had been doused in ice water, "You're right, Katherine. Very right. He might be trying to get a new start and we should help him."

Katherine smiled, "I think you're just worried because Elton isn't here."

Nora nodded, "I am."

"What do you think Elton would do?"

Nora sighed, "He'd have had the bed put up before the guy got to town!"

The man was barely awake when they brought him in and put him to bed. After he was settled, Zach and Carl came out to the kitchen. "Before you say another word, Nora, we wouldn't have done this if there was anything dangerous about it."

"How can you say that? He's been in prison and Lord only knows what he had to do with that poor woman's murder! He is a drug addict! How can you tell me that it isn't dangerous?"

Zach hugged her, "When you say it like that, it sounds worse."

"Drink your coffee, while I still have a mind to give you some."

"Look," Carl said very seriously. "If you don't want to do it, I completely understand. We can move him over to our house, but we have to borrow the hospital bed."

"You're crazy! You have all those little kids at your house all day! Are you out of your mind? The neighborhood babysitter is not the place for a drug-addicted ex-con! Mo is up to her elbows in baby bottles and laundry! Another patient is all she needs!"

Both men listened to her rattle on, until she pursed her lips. "No, you're right. We have known Effans for years and they were good people. We can't turn our back on their son, but you both better be here to help until the men get back from Fargo. Then I won't worry. I'll have Andy, Jackson, and Elton around."

Zach got up and gave her a kiss on the cheek, "I'll call Suzy right away. We'll come over and just stay here. We give you our word; we won't leave you alone with this."

"Thanks. I was so frantic this afternoon when CJ was missing, I still haven't calmed down from that!"

Carl nodded, "Doubt CJ will ever do that again. Where is everyone?"

"Doing chores."

"You okay, then?"

"Yah, Katherine gave me the business, so I'll be fine. I better go in and welcome him to our home."

"Want one of us to come with?" the very tall, fair-haired pediatrician asked.

"No, Zach. I think I need to do this on my own."

She knocked at the door and there was no answer. Finally, she said, "I'm coming in. Okay?"

There was still no answer, but she went in. The man was asleep. He looked very thin and fevered. She went over to him and instinctually took his hand. "Hello."

He jumped awake and then tried to focus on her. "Who are you?"

"Nora Schroeder. I wanted to welcome you to our home. We'll be watching over you until you are on the mend. If you need anything, just cry out. We'll try to help you."

"Huh?"

"I'm Nora Schroeder."

"I got that," he snarled at her weakly but suspiciously. "Why?"

"You need some help right now. We were neighbors when you were a little boy. Remember?"

He hesitated before he answered, "Does that kid live here?"

"You mean CJ?"

"The Indian kid. He gave me his sandwich."

"That is CJ."

"Your kid?"

"Yes, my foster son. He was worried about you."

The guy mumbled, "He was mad as hell at me cause I took his eggs."

"Yes, he was. It's his job to take care of the chickens and he was afraid he'd be in trouble." Nora nodded. "The men brought your clothes and backpack here. They're in the closet. We locked up your motorcycle in the garage for you. Grandma and I will wash your clothes tomorrow. Okay? Is there anything you need right now?"

"No. I want to go."

Nora raised her eyebrows, "How is that?"

"I said . . ."

"I know what you said. Look, Harold, you and I can't pull any punches, okay? We both know that neither of us are thrilled about this arrangement, but we'll make it work the best we can. Right? Can I count on you for that? You don't try to buffalo me and I won't try to buffalo you." Nora spoke directly, "Around here, we have some rules. We watch out for each other. Got it?"

"What is this—a halfway house?" the man asked weakly.

Nora smiled, "No. It's our home. I know you've bad tummy problems. The bathroom is right over there, and the light will be on for you. There is extra toilet tissue in the cabinet if you need it. Zach says you might. There is also a bedpan here, in this cabinet. Let me bring it over by you. If you need it, don't be shy about using it. We understand. Zach said that the diarrhea should settle down in a couple days. It might be better to keep the bed lower to the floor instead of high like a hospital bed. That way, it should be easier for you. The mattress is covered if you have an accident."

He just watched her as she talked. She was a very pretty woman, light brown hair and dark brown eyes. She was slender and had a warm smile, but one could tell that she was no one to mess with.

She continued in her soft voice, "Would you like something to eat, now? Zach gave me a list of things you can eat for the next day or so, until you go on the normal diet. Hungry?"

"My gut hurts like hell. Is that doctor here?"

"He is staying here for you for the next couple days. Then my daughter-in-law and nephew will be home. They are paramedics and they'll help care for you. Okay?"

Nora brought him some rice pudding and hot tea on a tray. She gave him a few spoonsful of rice and some tea from the spoon, but he didn't eat very much.

Zach came in and said, "I'll take over for you, Nora."

Nora stood and patted the biker's arm, "Rest now."

Zach encouraged him to eat a little more, but he wasn't hungry. After one of their several trips to the bathroom, Zach said, "Tomorrow I'll set you up with an IV to help you get some hydration. I don't have the stuff with me now. So, try to drink some water or tea."

"It makes me sick."

"Look, you're going to die if you don't keep your fluids up and it won't be a pleasant way to go. Now, drink some water. This water is good and won't make you sick."

Glaring, the man took a drink and then doubled up with cramping. "I have to go to the can."

Zach helped him to the bathroom and let him sit there while he took the tray out to the kitchen. He knocked on the door a few minutes later. The biker was just coming back into the bedroom, looking very pale and shaky. He almost lost his footing, but Zach grabbed him. "You okay? Here, let's get you over to the bed."

They no more than got him in bed and he said, "I have to go again. God, why don't I just die?"

Zach chuckled, "God doesn't make it that easy for us, most of the time. Let me help you."

About twenty minutes and two trips later, the man was exhausted and finally able to lie on the bed. "I can't stay here."

"Where do you think you should go? The water on your place made you sick."

"I figured that."

"Kevin and Harrington are going up tomorrow to dump some chemical in there. They'll get it retested in a few days."

"Why?"

"They have a thing about bad water. Now, let's talk about you. Okay?"

The skinny man glared out of his hollow, sunken eyes.

"Look, I need to know some things to care for you. Doctors can't go telling everyone what we talk about, so you're safe with telling me anything." Zach pulled up a chair, "What kind of drugs are you using and how much?"

The biker stared at him, but didn't answer.

Zach repeated the question, but still no response.

Then Zach stood up, "Fine. Your decision. I'll give you the same dose of pain meds as any patient who isn't a user and hasn't built up a tolerance. You'll be in a great deal of pain, but no one will know what you were taking."

The biker blinked, "You won't like it."

Zach sat back down and spoke persuasively. "Let's get this straight, right off. It isn't a doctor's job to like or dislike the way his patients lead their lives. We are just to treat them as best we can. I could say that you were an idiot for falling off a fence stealing eggs, drinking unsanitary water and using drugs at all, but that won't stop you from being sick. Now would it?"

The patient watched while he talked and then slowly shook his head with deep chagrin.

"You still haven't told me what you are on."

"Smack—heroin," Harold watched Zach's face for a reaction.

Zach nodded, "Figured. That's why the shots you were given when we set your arm had almost no effect. Anything else?"

"Only pot once in a while. I'm not much of a drug user."

"Heroin is not a small time addiction."

"Did LSD once. I'll never do that again. I'd rather blow my head off." Harold shook his head. "I haven't been able to sleep since I got back from Vietnam. Started using smack when I got back. I just wanted everything to go away. It's been downhill ever since."

"Did you quit dugs in prison?"

"Hell no!" Harold snarled, "Didn't quit having nightmares either!"

"I've heard drugs are available in prison before, but I don't get it. Can't the guards stop it?"

"Where I was, a couple guards sold it."

Zach shook his head, "When is the last time you used?"

"I used my last smack last night after I fell off that damned fence! It hardly helped the pain. I'm so damned sick. I can't sleep. Man, I haven't got one damned reason for being alive!"

Zach was matter-of-fact, "We'll try some things to help your sleep problems; but you have to get healthier first."

"How am I supposed to get healthier before I get healthy? What kind of quack are you?"

"The only one you got."

Harold stared at him again. Then his stomach started cramping again, "Damn. I have to go."

Zach helped him until he got settled down again. "I'm going to give you a few shots now. One will slow down the diarrhea, the other is to kill off your little intestinal friends and the other for pain. It should also keep the symptoms of withdrawal controllable. It isn't heroin, so don't get any crazy idea of swiping them to get high, because you won't. I might be dumb but I'm not entirely stupid."

"I'm too damned sick to care."

"That you are, my friend."

As Zach gave him the shots, neither said a word. Afterward, Zach left the room to put the medication away. When he came back in, he found his patient weeping. He went over to him and put his arms around him, "It's a hell of a mess you are in; but things aren't as bleak as you think. You just need to rest. This medication should put you to sleep for a few hours, so you can get some rest."

The man looked at him in panic, "You mean completely out?"

"Yah, why?"

"What if I have to go to the can?"

"That other shot will relieve that, so you can just sleep. How does that sound?"

"I wish I was dead."

Zach smiled, "Must not be your time yet or the Good Lord would have carted you out of here already."

"Bull."

"Whatever, Tough Guy. Just get to sleep. I'll see you in a couple hours."

As he started to leave, Harold grabbed his hand and squeezed it in gratitude.

"Go to sleep," Zach smiled.

-5-

That began an agonizing night. Thankfully, Mo and Carl had decided to have the Grey Hawk kids sleep over at their place, the Petunia Patch. It was right across the road. Everyone thought it would be prudent, since no one knew what to expect from Harold Effan.

After a couple hours sleep, the man was sick the rest of the night and spent most of his waking hours screaming in terror or in the bathroom. By the time the morning alarm went off, everyone knew why he wanted to live off by himself and stay drugged up most of the time. Amazingly, as they gathered around their trusty coffee pot, the only two who were sleeping soundly was Grandpa, who was deaf enough so the noise didn't bother him, and Harold, who was now sleeping soundly.

Zach looked at Nora, "I had no idea. When he talked about nightmares, I was thinking like Andy and Horse. Those are bad enough, but this is something else!"

"Think it's from Vietnam?" Diane asked.

"Some of it, yes. But with his time in prison, the bikers, a broken arm, and being sick, he has himself in a real state."

"I have to hug Mo for keeping the kids. That would've been a fright with them here. Do you think he'll be settled down enough in a few days, so that the kids can come home?" Nora asked.

"I hope so. The worst of the cramping should be resolved in another day or so. The pain from the arm will lessen and we should start seeing the light of day." Zach said, "I called the hospital and Keith is picking up some meds to bring out this morning. I want to knock him out as far as we can and maybe get him through the worst of this. He is also having some withdrawal, but not much because of the pain medication. I'm sorry, Nora. I really didn't think he'd be this unsettled," Zach put his arm around her.

Nora grinned, "I'll forgive you if you get out there and do the chores. I see Carl and the kids walking across the road."

The kitchen door opened and in came the troops. Carl, CJ, and Clarissa were there and Kevin came in right after them. "How's it going?"

"Tough night," Zach answered and looked out the window as a car drove in. "Who is that?"

"Harrington. He said he would help, too."

Nora smiled, "You guys are the best."

The very pregnant Suzy, Zach's wife, giggled, "I'm hungry. What are we cooking for breakfast?"

Zach kissed her cheek, "That's my girl. Always hungry."

"You would be, too, if you had to eat for three."

Everyone stopped and Nora beamed, "Did we hear right? Are you having twins?"

"The doctor thinks so, but he isn't sure. Anyway, however many there are, they're always kicking! My goodness, I don't sleep much better than your guest."

Zach was going out the door to help milk, when they heard Harold. "You go ahead. I'll see to him," Nora said. "That is unless he needs medication."

"No, he should be good for a couple hours in that department. I'd be glad to stay and help."

"You need some fresh air. Get out," Nora laughed.

She knocked on the door, but there was no answer. She knocked again and said, "I'm coming in."

She entered the room and he was in the bathroom. "Do you need any help?"

"Is that guy here?" Harold asked through the door.

"He's outside. I can help you."

"No, I'll wait. He's coming back, isn't he?"

"Yes, he'll be back up to the house in about hour and a half. That is a long time to sit there."

"You don't want to come in here! It's awful."

"Good grief, Harold. I'm almost sixty-years old and have raised a pile of kids. There probably isn't much in the way of a mess that I haven't seen. Get over it. I'm coming in."

He yelled no, but she entered the bathroom. She looked at the feces on the floor and all over him, and her face broke into a smile, "You did a bang up job!"

He looked at her through tears and humiliation, "You're blanking crazy!"

"Okay, where to start? I'll have Grandma find some pajamas for you. Can you stand by yourself?"

He shrugged.

"You stay put. I'll come right back to get the shower running. If you can stand by yourself, we'll just have you step in there. That's the plan, okay?"

"Jesus," the ex-con muttered.

"I wish He would help you with your shower, but looks like He left the details for us to work out."

"I don't want you to see this."

Nora put her hand on his shoulder, "Harold, we all have astoundingly, amazing, wonderful souls, but God put us in these animal bodies to keep us humble. I think it works, how 'bout you?"

He growled, "I should go to the hospital. The nurses there could help me."

"Then they will see you at your finest. Would that be better?"

He sighed, "Ah, shit!"

"That's the word I would use!" Nora giggled. "Hold on while I talk to Grandma."

A couple minutes later, she came back in with a scrub pail, mop and some clean towels.

"Okay, Sunshine, do you like the shower water hot or cold? No answer? I'll fix it the way I like it, then."

Harold was hardly able to stand, but Nora used the stool they used for Grandpa, so he could sit in the shower. While Harold tried to wash himself, Nora cleaned up the bathroom. Grandma came in the bedroom, changed the bed, and opened the windows to let the fresh, spring air fill the room.

After most of an hour of total mortification, Harold was back in bed. He was cleaner than he had been in some time, except for his broken arm, which spent the shower wrapped in a large plastic bag. He looked around the room, "Who fixed this bed?"

"Grandma Katherine, while we were in the bathroom. Looks nice, but I think it is a little chilly with the windows open. How about you?"

He frowned. Nora closed the window and then came back over to the bed, "How you feeling, Harold?"

He glared at her.

"Let me tell you something. Pride and dignity are great things, but reality is still more important. We all have our weaknesses and diseases. We need to recognize them, deal with them, and put them in perspective. I will make you a deal, okay? You put this episode in your back pocket and forget it for now. When you're feeling better, we'll have a good chuckle over it. Best deal in town, what do you say?"

"You're nuts."

"I'll take that as a yes." Nora patted his arm. "Let me help you set up and bring something to eat."

Harold Effan sat there in the fresh bed looking around the room. He couldn't imagine what made these people tick. He was pretty sure they had an agenda. They were somehow going to throw the screws to him further down the road. His gaze went to the bathroom. What a terrible mess he had made! Now, it was all cleaned up and this woman was even nice to him. He shook his head. There was a knock on the door and a soft voice asked, "May I come in?"

In came a tiny, elderly lady, not even five feet tall. She was a bit of thing with snow-white hair piled up on her head and Mrs. Santa Claus glasses. She had bright blue eyes and a big smile, "I heard there's a kid in here that wants his breakfast. You wouldn't happen to know him, would you?"

Harold looked at her in amazement.

"Good, if I leave this here, will you see that he gets it?" she teased.

After she set down the tray, she held out her hand to him, "I'm Katherine Engelmann, Grandma to you. I heard you don't like to be called Harold. Don't blame you. Guess you'll just be Kid. Need me to help you with your one hand, or can you manage alone?"

"I think I can do it."

"Here, want milk on your cream of wheat?"

He didn't answer and she just poured some on the hot cereal over a couple teaspoons of brown sugar. Then he smiled.

"You have a nice smile under that bird's nest," she said as she put some jam on his toast. "One scoop or two?"

He chuckled, but didn't answer.

"Okay, you get two. Zach said no butter yet, but we need to keep your sugar up." After she got his plate organized, she said, "Want a radio on or something?"

"No thanks."

"Someone will be in to check on you in a little bit. You need anything before, just yell!"

-6-

The scruffy patient finished all his breakfast and pushed the tray table back. He slept until he heard a knock at the door. "May I come in?" a lady asked.

"Yes," he answered weakly.

"Hi." A pretty, pregnant lady with blonde hair asked, "How was the breakfast?"

He gave her a puzzled look, "You look familiar."

"Yes," she smiled. "I used to be Suzy Heinrich when we were in school together. I'm married to Zach, your doctor. My name is now Suzy Jeffries. Are you finished with your breakfast? How is the old gizzard?"

The biker's face reddened, "I suppose Nora told you about the mess."

"Didn't even know about it until you just said." Suzy smiled, "That's what happens when you get water-borne bacteria."

Harold scrunched back down in his bed, "Is your husband back yet?"

"No, he will be soon. Want a radio on or something? A book to read?"

"No. My arm is beginning to hurt like hell."

"Zach will be in soon. I'll let him know. You rest, or do you need help going to the bathroom?"

"You can leave."

"Okay, Kid. See you later."

She left the room, but the door wasn't closed all the way. Harold lay in his bed and listened to the ladies visit while they were making breakfast. They weren't talking about him, but about some birthday party they were planning. He couldn't remember the last time he had heard anyone talk about birthday cake. It reminded him of when he was growing up. Before he realized it, tears were rolling down his cheeks.

The door opened and a tall, gangly old man shuffled in the room. This guy came over to the bed and peered at Harold. "I'm Lloyd Engelmann. Who are you? Are you a relative?"

Harold never moved while the man gaped at him. After studying him, the elderly man said, "I guess you can sleep here if you want. This is my house, you know. You look like a screwball with that mess on your face. Never get a woman that way! I'm telling you! I can go get my razor, if you don't have one."

"I like it this way," Kid answered flatly.

Lloyd cleaned his glasses and squinted at the man. "You must be the only one, then! It looks like hell!"

Grandma Katherine came in and took Lloyd's arm, "Be nice, Lloyd. The Kid is sick. He's had a bad time. He got back from the war and is trying to get his life back."

The Alzheimer's patient frowned and asked, "Where did you leave it? I can send Elton to get it."

"No, Lloyd. He has to build a new one."

"I'll get my tools right after breakfast. Okay Kid? You should shave off that beard though. I'd hate to get it caught in the saw!"

Katherine frowned, "Lloyd, mind your own business."

"If the kid is sleeping in my bed, he is my business!"

Harold groaned and began to curl up. "I have to hit the bathroom."

"Need help?" Katherine asked.

"No."

"I can help you, Kid," Lloyd offered.

"That's okay, Gramps. I can do it."

"See, I thought he was a relative," Lloyd took his wife's arm, "You got coffee made?"

"Come, I'll get you some," Katherine patted her husband's arm.

Zach came in to check on Harold, who was becoming restless and in pain, again. "How's it going? You made it about two hours this last time."

"My guts are torn up," the man said, "It was awful! I messed myself, the bed and the whole damned bathroom. Nora and Grandma cleaned me up like a baby. I gotta get out of here! They are all blanking nuts around here!"

"You can go, anytime you want. I have to warn you, we aren't bringing you dinner or medicine."

"Talk about extortion!" He threw his covers back, "Now I have to go to the can again! Will this ever end?"

Zach helped him up, "Another thirty-six hours should do it. Then your stomach will be fairly back to normal. The withdrawal from smack isn't helping that either. You have the chills?"

"Yah, but I'm hotter than hell. I had such night terrors and my throat is sorer than hell this morning. Must have been screaming, huh? You should've left me in the old house."

"About four this morning, that was being considered!" Zach laughed. "As soon as you get back to bed, I'll get your shots. I phoned one of my colleagues who told me about some stuff to try. It should calm you. I'll have someone bring it out from town this morning. But, he also gave me some ideas of how to knock you out for now. You need to rest."

On the way back to bed, Harold asked, "How am I supposed to pay you for this?"

"Don't worry your pretty little head about it right now."

"Tell that old man! Boy, did he tear me a new one about my beard!" the patient grumbled.

Zach chuckled, "Grandma told me! I have to warn you, he'll keep it up, too."

"What's wrong with him?"

"He has Alzheimers. His mind is gone."

"Can they give him anything for it?"

"No, there is nothing we can do for it. Maybe someday. We give him some things that help him sleep and such. It only works periodically, but we try. He has good days and bad days."

"What the hell kind of doctor are you anyway?"

Zach laughed, "I don't know if I should tell you! You'll be mortified."

"Worse than this morning?" Then Harold squinted suspiciously, "You aren't a veterinarian, are you?"

Zach almost doubled over in hysterics, "No, I'm a pediatrician."

"My god! This is worse than prison!" Harold grumbled. "What the hell did I get myself into?"

"A place the serves the best breakfast in the world. Did you eat much?"

"Cream of wheat and toast with jelly. I can't eat. I want to, but my guts are so torn up." Then he looked at Zach in misery, "I'm so miserable and confused. I hurt, itch and my guts feel shredded."

The pediatrician gave the tough outlaw biker a fistful of shots and then said, "I'm out of lollipops, but I have a dog biscuit."

"You SOB! Just wait until I get better." Harold pulled the blanket over his shoulder defiantly and got it tangled in his cast.

Zach chuckled as he helped him straighten it out. "Want the shades pulled so you can sleep?"

"Oh my god," Harold groaned. "I have to go to the can again."

The next half an hour was punctuated with numerous trips to the bathroom, cramping and moaning. Finally, the shots began to work and he was able to just rest.

Zach said, "When you wake up next time, I'm going to set you up with an IV. Right now, you're too restless. I want to see if this combination can settle you down. Okay? You need to drink water, for me."

Harold shook his head and stated defiantly, "No."

Zach held the glass to his mouth, "I didn't ask. Just do it."

The biker gave him a dirty look, "No."

"Okay, get dehydrated, you big idiot. See if I care!" Zach glared back.

Harold's eyes never broke their gaze with Zach, but he did drink the water. Then Zach set the glass down and stated, "I'm giving you one warning. You want to give me grief, you can! Don't you dare try it with the ladies! I'll come in and twist your cast backwards. Hear me."

Harold continued to glower, "Yah, I hear."

Zach sat with him until he fell asleep a few minutes later. He shook his head, 'This is going to be a long haul for you, Kid. A damned long haul."

-7-

Keith, Schroeder's oldest son, arrived from Bismarck. "Here's the stuff from the hospital. I had to darned near sign my life away to get this. Must be some serious meds, huh?"

"Yah, it is. I really appreciate you bringing this out for Harold. If I can get his gut straightened out, he should almost be like normal," Zach answered as he looked over the box of supplies.

"You know, I went to school with him. He was a nice kid and we were friends. We had shop together. His folks had all sorts of range cattle and a few horses. Come to think of it, he was a good rider."

Zach said quietly, "That's good to know. We need to think of something to get him interested in living again."

"I was floored about the biker gang business. Harold was never anyone that I'd have figured for that. He loved mechanics and was more thoughtful than most guys in school. In fact, he was very quiet. He went into the Marines before I did. He was the reason I chose the Marines. Dad rented that pasture from his parents for years, and they told Dad he signed up. That set me to thinking about it. That damned war business really made a mark on a lot of guys."

"Yes, but they all didn't join biker gangs."

Keith was a year older than Kevin, but looked a lot like him. He was a bit shorter, darker, and more reserved. "No, but look how Andy was when he got home. If it hadn't been for Annie and the fact he got help, it wouldn't have surprised me if he went off the deep end."

Zach shrugged, "Well, Harold is our focus now. Want to go in to say hi?"

"Isn't he sleeping?"

"Yes, but he only has very short times when he's civil. When he wakes up on his own, the meds are beginning to wear off. It doesn't take long for him to get edgy. Suzy introduced herself. I think it'd be good if he knew there were people around who remembered him when he was a kid, before his life went to hell." Zach pointed out, "He'd never admit it, but he is not only sicker than a dog; he is scared to death. Having that gang threatening to kill him, no family or friends and then the physical mess he is in—can't be fun."

"Sure, I wouldn't mind seeing him. How long should we talk?"

"Oh, not more than a few minutes. It would be good for him."

Keith knocked on the door but there was no answer. Then he opened it and came in. There was the man about thirty sleeping with his arm in a cast. He was extremely thin and rugged looking, Keith would've never recognized him. He went over to the bed and sat down. Then he touched his arm, "Harold? Harold Effan?"

The man opened his eyes with a scowl and took a minute to get his eyes adjusted. He looked at Keith trying to place him. "Do I know you?"

"Yes, you do. Keith Schroeder. We had shop together, remember?"

Harold tried to place him and then he smiled slightly. "Keith. Yah, we were in shop."

"Mom told me you were here, so I thought I'd stop in and say hi."

"Mom?" Harold frowned, "Oh yah, Nora. Grandma?"

Keith smiled, "So you met my little Grandma? She is a real sweetheart."

Harold nodded and closed his eyes. Keith sat a couple minutes and then said quietly, "I can go now and let you rest."

Harold opened his eyes, "Please stay."

"Okay. You know, Darlene and I will be staying here all weekend. Maybe we can play chess like we used to do?"

"Darlene?"

"You should remember her. Darlene Olson. Her brothers were Dave and Don. She is my wife. We have a little boy named Nathan. You have to meet him."

"Dave Olson. Yah," he nodded.

"Dave was killed in Vietnam about three years ago. He was 82nd Airborne. I heard you were over there."

"Yah. You?"

"Yes. Marines. I joined up because I heard you did! Did you know that?"

Before he was simply looking straight ahead; but now Harold's eyes moved to look at him. When their eyes made contact, he shook his head. "Bad idea."

"I was fortunate. Many had a tough time. We can talk about it anytime you want. Let me know. It's best to talk it out with someone who was there. You need to get it out. I had a hell of a time when I first got home, so I know it can be hard. My little brother, Andy and his friend are still having trouble."

"You?"

"I'm okay now. Never give up. Things do get better."

Harold shrugged, "Depends how bad you screwed up."

"I suppose, but it can still get better." Keith changed the subject, "I hear you have a bike. What kind?"

"Harley '69 XLCH Sportster. Just got it, when I got out of prison." He looked his old friend in the eye, "Keith, I screwed up bad."

Keith nodded and squeezed Harold's hand. Then he said, "I heard the XLCH is a good ride, but the kick start is a bearcat."

"Yah," Harold smiled weakly, "It is. You ride?"

"I'd love to, but don't tell anyone." Then he leaned ahead and whispered, "I drive a station wagon."

Harold smiled, "It's over for you, Dude."

"Well, I better let you sleep. I'll see you this weekend." Keith said, "You try to get well enough so I can beat you in chess. Okay?"

"I might not be here."

"Afraid you'll lose, huh? I know Darlene will want to say hi to you."

Harold's face became very somber, "No, she won't."

Keith frowned, "Just how in the hell do you know?"

"You don't know me anymore, Keith. I'm no good."

"Nothing stopping you from being good again, if you're of a mind." Then Keith patted his shoulder, "Why don't you give it a chance?"

Harold shook his head and his eyes reddened, "Things got way out of hand."

"Want to talk about it?"

"No, I'm too tired."

"Don't try to do it all at once. First, you get to feeling better; then we'll talk."

Harold shook his head, "It was good to see you."

"It was. See you."

The patient slept another hour or so before he woke up screaming. Zach went in and talked calmly to him until he could settle down. They made a few trips to the bathroom. It seemed that things in that department were beginning to get under control.

Harold looked at Zach while he was perched on the throne, "I never want to go through this again."

"When we get this bout settled, I'm going to set you up with an IV that Keith brought out. I'll give you the meds that way. Then you shouldn't have such severe fluctuations."

"Is that what you call the diarrhea? Fluctuations?"

Zach cracked up, "No, but it might be a good name for it at that! I meant you'll be sleepier and more comfortable with less pain and cramping. It should level you out. Hopefully, we can ride out the rest of the withdrawal and stomach problems easier."

"What if I wake up swinging?"

"That's why I didn't do it before. We'll try to fix you up so you don't get so wild and tear your IV out. Will you mind being mostly asleep the next few days?"

"Hell no! But I sure don't want to mess the bed again!"

"The meds should control that. Hopefully. But if it happens, it happens. Life is like that."

Harold glared at Zach and then said, "Knock me out."

Within twenty minutes, the patient was asleep. Zach was relieved that everything seemed to be going better and he decided to take a nap himself. Since he wasn't sure how his patient would react to the IV, he slept in the recliner in his room. Zach had to make a few adjustments to the IV, but things were more balanced. The patient was able to relax and his sleep seemed more restful. He wasn't quite as antagonistic when he was awake. His trips to the bathroom were much less frequent and more controllable. Zach was relieved.

That afternoon, Sheriff Bernard came out and asked if he could speak to the patient. Zach said he could, but wanted a few minutes to get ready for company. Zach woke Kid and helped him go to the bathroom and get ready for his guest.

"You gonna stay in here?"

Zach glanced at him, "Want me to?"

"Nah, I guess not."

"Look, if you'd rather I did, I can. I don't want to intrude."

"It wouldn't hurt if you were here. I mean, if I need to go to the can."

"Okay, I will. I'll tell Bernard to come in. Want to try some tea?"

Harold shook his head no, "What about a beer?"

"Yah," Zach poked. "That's just what you need!"

The middle-aged small town sheriff came in and held out his hand to the biker. The biker gave a quick nod, but watched him like a hawk. All the while he shook the sheriff's hand, his wary, antagonistic expression never changed.

Then the sheriff sat in the chair Zach had set by the bed, holding his coffee mug in his hand. He had a friendly but no-nonsense demeanor. He was a bit on the pudgy side, with graying hair and a tanned complexion. "Okay if I put my mug on your tray?"

"Harold asked me to stay in here in case he has some medical issues. Is that okay? I'll sit back here on the recliner," Zach interrupted.

"No problem. This isn't an investigation." Then he smiled at the patient, "Or an inquisition. I just need to get a handle on some things and would like your help."

The sullen biker's expression never changed.

Bernard smiled, "Okay, so let's start. Looks like all your papers are copacetic, but no driver's license. You are the sole owner of your Dad's farm, bike title is here and all that stuff you need to hang on to are in this packet. By the way, I want to say I was sorry to hear of your father's passing. He was a nice man."

The biker continued to stare into nothing.

The sheriff continued, "I put the papers in this manila envelope. You can check them if you want or I can give them to Nora. She'll keep them in their safe for you. Want to check them?"

The biker never responded, nor did he make a move.

"Okay, then I'll have Nora keep them while you're under the weather. Seems you aren't tied to parole or anything, so you're free to do what you wish. Have you made up your mind what you want to do?"

The biker ignored his visitor.

"I imagine that means you aren't sure yet. I can check back with you when things are more settled. Zach tells me you're doing pretty well. Kevin and Harrington are going to try to fix your well with chemicals, so the water is potable. Otherwise, you'll need to dig another one. It is really a hazard now; it is so polluted. They are going to have the state lab check it again in a couple days. Just thought you should know."

The biker remained unmoved.

"Now, about the Satan's Horde."

The biker's eyes darted toward Bernard, but he never said anything.

"From what I found out, which isn't much; they have no formal connection with the Sons of Silence, whose territory covers the Dakotas. However, if they find you, well—you know. At any rate, I'll keep an ear on the ground to pick up on any interesting movement from either group. You should keep a very low profile. You might remember there's not much goes on country roads the neighbors miss. Biker gangs aren't common out here in the sticks; so if you drive your bike in daylight wearing your colors, you might as well take out an ad in the paper. I would appreciate any help I can get from you."

Harold glowered, "Why?"

"I have little experience dealing with biker gangs."

"I mean, why help me?"

"You're one of my citizens and it's my job to keep the peace. Besides, like I said, I liked your folks. If you want to go it alone, I'll still have to keep a watchful eye because I don't want to have a band of bikers nesting in the neighborhood. If you want help, I'm here and I know Schroeders and Kincaids are here for you, too. If you want to cause trouble, then you'll be on my other list. I really don't like that idea."

Harold sighed, "I can't see me helping Johnny Law."

The sheriff studied his face for a bit and tried to get a read, but he couldn't. Then he said, "Okay, let's do this. I'll assume you want to be a righteous citizen, until you prove otherwise."

Harold gave a sarcastic laugh, and said, "Man, I don't even trust me. Why the hell would you?"

"Because, Hot Shot, I know what you've been through and what a damned mess you are in. If you wanted to stay with the gang, you wouldn't have spent so much time in isolation at the prison because you didn't help out your buddy."

"Scab was never my buddy!" Harold snapped angrily. "I never could stand the SOB! I always tried to avoid him on the outside! He's an unhinged, sadistic bastard! Scab was asking for it. He kept riding this mousy guy and antagonizing the hell out of him! I told him to knock it off, but Scab thought it was funny. I knew the mousy guy had friends in the 'Nation'

45

and so if he kept it up, he could get his teeth kicked in. The arrogant ass didn't listen. A couple days later, sure as hell, he had his jaw flapping. Next thing you know, he and I are walking back from the laundry and four big brutes were all over him. There was no way in hell I wanted to take a beating for him. I just kept going 'til the guards showed up."

Sheriff Bernard inserted, "That's the story I heard."

"The club members didn't see it my way. They made it clear I was a dead man, so the prison put me in isolation until I got out. If the members find me, I'm dead. I don't know if I'm worth looking for, but I know if they ever got a hold of me, they'd kill me." The Kid spoke quietly and without emotion.

"I don't know if they'd come looking for you way up here or not. I know there is an outlaw gang in the upper Midwest, the Sons of Silence. I think they're into trafficking of drugs and firearms. I don't know if they do contracts for other clubs or if they would even allow another club into their territory to do a hit. Do you?"

"No. I know it's my own damned fault. If they'd kill me, it'd be over. I wouldn't have anything more to worry about."

"Yah, but I'd have a lot of questions to answer!" Bernard asserted. "You might disagree, but I like our backward community the way it is. We manage to get into enough trouble."

The biker gave him a weary look, "You're telling me to move on, I take it."

Bernard shook his head, "You damned fool, I'm not saying that! I'm racking my brain trying to figure out how to give you a square chance, if that's what you want. Maybe you are so cynical and leery that you don't believe that, but that's not my problem. I'm being as square and frank as I can. You pull any bull on me, or the neighborhood, and my stance will change immediately. Know that."

The biker's eyes dropped, "What can I do if I stay?"

"First, get well. I took the liberty of talking to Carl Kincaid. We know you'll have to be here to heal up. If the well can be cleaned, we could help you fix up the old house to be livable. You might want to consider buying your own chickens and a cow. Poaching won't make you very popular. Anyway, I just wanted to touch base with you. Your papers will be with Nora and your firearm is in my safe because you can't legally be carrying it."

"What the hell?"

"When you get straightened around, you talk to me and we'll work out what you need to do to make it legal. Okay? Until then, no gun."

The biker just glared but the Sheriff continued, "Very few know you are here and we'll try keep it that way until we see if there is a threat from that Satan thing. If I was you, I'd get rid of my patches on my leathers. Hell, they might as well be neon around here! You won't be riding your bike until your arm heals up, so by then we should know if you are safe. Anything to say?"

"You'll let me stay?"

"You are a legal landowner. Yup. Now if Nora wants you to stay here, that's up to her."

"What if she doesn't?"

"If I was you, I'd make damned sure she didn't have a reason to throw me out!"

Harold didn't even notice the Sheriff was smiling.

"Well, I have to go. Get any ideas, hear anything or have any questions, call me. Can I ask you for that much?"

Harold nodded, "Yah."

"Bye now."

"Yah."

The sheriff went out and Harold didn't move for a full five minutes. Then he scrunched over with the cramps, "Zach! I need help."

Zach took him to the bathroom and when they got back to bed, Zach raised some of his meds. The guy was obviously very distressed by his talk with the sheriff, but had no intention of talking about it. Before long, he was back to sleep.

He only slept a couple hours. Zach went out to join the rest of the family with chores and then brought a tray with some food. He set it on the bedside table and roused the man. "Hey Kid, you hungry?"

"Huh? No food. I need the can."

After they got him comfortably back in bed, Zach said, "You really need to eat. If you do okay, tomorrow I can see about getting you something that isn't as bland. Grandma is making caramel rolls for breakfast."

The biker's eyes lit up, "Really? I haven't had them since we left North Dakota. I could eat them, you think?"

"If you can handle supper tonight."

47

"I haven't even thought about those rolls for years. They were killer! I loved them. I remember Keith used to bring them in his lunch pail sometimes. He'd share with me." Then he looked at Zach, "You know he was a good guy. We were friends, I think."

"Keith thought so," Zach smiled.

"He said he wanted me to see his wife and baby. That's just because he doesn't know me anymore."

"Look Kid, he knows about the gang and prison. It isn't like he doesn't care, but you don't throw a person under the bus first time something goes sour."

"Does he know that woman died in California?"

"Yes."

"He still wants me to meet his wife?"

"He knows you didn't do it. You weren't hanging with very good people. Harold, we've all had our moments of splendor. He's willing to give you a chance. I wouldn't take that as a free pass, though."

"No, I remember Keith that well." Kid nodded, "Do you think he really meant that he would talk to me about the war and all that?"

"Yes. If he said it, he means it."

"What do you think? Can talking really help with the night terrors?"

"Yes, but not all by itself. You need to watch your diet. A low blood sugar is a no-no. That will bring on nightmares. Even though the smack and booze help quell them for a bit; when you go past the high, it compounds it. You need to treat your body as well as you treat your bike. Then you should be able to sleep better. We can work on other things to help, but not until we get this first mess under control. Back to your question, talking does help, a lot. So, find a few trustworthy, willing souls that have an idea what things were like and talk to them. May I ask if you have a church?"

Harold snorted, "What the hell kind of church would want the likes of me?"

"They all should. If they don't, it is their problem, not yours!" Zach responded simply. "Did you ever belong to a church?"

"Last time I set foot in a church was here at Trinity in Merton." Kid squinted at him, "You a Bible thumper?"

Zach chuckled, "Not hardly, but you asked me what helps and I told you. I go to Trinity regularly. Believe me, it saved my sorry ass. What you do is up to you. Anyway, get some rest."

-8-

That evening, the house sounded different. Harold lay awake, listening to the banter among the family members. A few folks stopped in to say hello to him; Carl, Harrington, and Kevin. Their visits were short, friendly, and mostly just to see how he was doing. The ladies came in and out a few times, and chatted a little. Harold woke once and saw the old man sitting in the recliner, watching him sleep. Harold said hello, and the old guy nodded, smiled and went out to get some coffee.

He heard the folks getting ready to go do chores and could smell something fantastic cooking. Then Suzy came in, "Hi Kid, just thought I'd let you know the plan around here for the next few days. The guys will be home tonight and then Friday night the clan will all be here for dinner, Saturday night is a barn dance, and Sunday, we'll all have dinner here again. There is a birthday every day! So, get ready for birthday cake. Okay?"

Harold kinda grinned and tried to sit up. Suzy elevated the back of the bed so he was more comfortable. She sat down on the chair next to the bed and put her swollen feet on the side of the bed frame. He glanced at the bloated feet that looked so painful. "Don't mean to stare, but you walk with those?"

Suzy giggled, "Almost have to! I forgot where I left my other feet. I doubt I could run if you paid me."

Harold nodded. Then she smiled at him, "That's one of the reasons why Zach and I will be here Saturday night with you, Grandpa, and maybe some of the babies while everyone else goes to the barn dance."

"Barn dance? I haven't heard about them since we left here! They used to be at your folk's place, huh?"

"Still are. Old Heinrich's barn! But don't worry, we'll have more later, so you can come to those. Zach didn't think you were well enough to go to this one yet. You remember the outhouse is a long ways from the dance floor."

Harold gave a weak smile, "Be honest, you guys don't want me around, but thanks for giving me an excuse."

Suzy frowned and gave him a dirty look, "Listen here, we aren't judging you by the same criteria you're judging yourself! Don't tell us how we feel!"

The biker grimaced and mumbled meekly, "Sorry."

"Oh don't worry. I get mad fast and over it faster. Once you're well enough, you'll be invited. If you act like a jackass, there'll be hell to pay. The same as the rest of us! Anyway, we are celebrating a bunch of birthdays this weekend. It will be Father Vicaro's on Friday. Remember him from St. Johns?"

"He's still alive? How the hell old is he anyway?"

"Don't let him hear you say that!" Suzy laughed. "He's still spry. We have gotten to know him very well. In fact, he is one of the clanners."

Harold's eyes darted toward her, "Ku Klux?"

Suzy went into giggle fits until she was holding her stomach. "That's hysterical. No, it is what our family calls itself. You know Grandpa Lloyd Engelmann thinks that we are all his kin, so we are the Engelmann Clan. There is a bunch of us and he thinks we are all related."

Harold nodded, "He told me that he thought I was his relative."

"See, now you are a clanner, too. It is an honor actually."

"What do you do if you are a clanner?"

"We all get together every Sunday after church or mass and eat here at Schroeders. We get together for every holiday, birthday, wedding and any other reason we can dream up."

Harold watched her beam as she talked about it. He smiled warmly, "Sounds easy enough."

"Well, we have a few unwritten rules. We help each other, give each other hell when we need it, have fun together and share our lives. We don't lie or break our word to each other, if we can help it. That's about it."

"How does that work?"

"Pretty well. Once in a while someone goes off the reservation, but that's life. Anyway, you have apparently been through the initiation."

"What was that?"

"Grandpa thinks you are his relative." Suzy smiled. "Easy, huh? Seriously though, it is like a big family unit, whether we are related or not. We learned from the little Sioux kids, the newest clanners, it is like tiyospaye (tee-YO-spa-yae). That is Sioux for extended family. It is one of their four main virtues."

"Didn't know that."

"Anyway, their groups can extend up to two hundred people!"

Harold crinkled up his face, "How many clanners do you have? There aren't two hundred people around here, are there?"

"Oh, we have about forty, I guess."

"They all eat here every Sunday?"

"Those that can make it. You know, I can make you a list of the Engelmann Clan. It'll make it easier to figure out."

"I don't want to."

"Maybe not, but I will anyway. You can figure out who is who. I'll be back in a minute."

With that, she went out and returned minutes later with paper and pen on a tray with a pot of tea and two cups.

"You guys are determined to make me drink tea like a prissy, huh?"

"Up to you," she smiled as she poured it and asked, "Sugar, milk, or lemon?"

Harold watched her and shook his head, "Sugar, I guess."

She handed it to him and then set the tablet out. She started writing and soon had a list of folks. He observed her in amazement. Then he said, "You guys are certifiable, know that?"

She didn't take it as the insult it was intended, but handed the list to him to look at.

===

ENGELMANN CLAN MAP
1971
Lloyd and Katherine Engelmann

Pastor Byron and Marly (Jessup Petfarken) Ellison,
    Ken (Petfarken) Ellison
    Katie Ellison
    Ginger Ellison, 8
    Charlie Ellison, 7
    Miriam Jeffries, 3

Elton and Nora (Spanner Grainger) Schroeder*
    Keith (Spanner) and Darlene (Olson) Schroeder   Bismarck
        Nathan, 18 mos.
    Kevin (Spanner) and Carrie (Jessup) Schroeder
        Holly, 4 mos.
    Andy (Grainger) and Annie (Packineau Grover) Schroeder*
    Christopher and Victoria (Grainger Schroeder) Holloway   Grand Forks
    Clarence Grey Hawk, 8*
    C J Grey Hawk, 7*
    Clarissa Grey Hawk, 5*
    Claudia Grey Hawk, 3*
    Clancy Grey Hawk, 20 mos.*
    Jackson (Horse) Fielding*

Pastor Marvin and Glenda (Owens) Olson
    Clark Olson, 8
    Maddie Lynn Olson, 5

Doug and Julia (Heinrich) Anderson
    Rodney
    Little Bill, 9

Jerald and Elsie (Gertz) Oxenfelter   Bismarck
    Rebecca   Bismarck
    Junior Oxenfelter, 10   Bismarck

Eddie and Lucy Schroeder   Bismarck
    Danny and Jenny (Jessup) Schroeder
        Baby Matthew
    Marty and Greta (Heinrich) Schroeder
    Dick and Megan Elizabeth (Schroeder) Heinrich

Darrell and Jeannie (Frandsen) Jessup
Mervin (Chatterbox) and Eve (Jessup) Olson
Zacharias and Suzy (Heinrich) Jeffries
Carl and Maureen (Finn Harrington) Kincaid
    Ian and Ruth (Jeffries) Harrington
    Matthew Harrington—fiancée Diane (Berg) Waggoner*

Father Frank Vicaro
Father Bartholomew Fedder
Father Landers
Sister Abigail
Randy Berg—fiancée Beatrice Fedder   East coast
Josh Perkins
Joallyn Frandsen
Jeff Wilson
Harold (Kid) Effan*

==

Harold looked it all over and shook his head, "There are more than forty people here, and I don't think they will want me. Doubt any of these folks were heroin addicts."

"We don't do blood tests, but I know two of them used drugs, went through treatment and stuff. Some of these folks are little kids or live out of the area now. I made a note by their names. So, it isn't so many, really. Besides, most of them live right here, with Schroeders! I put a star by their names."

"It is awful quiet around here for that."

"Andy and Horse had to go to the VA in Fargo with Elton and Byron. So they aren't home until tonight. The Grey Hawks are staying over at Carl's until you get settled."

"That's not right. They shouldn't have to leave because of me."

"Diane lives here, but she is a rather quiet person. If you heard piano, that was her."

"I did hear some piano. I thought it was a recording or something because it was so good."

"That would be Diane. Andy's wife, Annie is a paramedic and stays in Bismarck when she works."

"Does Pastor Ellison still have Trinity?"

"Sure does. Did you belong there?"

"Kinda."

"Well, he'll be home later tonight and I'm sure he'll stop in to see you."

"Why did he go to Fargo?"

"He is power of attorney and legal guardian for Jackson (Horse) until he's of age. He's a good kid. Well Sunshine, I have to go help with dinner.

We had only a bite earlier, because the guys will be hungry when they get back from Fargo."

Suzy got up and Harold watched her, "Suzy? Thanks. You didn't have to do that. I appreciate it."

"Can't have you being confused. That's Grandpa's arena. Oh, but if you value even a morsel of your life, you better never treat Grandpa with anything but respect. He would do anything in the world for his family and none of us want him to be hurt."

"What kind of person do you think I am?"

"A nice one, but you'd be surprised how some people treat people who have Alzheimers. They should think twice. None of us know what's in store for us."

"You're right."

Harold woke later when he heard Nora saying, "Kid, can you wake up for a bit? We'd like you to meet the little kids that live here. Okay?"

He was very tired, but went to the bathroom, splashed some water on his face, and came back to his bed. Nora had straightened it up for him and had the back up some. It had been moved higher than a regular bed since he went on the IV. He got in and then asked, "Did you find a comb in my bag?"

"No, I don't remember seeing one but I can get you one."

She went out and came back in a few minutes with a comb and brush. "You might want to use a brush first. It is rather tangled and I don't know if you could get a comb through it."

He reddened a bit and just took the brush. Then he combed it, "I suppose Gramps told you about my beard. He doesn't like it."

"Yes, he has told us, but he thinks Matt is a dumb one because he still goes to school. He doesn't get that he teaches. Don't worry about it. However, if you like, when Marty gets home tomorrow, he can trim it for you. Then it wouldn't be so shaggy."

He watched her expression, "You think it is ugly too, don't you?"

"Not ugly, but shaggy."

"I never thought it mattered. Sheriff Bernard said to behave and not wear out my welcome. So maybe I should."

Nora surprised him as she sat down next to the bed and looked directly at him. "Harold, you be yourself. I'd rather you do that. You and I had a rough start, but I think we're doing okay now. I would hate to think that you aren't sincere, just so we won't throw you out."

Harold's mouth dropped open, "No. I didn't mean that. But Gramps thinks I should get rid of the beard, so maybe I should."

"Okay." Then she took his hand that was in the cast, "I should've been nicer when you came, but I had my judging meter on high that day. I was so panicked when CJ was missing, I could hardly think straight. I want to apologize."

He squeezed her hand with the part of his hand sticking out from the cast, "I'm the one who owes that kid an apology. I owe one to your whole family. I did steal from you and I had no excuse."

"It would've been better if you had just asked us. But hey, it's over now; although it might go a long way with CJ. He was pretty rattled by the whole thing."

"Want me to stay away from your kids? I get it if you do."

"No. Watch your language. I really would rather not have them going to school with biker talk. You live here, and they need to accept you like they were accepted."

"Do you trust me?"

"Yup. If you hurt them, I'll hang you from the highest tree like I would anyone else. Harold, you're still the same kid that we knew before. You just sorta stuffed him in the back seat . . . or what is it bikers have? A side saddle?"

Harold laughed, "A side car."

"Same difference. I'll go get them and by the way, they know to keep quiet about you being here. We told them some bad guys are looking for you, so they are on board."

"I wish to hell I'd never started buying from Diablo. That really was my end gate. I didn't realize how deep I was getting until I couldn't get out. I really hate things being this way, but I have no idea what the hell to do."

"I can imagine that. I know how both Andy and Jackson suffered when they first got home from the war with nightmares and all that. It was wrenching for all of us. I have no idea what it would be like to try to deal with it all alone. I do worry about the influence of the gang. I don't go for violence."

"I know you didn't ask, but I want to tell you. Nora, you have my word, I didn't know what they were doing to that woman that was murdered. I was so stoned, I didn't even know where I was. I know it's no excuse. I'll be honest, if I had known what they were doing, I still wouldn't have tried to stop it. Some things you can't really stop. I'm for sure no damned saint, but I don't like hurting people unless I have to. I promise I'll get out of your hair as soon as I'm well enough."

"Harold, that makes no sense. You'll only stay here when you are sick, but when you are well enough to be good company, you want to leave! You knit wit." Nora smiled, "I'll go bring the kids in."

Harold was amazed, but he actually felt nervous while he waited for the kids to come in. He guessed it was because of things with CJ, but he wasn't certain. Then the mob came through the door. Zach was carrying a toddler and four other little kids followed with Nora. They looked like they were going to see the Freak Tent at the circus, except the middle one, a girl, who was grinning from ear to ear.

Zach introduced the boy in his arms, "This is Clancy, also called High Pockets. Clancy, this is Kid."

"Hi," the little boy smiled, and then shouted, "Iwo Jima!"

Harold chuckled, "Did he say Iwo Jima?"

"Yes," Zach explained. "He and Grandpa talk wars and Grandpa taught him that."

Harold smiled and said 'Iwo Jima' back at him. Zach put the boy on the floor and he took off out of the room like a shot. "Did I scare him?"

"No, he just does that," Zach explained, as he picked up the littlest girl. "And this little sweetheart is Claudia. We call her Kitten. She is going to be four in a couple days. Oh, Kid, she just got hearing aids, so she has a small vocabulary."

Harold held out his free hand to her and said, "Hello, Kitten."

She considered his every move with a studious gaze and then smiled, "Hello."

"It is good to meet you."

Nora added, "Kitten, we are going to keep a watch over Kid until he gets well. Okay?"

"Okay," she answered shyly. "Watch Kid."

Then she turned into Zach's arms and hugged him. Next, Clarissa stepped forward, "Hi, Mr. Kid. My name is Clarissa and I'll be your friend, butcept if you take my calf cause his name is Sneezy and he would be very sad if you taked him from me and so would I bite you."

Nora frowned, "We don't go around biting people, Clarissa."

"I would so, if he taked my Sneezy."

Harold told her, "I won't take Sneezy."

"Is that a cross your heart promise?" the little girl demanded.

"It is."

Then she giggled, "Okay. We can be friends and I can tell you about everything because I like to talk and I know about a lot of stuff, but Missus said that we must never say to anybody that you are here because some bad guys will put you in the ground. I just hate that. But I did get a feather when they put my Daddy and my new Mommy in the ground, butcept I got Missus now."

Harold grinned, "I see."

"Yah, it would be most hardest to keep a big secret like that butcept for the ground part. So I won't. But when I can, will you let me tell everybody because I am the most goodest at it?"

"I bet you are. What was your name again?"

"I am Clarissa Grey Hawk and I'm five years old."

Clarence was rolling his eyes, "Clarissa! You are talking so much my head hurts."

Clarissa squinted her eyes at her big brother, "Well, you haven't said nothing!"

"I couldn't. You were talking too much!" Clarence said. "I'm Clarence and I'm eight. I hope you get better Mr. Kid and you feel fine again. If Clarissa talks too much, just put your pillows around your ears. You won't have to listen."

"Clarence Clayton Grey Hawk!" his sister reprimanded him, "You are a bad boy! You tell him, Missus."

"Come on kids, let's get out of here before we drive Kid crazy."

They all left except CJ who was standing behind them all. When they left, he came over to the bed. He stood there looking him over and finally asked quietly, "Is that big thing on your arm made out of rock?"

"Kinda. Come around and feel it. It is a plaster cast. The doctors make it like a mud, then put it on, and let it dry. It gets hard as a rock. Feel it."

CJ did and then asked, "Does it hurt?"

"It is getting better."

"Will you have to carry that rock on your arm forever?"

"No, three months or so, if I take care of it."

"I hope you do." Then CJ looked at the biker, "You mad at me yet? I shouldn't have looked through your window and been so sneaky. I'm sorry."

Harold was shocked, "You're sorry? I shouldn't have stolen your eggs and milk!"

"That Sheriff guy said two wrongs don't make it right."

Harold watched this kid in awe, "No CJ, it doesn't. I was wrong. I didn't have to act like I did. I'm sorry."

"Me, too." CJ climbed up on the bed and hugged the man before he climbed back down, "Are we friends now?"

"Do you want to be my friend?"

"Yah, I guess so. I mean we're going to be tiyospaye, so I guess we should be friends. It's easier," the little boy explained. "What do you think?"

"It's always easier to be friends. CJ, when Nora comes in again, I'm going to ask her to get my wallet and give you the buck fifty for the eggs and milk."

"No, that is Mister's money. I just didn't want to get fired. You remember Kevin? He, Charlie, and me are going to raise rabbits and I need to pay him. See?"

"Oh, should I give the money to Kevin?"

"No, I think we can talk to Mister about it. Okay? Do you know anything about rabbits?"

"I had some when I was a boy, actually."

"If you promise not to cook them, I'll show them to you when they come. Okay? Would you like that?"

"I would."

Zach came back in, "Nora says you should get cleaned up for dinner, CJ. The guys will be here soon."

CJ looked at Harold, "I'm glad we're friends. I know you are an okay guy because you helped my foot. I'm not ascared of you. I hope your hand gets better real fast. Bye."

The boy dashed out of the room and Harold's face was a study. Zach sat down next to the bed and then said, "Want to talk about it?"

The man started to weep, "He apologized to me! I scared him half to death and he apologized! Zach, I think I'm going crazy."

"Nah," Zach put his arm around him, "You're not. My practice is all kids and I tell you, they're so honest and open, sometimes I think it is a shame that people grow up. It usually is not an improvement."

-9-

Harold put his bed back and thought about what had just happened. Those kids were pretty neat, especially that CJ. It was really something that he would apologize. Harold knew the boy thought he was going to kill him. He also figured he was still afraid of him, or he would have never said he wasn't. If he hadn't known himself so well, Kid might have felt good about it. Then he raised his eyebrows, 'Yah, I'll end up letting him down like I always do. I need to get out of here.'

Later, Kid woke screaming, and Zach and another guy came rushing in to help him. Zach gave him an injection into the IV while the other man talked calmly to him. He reassured him that he was safe and helped him relax.

When Zach got finished, he said, "That was my fault. I didn't get your IV fixed up in time. I'm sorry. I want to change that IV bag and then you'll be good to go again."

He frowned, "Does that mean that once these IV's are done, my terrors will be back?"

Zach sat on the edge of the bed, "Sorry to say, most likely, but not as bad. Right now, they are just dormant. We need to use this window to try to get other things working better for you, before we have to take the IV's away. If you can get your body healthier, that will help a lot. It will take longer, but you should be able to work on whatever is making you have those nightmares."

"I guess I thought things would just be this way from now on," Harold mumbled with disappointment. "Not realistic, huh?"

Zach said, "Would be nice, but no. Let me put these meds away. Oh, this is Matt Harrington."

Matt smiled, "Hello. Do you go by Kid or Harold?"

"Harold was my grandfather's name!"

Matt nodded. "Okay, Kid, I'm around here a lot because I am engaged to Diane and she lives here. You've met my brother, Ian. He's called Harrington."

"Oh yah, we met. He is related to that Carl."

"Yes, Carl is our step-dad."

"He was FBI, right?"

"He was and Ian was a detective with Boston PD."

"Were you a cop, too?"

"No, I was a Catholic priest. Now, I teach high school in Merton."

"I didn't think that you could quit being a priest."

"You can and you can't."

Harold shook his head in bewilderment, "Clears that right up!"

Matt chuckled, "I'm sorry. I didn't mean to be obtuse about it. I'll explain it to you later. I think the guys will be here from Fargo soon, so I should get you set up to eat before they come driving in. The house will be chaos once they arrive."

"I can take care of myself. You go ahead."

"I see that. Or, I can help you."

Harold gave him a dirty look, "Well, I guess I might need a little help. I should go to the can. What can I do with this IV?"

"I'll help you with that while Matt fixes up your bed." Zach said as he came back in, "Hey, I like what you did with your hair."

Harold glared at him, "Jackass."

In a few minutes, the patient was cleaned up and his bed remade. The IV was doing its work, and his mood was improving. The men said dinner would be there shortly and he was looking forward to it.

A couple minutes later, there was a rap at the door and Matt returned carrying a small coffee pot. With him was a beautiful young woman. She looked like a younger Nora, slender, soft brown hair, and big brown eyes. She had his dinner tray. Matt moved the bedside table around. She put it down and held out her hand to the man.

"Hi. I'm Diane, sometimes called Tinker. I live here, too. Matt is my fiancée."

"Damn, what a fox!" Harold blurted out and then felt extremely stupid.

His eyes darted to Matt who just grinned back, "I think you are recovering!"

"I shouldn't have said that."

Diane giggled, "Better than having you say, 'Yikes, what a dog!'"

"I might kill myself now." Harold muttered.

Matt laughed, "You almost succeeded on that earlier this week from what I heard."

"Just about."

Diane smiled, "Matt will visit with you, but I better get out there and help with dinner. Just think, soon you'll be able to join us."

After she left, Harold said to Matt, "You can go, too. I know you don't want to sit here with me."

"You psychic?"

"Why?"

"If I go out there, I'll get put to work! How many of the clan kids have you met?"

"The Grey Hawks. They seem nice."

"They are all nice, but when they get together with the Ellison kids, who are also all nice, insanity prevails."

"How many kids do they have?"

"Five. Well, Miriam isn't their kid, but she lives with them. She is Zach's niece. The oldest two are wonderful teenagers. Ginger is a sweetheart, but she and Clarence are at loggerheads with each other. They squabble about everything. Then Charlie and CJ are like two little whirlwinds. Miriam calls herself Gopher and she is Kitten's best friend. They are all pretty well-behaved, but they are goofy."

"Want to share my IV?"

"Might just," Matt grinned.

"I'm sorry Man, I didn't mean to make a crack about your old lady."

"That's okay. I think she is nice-looking, too." Matt sat down and grinned at Harold, "Want to hear what I did? Last week when I was in the hospital, I was all drugged up and in front of everybody, asked her if she wanted to make out. Needless to say, she said no."

"Must be the meds," Harold nodded. "Why were in you the hospital?"

"Her Mom poisoned me." Matt said matter-of-factly, "She wanted to kill me."

Harold looked at him in shock, "You giving me bull?"

"Not in the least," Matt replied. "Someday, we have to chat."

Harold studied this guy, "Are you a—what do they call it—clanner?"

"Yes. I hear you are, too. Grandpa doesn't like your beard, but he thinks I'm the dumb one. We must be picks of the litter!"

The biker laughed, "Nora told me about that! I think I'll get my beard trimmed when this one guy gets off work. He is an ambulance driver."

"Marty. He is a paramedic. You'd have to get up pretty early in the morning to find a nicer guy. Oh, and here I sit, holding on to the coffee pot. Zach said you can have a little bit if I dilute it down with milk. Otherwise, you can have just milk or I can get you some tea."

"I would love a cup of black coffee or a brew."

"No can do. Sorry, but Zach would boil us both in hot lard."

"Yah, I guess. Coffee with milk then."

The biker watched as this slim man with dark auburn hair and bright blue eyes poured his coffee. He couldn't imagine what this guy was. A priest, victim of attempted murder, and fiancée of a beautiful woman he had just made a pass at—and here he sat visiting with him like a long, lost friend. These last few days were a hallucination.

Matt held the cup out for Harold. "What? You have something on your mind?"

"Nothing."

"Liar."

"I was wondering if this is a hallucination."

Matt laughed, "It might be, but then we are all having the same one. How's the coffee?"

"It'd be better with less milk and more coffee."

"Yes, but it would tear up your gut. You have enough trouble in that department. The guys went up today to put chlorine in your well. Kevin said the one whole side is caved-in. You might consider just filling it in and starting over. They'd be glad to do that for you, if you want. The Sheriff isn't very happy about just leaving it, because someone might come by and get sick like you did. You can think about it."

"Matt? That's your name, right?"

Matt nodded.

"I don't have enough money for that."

"Oh, they won't charge you for it."

"What am I supposed to do, just keep taking from the people I stole from?" He was agitated.

"Don't get all bent." Matt put his hand on his arm, "No, Kid. You can pay them back later. There are a lot of ways to pay folks back besides handing out dollar bills. I think you know that. God doesn't give us all a fat bank account, but He gave us all something that can be shared."

"You giving me a sermon?"

"I'm out of that business. Nope. Just the facts. You can help with stuff, listen to people, be a role model, cook—,"

"A role model? Hell, you must be smoking something stronger than I got!"

"You know, people that come out of messing up their lives can be a better role model than ones that didn't."

Harold looked at him for about a minute flat without an expression and then slowly shook his head, "It was a good idea you got out of the sermon business!"

"Didn't I make sense?" Matt chuckled.

"I guess you kinda did. I'm just not in the mood to think about all that crap."

"I believe that. Well, you have a couple weeks, like Zach said. If you want to talk, anytime except when I'm at school, say the word. I'll be happy to listen. You already know I give wonderful advice! Really, I know that life isn't like a Hallmark card."

Harold considered this man, "You're different."

Matt grinned, "Good or bad different?"

"Don't know yet."

"I don't know about you yet, either. Gives us something to look forward to. Hey, Keith said you used to ride horses, huh? We go riding a lot and Diane's brother has a fine horse, but he is in the Air Force. He could use the exercise."

"If he's in the Air Force, he probably gets his exercise," Harold poked.

Matt scrunched up his face, "I'm thinking that bad-different is definitely winning!" Then he laughed, "I was going to ask you if, as soon as Zach says, you'd like to ride Lightning. Now, you'll have to beg."

"Man, I haven't been on a horse since the beginning of time. I'd probably fall off and break my other arm."

"Look at it this way, then you could be on IV's longer!"

"You're totally insane!"

"Hey, I'm not the one with my arm in a cast."

"If I ever get well, you might be," Harold grinned.

"Careful, I'll turn Diane's mother lose on you."

"Oh," Harold doubled over in cramps. "I gotta go."

After they got the bathroom trip all settled, Matt started to pick up his dinner things on the tray. He stopped and held out his hand to him, "Kid, it's been fun visiting with you. Hope you'll let me stop by again."

Harold shook his hand and said, "I'd like that."

"Okay, anything else? Bed down?"

"I think so. I'm awful tired again. Matt, I'll think about it."

"What?"

"Yea gads, good thing you quit being a priest! Being a role model, you bozo!"

"Oh that," Matt smiled. "There's no thinking to it. You already are. Everyone is, every day. Good or bad. So, all we need to decide is what kind of role model we want to be."

"Oh."

Harold slept awhile until he heard a knock. A short, slight man with a shock of salt and pepper hair came in. He held out his hand and smiled, "Hello. I'm Elton Schroeder. Welcome to my home. I hope they're treating you well."

"Oh, uh." He sorted himself around, "Mr. Schroeder. Everyone has been nicer to me than I deserve."

"Call me Elton." Elton chuckled, "If most of us were treated like we deserved to be, it wouldn't be nice. I was so sorry to hear about your Dad. He was a good man and I considered him a friend. I didn't know we were going to be neighbors again."

"Neither did I. Mr. Schroeder, I shouldn't have stolen your eggs and milk. I was wrong and I apologize."

"Accepted. In the future, if you need something, just ask. Okay? CJ was certain we would have to hang a poacher!" Elton laughed. "Kevin explained we don't do that. I hear your situation has been lousy lately. Let's get everything fixed up for you and then we can work on being good neighbors."

"Dad would kill me if he knew what I did to you all."

"Don't worry about it. I understand that you have problems sleeping. You'll fit right in with the Nocturnal Engelmanns around here."

"The what?"

"We have a bunch of night wanderers among us. Zach was a good one."

"I thought he lived next door?"

"He used to live here. Now we have Andy, Jackson, and Diane. Of course, Grandpa thinks nighttime is when he can rearrange the pantry. We have more going on at night than most people do all day! Oh, and have you heard Clancy's wolf howl yet? He howls and the little girls start to cry. Why, it makes me want to take up drinking again!"

Harold listened and then said, "I'll be on my way and out of your hair as soon as I can."

"No need. I hear that most these guys are getting attached to you. I just wanted to say hello and let you know that you're welcome here. Okay?"

Harold looked at him, "Dad always said you were a good guy."

"He was, too." Elton patted his arm, "Well, Pastor Byron wanted to say hi before he goes home. So, need anything?"

"No, I guess I could have the bed up."

"Okay, Kid. You got it."

Elton cranked him up and then said good night. A minute or so later, there was another knock and Byron came in. The middle-aged man was about 5'10" with fair hair and blue eyes. "Hello Harold. I mean, Kid."

"Hello Pastor," the embarrassed biker replied.

"May I sit down?"

"Help yourself."

"It sounds like you've had some interesting times. If you ever need to talk, I'll be here as soon as I can. I'm only five minutes away. I mean it. Okay?"

"What would I want to talk about?"

"I don't know. But if you call me at two AM, it better not be about corn flakes! I know you've been having those night terrors since the war, like these guys did. If you want to talk, that's what I'm here for. I know it isn't quite the same, but I was in Korea. That was no cakewalk. It is extremely difficult to be thrown into a life style that contradicts everything you believe and then leave it again without some hangover."

"Pastor Ellison, I don't even know what I believe anymore."

"I'll tell you a secret. Life is a contradiction for most of us. If you want, we can spend some time sorting through it when you feel up to it."

"You don't want to mess with me."

"Who told you that?" the Lutheran minister asked pointedly.

"Ah, well . . ."

"I plan on messing with you, a lot, as your preacher and your friend!" Byron grinned, "I hear you are our newest clanner! Grandpa Lloyd wanted me to talk to you about shaving your beard. He thinks you lost your razor."

The biker smiled for the first time, "He offered me his. He said I'll never get a woman with this beard. Little does he know."

"Oh, does it attract a lot of women?"

"Hell, no self-respecting woman would want to be around me."

"You know this how?"

"Did you hear about California?"

"Yes. Did you murder that woman?"

"No, but . . ."

"But you planned it?" Pastor Ellison interrupted.

"Of course not!"

"You know Harold, you can hold on to your guilt as your anchor as long as you want, or you can put it away and go about your life. If you told God you're sorry and mean it; it is over. He's forgotten it. Humans are a lot less forgiving, but you paid your debt to society. We've all done all sorts of stuff we aren't and shouldn't be proud of. It can be an excuse or not."

"I was an embarrassment to my family. My sisters won't have anything to do with me. They said I was the reason Dad died."

"I thought he died last year. Weren't you in prison for six or seven years?"

"Yah. Why?"

"If he died because he was embarrassed you were in prison, wouldn't he have done it when it first happened?"

Harold turned and looked Byron in the eye, "Never thought of that. You know, Dad and I had a lot of talks after I was in jail. He wasn't proud, for damn sure, but he was rather matter-of-fact about it. He told me to get my head out of my, ah, well you know."

"Yah. Harold, when you talk to me, you don't have to butter it up. Okay? Oh, I forgot, I'm to call you Kid. That is probably good because then no one will know you are back."

Harold got a bit of a weak smile, "You know Matt?"

"One of my best friends."

"He told me I'm a role model. He said we all are. It's up to us if we are a good one or a bad one."

"He's right."

"How can I be a good one? These rugrats all think I'm a poacher and should be hung! That little Clara or whatever . . ."

"Clarissa."

"Yah, she told me that if I take her Sneezy, she'll bite me."

Byron chuckled, "No doubt, she would, too!"

"I always liked kids, but I scared CJ to death the other day." Then the skinny man looked vacantly across the room. "I wanted to. I want to make him go and stay away! But as terrified as he was, he stayed by me when I was so sick and even gave me his sandwich! Not many grownups would do that. Tonight, he apologized to me for sneaking on my place!" Then he eyes reddened with tears, "Can you believe that?"

Byron nodded, "Yes. I can. Those kids had quite traumatic lives. They know everything isn't always pretty."

"I have to go to the can."

"Need help?"

"The IV is on this wheel thing. I usually knock it over, if you could help me with that."

When he settled back in bed, he said, "Thanks. I just have to get on my way and out of your lives as soon as I can."

"Any plans on what you're going to do?"

"Nah. Doesn't matter. Guess if it gets too bad, I can just go to California and let the Horde take care of it. Then I'll be done."

Byron watched this dejected man without a reaction and then said, "We all have a similar option, I guess. Trouble is, it isn't retractable. Anyway, my suggestion is to not think about it. Cool it for a while. You have a place to be, good folks around you, and great food. Enjoy it for a while. Once you recoup a little, you'll be able to decide what to do rather easily. You know, Harold, there isn't a clanner than wouldn't be willing to listen if you want to talk. So, make it a point to do that, or at least try. You might be surprised at the options you have. You rest now and I'll tell my kids to see you tomorrow."

"No. That's okay. The Grey Hawks got to see the freak; they should, too. Drag them in here if you want," he snapped.

"I don't want them to see you with that attitude."

Byron left the room without a word. Harold looked down at his cast and wished he was dead. Harold couldn't believe that he had shown such disrespect to this man, a minister no less, for no reason. He banged his fist on the bed and then wiped his face with his free hand. He felt himself getting wound up. He wanted to scream, but felt he had caused enough baloney that night.

A couple minutes later, there was a knock at the door and Byron poked his head in, "Ready?"

Kid frowned, "I thought you didn't want them to see me."

"Here they are." Byron grinned, "This pretty lady is my wife, Marly. There is Ken, Katie, Ginger, Charlie, and Miriam."

Kid nodded and Marly reached for his free hand, "Glad to meet you. I have to admit, I don't remember you from years ago. Nora and I are best friends, so I know I'll get to know you now. Okay?"

Seventeen-year old Ken shook his hand, "Hi. I'm Ken. Maybe if you have time, we could talk about your Harley. I work at Uncle Elton's garage in Merton and I like that kind of stuff . . . If you want to."

"Are you going to be a mechanic?" Kid asked.

"I don't know what I'm going to be, but I like that stuff."

"Me, too. Yah, when I get more awake, we could do that."

"I'm Kate," a pretty, blonde teenager said. "I hang around here a lot so you'll see me again for sure. I like baking and sewing, so we probably don't have a lot in common. Maybe we can find something."

"I like eating," Kid smiled.

Katie giggled, "That will work! I'd better go help Grandma right now. See you soon."

The two teenagers went out of the room and a little red-headed girl with a face-full of freckles came up by the hospital bed. "My name is Ginger and I just turned eight. I bet you hate being in bed, huh? I know I did. See, I did something stupid and burned my face off. I had to be in bed forever. It is boring! So if you get bored, you can tell me about it. I used to tell everybody how much I like dirt and I still do, but I found out that most people don't. So, I don't mention it so much anymore. But if you want to read a book about dirt, I have lots of them. Okay? Clarence said you probably won't like dirt. Be careful of Clarence, because he thinks he is the boss of everybody."

"Thanks for the warning."

"I mean, he's okay." Ginger said and then shrugged, "I'm nicer though."

Kid nodded, "I might just look at a book about dirt. But in a few days, I'm pretty worn out today."

The littlest girl with black, curly hair and long black eyelashes smiled at him and patted her chest, "Gopher. Me and Kitten friends. Watch you. Okay?"

"That'll be nice."

"Good. Bye bye."

The man chuckled, "Bye."

Gopher went out of the room and the tow-headed boy with blue eyes and a few freckles came up to the bed. He scrutinized the patient and then leveled his gaze at the man, "It wasn't nice of you to take those eggs. It made me and CJ worried; but Daddy says that you're sorry, so we're over it. CJ told me that you know about rabbits, huh? We're going to get some. Maybe you could help us with the rabbits. See, CJ and I have lots of animals to take care of. We're awful busy, but since we don't have to worry about poachers no more, we'll have more time for our rabbits."

"I see that. When I can get around better, I'll try to help you with your rabbits."

Charlie squinted his eyes, "Does that mean you will steal them?"

"Nope. I won't steal your rabbits."

"That's good." Then the little boy studied the man, "When you get better, can you help us dig? Are you a good digger?"

"It will be a while, but I suppose I could. Do you like to dig?"

"Us kids are all good diggers, but we can't dig in the cemetery. My Dad gets mad about that. We are going to build a big dam in the pasture to make a lake. You can help us, if you are better. I can borrow a shovel for you."

"That'd be nice. When I get well."

"I have to go now. I'm glad you didn't shoot CJ. He's my best friend."

The boy took off out of the room and Byron pulled up his chair, "See, look how many new friends you have made already!"

"There isn't a one of them that trusts me. Is there?"

"Not right now, but they'll give you a chance. I hope it doesn't bother you that they mention the poaching so much. They aren't trying to put you down; it was just a lot of excitement."

"I know that. Hell, I deserve it. Thanks, Pastor Ellison."

"When we're home, I'm Byron. Okay, Kid?"

The biker nodded and then tried to scoot down on his bed. The minister helped him get ready to rest. "Zach said to tell you he is getting your medication ready, so you can rest for the night. See you tomorrow."

Harold Effan leaned back on the bed and listened to the hum of the household. After a few minutes, he realized how much he had missed that. When he was a kid, he was used to the sounds of stoves, furnaces, chatter, and the other sounds of living. However, from the time he went to Vietnam, it was missing. There was no sound of coffee perking in a kitchen or dishes clinking on a table. With Satan's Horde, there was nothing domestic about the sounds. Partying, swearing, or hangovers about covered it. He never slept in the same place more than a night or two. Then prison. That had its own background noise, no doubt; but it wasn't comforting.

He had always liked kids. In Vietnam, one of his best friends died when a small, sweet child gave him some water laced with poison. He bled to death internally in Harold's arms. Harold knew better than to blame the child, but he never trusted them again. He didn't trust anyone or anything, most of all himself.

His head was really a whirl. He was very grateful for the IVs. They made him more relaxed then he had been for this last half his life. These folks were all nice, but he knew he would mess that up before long. In spite of the fact he was relieved, he was still more frightened than he had been in his life, and he knew fear. He felt alone and lost.

Zach gave him his medications. "Suzy and I are staying tonight, but Annie will be home tomorrow. I have to get back to work. Between Annie and Marty, you'll be in good hands. Questions?"

Harold shook his head. Zach studied him, "What is it?"

Harold Effan, formerly known as Geraldo, in the tough Satan's Horde Motorcycle club from California, just shrugged, "Nothing."

Zach sat on the edge of the bed, "It'll take a while. Your body hasn't even begun to heal. You just got off a long roller coaster. Can I ask you a huge favor?"

Kid wrinkled his eyebrows, "What could I possibly do for you?"

"Take it easy. Just take it as easy as you can for a week, anyway. Please promise me that you'll take advantage of the offers of friendship. One thing about the clan that took me forever to believe was that they not only will honor your privacy, but they will also go the extra mile for you. They won't pull any punches, if you keep it square. You need help, say so."

"Why?"

Zach grinned, "Why not? You got something else going?"

- 10 -

Harold was asleep before very long, but it was more restless sleep than before. It wasn't noisy, just more commotion. A while later, he opened his eyes to find Grandpa leaning over him, "Still has that mess on his face," the old man mumbled to himself. "I should shave it for him. I'll get my straight-edge."

Kid's eyes flew open, paralyzed in panic.

"No, Lloyd!" Elton intervened, "He's getting it trimmed tomorrow. He is too sick today. You don't need to shave him. That is the last thing he needs."

"You just think I don't know how," the old man grumped. "You think I don't know anything."

"You know a lot of things. Come on, Lloyd. Let's not wake Kid. He is so sick. I can walk you back to your room."

"Will he do it tomorrow?" The elderly man worried.

"Most likely. Anything I can get for you, Lloyd?"

"No. You should bring the team up. I need to get that seed corn."

"I know. We'll do it after the sun comes up. You might want to take a short nap so you have more energy later."

Harold heard Elton walk the man to his room and inveigle him back to bed. Then Elton came back into Kid's room. "Need anything before I go to back to bed?"

"No." Kid said seriously, "Thanks. He could be dangerous with a razor."

"For sure! If you need anything, don't be shy about yelling. Like if he shows up with a razor! Okay? Want to go to the bathroom before I leave?"

"Suppose I should."

As he was getting back into bed, he looked at his host, "Mr. Schroeder, are those veterans home tonight?"

"Yah, they're both sleeping. Do you want to talk to them?"

"No. I just wondered. How are they doing?"

Kid wondered why he hadn't met the veterans, Andy and Jackson. Everyone had mentioned them, but they never came by. They were probably war heroes, not some loser like him. If these folks had a clue how much courage he lacked, they would have left him in the farmhouse.

Elton pulled up the stool next to the bed and sat down. "They're doing pretty well. They were both worn out when they got home tonight. Andy, my son, got a good report on his legs. He had both knees shot out. He has artificial knees and many injuries on one leg. But his biggest problem was from some of the chemicals used over there. Turned out, Andy had a high level of arsenic in his system! They finally got that about back to normal. Kid, it was a fright. He couldn't sleep, snarling, and snapping at everyone. He had alienated nearly everyone. He is doing so much better now. However, when he gets too tired, he still gets very edgy. Now he has learned to just get some sleep before it gets out of hand."

Kid nodded, but never said how well he understood that. Elton continued, "Now Jackson has some of that, but not as much. He had to have his foot amputated after he got back to the States, because the infection just wouldn't give in. Until recently, the doctors thought he might have to have to take more of his leg. The infection finally relented. He was fitted for his artificial foot this time. He will get it in a couple weeks. He had quite a work out while we were gone and was in a good deal of pain tonight. He took his pain pill and went right to bed."

"Lost his foot?"

"Yah, about mid-calf."

"What do the guys do?"

"They work down at the shop, here at home. We got a little appliance/ small engine repair shop set up for them. They are actually doing quite well with it, considering their injuries. What sort of work did you do?"

"Honestly?"

"Well, if it isn't going to be honest, there's no need to ask. I could just make something up in my own head."

Kid looked at Elton and grinned, "I guess. I used to tinker with motors and bodywork. After the service, I mostly just got high, sold drugs, and raised hell. Not much of a resume."

Elton watched the man, "I imagine you worked on motorcycles, huh?"

"Yah. Love 'em."

"Oh, by the way, Kevin mentioned that Sheriff Bernard thought you should get rid of the 'colors' on your leathers. I don't know how you feel about it, but if you want, Katie offered to take them off for you. Then we can get the leathers all oiled and cleaned up. Some of it probably means a lot to you, so you'll need to think about it."

Kid snorted, "It doesn't. I don't have much that means a lot to me."

"Yah, you do. You're just too tired to realize it now. Once you get well, you'll find your interest in things again."

"You sure?"

"No, but you don't know I'm wrong, do you?" Elton chuckled.

"No."

"Well, I should wander off to my room. Good night, Kid."

"Thanks Mr. Schroe—,"

"Elton."

"Thanks, Elton."

It was a while later, Kid thought he heard his door open, but wasn't sure. It was dark in the room and no one said anything, so he went back to sleep. Once he woke up and became restless with the sense that someone was in the room. He thought he heard movement or breathing, but didn't see anything. He decided it was the medication.

Later he became very uncomfortable and knew he had to get to the bathroom in a hurry. He tried to sit up, but got tangled up with his IV. Just then, Zach came in and helped him. After things were settled, Kid asked Zach, "How did you know I needed you?"

"Kitten came to get me. She took my hand and said, 'Kid'."

Kid gave him a surprised look, "How did she know?"

"I don't know," Zach shrugged, "But it worked out well. You doing okay?"

"Yah. Is the medication different tonight? I'm restless and feel like someone is in the room, but I don't see anyone. I'm going nuts."

"Meds are the same. Kid, I'm going to keep you rather knocked out for the next few days, unless you disagree. I want your body to get a chance to heal in peace. When you're on the mend, we can talk about your withdrawal from smack. The more healing you get before that, the easier that will be."

"I have done it cold turkey a couple times. It's no picnic, but I don't feel at all like that now. Why?"

"Because of the medication and pain meds. I hope that we can get the other things in place before we withdraw it all."

"What things?"

"Your overall health and your emotional condition."

Harold squinted suspiciously, "You saying I'm crazy?"

Zach grinned, "Everyone is a little crazy. You know you can't sleep all night. Waking to night terrors is not normal. We want to get that sorted out, so at least you can get your rest. Your body needs that to survive."

"How long will that take?"

"I don't know. I'll talk to my colleague tomorrow and see if he can come up with something to take the edge off. Is the restlessness something that you find too difficult to deal with?"

"Nah. I feel antsy, like I'm being watched."

Just then, the bedroom door opened. Cotton, Kitten's cat, came in and jumped on the barrel chair by the door. Cotton made herself at home and stretched out. Zach chuckled. "I think the mystery is solved!"

Kid was visibly relieved, "I'm glad it is the cat. Grandpa came by earlier and thought he should help me shave my beard!"

"Yikes!" Zack scrunched up his face, "Want me to build you a moat?"

"Might be a good idea."

"Want me to put the cat out?"

"No, that's okay. I like cats."

Different times during the night, Kid heard various noises or movement in his room. He thought to himself, 'Just the cat.'

In the morning, the family alarm went off and the routine began. Zach stopped by, gave Kid his medications and told him that Annie would be home about seven. She and Marty would take over then. Then he grinned, "If I were you, I'd have Marty cut my beard. Grandpa doesn't give up."

Kid smiled, "I thought of that. A guy could get his throat cut!"

"For sure!" Zach grinned. "I see that Kitten was in here this morning."

"You mean the little girl? I only saw the cat."

"No, Kitten left her blanket on the chair. She was probably looking for her cat."

"Zach? Will her hearing ever get better?"

"No, the damage that was done is permanent. At least she isn't losing more. Those kids have had a struggle just existing, up 'til recently. They are doing very well. I think I hear breakfast coming."

Sure enough, in came Grandma with a tray. Zach helped her set up the bedside table and said goodbye. Grandma smiled, "I heard that you like caramel rolls. Is that a fact?"

Kid grinned broadly, "Yes, it is. Keith used to bring them to school for me."

"I remember that he used to bring an extra one every so often. Glad you liked them. This one is fresh out of the oven. Would you like me to cut it up for you?"

The man looked at the golden brown roll that was about four inches in diameter and over two inches deep. "Man, it is making me drool."

Grandma cut up the roll and Kid smiled as he put his first forkful of caramel roll in his mouth. "Oh! This is wonderful. I had forgotten how wonderful this is!"

Grandma watched while he ate, "Zach said you can start a regular diet soon. What would you like as a special treat?"

His eyes moved toward her and his face froze, "No one has asked me that for years. I have no idea. You don't need to make anything special for me."

"Young man," the elderly lady pointed out, "I have prepared meals for over eighty years. I enjoy a good suggestion from time to time."

He smiled, "Okay then, what was my favorite? When I was a kid, I always ordered breaded pork cutlets and mashed potatoes with gravy for my birthday dinner."

"Hm," Grandma smiled, "That does sound good. As soon as I get the word from Zach, we'll have that. Okay?"

The young man nodded, and then said very quietly, "May I ask you something?"

"Certainly."

"Why is Zach doing all this for me? He even paid my bill at the hospital."

"He wants to help. Zach's family life was a mess and he had a terrible time. It took a while, but eventually, everything got sorted out. He knows what it's like."

"I can't imagine that it was that bad. He seems like a nice guy."

"He is," Grandma sat down. "Kid, it isn't my place to tell you. Ask him."

"I don't want to get involved in something that I can't ever pay back."

Grandma patted his shoulder, "Don't worry. Zach wouldn't do that to you. You can count on that."

He studied her and then nodded slowly, "Okay, I'll take your word for it."

He was eating his roll when Clarissa, the bubbly, five-year old, came into his room. "Hi!" the little girl said. "Is your roll good?"

"Yes, it is. Have you had breakfast yet?"

"No, I was helping milk. I just washed my hands and I'm going to eat. You get to eat first cause you are sick."

"How did chores go this morning?"

"Pretty good. You know, Diane and I are the bestest at feeding calves. Did you ever do that?"

"Yes, when I was a boy."

"I bet we're more gooder than you were, huh? Cause we do it every day."

The young man smiled, "I suppose."

The little girl climbed up on the stool and looked at him seriously, "Mr. Kid, was you really going to shoot my brother?"

He shook his head no, "No. I just wanted him to go away."

"You should have said 'shoo!'"

"I guess I'll do that next time."

"I didn't think you wanted him to go away anymore. I thought you liked him now."

"I do. I just meant . . ."

"Clarissa, Nora is waiting for you to come eat breakfast," a young man on crutches told the little girl. "Hi, I'm Jackson Fieldng."

Kid shook his hand, "Pleased to meet you. I've heard good things about you."

"Thanks. Go Clarissa. I'll be right there." Jackson smiled and then shook Kid's hand. "I hope she doesn't bug you too much. She is such a blabbermouth."

"She is only saying what everyone else is thinking."

Jackson raised his eyebrows and chuckled, "I don't know about that. She says stuff all the time that nobody in the world ever thought! Well, I better go eat now. I just wanted to say hello."

Kid lay back in the bed and was almost asleep, when a young woman came in. "Hello, I'm Annie."

He tried to sit up and she raised the back of the bed. "Hello. You are Andy's wife?"

"Yes. Have you met him?"

"No."

"He was quite messed up yesterday when he got home, so he said he went straight to bed. He still gets real cranky if he gets too tired. Have you met Jackson?"

"He stopped in a bit ago."

"He's a great guy. He and Andy were best friends over in Vietnam. He helped my Andy through some hard times."

"Friends are good over there."

"Did you have a best friend over there?"

"The first tour, I did. He died there. After that, I made it a point to not make a friend."

Annie sat on the stool, "Must have been lonely."

Harold Effan looked at her and answered flatly, "I wasn't sent over there to make friends."

"That's true." She nodded, "You weren't. Marty and I talked to Zach. We have worked out a plan to let your body rest for a few days. You will have a say in it, but we have the meds!"

"Blackmail."

She teased, "Oh, let's settle on coercion."

"Is that better?"

"Not really." The gorgeous young woman giggled, "Marty and I aren't doctors. You have to tell us exactly what's going on with you, so we can tell Zach. Okay?"

"Okay."

"I did hear that Marty is going to give you a haircut or something so Grandpa doesn't. I can tell you, I'd be terrified if Grandpa came after me with a scissors!"

"He wanted to give me a shave with a straight edge!"

"Kid, seriously, would you like to have the door locked?"

"No. When I need help, I can't get to the door."

"Good point." Annie agreed. "Well, I'm going to check your temp and then go snarf up some caramel rolls. I'll stop back later. Marty was going home and said he'll be here later this morning unless you need him earlier. He'll help you with your shower. Your meds should allow you to sleep most of the morning. Anything you need?"

"Nothing. Is today that birthday party?"

"One of them. Father Vicaro's birthday dinner is tonight. Tomorrow is Kitten's and then Sunday is Elton's."

"Kitten?" the biker asked, "How old will Kitten be?"

"Four. Want your bed back down?"

Kid had slept for a while when he heard the door open. No one said anything, but he had the feeling that someone was in his room. Within a few minutes, he fell back asleep.

A bit later, the young girl, Katie Ellison, came in to his room. "Hello."

"Hi. You're Kate, right?

"Yes. I don't know if you had time to think about those patches on your biking clothes. I haven't worked a lot with leather, but some. I'd be happy to take them off for you if you tell me which ones."

"I guess all of them."

"I'll put them all in a bag and you can look them over later. If you change your mind, we can replace them. Okay?"

The young man frowned, "I don't think I want them."

"Well, you can throw them later." She smiled, "Then Uncle Darrell and the boys will clean and oil the leather for you. You will be all spiffy."

"Darrell? Is that the kid that liked goats so much?"

"Yes. He is my mom's brother, Darrell Jessup. He has a dairy and raises goats and milk cows. Are there any tears that need repair?"

"Only on one leg. Don't worry about it. It's good enough."

"If I can, I will fix it. Okay?" Katie opened the cabinet.

She rummaged a bit and then found the leathers. Kid watched her expression. She was unable to conceal the fact that the leather jacket and chaps smelled foul. The jacket had patches all over it and some were quite offensive. He could have died of embarrassment. She never said anything but busied herself looking at how the patches were sewn on. She came over to him and giggled, "Did you sew some of them on yourself?"

He nodded, "Yah, you can tell? They were in storage for over six years. They stink."

"We'll try to get them cleaned, okay? It looks like I can get them all repaired, even the leg. There will be a problem with the big patch on the back. I think it will leave pinholes in the outline, because it was put on with a huge needle. I don't know if taking it off will make it unnoticeable. We might want to think about what we can do to cover it."

"You mean a different patch?"

"I don't know. I'll think on it, okay? You might want to think about what you would like on there."

"I have no idea."

"I'll take them now and get started. After Uncle Darrell gets them cleaned, we have plenty of time to decide what to do."

She left the room and the door was closed. Right before he fell asleep, he heard the door open again. A few minutes later, the cat jumped up on his bed and curled up on his feet. He smiled and closed his eyes.

A bit later, there was another knock on the door. "Come in."

"Hi," a young man said. "I'm Andy Schroeder."

"You look like your brothers," Kid said. "Is the cat in here?"

"No. Was she?"

"Yah, earlier. I keep hearing the door open and then don't see anyone. I think it is the cat."

"Could be. I know Kitten was in here. See, her doll is on the chair by the door."

"I can't see it from here." Kid tried to sit up.

Andy cranked up the bed, and Kid looked over, "Oh, now I see it. She never said anything. I suppose she was looking for her cat."

"She is a very quiet little girl. Zach says it is because she couldn't hear. She is starting to talk a bit now. Anyway, thought I would stop in and say hi. Need anything?"

"I guess I could go to the bathroom. I always get my IV tangled up."

"Let me help you."

After he was back in bed, Andy said, "I kinda remember you from when I was a kid. You and Keith were friends, right?"

"We had shop together."

"He joined the Marines because Dad said that you did."

"He told me that. Don't know if that was a good idea," he said quietly.

"That whole mess over there wasn't a good idea to my notion. Horse and I—."

"Horse?"

"Jackson. That's his nickname. We had one tour of duty there. Damned near did us in. Dad said you had two?"

"Yah. And it was my undoing, or my excuse for undoing."

"I guess we can all say that. I know I wasn't a pleasant person to be around when I got back. If my family hadn't been so stubborn, I'd have been out the door in a heartbeat. I was a royal ass. Still am sometimes. I have learned that when I get too tired, my wonderful nature is the first thing to go," Andy chuckled.

Kid smiled, "At least you have one to start out with! I go from sullen to impossible in two seconds flat. By the time I got back from Vietnam the last time, I hated everybody. Mostly myself. Did you ever feel like that?"

"Kinda. Mostly, I just hated myself and God. Figured that would cover it."

Kid shrugged, "I gave up on God. He wasn't there that I could see. I think it's mostly bunk."

"I finally came around to realize that the God I went over there with was rather simplistic. Now I'm beginning to understand there is more to Him than that. Sounds dumb to say. When you get to know the clan better, you'll see that no one has a clear path of it or made all the right choices. Nothing is simple. Uncle Byron says that's when you look at God in a grownup way. You begin to realize that most of the time, His answers aren't that simple. Anyway, you should talk to him about it because I don't make much sense."

Kid raised his eyebrows, "I think you do. I just don't know how I feel about it."

"Well you certainly don't owe me an explanation. I'll leave you to sleep now. I have to go down to our little shop and get some work done. Have you ever fixed a heavy-duty mixer? I have one that's motor is burned out. I think that lady must have been trying to whip rocks with it! It is really fried! Anyway, the new motor came in yesterday, so I better get it done. When you feel good enough, come look at our set-up."

"I will. Andy? Thanks for stopping in. I wondered if either of you guys were going to talk to me after what I did to CJ."

"Like I said, nobody's a saint. You didn't hurt him and you were in a tough way." Andy smiled, "Bed down? Should I leave the door open?"

"Yes please. You can close the door. Okay?"

"Later," Andy pulled the door closed.

Kid lay back in bed and thought over what Andy said. 'It might be true of him, but he was never in a biker gang or prison.'

-11-

He was in a deep sleep when he felt someone touch his shoulder, "Hello?"

"Huh?" He opened his eyes to see a dark-haired man with bright blue eyes smiling down at him.

"Hi, sorry to wake you. I'm Marty Schroeder. I came over to help you with your shower and give you a shave so Grandpa doesn't," he grinned.

"Good idea. I can wake up. All I do is sleep and eat."

"That's all you're supposed to do. You were wearing out your body. Now you have to be good to it for a while."

"I'm glad that stomach stuff has subsided. I've never had anything like that in my life and I don't want it again."

"I know I wouldn't. I see that Danny sent some clothes over for you. Grandma said that you are his size."

"Danny?"

"My brother. He is such a clothes horse! Elton is our uncle. Our dad is Eddie Schroeder who runs the Cheese Factory in Bismarck. Danny lives across the road from Ian Harrington. So, you pick out which pair of jammies you want to wear and I'll get you set up for your shave. You want your hair cut too?"

"I guess. Nora said it was straggly. I think that means it's awful."

"Ah, it isn't so bad. Let's get it cut and then you can take a shower."

While he was cutting Kid's hair, they chatted. The door opened and CJ came in with a long face. "What's up, Little Buddy?" Marty asked.

"I thought we were going to do boats today; instead you are playing with Kid. I think I don't like it," the little boy pouted.

"CJ Grey Hawk! What are you saying? You know there is always room for another friend. We'll work on our boat after I'm finished helping Kid."

"But Marty, he is a poacher. Now, he is a friend-poacher!"

Marty put the scissors down and knelt down in front of the little boy, "That was naughty. I'm disappointed in you, Man. We don't act like that."

CJ dropped his head and the tears fell as he ran out of the room. Marty stood up and apologized to Kid. "He is really a good kid. This isn't like him. I should go talk to him."

Marty went upstairs and found CJ thrown across his bed, crying his heart out. Marty gathered him up and pulled him on his lap. "CJ. You have a good cry and when you are done, we can talk. Okay?"

It only took him a little bit and a couple hugs before the boy said to Marty, "I thought we were special friends. I thought you liked me."

"I do. Greta and I are going to be your Godparents. We love you, CJ. I know that you were very upset about what happened; but right now, we need to help Kid. He doesn't have any friends and he is sick. You know, instead of being a baby about this, you could help us. Then you would feel better. I think that Kid feels awful about what he did. Have you ever done anything really stupid?"

"Yah, but . . . He is sick because he was dumb. He shouldn't have drank that yukky water and sneaked over the fence to break his arm. Then he is taking that bad dopey stuff that makes him crazy. It is all his own fault, but everybody is fussing over him. Nobody cares about me."

"You, Lunkhead! We all care about you and you know that! Do you want us to fuss over you?"

"No. But . . ."

Marty patted his back, "I know what you mean; but let's try something. Okay? Will you try for me?"

"Yah," CJ pouted.

"Okay, I'm going to go back in and finish his haircut and shower. I'd really like it if you could think of something to come in and talk to both of us about, like Bruno or bring our boat in to show it to him. If he is rude to you, then you can be mad. Deal?"

CJ stared at him, "You know he won't be that rude thing. That is why you said it. Besides, what would he know about boats?"

"I don't know. You should ask him. CJ, I'll always care about you, but I don't want you to be a jerk. Please be the great guy that I know you are."

"I still think he is a friend-poacher." CJ grumped, "I'll show him our boat and you'll see he won't like it."

Marty went back and was just finishing Kid's beard when CJ came back in carrying their model boat. He came in and stood in front of Kid, "This is the boat that Marty and I are building. I suppose you didn't have one of them when you were in jail, huh?"

Marty gave him a dirty look, but Kid answered, "No. I didn't. I used to build them when I was a kid. I had one like this except made out of balsam wood. When I got it done, I floated it on the creek. It worked until it went into the rocks."

CJ was shocked, "You had one that floated? We hope this one will. That's why we're building it."

Kid looked it over, "It is a fine ship and you did good work on it."

CJ sat down cross-legged on the floor and looked at his ship, "I don't suppose you'd want to help us do the ship?"

"I'd love to help you, but I pretty well messed myself up. I wouldn't be much help, I'm afraid. CJ, I was stupid and made a lot of bad mistakes. I have to get that fixed now. But if you have a book about ships, I'd be happy to help you read it."

"I don't have a book like that, but Mr. Matt could get us one. Right, Marty?"

"Yes, he could do that. I think I'd like to learn more about ships, too. When Kid gets well, he can help us build another ship. What do you think?"

CJ smiled, "That would be good."

Kid shrugged, "If I'm around, I would like it."

"Where you going?" CJ frowned. "I thought you are one of us guys now. Grandpa says."

"He just doesn't know what a louse I am. Once he does, he won't want me around. You know that, CJ."

"You didn't shoot me."

"I was never going to shoot you. The gun was on the table and I put it away, but I wasn't going to shoot you. CJ, I'm sorry I was so mean to you that day. I'd like it if we could be friends."

"Yah, but I got cranky when I thought you were going to steal my friend. Marty is way cool."

"Yah, he is. I can tell. I promise I won't steal him. I'm glad you'll give me a chance."

"Only if you don't take too much of Marty's time." CJ nodded, "I think Charlie is going to be here pretty soon, so I have to go now."

Marty raised his eyebrows, "Does that mean that he is a friend-poacher?"

CJ dropped his head and then gave Marty a big hug, "You're right. I was a jerk."

"Go play, I'll call you after I make Kid beautiful."

CJ teased, "Boys aren't beautiful."

After CJ left the room, Kid was quiet. Then he asked, "Think he will ever accept me?"

"He will. He was really scared that day, not only because of you but because he didn't do like he was supposed to. He didn't tell Nora he was leaving or where he was going. Then Sheriff Bernard told him he was trespassing. That threw him for a loop."

The two men were trying to figure out how to get a sweatshirt on over his cast, when Katie came in. One look and she laughed, "That won't work. If you give me the sweatshirt and about fifteen minutes, I can fix it for you."

The blue-eyed girl took the sweatshirt and left the room. "How is she going to do that?" Kid asked.

"I don't know. She is quite a seamstress. You should see the beadwork she does. She makes fantastic wedding dresses and all sorts of stuff."

Kid frowned, "She seems too young. How old is she?"

"Fifteen. She and Horse are sweethearts."

"Jackson?"

"Yes. He is nineteen."

"He seems a lot older than that."

"You should see his sketches. He is a very talented artist. He sells them at a gallery and has quite a following."

"I thought he worked in the machine shop."

"He does, and he helps out at Trinity, at the church office."

"When does he find the time?"

"The time is there; it is all in how you want to use it."

In less than fifteen minutes, she was back. She had put Velcro on the sleeves and shoulders of the shirt. "I think this will work."

"What about the IV's?" Marty asked.

Katie showed him how to open the Velcro seams to fit over the cords. "There you go. You look pretty snazzy. Grandpa will be pleased that your beard is gone. Are you going to join us at the table for lunch?"

Marty looked at him, "What do you think? Up to it?"

"Not really. I'm starting to get edgy and hurt again. I think I need to sleep."

"Okay, but maybe after a nap, I can give you a tour in the wheelchair. Would you like that?" Marty asked.

"I guess it would be good to get out of this room."

Katie smiled. "I just stopped in to tell you that Mom took your leather stuff over to Darrell. Do you have an idea of what to put on the back of the jacket?"

"I have no idea, Katie."

"Jackson and I took an imprint of the back patch and have an idea what we can do with it. We'll show it to you before we do it."

"Okay."

Marty helped him get settled for his rest, pulled the curtains, and then left the room. Kid heard him talking to CJ and Charlie while they worked on their ship. Before long, he heard the door open. Soon he felt the cat jump on his bed and curl up on his feet. He smiled and then fell asleep.

Later he woke up to the sound of little girl giggles. He looked over and saw Kitten and Gopher sitting in the barrel chair by the door. They were playing with their dolls. They noticed him and he smiled, "Hello."

Then they ran out of the room. A couple minutes later, Nora came in. "You feeling okay?"

"Yes. I just woke up. I think I scared the little girls. They were playing with their dolls in that chair. When I said hello, they took off. Are they afraid of me?"

"I don't know. Kitten sits in here a lot and 'watches Kid'. I think she got the idea because I said that we were going to watch over you. She took it literally. If it bothers you, I'll make her stop. Those kids shared one mattress at their home and have no concept of bedroom privacy."

"It's kinda sweet of her. I think that she sits in here at night. At first, I thought I was losing my mind, but very often, see the door open. I can't usually see her from my bed, but she has got me help a few times. She shouldn't think that she has to stay awake all night to watch over me."

"Elton finds her in here and carries her back to her room. When he gets up again later, she is back in the chair, sound asleep."

"He sure is up a lot at night."

"Yes, he has been the last few years. Grandpa gets quite ambitious at night. I guess it goes with his Alzheimers. Elton has the best luck getting him back to bed, although Zach is good at it too."

"Nora? Can I talk to you about something kinda private?"

"Sure." She sat on the stool. "What is it?"

"I don't want to sound ungrateful, but I'm worried. Everyone has been real good to me. It makes me wonder what you want."

Nora smiled, "We want to give you a helping hand."

"I don't believe that. You know, Zach paid my hospital bill. That cost a lot of money. If you want to rent the land like you did from Dad, I'll do it. You don't have to take care of me to con me into it."

"Kid, Elton understands that you might want it for yourself. He rented Olson's pasture across the road."

"That isn't very handy."

"No, but he's going to put the range cattle over there. He'll use our pasture for the milk cows. We aren't doing this for that. Everyone in the clan had someone help us at one time or another. We try to do it for someone else."

"Just to be nice?"

"Not really. We believe that is why we are here." Nora studied him, "You know, folks don't get a practice run at life. Usually a person is knee-deep in it, before he realizes what's going on."

"Amen."

Nora gave him a big smile, "I believe that sounds like a revival!"

"Not quite."

"By the way, I like your hair cut and shave. You're a nice-looking man. Now if we can get some meat on your bones, you'll be downright handsome."

"Could you put that in writing?"

"No way!" Nora laughed. "Marty said you might want to come out and join us. Would you like to have something at the table for lunch? We have some of Grandma's homemade chicken noodle soup today."

"That sounds good." Then his face fell, "Nora, I don't feel right around people."

"That is because you have been in this room too long."

"I'm a loner. I spent the last months in prison in isolation."

"I know. You had a reason for that. Being alone all the time isn't so good. And besides, we aren't people. We are just us."

"I haven't been an 'us' for a long time," Kid mumbled quietly.

"Guess you can't start any sooner, can you? If you want, I'll get Marty so he can help you come out. If you really don't want to, then I'll just bring your lunch."

"No, I'll come out. I hope I don't embarrass you."

Nora got off the stool and patted his hand, "And I hope I don't embarrass you."

Kid was fascinated by the number of bedrooms and the huge dining room that seated seated so many people. "You guys! This is enormous!"

"We need a place to hang out when we are all together," Marty answered.

"Once a year?"

"Try every Sunday, at least!"

After a tour of the main floor, Marty brought the biker to the kitchen. There was a lot of commotion, but a spot was set at one end of the table for him. Marty parked the wheelchair and shook his head, "I think there is more frosting here than cake!"

"No Mr. Marty! We are making the pink frosting for a surprise cake," Clarissa explained. "I know the mostest about pink, so Missus says I can decide which color is right."

"So, what is your decision?"

"It's hard. See, this is too red and this is too white. I like pink, but I like it soft. Missus said we can't promise it will be soft because it will set down."

"It will set up," Nora corrected her. "The frosting will set up."

"So we just have to get it the bestest pink."

"How are you going to decide?" Marty asked as he put a mug of coffee with milk on the table for Kid and sat down to drink his own.

Clarissa continued, "I need to think it. You can help me think, if you want."

"Okay, but I'm not a pink expert."

"I know. You think your puppy is blue, but it's gray. We can help you learn your colors more gooder."

Marty responded, "I know Bruno is gray. The people who have Great Danes call that blue."

"Don't any of them know their colors?"

"It is just a nickname." Marty mumbled.

"That's okay, Mr. Marty. Bruno is a nice puppy."

"You have a Great Dane?" Kid asked. "They are wonderful dogs. Between deployments in Vietnam, I worked for a while with the canine unit. I really liked that."

"Wow! That's good to know. I'll need some help training Bruno. I read that you need to train Danes early because they get so big."

"If I'm around, I'd love to help,—what I can remember of it. Maybe CJ could help, too?"

CJ had been listening to the conversation while eating his cookie. "You want me to help?"

"Of course." Marty answered, "You take care of Bruno all the time."

"That'd be good," the boy nodded.

Clarissa moved over between Marty and Kid with her cups filled with frosting in various shades of pink. "Okay, see. This is what I need to decide. I need it to be the most best pink ever, cause Kitten likes pink. She says she doesn't, but I know she does. She thinks she likes green, so Missus is going to write her name on top with green. I have to pick the best pink ever for the rest."

Marty looked it all over and said they all looked fine to him. Clarissa rolled her eyes and then asked Kid. "Mr. Kid, which would be the bestest? I can't make up my mind."

"How about making the frosting white all over and then having different colors of pink flowers around the outside and on top? Then all the pinks would be there. It would be very pretty with green writing on it."

Clarissa's mouth fell open, "Missus, do you think that we could do that?"

"What kind of flowers?" Nora asked.

"Mom used to make stiff powdered sugar paste. We kids made flowers out of that. We made them separate and then she would put them on stuff. She froze the ones that she didn't use right away."

"Could you make them?" Nora asked.

"I could, but not with my hand all banged up. My sisters and I used to do it all the time. We made roses, carnations, and prairie roses."

Annie had been helping Clarissa, "Do you think you could give me the instructions so I could do it?"

"I can try. Really, you guys just go ahead and do like you were going to."

Clarissa decreed. "I think your idea is the goodest."

"Okay, I'll try to tell you, but it has been years."

While he ate his soup and homemade rolls, he gave Annie instructions on how to craft the sugar flowers. By the time his soup was gone, several flowers had been created. Even Clarissa made a couple. Annie and Clarissa were making green leaves when Marty took Kid back to his room.

After he was back in bed and had his shots, Marty said, "That was neat. Maybe you could show Greta how to make those. I think she would like that."

"Ah, it was just something us kids used to do to pass the time. Mom decorated every cake, cupcake and cookie she ever baked."

Just like that he started to cry and Marty put his arms around him. "I think I let you get too tired. Zach will have my hide."

"No, I suddenly missed my Mom, so much. I wasn't there when she died. I was sent home for the funeral from Vietnam, but never got to tell her goodbye. A few years later, Dad died while I was in prison. I really let them down. I hate myself for that. Being here today has made me homesick. When I had a chance to be with them, I blew it."

"I think you got too tired." Marty sat on the stool.

"The best thing I can do is get the hell out of here as soon as possible."

"After Bruno is trained," Marty chuckled. "Not before. Get some sleep."

-12-

He had slept a while when he heard a knock at the door. "Come in."

Elton came in carrying his coffee mug. "I brought you some tea. I know you'd rather have coffee, but Zach wants to limit that for a while yet."

Kid sat up and Elton cranked up the bed, "Nora said I should talk to you about the pasture. We can now, if you feel like, or later. You need to go to the bathroom?"

"I should."

When he was settled again, he took a sip of tea, "You know, I'm beginning to like tea."

"That's good. It isn't too bad. I'm still fighting Whipple's disease so I had to be on tea for a while. It is good, but not coffee."

"What is Whipple's disease?"

"Some intestinal bug that lives in feedlots. I was repairing a conveyor last year and waded in a feedlot for a couple months. Sure as shootin', I got this weird bug. Have to have antibiotics for two years! Can you imagine that?"

"What kind of a disease is it?"

"Makes it so you can't digest anything. I was starving to death and still eating like a horse. I started to get real sick from it. Of course, Matt and Zach got a hold of me and slapped me around until I went to a doctor. I'm still on antibiotics. I had to have IV's a couple times a week to keep up my electrolytes for a while there. It was a major pain."

Kid watched him while he talked and then smiled, "You better now?"

"Yah. I do appreciate a little of how you must feel. Gut explosions are not fun."

"I bet your wife could have killed me that first day! I made such a mess."

"Nora is patient. Word of warning, you don't want to get her mad. When she is, the frying pans fly!"

Kid chuckled. "She seems like a great lady."

"She is. I couldn't make it without my Nora." Elton smiled at the patient, "She said that you were worried about the pasture?"

"I was trying to figure out why you were being nice to me and thought maybe it was because you wanted to rent the pasture."

"I told your lawyer I wanted to rent it months ago. I rented Olson's when I didn't hear back. No problem."

"Elton, what would I do with the pasture?"

"You need to decide what you want to do. Do you have any idea?"

"No. I think I need to get out of your hair around here as soon as I can. I thought if I could rent the land to you, I could pay Zach back. Then I could clear out."

Elton listened intently, "What are you going to do?"

"Dunno."

Elton studied him for a bit and then suggested, "Kid, it's not my business; but honestly, that has never stopped me before. Since you don't have some pressing thing you want or need to do, why don't you just coast a while?"

"A couple people told me that. How do I coast?"

Elton shrugged, "You just sit back and take it cool. From what I figure, you got yourself rather torqued out of shape when you got back from Vietnam. Maybe you need to rewind to that point and sort that out. Then you can move on. What do you think?"

"Sounds easy, but how do I survive in the meantime?"

"You surviving now?"

"Yah."

"There you have it."

"I can't sponge off you until I get my life sorted out! You'll get sick of me long before then."

"Just how damned bad is your life anyway? I think you have built it up in your mind to be insurmountable. Maybe if we whack it into smaller bits, we might get it down to something you can handle."

The biker frowned at Elton, "I just don't want to be beholding to Zach and you."

"Why not?"

"Huh? Cause I don't. I don't like it that he paid for my hospital bill."

"Look, you need to talk to Zach about that. He'll be home later tonight."

"I tried to before, but he told me not to worry about it."

"So, you went right ahead and worried! Right?" Elton shook his head. "I'll let Zach know that he needs to explain about the money. As far as the land, if you want me to rent it, I will. Do you have a checking account or do you want cash? How long do you want me to rent it? What are you going to do when you go back to your farm?"

The biker glared and then barked, "Don't ask me all that shit! I don't know! Don't you get it? I don't know what the hell to do! I just don't know!"

"I'm sorry, Kid. I didn't mean to badger you. Let's think this out. Before you go home, you need to fix your well and your cook stove. That thing will burn the house down. I take it that you didn't have a fire in it since you've been back."

"No, I started a small one and the smoke came right into the kitchen. I almost choked to death." Then he started to tear up, "I just wanted to come home. Back to my old home. That's all I wanted. It just isn't here anymore. I should've known better."

Elton put his arms around the kid and gave him a hug, "None of us can go back. But it tells me that you do have a plan."

"What the hell you talking about?"

"What did you want to go back to? Explain it to me."

"Well, I had a family and I wasn't a freak. I enjoyed being on the farm. I hadn't made a mess and half out of everything. Now, that is all I have—a mess."

"I'm not going to respond to that last comment. When you get better, there is a family right outside this door. Your parents have passed over, so we can't bring them back. You have to make a new family. We ain't much, but you already know us. Build on that until you come up with something better. We have chores when you are well enough and a kitchen that is always open. The ladies were impressed with your flowers! Did you cook a lot?"

"At home, I did. I liked cooking. I know, it's a girl thing."

Elton responded, "Most chefs are men. I like to cook and am pretty darned good, if I do say so myself! Hey, we'll be expecting big things from you in our July cooking contest!"

"What's that?"

"Carl and I started it last year. He thinks he can cook too, but he really isn't that good. He baked biscuits once and thinks he is Bobby Crocker! So, we ended up with this big contest. Everyone in the clan got into the act! I imagine you'll be taking that grand prize this year."

"I'll be gone by then."

"You keep saying that. Kid, I have to go back to work. When I get home today, I want you to tell me where you're going. If you have no idea, you just stay here. Got it?"

"Right now I'm on this IV. From what Zach says, that is keeping my cravings and terrors away. Once I get off that, I'll become the fiend I know I am. You won't want me around."

"No, I don't want a fiend around. I also know you don't like being that guy. That is what we need to work on. Hear me?" Elton patted his hand. "Every single one of us has a frightful creep inside. We all have to keep a lid on the fiend. It can be done. The more you do it, the easier it gets."

"I'm an addict."

"So, I'm an alcoholic. I haven't drank now in fifteen-sixteen years; but mind you, I consumed more than my fair share when I did! I'd drink until I got a whole new set of brains. I would pick fights with brutes twice my size or shack up with some sleazy broad who would unload my wallet. There are times, I'd still like a drink, but then I think about letting that monster loose. I don't want to. The monster didn't do anyone any good."

"I'm addicted to heroin and booze. That is the only way I can sleep."

"I heard you didn't sleep."

"I don't."

"Then you must be barking up the wrong tree."

The Kid leaned back on the bed, "Did that even make sense?"

"Probably not." Elton grinned, "Look, I'll talk to you after work. We'll work out something on the pastureland. I'd like you to think of just one thing that you'd like to do. Even if it is a little, tiny thing. Okay? That should give us something to work on. And quit telling everyone you are leaving until you can tell me where you are going and why it would be good for you."

"Ah, shit. You sound like a shrink."

"Most folks think I'm crazy, so that's a step up!" Elton patted his shoulder with a chuckle. "I'll let you rest now and then bug you again when I get home."

"Yippee," the biker groaned as he slumped down in bed.

He was feeling very anxious after Elton left and was relieved when Annie came in. "I was about to call you. I don't think I can stand this. I feel like I'm going crazy."

Annie was matter-of-fact, "Your shots were due. That's why. You aren't going crazy. Zach wasn't very happy that we had you up so long. He gave us the business."

"He shouldn't have. I wanted to get out of here for a minute. I hope he didn't give you too bad a time."

"Nah. We all know each other so well; we'd have been disappointed if he wouldn't have. We knew you were up too long. Next time, we'll cut it shorter—by five minutes," she winked.

"I don't understand you people. If someone gave someone hell where I'm from, there would be a beating."

"That would be silly."

"Yah, but what about respect?"

"How can you respect yourself if you have to make someone else compromise what they believe, especially if you agree with them?"

The biker shook his head, "You make as much sense as Elton. I know I'm going crazy."

"Most of us get a little crazy around Elton! But he is the best guy in the world to have in your corner. We all know that. I'll tell you a secret. He and Byron sound a lot alike. It's really scary sometimes."

"Oh, I almost forgot him. He said he'd be back today. He must have decided he had better things to do."

"No such luck, Hotshot. He already called and asked when would be a good time."

"Help me get out of bed and dressed. I have to get out of here."

"Yah, right. I'll have Horse tap dance for you, too. What is it with men, they all think they are superhuman?"

"I don't think that. I just don't want everyone to know what a loser I am."

Annie sat down on the stool and leveled her eyes at him. They stared at each other and after a couple gut-wrenching moments, Kid nodded, "Okay. So, you already know."

"We know what happened, but we don't know the end of the story yet. It isn't over. You can change the ending."

"That is a load of crap."

"Or high quality fertilizer, depending on the salesman!"

"Are you guys ever pessimistic?"

"Oh yah. I was the queen of gloom, doom, and utter despair. My first husband was killed in Vietnam. Later, when I had a brother and Andy over there, all I could do was moan and groan around. Pastor Byron got ahold of me. He told me that if my whining could change one damned thing, he'd help me. Otherwise, I owed it to everyone concerned to brighten up. I tried and you know what? It worked. Not only for everyone else, but for me, too! Anyway, you don't want to hear my tale of woe. I'll let you sleep. Byron said he'll be here about two. I will wake you before then and see how you're feeling. We can always cancel if you aren't up to it. Or, he may come anyway because he is like that."

"You guys don't give me much wiggle room, do you?"

"Is that what you want?"

He started to tear up, "I don't know what I want."

Annie gave him a quick hug, "Let me get Jackson. Okay?"

"You don't need to."

"Yes, I do."

A minute later, Jackson came in, "Having a hard time? Wanna talk about it?"

"No. There is little to say."

"Then say a little. Let me get my hinder balanced on this stool before I tip over, or we will have a lot to say!" Jackson said as he sat down. "Look, you can tell me anything. I'm not a doctor, lawyer, or even an Indian chief. Just an Indian. It's kinda neat nowadays. White folks call most of us 'chief'. It is really funny. It'd be like us calling you all President."

Kid frowned, "Never thought of it that way before. Do they call you chief?"

"No, they call me Horse because I come from the area where they are building that Crazy Horse monument. At least they don't call me Crazy."

"Jackson, how long have you been with these people?"

"Since December. Why?"

"Do you understand them?"

"I didn't at first. I have to tell you, I have never met people like them before. I did know Andy though, so I wasn't that surprised. It should be easier for you, you knew them before."

"I was a kid then. I was Keith's friend at school. I was almost fifteen when my folks moved to California."

"Annie said something was bothering you. Want to talk about it, or do you want to talk to someone else about it?"

"I don't know. Elton told me that I have to think about just one thing that I want to do. Jackson, I can't think of a thing except get out of here."

"I was determined to go back to Pine Ridge when I got here! I couldn't walk or anything, but that was my plan. I think your chance of getting out of here now is about as good as mine was then. Huh? Maybe you can soon, though. At least you have all your parts!"

The Kid watched him and said quietly, "Do you know your little sister comes in here and watches me sleep? She thinks she is watching over me. In fact, she really is. She has got me help several times. Does that bother you?"

"No. Kitten has always been a watcher. She feels that watching you is her important job. Every little kid likes to think they have something worthwhile to do."

"Really? I thought they just wanted to play."

"Well, she is playing with Gopher right now, but she takes watching over you seriously."

"Does it worry you? I mean, her sitting in here when I can get so out of control."

"You haven't done anything that Andy and I haven't done. You have to understand, my Mom and Clayton, their dad, used to be drunk for days on end. What they saw while all that was going on, I'm sure neither you or I have ever seen! Good grief, they had people over who they hardly knew who drank with them, ate everything, like locusts, and when it was gone, they moved on. Mom and Clayton would go to their place and leave the kids alone with nothing. Sometimes, they even took their clothes to trade away for more booze. You know, these kids wouldn't take off any clothing they liked when they first came here, because they were afraid it would be given away! When we went down after the car wreck, the house was cold because the folks had traded away a full fuel tank for booze. I had paid to have it filled and they traded it away! It still makes me mad."

"I can see that. It is too bad the kids had to face that. Then I come along and scare the devil out of CJ."

"Well, now he learned how important it is to tell a grownup where he is going!"

"Doesn't make it right. You know, he fed me his sandwich!"

"You should be honored." Jackson smiled, "He always was the food packrat. He has stashes all over and rarely goes anywhere without something to eat in his pocket. He must have cared about you to want to feed you his last sandwich."

"No, he was scared of me and he still shared."

"Elton always tells us that we are here to help each other. Nice to know some filtered through. As far as Kitten, if you want her to go, just tell her. Okay?"

"Honestly? I kinda like it, now that I know it's her. I was freaked at first because I kept hearing noises and couldn't figure it out. I think it is sweet that she is so caring, but is she getting enough sleep?"

"Oh yah. If she isn't watching you sleep, she is watching me. Or Clancy and Grandpa. She naps whenever she wants. Don't worry. Nora won't let her get too tired."

"Okay. I don't want you to get mad about it."

"I won't. If I find a problem, I'll let you know, first thing. Okay?"

"Okay. Jackson, thank you for taking time to talk to me."

"I didn't do anything. Whenever, but remember, I might call on you sometime."

Kid got a puzzled look on his face, "You would call on me? Why?"

"For someone to talk to."

"How could I possibly help you?"

"You solved Clarissa's dilemma about the pink frosting nightmare. The rest of us were about ready to jump out the window!"

"She sure gets excited, doesn't she?"

"That she does. A total opposite of Claudia."

"I don't think I have met Claudia."

"Kitten's real name."

"I wonder if I knew that." Then the man's eyes started to redden with tears again. "I don't know what's wrong with me. I can't remember a darned thing."

"See that bottle hanging there? It is full of medications. Trust me, Man. They can mess you up. They can do a world of good but they sure can mess up your perception."

"Elton said you had dreams too, but not as bad as Andy's."

"Andy had been gassed in a tunnel real bad one time and darned near died. He was something else after that. His skin itched. He said it was like ants crawling under it and he was like a caged badger. He told me off more often than I care to remember. He made Nora cry more than once. Zach figured out there was a lot of arsenic in the gas and put us both on chelation therapy. That takes the heavy metals out of your system. I tell you, that's no picnic. Andy even had convulsions and everything while doing that. Now that it is over, it was worth it. I know you have no reason to believe me, but I trust these guys with my life. I know because I have."

"Why would they do it for me?"

"Why did they do it for me? They didn't have to and then take in the kids, on top of it all! But they do expect something from you."

"What? That is what I've been wanting to know. Why are they doing it?"

"Why and what are two different things. The why is because they believe that a person should try to help when a problem is put in front of them. The what—they expect that you will be there to help someone else when it is needed."

"Then they should stop right now. Jackson, I have let down everyone I've ever met. My sisters won't even talk to me because of that business with that woman's murder."

"I can see that, but they haven't thought it through. I've seen people who were stoned. Hell, the world could cave in and they wouldn't know."

"Yah, that's where I was at. Actually, I was sitting outside the bar by the dumpster and had shot up. I didn't even know when I was arrested, let alone what was going on. But seriously, if I hadn't been high, I wouldn't have said anything. I wouldn't have taken part, but I sure as hell wouldn't have tried to stop them."

Jackson studied the man a minute and said, "Between you and me, I don't think that I would've either. I'd probably have run away."

"Not in that crowd."

"Well, then, I'd have wished I could. Is that what you dream about?"

"No. Well, sometimes. I dream about other stuff we did though."

"Not Vietnam?"

"Mostly. I hated some of the things I saw there, and that we did. Makes me sick, us and them."

"I know. We weren't saints for damned sure."

Harold shook his head, "I couldn't understand how God could pick and choose."

Jackson smiled, "Andy used to say that. He wondered where God was. I didn't have that problem. I believe in Wakan Tanka."

"Who is that, the Great Spirit?"

"Actually we don't call it that, but yes. We believe that everything and everyone is part of Wakan Tanka's creation, so we know He is on both sides. It makes sense to us."

"How can that make sense?"

"We believe that Wakan Tanka is all things mysterious. The fact that we don't understand it, is part of it. He created both the coyote and the rabbit. He is on both their sides. Some things, we just don't understand."

The biker yawned from the meds, "I have to think about that. Thanks Jackson."

-13-

Harold Effan fell asleep and was besieged by many crazy dreams that afternoon. He dreamt about coyotes watching baby rabbits, the psychopath Scab eating his frosting flowers, and then he dreamt he was in the old farmhouse with his Mom baking cookies on a rainy day. He woke up crying.

Nora came in as he woke up, "How's it going? Kitten said you were sad."

"She must think I'm nuts."

"I often wonder what she thinks about any of us. Is there anything I can help you with?"

"I have been so homesick today, I can't stand it. Why is that?"

"Homesick for what?"

"The farm; the way it used to be. I miss Mom and Dad."

"I'm sorry. I call that the blues. I still get lonesome for my Mom and Dad. It has been years since they passed away. I just have to remind myself they're in a better place. And if I'm really in the dumps, I think it wouldn't have to be very good to be better than here!" Nora laughed.

"I can't believe you said that! You guys are so upbeat about everything."

"No, we just try not to burden you with our baloney." Then she frowned, "And you, young man, are on my list!"

"What did I do? I mean, which thing?"

"You told Clarissa about making flowers! Now she thinks she needs to make flowers out of everything. Her last idea was using mashed potatoes! What did you start?"

Kid chuckled, "That would be kinda cool. A guy could make potatoes in shapes and it would make a plate look real neat!"

"You aren't allowed to talk to her again!" She laughed, "Thank goodness, we are having spaghetti tonight for supper."

Kid teased, "I could give her ideas on what to do with that."

Nora raised her eyebrows, "I just bet you could! Please don't. I talked to Zach and he said you could have spaghetti with us tonight, if you think you can handle it. Otherwise, I'll make something not as spicy for you."

"It sounds good. I'd like to try it." Then he looked at her seriously, "Do you really want me to stay away from her?"

"No. Although if we start making flowers out of potatoes, I may change my mind! She does want to show you her collection, if you feel up to it."

"I think I should go to the bathroom and maybe wash up first. Man, I was sweating. Why does a guy have dreams like that?"

"I don't know. Someone told me it is your brain trying to work out things."

A bit later, Clarissa came in carrying a cookie sheet filled with 'flowers'. She wanted Kid's opinion on them and he looked them over seriously. Then he decreed, "Some of these are very good. I can see that you were getting better at the end."

She frowned, "You mean some of them aren't good? Are they the most baddest?"

"Clarissa, when you learn something new, you need practice to get good. Everyone does. You had never done them before. Look. Can you tell me which ones you did first?"

She looked at them and then sighed, "I guess I was sloppy when I was first did it."

"Not sloppy, you just weren't used to it. And now, look at the last ones! They are very good and you only did it one day! I think you'll be an expert at it in no time."

She looked at him expectantly, "You mean that for real?"

"Yes ma'am."

"I'm a girl, not one of those mam things," she corrected him. "I want to get to be a spurt. Can you help me?"

"An expert?"

"Yah, that's it. When I do, will you help me? I told Missus we should do mashed potatoes. Can you help me?"

The man watched the little girl who was so excited about the idea, "As soon as I can use both my hands, we'll do that."

"A heart promise?"

"Now, what's that?"

"It's a cross your heart forever and for real promise."

"Yes, I give you my word. Cross my heart."

"You didn't do it. You know, make that mark on you."

"I have trouble moving my arms with the IV and cast."

The little girl nodded, "I bet you wish you hadn't poached those eggs huh?"

"That's very true," he smiled.

"I'm kinda glad you did cause I learned how to make flowers. Do you think we could put Missus' perfume in them so they smell nice?"

"No, no. Then we couldn't eat them."

"But we could smell them."

"If it is food, we want to eat it."

Byron came to the door, "I like to eat stuff that smells good."

Kid looked at him and crossed his eyes, "Clarissa thought we should make them smell like flowers, not food."

Clarissa was excited by Pastor Ellison's remarks, "Like what do you want it to smell like?"

"Ah . . ." Pastor Byron made a face, realizing the pit he had stepped into up to his knees.

"Yah, like what? Roses, lilacs?" the biker asked.

"Ah, lemons," Byron thought quickly before he said, relieved that something came to him.

Harold nodded, "I guess we could do that, but we won't use Missus' perfume. Okay?"

"Okay. I'll ask Grandma." The little girl dashed out of the room. "Maybe Mr. Byron could help us."

After she closed the door, Byron sat down, "Do I want to know what just happened?"

"You volunteered to help us make mashed potato flowers that smell like lemons."

"I really have to learn to keep quiet until I know what's going on. How you doing?"

"Okay."

"Let's try that again. How are you doing?"

"Not worth a damn." The biker glared, "Does that make you feel better?"

"No. Nora told me that you had the blues, so I knew that you were feeling down. So, I cheated. Should we talk about it?"

"No, but you guys won't leave me alone unless I do. Will you?"

"If you seriously think you don't want to, I'll let it go. Otherwise, I'm here. Nora is bringing us some tea."

"What I wouldn't give for a beer! And then if I could, I'd beat somebody to a pulp."

"Sounds exciting," Byron said nonchalantly. "I think I'd rather drink my tea. It is easier to heal up from it."

Harold scowled at him, "I feel like a potted plant!"

"Carl used to say that he was surrounded by petunias."

Harold's eyes darted to him as if he suddenly realized who he was talking to, "I'm sorry, Pastor."

"No, you're not. You do feel that way. I have rarely met anyone who likes being tied to a bed for any length of time. I think Zach said a couple weeks, huh?"

"Yah, how long have I been here?"

"A few days, so you have a while to go yet. The good thing is that your stomach is healing. Aren't you glad about that?"

"Of course I am. I hated that." His eyes filled with tears, "I can't stand being such a bawl baby. I'm acting like some woman."

Byron shook his head, "Man, don't say that very loud! These ladies will have you hung, drawn, and quartered in a heartbeat! Seriously, most women are stronger than men. I think it is because they don't try to act like stuff doesn't bother them. Men try to cover it over and then it eats us up. Women will talk it out, determine the cause, and extract a high penance. And please, don't tell Marly I said that!"

"I don't imagine you stray too far."

"I get into trouble, but mostly for not talking to her and she is right. It might be a real John Wayne thing to be silent and tough. It works well with everyone but a wife or girlfriend. Do you have someone special?"

"No. Never did. I dated in high school and when I was stateside in the service. No one for very long or steady. When I was with the Horde, there were women around. Nothing you'd call dating. Then prison. Now, I doubt anyone I'd want to be with, would want to be with me."

"Well, then you need to be someone that a girl you'd want, would want to be with," Byron smiled.

"Annie was right," Kid chuckled. "You do sound like Elton."

"Could do worse!" Byron laughed.

Nora knocked at the door, and Byron took the tray. After he sat down he asked, "Does that sound like something you'd like to have as a goal?"

"What? A girl? Not hardly. I'd be happy if I could just make it through a day without wishing I was dead."

"Why do you wish you were dead?"

"I've screwed up my life beyond repair. I know Elton said I can fix it, but he just doesn't know."

"He probably has a better idea than you think. Okay, let's pick one thing that you don't like about yourself and we'll talk about it today."

"I don't want to."

"Okay. You sure don't have to, but don't tell me that you want to quit feeling the way you do. You're holding on to it with both hands and a leather belt."

"What the hell do you know about it?"

"Nothing, because you aren't telling me. That's your affair." Byron looked out the window, "It looks like it might rain. Real low clouds. I hope it isn't more snow. Oh, Kevin and Harrington took another sample of your well water in to the State Lab. We'll hear by mail if the chemical treatment worked. Kevin was concerned because the inside is caved in. He didn't think treatment would do it."

"Someone told me that. I guess I'll have to have it closed in."

"Yah, Sheriff Bernard worries about an open well like that. I imagine one of the guys would do it for you."

"I'm not getting in any deeper. I'm beholding to everybody. I hate that worse than you can imagine," Kid growled.

"Yah, like you hate yourself. Will you live with that too?" Byron asked pointedly. "Look if you want me to leave, I can. I don't want to upset you too much."

Kid smirked, "But you would upset me a little?"

"Caught that, huh?"

"I'll be leaving here as soon as I can!" Kid explained. "I'm not hanging around here to be the freak show."

"You just promised Clarissa you'd help her make mashed potato flowers."

"Ah, she'll forget that in no time."

Byron leaned back, "You'll have to tell her. I won't let you get away with that! All their little lives, people have lied to them. They are just learning to trust people. Now you come trouncing in and start breaking your word. You're really something!"

"Maybe they shouldn't trust people. You're only hurting them by teaching them that people are trustworthy."

"Who betrayed you, Kid? Who hurt you so?" Byron asked compassionately.

"No one. Everyone," Kid glared at him and then started to weep. "I did."

Byron put his arms around him and let him sob.

After a minute, Kid pulled back. He wiped his face and said sarcastically, "Now, do you feel better?"

Byron shook his head, "The question is, do you?"

Kid's face contorted in tears again, "No. I feel horrible. I hate this so much."

It took him about five minutes of deep breaths to get settled down again and when he leaned back in bed, Byron asked if he wanted him to see if Annie could give him something.

"I don't know why I'm doing this. I've never been like this in my life."

"My guess is medication, ill health, and everything that has been stored up. Eventually, it will break out; one way or the other."

"I just wanted to go back home, Pastor Ellison. I wanted so much for things to be like they were before I messed it all up. Now, I know it can't be."

"Is that why you came back here?"

"Yah, and besides, I had nowhere to go or nobody that even wants me around. I've ended up mooching off someone I stole from. I'm supposed to simply turn over and be good. Don't you guys get it? I can't. I couldn't do it before! What the hell makes you think I could do it any better now?"

"Don't know. My idea was it just swallowed you up before. You have a chance to start again. I thought maybe you'd take the chance. Harold, it'll never be like it was when you were a kid again, because you aren't a kid anymore. However, it can be good if you want it to be. You have to want it though."

"I do, but I don't."

"I'm going to get us more hot water? Want another tea?"

"I guess."

When Byron came back in, the young man was staring at his blankets in deep thought. He didn't make a move when Byron came back in and poured the tea. The minister sat down and asked him if he wanted sugar. The biker nodded.

"Pastor Byron, I really want to be respectable. You know, someone that Mom and Dad wouldn't be embarrassed to say they was their kid. Do you think I can do that?"

"Yes, I do."

"I don't have to be good or nothing like that, just passable."

"Good idea. Aim real low."

Kid scowled, "Look. I'm trying here!"

"I know. I take it that you really want to live on your home place?"

"You know, this is all stupid. Once Scab figures out that I'm here, he'll finish me off. So, it doesn't really matter. All this messing around trying to get better is just a wasted effort."

"Are you sure he'll come after you? Sheriff Bernard wasn't very sure the Horde would look for you."

"The Horde won't, but Scab is a sadistic bastard, simmering with revenge. He will if he has to crawl after me."

"He is still in the pen, right?"

"Last I heard."

"With your permission, I'll ask Bernard to keep track of his status for you. However, it would be better if you'd ask him."

"Me, ask the fuzz for help? You nuts?"

"Are you? He is the one who has the connections and he offered to help you. What do you want folks to do? Beg to help? Boy, you must really think you're something!"

"No, I don't."

"Think about how you're acting!"

Kid stared at the preacher for a full minute, "Boy, you really slapped me upside the head! I didn't mean it that way. I do appreciate that everyone has been so nice. I just don't want to be beholding to anyone."

"I think you don't want to feel you owe the same decency to others that they are offering you. Think maybe I'm right?"

"Hell, I don't know. I really don't. Can't you leave me alone?"

"Yes, I can. In fact, I think this conversation went awry. I had no intention of coming in here and giving you a bad time, but I did. I apologize. You didn't ask me to dive into your life with both feet. I should've waited. Will you forgive me?"

Kid glowered at first and then shook his head, "You ass. You know if you ask me that, I'd have to be a genuine jerk to say I won't. Don't you?"

"Not really. I honestly wanted to help you, but I shouldn't have presumed you wanted me to. I'm really sorry." Byron said sincerely, "I'll go now. If you can see your way fit to give me a chance to just be a friend, let me know."

Byron started to pick up the tea things and Kid stopped him, "Don't be a sap. You aren't the one that was impossible. It was me. I know that. I'm just so confused. I really appreciate that you cared enough to stop over to see me. I have no right to be rude. Pastor Ellison, I don't know what to do anymore."

"How 'bout I talk to Annie about something to help you calm down and then we can just visit awhile."

Kid nodded and slumped back into his bed. Byron took the tray out. It took a while before Annie came in with a syringe. "I talked to Zach and he had talked to his colleague. They were worried you might get weepy with this combination. He told me to give you this so you can relax more. Okay?"

"Will it make me sleepy?"

"Are you tired?"

"I'm jumpy, but I wanted to talk to Pastor Ellison unless he left already."

"No, he is here. Clarissa is explaining to him about how to make potato petals! Yea gads! She was so disappointed when Grandma told her she couldn't put perfume in her potatoes. Did you really tell her that?"

"I said no, but Pastor said to use lemon or something. She said she would ask Grandma."

"Oh, that is what he was trying to explain. Anyway, he is trying to talk his way out of that quagmire now. He is planning on talking to you again."

"Annie, can you answer me something honestly?"

"I can try. What is it?"

"Is there a chance for me?"

Without hesitation and with a big smile, she answered, "Of course, Harold. Absolutely!"

"You sound certain," his response was one of shocked surprise.

"Well, you aren't the worst guy I've ever met by a long shot!"

"What are their names? I might know some of them," he laughed.

Annie laughed, "You have a nice smile. Use it more. You should be feeling better in a few minutes. I'll get Byron now. Okay?"

When Byron came back in, he chuckled, "Thanks for saving me. Clarissa had me so confused! Yikes. She is quite the kid."

Harold chuckled, "She asked me today, if I was sorry I poached eggs."

"You know, you might be right. You should leave soon and if I had a brain, I'd go with you! Charlie always tells us that he and CJ think she is squirrelly. I told him to quit saying that, but between us, they might be right!"

"I think she is cool. No one could ever accuse her of not getting excited about things!"

The men visited about the upcoming birthday parties and the big Italian dinner that night for Father Vicaro. Then the subject turned to Claudia's birthday party. Suddenly, Kid turned pale. "What is it?" Byron asked.

"Did you know that she sits in here when I'm sleeping to 'watch over me'? I don't know how many times she has gone to get me help. She never sits in here if I'm awake or have company, just while I'm asleep. Isn't that something?"

"Marly told me about that because when Miriam is over here, they both sit in here, in that chair."

"I know."

"So, what's the problem?"

"It's her birthday tomorrow and I don't have anything to give her."

"How about potato flowers?"

Harold made a face, "You sure you're a real preacher?"

"Lucky everyone doesn't know me very well, huh?"

"I'd say."

"Well, I could pick something up in Merton for you tomorrow. What would you like to get her?"

"I have no clue."

Pastor Ellison offered, "Why don't you talk to Nora and let me know tonight? I can get it tomorrow and Marly can wrap it."

"I'll talk to Elton and work out how to pay for it. I don't want to be . . ." Then he shook his head, stopped and then teased, "I don't want to have to be nice to you."

Byron laughed, "Don't worry, we'll work something out. Maybe you can clean the pews at the church for me."

"Lord have mercy."

"I better go now. I still have some work to do. Let me know what you want to get for her. If not, I can ask Marly. Deal?'

"Deal."

"Mind if I say a prayer?"

"No, I don't mind."

"Heavenly Father, Thank you for sending Harold back to us. Give him the peace in his life he is searching for and show us how we can help him. Please help him understand that You have forgiven him, and now he needs to forgive himself. Help us all to accept Your ways and Your wisdom. In Jesus name we pray, Amen."

Harold grabbed his hand, "Thanks. I don't know if I believe what you said, but thanks for saying it."

"If you don't believe God can forgive you for what you've done, you find the places in the Bible that backs up your opinion. We'll have a conversation."

"I'm not about to bite on that."

Byron grinned, "It was worth a try."

-14-

Kid slept soundly for a while but woke when he heard a knock at his door. Kitten hopped off her spot on the barrel chair where she had been napping and smiled at Carl before she ran out to the kitchen. Carl smiled, "I see you have your sentry stationed by the door!"

Kid almost felt proud when he said, "Yes, she watches over me. Isn't that something?"

"It is," Carl chuckled. "I brought you some coffee. It has so much milk in it that I should say I brought you some milk in a dirty coffee cup!"

"Zach's orders," Kid nodded. "He's keeping the reins on me!"

After Kid went to the restroom and washed up, he returned to his bed that Carl had straightened up for him. Carl sat down and made himself comfortable with his coffee, "I just got off the phone with Bernard before I brought Mo over here."

"The Sheriff?"

"Yah, nice guy. He had talked to Byron about keeping an eye on that Scab character. He asked me what I thought he could do to gain your trust. I told him I don't know." Carl's look penetrated the patient, "I offered to talk to you and see what you think. Now, I was planning on visiting with you today anyhow, but I can promise you—I will not be your go-between."

Kid's brow furrowed, "I told Ellison that I don't talk to cops."

"Your choice. I sure can't tell you who to talk to, but you might want to think it over."

"What's to think about?"

"See, that's the problem. I don't know why you think you shouldn't, so I can't tell you why you should."

"I don't trust the heat. They are always looking for something to bust you for."

"I wasn't aware that you had anything you could be busted for." Then he grinned, "I take that back. If you saw what Clarissa was doing now, you might be treading mightily close to getting in trouble with Nora. It could easily degenerate into mayhem."

"Is she still making potato flowers?"

"No, she has moved on to bigger and better things. Seems the potato flowers led to a discussion of Mashed Potato Candy. Somehow, it ended up that Annie is helping her make the candy now. Good grief, there is wall-to-wall powdered sugar in that kitchen. A guy almost has to wear a mask to breathe!"

"Mashed Potato Candy? I had forgotten all about that. That's the stuff with peanut butter, huh?"

"Yah. Miss Clarissa is in it up to her elbows. You should see her, Kid! She even has powdered sugar on her eyelashes!"

"How can that be my fault?"

"Don't know, but Nora was mumbling your name under her breath." Carl laughed, "I can't wait until the cook-off this year!"

"Elton mentioned that. He said it was a big deal, but I doubt I'll be here for it."

"Leaving, are you?"

"Likely." Kid nodded, "I should just move on."

"Afraid of Scab?" Carl asked bluntly.

Kid recoiled at that, "What's that supposed to mean?"

"If it was me, I'd be! If you aren't, you're stupid. Bernard talked to the warden. That guy sounds like big trouble."

Kid snapped, "He's a sadistic bastard that never lets go."

"I imagine you'd need to find a safe place to hide then."

"There isn't a place."

"You planning on just facing up to him, then?"

"No. Hell, I don't know! What do you think I should do?"

"Beats the hell out of me. I'd build myself a fortress right here. You're already planted and have some land. You don't want to give that up for some psychopath."

"Yah, I was so safe on the farm that a little boy overtook me!" the patient pointed out.

"You were drugged up and sick. Of course, he did. If you were clean and healthy, you would've had a better chance. I don't think you should go back to the old farm alone until you're healthy. Hey, want us to go cover that well? The water's no good. You'll need a new well."

"Not surprised. I have no money to pay you guys for that, but I'll talk to Elton. I may rent him the place."

"He already rented Olson's instead. I don't think he has that much money to be renting everything in the county."

"Never thought of that. Do you know anyone that would want to rent it?"

"You talk to Elton, not me. I'm a novice to all this. I only moved here last summer, so I haven't got a clue. My life used to be the FBI. Now, I'm raising ducks and kids! I still wake up in shock most days!"

Kid watched him closely and then grinned, "I think you love it."

Carl nodded, "Yah, I do, but I have to maintain my image. So keep your trap shut about it or Magpie will give me no peace."

"Who is Magpie?"

"Elton. That man talks more than anyone should be allowed! I'll get the guys and take care of that well for you this weekend. Okay? No need to pay us. We'll extract payment from you."

"Like what?"

"Don't know yet." Then the older man looked at him, "Kid, I do know. I personally want something from you. I'd really like it if you'd give this place a chance. You know?"

Kid watched him, "You have no idea what the hell you're talking about."

"We aren't so different, you and I. I devoted my life to crime. Albeit the other side, but in the end, it was as consuming. I discovered it is just as debilitating to think that everyone is a slime bag as to being one."

"I don't get that. I was selling dope; you were trying to stop it."

"Yah, but in the end, we both spent all our time thinking about it, and little looking at the good in life."

"There's little to see."

"Bull. I used to think that, until Zach drug me up here. You're lucky. You have your own room. I shared one with Byron's cantankerous old father, Bert. We argued steady. What an old buzzard! Then he died and it broke my heart."

"You lived at Ellison's place?"

"Nope. Right here in the room Andy and Annie have now. I was recuperating from a gunshot by Miriam's deranged old man. Her mom shot Harrington."

"Here?" Kid frowned, "What the hell?"

"No. See, I was quietly working at my office in San Antonio when I got a call from this Boston detective named Harrington. He had a man there who was concerned about his father's death. Turns out, that man was Zach. The investigation was very contorted. Long story short, Zach's father was a deranged, evangelical minister with some off-the-wall religion. He and this Ezekiel, his son-in-law, were partners. They were involved in blackmail, murder, and extortion. Probably make your Horde look like playschool! It turned out, Harrington and I uncovered murders all over the country. Zach's old man beat his wife and watched her die slowly. He murdered his oldest son with a rattlesnake while making the other kids pray and watch! He was a sick bastard. How Zach or Ruthie ever survived is beyond me! I can't even begin to explain it all, but it was sick. In the end, Ezekiel and his wife, Naomi, murdered the old man. When law enforcement finally moved in to shut them down, Ezekiel tried to shoot Miriam. She and I both got shot by the same bullet, me in the upper chest and her in the hip. Then Naomi shot Harrington and herself. So, we were all laid up in a Shreveport hospital! Who comes be-bopping in but Zach the Petunia, dragging Byron and Elton with him. They set up shop and took care of us. Damnedest thing you ever did see! Hell, a few months later, I was sitting in North Dakota wondering what the hell happened. I'm still not sure."

"I thought you were married to Harrington's Mom."

"Old Mo? Yah, best part of the whole damned thing. I met that Motor Mouth in Shreveport and for some reason, she actually thought I was worth the time of day. I don't like to let on, but I've never been happier."

"Good for you. I've met both Harrington and Matt. They seem upstanding. But I'm on the other side. I can't just walk away from my past."

"If it isn't that you still want it, why not? Tied to it?"

"I'm an addict and I've done some rotten stuff."

"You paid your debt to society. I'm pretty sure you weren't arrested for everything you did, but seriously, none of us are. And that's a blasted fact, as Harrington would say. There are a lot of addicts who manage to rebuild their lives. You have to try."

"What if I screw up?"

"Try again! I never saw where you get only one chance. Most of us are trying all the time."

"You're an addict?"

"No, but I screw up. No one is immune to that!"

"Some are worse than others though."

"Well, I'll talk to the boys and get that well covered. I can't tell you what to do. You're the guy that has to live it. You want help, just yell! I told Bernard to get his butt out here and talk to you himself. He said he will tomorrow. At least, listen to him. That's all I ask."

"I will, Carl."

"Hey, is it okay if I drag Jeff and Mo in here to meet you?"

"Who is Jeff?"

"He is Matt's friend. He used to be a priest out in Boston. He got sacked the same time as Matt over that pedophile. Those two complained about that creep, and they got put on suspension. Jeff is a great guy and living with us now."

"One thing about the Horde, they tolerated everything but pedophiles," Kid said.

"Honorable."

"I didn't mean it that way."

Carl smiled, "Neither did I."

Carl went out and came back a few minutes later with a man about Harold's age in tow. "This is Jeff Wilson. Jeff, meet Harold Effan."

"Hi," Jeff smiled, "Hear you're called Kid."

"Yah, Grandma named me that," Kid's grin portrayed a bit of pride, as he shook Jeff's hand. "I kinda like it."

"Okay, it'll work. So Carl has been jawing at you, huh? I was glad he came to rescue me because it's getting pretty crazy in the kitchen."

"Are they finished with the candy?" Carl asked.

"Just about. Annie was done with it an hour ago, but Clarissa is wound up enough for a marathon. They have to put it away though, because of Father Vicaro's party tonight. A big Italian dinner!"

"I heard they are having spaghetti with meatballs?"

"Don't know," Jeff frowned. "I know they've been cooking up a storm. Grandma is making breadsticks. I think I ate forty of them!"

"Any left? I might want to get me some," Carl stood up. "How 'bout you, Kid?"

"Sounds good."

Carl left the room and Jeff grinned, "How's it going?"

"Okay. How long you been here?"

"I came here to visit over Christmas and then got a job at the state reformatory. I finished my job in New Mexico early, so I got here two weeks ago but I don't start until first week in May. Since I'm living with Coot and Mo, I've been drafted to help him with his yard." He looked at Kid, "I wish you felt better, I could use your assistance! He is planting an orchard! I don't think the man realizes this isn't orchard country! I've dug so many holes, I'm dizzy."

"Is that why the kids asked me if I was a digger?"

"No. But those crazy kids dig all the time! Even the little girls helped with some of the tree holes! Sometimes it's more trouble than help, but they're working."

"I guess that's good," Kid nodded. "Are you a guard at the reform school?"

"Me?" Jeff laughed, "No. I'm a counselor. I also teach and coach. Most those kids just need to get their heads cleared and make new friends. Sometimes I think friends do more to mess a person up that anything else. As a priest, I noticed that if a married couple was hanging around with a couple that was fighting; before long, they were fighting with each other, too! Weird, huh?"

"Yah, really. Matt said he'd been a priest. I thought that a person couldn't quit being a priest."

"Yes and no."

"Oh Lord, that's what Matt said. Can't you give a better answer?"

"See, we ask the Vatican to be returned to the laity, or congregation. We also ask separately for a dispensation so we can marry. If it is granted, which it usually is, then we aren't allowed to do any priestly duties except the Last Rites under certain circumstances."

"Like what are those?"

"If you're the only priest around and the person's dying. In fact, I did that out in Montana last week! I felt uncomfortable doing it. In the end, I was glad I did."

"Going back to the priesthood again?"

"Not really. In fact, I'm just busting to tell someone, if you promise to keep quiet about it! I met a girl." Jeff grinned like a kid with a Christmas stocking. "I suppose you've had dozens of girlfriends, but I have never felt this way before in my life! She is all I can think about! In fact, I have to learn how to dance before Matt's wedding, because I asked her to be my date."

"Does she live here?"

"No, she lives in Montana! I just met her last week."

"When is Matt's wedding?"

"They haven't set a date yet. I have to talk to that boy so he gets on the stick with those nuptials! It is critical to my love life!" Jeff chuckled.

Kid laughed, "That's cool, but you're wrong. I've never had a real girlfriend."

Jeff nodded, "You too, huh? Well, if I can get hooked, you shouldn't have any problems."

"You kidding? Yea gads, with my background it is almost impossible!"

"Not really. I'm so doggoned shy when it comes to girls. I act like a total dipstick." Jeff admitted, "You'd swat me upside the head if you saw me in action!"

Kid cracked up, "You should have hung around the Horde! Some of those broads wouldn't give you the chance to be shy. They were on the prowl and ready to pull a train."

"Pull a train?"

"Oh my god, I can't believe I said that. Forget it."

"No, really, tell me."

"Like take on a string of guys, one right after the other."

Jeff looked at him, "You mean . . . really?"

"Yah."

"How can . . . I mean . . . wow. I can't imagine."

"It isn't pretty. I've seen it, but between us, I never took part. It always made me sick to my stomach. No matter how drunk I got, it always reminded me of cattle in heat. That's not very enticing, to me anyway."

Jeff studied him, "I may call Kathleen and tell her to stay home."

"I can't see you going with someone like that."

"Likely not. That's over the top. I have to tell you, I'll never feel the same about railroad tracks!"

"You idiot!"

"I know, huh? Please don't tell anybody. I enjoy having them think I'm normal for a little bit."

"Your secret is safe with me."

"Hey, would you like to see a photo of Kathleen?"

"I guess. You have one?"

Jeff took out his wallet and pointed, "She is the blonde girl. Isn't she great?"

"Wow! She is a looker. I hope she is a good gal."

"I think she is. I'll be anxious for you to meet her. Just act stupid around her, so she thinks I'm brilliant."

"How long have you known her?"

"A few days."

"Sorry, she probably already figured out you aren't brilliant," Kid teased.

"Don't give up your job at the suicide hotline, there!" Jeff laughed, "I better go see what happened to your bread sticks. It was great meeting you, Kid. I hope to visit with you again."

-15-

Kid was almost asleep again when there was a knock. Carl returned with a pretty, short lady with auburn hair and a big dimpled smile who was helping Clarissa carry a dish of candies for Kid to inspect. Carl introduced the lady as his wife, Mo. She held out her hand and smiled broadly, "I see what Nora meant when she said you were a fine-looking laddie! It's good to have you here to spruce up the scenery."

"Mo, you're so shallow!" Carl frowned.

"Shallow as a wading pool! I'd just as soon look at a fine young man as a wrinkled old one!" she laughed. "How soon before your arm will allow you to get up?"

"I have to stay in bed because of my stomach, not my arm. Zach is trying to keep me from going into withdrawal before my gut heals," Kid answered frankly.

"And I'm being glad of that!" she exclaimed. "I can't imagine having it all going on at the same time! If you need someone to be rattling beads for you while you are healing, remember I'm good at that! We got prohibition repealed!"

Kid laughed, "I can see why Carl is so proud of you!"

"Sakes alive, can you repeat that for my tape recorder?" Mo giggled. "I have a leprechaun here that wants you to check out her candy."

Clarissa held the large plate of candies up to Kid expectantly and he took one. He popped it in his mouth immediately, but Clarissa went into a tailspin! "How could you do that, Mr. Kid?"

"It is great," Kid answered. "What's the matter? Why the tears? I thought you wanted me to try one!"

"You were supposed to look at it, not eat it! Now you can't say if I'm a spurt!" the little girl grumped. "Maybe I didn't do a good job! You can't tell me cause it's in your belly! I'm pretty mad about it."

Kid chuckled, "It looked very good! That's why I popped one in my mouth right away. Let's look at the other ones. Wow! I see how even they are. Did Annie help you?"

The little cook squinted, "Why, don't you think I can make them my own self?"

The man studied her, "How many did you eat?"

"Like four or ten," she answered. "Why?"

"I think you ate so many that you are thinking about crying, huh?" the biker asked.

"How did you know about that?"

"Because I was once your age."

"Did you do that, too?"

"Sure did. Once I ate so much Halloween candy that I got a tummy ache and cried myself to sleep. It was horrible."

"You know, you're pretty smart about some stuff." Clarissa looked at her candies, "Do you think I'm a spurt?"

"Let's check. Can you tell me the recipe?"

"See, we taked some mashed potatoes in a cup with lines on it and made them warm. Then we added enough powdered sugar to make it be dough. It took lots and lots of sugar. Then we rolled it out like cookie dough. We put peanut butter on it and rolled it up. It started to get too thick, so Grandma showed us how to cut them and start another one so they didn't get too big. Then Annie sliced the logs because I'm too little to use a knife. I mostly smeared the peanut butter."

"You put the peanut butter on evenly. That was a good job."

"Okay. Can I tell CJ that I am an even spreader?"

"If you want. You did a good job." Kid smiled. "And they taste good, too. But I think that now you should wash your face and get the peanut butter off your arm."

"Okay. I have to help Annie clean up anyway. She said she is going to throw me in the bath tub."

"Good idea."

The little girl crawled up on the bed and gave the man a big hug. "I like you."

"I like you too, Clarissa." Then he looked at his arm, "Yikes, now I got peanut butter on me!"

Clarissa giggled, "I have to go help now."

She and Mo left the room. Carl watched until they left and shook his head, "You handled that very well."

"I like ankle-biters, most of the time."

"Want to have a big family?"

"Yah, I'm gonna run right out and do that. By the way, where is my breadstick?"

Carl laughed, "Oops! I sorta ate yours while I was waiting for the ladies. Want me to get you one?"

"That's okay. I really need help getting to the bathroom again, if you wouldn't mind."

When Kid got back to bed, Carl picked up their cups, "Anything I can get for you?"

"Could you tell Annie I'm starting to hurt?"

"Sure thing. See you tonight."

"Carl? Thanks. I'll try to be decent to Bernard. If you say he's good guy, he probably is."

"I don't think you'll be sorry. If you are, let me know right off? Okay?"

"Okay."

Annie came in with the medications and smiled at Kid, "You and your mashed potatoes!"

"I'm not responsible for that! Really."

"Yah, yah. That's what they all say! I have so much powdered sugar on me, I stick to everything. You should've seen Miss Clarissa. She was in her element. She went after that jar of peanut butter like gangbusters! She never stopped talking for more than a minute the whole time! Zach will be here in a couple hours, for the evening. I hope he doesn't think that you've done too much today."

"I have slept a lot, but I had a lot of company. I feel a bit out of whack though."

"Like how?"

"My head is spinning."

"I'll tell Zach, but it is probably a reaction to Clarissa. What do you bet she marries someone who is extremely quiet?"

"Oh, I was going to ask Nora, but maybe you have an idea. What would Kitten like for her birthday? Any ideas?"

121

"Hm. She loves her cat, picture books, Miriam, and the colors beige and green. That is all I know. Why do you ask?"

"I want to get her something for her birthday. Byron said he'll pick up something for her in Merton tomorrow."

"Merton? Okay, I know what you should get her. I saw some neat pajamas in the Five and Dime that had feet in them. They had some with kittens all over them."

"That would be good. I'll tell Byron. Thanks, Annie."

"No problem. You should sleep now for a while."

"When will Elton be home?"

"In about an hour. Want me to tell him you want to talk to him?"

"No, he said he was going to talk to me. I just wanted to make sure I'd be awake."

"You should have a good nap before then. Want me to pull down the shades?"

"Yes, please."

Later, Elton knocked and came in. Kid was sleeping very soundly. Elton was about to leave the room, Kid woke up. "You should have woke me up."

Elton turned around, "You seemed to be really getting after it. Good dream?"

"No dream, and that's good! This new combination of IV stuff seems to really knock me out. I feel better than I have for a long time. If you have time, I'd like to talk to you."

"That's what I'm here for."

"I talked a lot today and I made a couple decisions I want to talk to you about."

"Good," Elton sat down. "Want me to get us some coffee?"

"Think I could really have some?"

"I'll see what I can do. Want to go to the can?"

A bit later, the two men sat down with their coffees. Kid was pleased because he got a little more coffee with his milk. Elton took a swallow and then said, "Okay, so tell me. I'm dying of curiosity."

"I talked to Pastor Ellison. I decided. It sounds dumb, but I truly want to be someone Mom and Dad wouldn't be ashamed of."

"What kind of a person is that?"

Kid frowned, "I didn't get that specific. I figured I'd know."

"Okay, what else?"

"I will talk to Sheriff Bernard about Scab and the Horde. I mean, I'll act like a normal person and be polite. I guess he is coming out tomorrow."

"Good. I'm glad, Kid. You know, he was a great help for us when Diane's father-in-law went bezerk."

"I didn't hear about Diane. You guys really have a lot of stuff going on. I thought you were Ozzie and Harriet."

"No, more like Dracula in the Haunted Forest!" Elton chuckled. "Anyway, I think you made some good choices."

"Well, I'm not done. I also ended up telling Carl that I'd like to have him get some guys to fill in my well. That's one of the reasons I need to talk to you. The other is CJ."

"What's with CJ?"

"He and I talked the other day and he told me that he needed to pay Kevin for his share of the rabbits. So, I offered to pay him $1.50 for the eggs I stole. He told me to give it to you, because they are your eggs and milk."

"You don't need to pay me. We settled that already. Remember?"

"I know you said not to mind it, but what about CJ's money?"

"He gets paid from me for taking care of the the chickens. He'll get his money. He gets paid from Carl for helping with the ducks. Don't worry about it."

"Can I help with the rabbits?"

Elton leaned back, "Do you think you need to?"

"I think that I should. My Dad would think so."

"Okay, then you need to talk to Kevin. He could use a partner. He is letting the boys pay him so much a month but he put up all the cost. I told him to keep records and explain it all to the boys. They need to learn how that all works. If you want to be a part of it, I'm sure Kevin would appreciate the help."

"Sure? I wouldn't be barging in?"

"I'm positive."

"Okay, I'll talk to him. Now, I need to talk to you. Carl said that you probably don't need to rent my land because you got Olson's. So, if you don't want to rent mine, do you know someone that would? I really want to pay my way as much as I can. I need some money."

"No, I don't know anyone. I can keep my ear to the ground. I was thinking today though, if you want to give it a try here, maybe we could work something out. You need livestock, right? You need someone to help you rebuild and some cash. I can always use another pair of hands around here and at the shop. I'm sure the boys would be interested in some help as would Carl and Darrell. He has a dairy, you know. Clarence has been over there almost steady since they started calving. He has school again next week."

"Does Darrell do it all alone? Someone told me he has about over a hundred head."

"That is just his milking herd. He has a lot more than that. Matt lives there as does Jeannie's sister, Joallyn. They help."

"I remember Joallyn! Eddie Frandsen's sister, huh?"

"Yes. She spent a lot of time in San Francisco, but she is back now. She lives with Darrell and Jeannie. She is going with this guy from Indiana, Josh Perkins. He teaches at St. Johns."

"Oh." Kid questioned, "Is it serious?"

"Seems to be. Were you interested in her?"

"No. I was too young, but I just remember she was so pretty."

"Yah, she is. She and Josh started going together about the same time that Diane moved in with us." Elton chuckled, "I tell you, it's almost like Peyton Place around here."

"I doubt that, very much."

"I'll talk to you in a month or so." Elton got serious, "I hope you're planning on staying around here. I forgot to ask you."

"Yah. I'll be here for a while anyway, and everyone seems to think that I should try to get grounded before I go taking off."

"Good idea. That's a relief."

"Elton," Kid became very serious, "I hope you don't end up being sorry. I still have to get off these meds and smack. I have a lot of fences to mend and I honestly doubt if you'll want to stick with me through it all. I don't expect you to, and I know how bad I can get. I don't want to, but I always have. I have never stayed off heroin if I had the money or wasn't in prison. I only got it there when it was available."

"Kid, would you mind if I asked Nora to join us?"

"No, I guess not. I'd rather talk to you alone, because I don't want her to think badly of me. Not that she thinks well of me as it is."

"Okay, let's us talk it out first and then we'll ask her to join us. I think that she should have input. And actually, she likes you. Don't know why? I'm so much nicer."

"I wouldn't know about that," Kid teased. "I won't stay here at the house that long. As soon as I can, I'll move back to my place."

Elton thought a bit, "Don't know about that. You'd be safer here than there. For one thing, you'd be alone and from what I've heard from some of the clanners that have fought addictions, being alone is not good. Also, if you're with a family, you'll have more protection from the Horde. Can we not carve that in stone until we have to?"

"I guess. Are there clanners who are addicts? I think Matt mentioned that there was."

"Yes. I know they're planning to talk to you on their own, so I don't feel like I should be the town crier. You know?"

"Yah, I get it." Kid shrugged, "They might decide not to get down with dregs like me."

"That's not at all the case. I don't know very much about heroin addiction except it's a tough one. We can go through this together, okay? You'll have a huge support system, if you want it. But remember, it's also a pain in the ass. I remember when I quit drinking, I wished that no one knew. These guys all let me know when I was crossing the line. Took all the fun out of it, for damned sure, and I wasn't very pleasant about it. We won't expect miracles, but we'll expect you to try."

"I hope you won't be disappointed."

"Will you stop borrowing trouble?" Elton finished his coffee, "Well, I need to get chores done. Big doin's tonight. Are you going to join us for dinner?"

"Zach says no. I stayed up too long at lunch."

"You have plenty of time to meet the whole crowd. All at once, we're a headache anyway. Should I call Nora?"

"Did we decide anything?"

"Of course, you are going to be another of our kids. Nora will get another baby chick for her nest!" Elton chuckled.

"Yah, bet she'll be thrilled."

Nora was very happy when they talked to her and gave Kid a big hug. "That's great! We'll be here for you. Grandma and I will keep you on a short leash until you work this out. You will, I just know it. You know Kid, you and I go way back. Don't we?" She winked.

He looked at her and started to laugh, "You mean like that first day?"

"You got it. I knew we were bonding."

"I don't imagine you'll let me forget that any time soon."

"Not if I can help it! I have to go help Kitten. She wants to fix your tray for supper."

"Really?" Kid asked, very pleased.

"When I left the kitchen, there was a cupcake, three pieces of mashed potato candy, two potato chips, a dish of pudding, and a cookie. She and Grandma were in a deep discussion about the menu."

After she left the room, Elton turned to Kid and said, "My girl is happy about your decision. I know that. I'm glad that we talked to her. We'll work something out with the money. As far as paying back the boys for covering your well, just remember it. There will be things that you can do to repay them in no time. Why don't I help you get set up for dinner? I might just stay in and watch you eat everything on your tray!"

"I won't really have to eat all those sweets, will I?"

"I imagine Grandma will explain it to Kitten."

A few minutes later, Grandma came in with his dinner tray and Kitten. Kitten was carrying another smaller tray. Grandma's tray had dinner on it and Kitten's had dessert. The ladies put their trays on the bedside table and Kid thanked them. Then Grandma sat down and took Kitten onto her lap. "She has something she wants to tell you, okay?"

"What is it, Kitten?"

"Me make 'zert' for you, okay?"

He looked at the tray she had brought, "It looks very good. Is it ice cream?"

Kitten looked to Grandma who said, "It is spumoni."

Kitten repeated to Kid, "Moni."

"Oh, I bet I'll like that, huh?"

"Taste."

He took a bit of it on his spoon and tasted it, "Oh, it is wonderful!"

Kitten smiled and crawled up into Grandma's shoulder. Grandma looked at Kid, "Thanks. She wanted you to like it. Well, we're going to get ready for tonight. I'll stop back later. Need anything now?"

"No, it looks good. Thanks, and thank you, Kitten."

"Bye bye," the little girl said as Grandma stood her on the floor and took her hand. "I go be pretty."

"That's right. We are going to get all pretty for tonight. Enjoy your dinner, Kid!"

"Enjoy!"

The dinner was good, but before he could eat much, he was getting very sleepy. He ended up going to sleep before he ate very much, but he was glad he got to eat something with some spice. He didn't wake when someone came in to get his tray.

-16-

Kid felt someone touching his shoulder and opened his eyes. There was Zach, smiling down at him. "Meds seem to be working pretty well, huh? You were really sleeping."

"Yah, it feels good. I'm glad you woke me up though."

"What's up?"

"I've been making some sort of plans today and worried I'm just enjoying the meds too much."

"You needed to make some decisions, meds or not. You'll feel better having a direction. You can always change them. Everyone needs a little direction. I've heard that you're still stressing about paying me back, huh? Didn't I tell you not to worry about that?"

"Save your breath. Elton already gave me hell about it."

"So, you quit worrying?"

Kid chuckled, "No. I need to go to the bathroom. Could you help me with that IV? Why do I have so much trouble with that?"

"It is unwieldy. They make more stable ones, but since this is a home, we go with the cheaper version," Zach chuckled.

"From what I heard, you must have a patient or two here all the time."

"Actually, we do a lot. I think this is the first time in a long time that we haven't had oxygen stored. I heard that you've been complaining about your coffee, huh?"

"I wouldn't call it coffee. More like milk."

"If you drink too much coffee, you won't sleep so well."

"Hot cocoa?"

"That wouldn't be much better than coffee." Zach laughed, "Let me go get something for us."

A few minutes later, the two men were settled and enjoying some hot tea. Kid shook his head, "I'm actually beginning to like tea now."

"I'm glad. You know, you can't have too much of that either."

"Stop already. Quit telling me what I can't have. I'd like to hear what I can have for a change."

"Good news! Nora is bringing you some breadsticks. She said you got swindled out of them earlier."

"That sounds good. She takes good care of me, doesn't she?"

"Yes, she's the best. Wait 'til she gives you hell! That's weird."

"How?"

"She cuts right through your gizzard and somehow makes you feel guilty that you made her feel bad enough to do it. It isn't fun."

"Doesn't sound like it. Carl told me how he ended up in North Dakota, so in the process I learned some about your family. He didn't say much, though. You guys all seem to have lines about what you'll tell about each other."

"Some things should be left for a person to tell about themselves. About paying me back, it's like this. I don't know what you know about my father and his so-called ministry, but he amassed a pile of money by horrible methods. When he, my brother-in-law, and my sister all met their violent ends, all the money was left to Ruthie, Miriam, and I. We're the last of the family that weren't murdered or had committed suicide! Nice legacy, huh? We put some money away for Miriam's college and stuff, but the rest we decided to use to help folks. We tried to repay the folks that it was extorted from, but the FBI couldn't find that many or figure out who they were. So, we just decided to move ahead. It isn't really good money or our money. So, your hospital bills, etc. were paid from that. If you ever want to pay us back, we'll put it back in the account or you can help someone else. Don't feel like you have to though. It was given without too many strings."

Kid wrinkled his eyebrow, "Too many?"

"Yah. We'd like it to be a step toward things improving for you."

"I imagine you have it all figured out how that should be."

"No, I don't. You see, I'm not you. I love having a model airplane hangar in my yard. You might not!"

"You have an airplane hangar?" Kid's eyes flew open.

"Not a real one." Zach laughed, "See, we used to build model airplanes in Elton's shop here. But we ran out of room to store them and so, when I built the house, I conned Suzy into allowing me to build a hangar with a workshop at the end."

"You mean small model airplanes?"

"No, the big ones, that fly. How we do it is anyone who wants—can chip in and then we get enough money, we buy one. Sometimes someone just buys one on his own or with someone else. Whoever has the time or inclination helps build it. We do have a few rules though. You have to be over 4'6" and present at the maiden flight."

"Why 4'6"?"

"Keeps out the Gophers, our name for the little kids! And we may raise the height requirement, because Charlie and CJ are getting close! They have helped from time to time but it is nerve-wracking. We'll be having another maiden flight in a few weeks. Hopefully, you'll be out and about for that one."

"Me?"

"Yah, you. Don't see anyone else in here. You're welcome to help whenever you want. I used to do a lot of talking to Elton in the middle of the night while we were working on our first one. Actually, that was a helicopter about six feet long. I'll show it to you when you can get around. Anyway, back to me telling you what to do with your life—I can't. I was so excited about the model planes, I told Carl about them. He said he'd rather shoot himself."

Kid laughed, "He sure acts like Billy Goat Gruff! Does he do them now?"

"He helps a bit, but he really doesn't care about them. Instead, he and Mo have turned their home into a daycare. That guy was mister crotchety and tough. Now he has a playground slide inside his house and at least three or four cribs and playpens! He has one whole room devoted to his 'Gophers'. The kids have their own tool shed filled with shovels and fishing poles! I would've never ever guessed that!" Then he laughed, "I don't think that Coot would have either, a year ago."

"Coot? I thought I heard someone call Carl that before, but I decided I didn't hear it right. How did that happen?"

"Mo calls him an Old Coot all the time and so do most of the Gophers." Zach continued, "It's your life and you have to live it, so it has to be your decision. Having said that, I don't think that using dope is a good way to find peace. What I'd like for you is to have you able to sleep like a normal person and not be addicted to heroin. How do you feel about that?"

"Is that the part you want from me so I don't have to pay you for the hospital?"

"That wouldn't be very realistic. If you remain addicted, you won't have enough money to pay anyone. We both know that." Zach leaned back in the chair, "Do you want to get clean?"

"Yah, and while I'm not looking forward to withdrawal, I have lived through it before. I trust you enough to think you won't let me croak. But Zach, then what? I've never stayed away from it for very long. I don't really see what would be different now."

"It is very treacherous in its addiction. I can't tell you what would be different, because I don't know. My ex-wife was addicted to heroin. Our marriage lasted about a year. She overdosed twice and was a physical wreck. She ended up moving in with her pimp. I never did hear what became of her after we split. She couldn't fight it. After a fix, it took her about eight hours and she'd start getting sick. It wasn't pretty. She would honestly think she'd just take enough to get her over being sick; one more time, but it never was. She told me once that she just couldn't get as high as she did at first. That's why she kept overdosing."

Kid spoke solemnly, "That's what happens. The first time, it's such wonderful oblivion, but it's never as good again. It soon becomes just getting a fix to keep from having your muscles spasm, roaring stomach problems, and drenching sweats. You feel good for a short time and then start to worry about where you are going to get the next fix because you know you'll be getting sick again. Then you lose your veins. You can have the syringe filled and not be able to get it into yourself. That's hell. Well, honestly, it all is. But Zach, I'll probably go back. We both know that, right?"

"No, I know it's a possibility. Kid, your body is pretty well wrecked. If this keeps up, you won't make old bones. Your body can't stand how you're treating it. You can't stay on heroin and keep safe from the Horde. Sure, you can keep out of California, but what are you going to do about Scab?" Zach responded, "You are too nice of a guy, with a fun sense of humor. Now that we know the real you, we don't want to lose you. So, don't give up on yourself, please! That is why I want you to start being serious about getting things sorted out as much as possible before next week is over. Somehow, we have to get your brain to figure out that heroin is not your hero, but your downfall. You'd have never gotten into the Horde without it, and then prison."

"I know that. I knew that before. It doesn't seem to help. Have you ever done something and hated yourself the whole damned time you were doing it because you knew that after you did, you'd hate yourself even worse?"

"Actually, I have. Don't know what that's about. Most of us do that about something. Sometimes, I would hear myself saying I'm not going to do something and all the while, be making plans to do it. I know alcoholics that feel the same way. When someone asks them why they had a drink, they say they don't know. They just did. I believe it. But it isn't just addicts. I have a friend who is a very bad diabetic. John would sit down and eat a half a box of candy at one sitting, knowing full well how sick he'll be." Zach shrugged, "Guess that's part of being a human. Anyway, I see a psychiatrist, Dr. Samuels. He is very good. I'd be happy to make an appointment for you, if you'd like. He has helped a lot of folks."

"Then I have to go to him forever, huh?"

"No. I used to see him once a week. Now, it's only when something starts to bother me. My problem is dealing with my childhood. Once I got some of those ghosts settled, I've been doing okay."

"Hm, I always thought it was just a crutch. If I did, I'd owe you even more. I hate that."

"When you get a better idea, let me know." Zach grinned, "Anyway, you don't need to decide it tonight. We can talk more later, if you want."

"Suzy said you are babysitting for me tomorrow night?"

"No, but babysitting for some of the littlest Gophers and my Suzy. She is having such trouble with her legs and feet."

"When is she due?"

"In a couple weeks. Just think, I'll be a daddy. I can't believe it."

"You'll be a good dad. I'm pretty sure of that."

"Thanks. You know, you have a knack with kids, too. Everyone has commented on it."

"Most folks would be good with kids if they were attached to a bottle of tranquilizers!" Kid laughed.

"Might be on to something there! Well, I think Byron said you were going to talk to him about something, so I'll go get him if you feel up to it."

"Thanks Zach."

"Hi," Byron said as he sat down, "You were sleeping like a log! I stopped in a bit ago and you were totally out."

"The best part, I didn't even dream!" Kid agreed. "I found out about Kitten. Annie said that she likes beige, green and kittens. Annie said there are some pajamas with kittens on them at the Five and Dime that have feet in them that would just fit the bill. So, if you could pick them up for me, I'll have Elton pay you."

"Not going to clean pews for me?"

"If you can wait until I get my cast off," Kid smiled. "They might be pretty dirty by then."

Kid was awake later when there was a knock at the door. Matt came in with Jeff. "Hi, we just got beat in whist, so we wondered if we could come in here and pout."

"I guess. How's the party?"

"Nice. Did you have spaghetti?"

"Yes, it was very good. Nora even brought me a breadstick a bit ago. Carl was going to bring me one earlier, but he ate it before he got here!"

"Nice, huh?" Jeff grinned. "We got skunked in whist by Father Vicaro and Carl. I think they cheated. Matt and I never made a single point! Seems awful fishy to me!"

"Oh, Diane and I are used to it, Jeff. We always get beat no matter what game we play. We have a little luck with Ian and Ruthie, because they are pretty bad too," Matt explained. "I think it is because we are from Boston."

Jeff shook his head, "I don't know, Matt. I rather doubt it is a matter of geography."

"Me, either," Kid agreed. "So, how are the dancing lessons coming, Jeff?"

"Haven't started yet."

"Dancing lessons?" Matt asked. "Why are you taking dancing lessons?"

"Because I have a date to your wedding, as soon as you set a date." Jeff said, "So you better get to work on that!"

"Diane and I are thinking of May before Elton and Nora go to the Grand Caymans on their vacation."

"What's the hold up?"

"My niece, Rain, is going to be a bridesmaid. We have to find out when she is out of school."

"How old is she?" Kid asked. "Is she in high school?"

"No, college. Freshman year. She'll be nineteen in June," Matt explained.

"What is she going into?" Jeff asked.

"She doesn't know if she wants to continue in college. She hates it. She was going into psychology."

"I should talk to her about that. It won't make you a millionaire, that's for certain," Jeff nodded. "What would she rather do?"

"Almost anything else, but math," Matt laughed.

Kid frowned, "Is her name really Rain?"

"Short for Lorraine. She hates that, too! She is a character. You guys will like her."

"What if she hates us?" Jeff asked.

"You are both nutty enough. She'll like you."

"That's one hell of a compliment there, Matthew," Jeff laughed. "No wonder I have an inferiority complex!"

"Who are you trying to kid?" Matt laughed. "Too bad you have a date, I thought you might want to go with Rain. So, are you going to tell me who you asked out?"

"You don't know her. It is Sister Abigail's niece. Her name is Kathleen and she is gorgeous."

"She is," Kid agreed. "You should show him her picture, Jeff."

"Here," Jeff handed her photo to Matt with pride.

"She looks short, chubby and bald!" Matt poked.

"That's her father, you jerk!" Jeff blustered.

Matt laughed, "I know. She is really nice-looking. She looks like a young Abigail."

"I saw a photo of Abigail when she was a girl and Kathleen could be her twin."

"You and Sister became good friends on that trip, huh?" Matt watched his friend as he carefully put the photograph carefully in his wallet.

"Yes. I really like her. She is one fine lady," Jeff pointed out the time, "Man, we better let this guy sleep. I'll see you tomorrow, Kid. I think I'm helping milk and then staying for breakfast."

"What else do you have planned?" Matt asked.

"Dancing lessons. Grandma and Nora are going to teach me tomorrow morning."

"You won't learn it all tomorrow," Matt announced.

"I'm a fast learner."

"Yah, and I'm a mountain climber!" Matt chuckled. "See you tomorrow, Kid."

-17-

The next time Kid woke up, it was quiet in the house. He felt the cat, Cotton, jump on his bed and curl up on his feet. However, this time he wasn't comforted. He was becoming irritable and crabby. It was getting very tiring to just lay there so much, but he was still too weak to move around. He determined that he needed to get up on his own.

He tried to sit up and managed to only disturb Cotton. He heard the door open as he tried to get out on the IV side of the bed, thinking that would keep him from knocking over the IV pole. He was wrong, and managed to knock it over, and jerk the needle out of his arm as he fell over onto the floor.

Elton and Annie were there within seconds and helped him up. Then he was even more frustrated. "Dammit, I wish I could do something on my own!"

Elton smiled, "I think you did! You gave yourself a black eye from where you hit the IV stand."

"Yah, to go with my new growth beard," his voice trembling. "I give up."

"Oh, come on Champ. We can handle this," Elton said as they helped him up. "Let me help you to the bathroom."

"I'll get your medication," Annie said as she left the room.

While Elton helped him, Annie got his meds and remade his bed. When they came back in the room and stared at the bed. "I wish I could sit up for a while."

"Tell you what, if you let me fix up your IV, you can sit up," Annie suggested.

"I could use some juice, myself," Elton smiled. "Let Annie get you rewired and I'll take you to the kitchen for some juice. Won't that be dandy?

Kid nodded, "Thanks. I'd like that. Can I have juice? Don't suppose I could get a beer?"

"Nice try, Hotshot." Elton laughed. "Zach would skin me alive!"

"You can have some juice, unless you have trouble with citrus." Annie said, "If you do, then I'd suggest some peach or pear juice."

"I get heartburn from grapefruit juice, but otherwise I'm okay."

"I think we have some apple juice out there." Elton suggested.

Annie ended up putting the IV in the back of his hand, "Your veins aren't very good."

"I know," Kid looked down. "I did that."

"Well, before long, you'll be free of this. There you go, Sunshine. You guys have fun. I'm going back to bed."

"Thanks again, Annie."

"No problem."

"Sorry to be such a pain in the ass," Kid said, as he sat up to the table and Elton poured his juice.

"We all are sometimes, even someone as wonderful as me," Elton chuckled. "You know, I should go wake up Lloyd on sheer principal."

"The poor guy. I remember him from when I lived here before. He was always nice to us kids. He helped me once when I fell off my horse and tore my jacket. He patched me up, fed me some cocoa, and took me home."

"Sounds like Lloyd," Elton said. "He saved my sorry ass more than once. He was always there, whether to give me hell or a hand—or both!"

"That's a good thing," Kid nodded. He was quiet for a bit and then said, "Elton, you know right now I'm still half-drugged up. After I get clean, I'll probably go back to using. Once that happens, I will lie, cheat, and steal to get my fix. I'm awful to be around. You'll have to kick me out before then. I don't want the kids to see that. Matt says we're all role models. I don't want to be that kind."

Elton scrunched up his face, "That is the most contorted line of bull I've ever heard! Look, if you are half-drugged up, that means you are half-clean! You act like when you get clean, the next logical step is to start using. You have that all planned out already! If that is all you intend to do, why bother? Don't get clean. That would be a stupid, waste of time."

"Huh? Don't you want me to get off heroin?"

"Yes, but not for ten minutes! When I drank, I quit drinking almost every time I passed out."

"That's not quitting."

"No, and what you are talking about isn't getting straight either! We need to get you lined up with other things to think about besides your big nosedive off the wagon!" Elton shook his head, "What can I do to help?"

"I guess I'd keep me from getting my hands on cash."

"That should be easy to do. Live in my world!" Elton laughed, "Let's see. We could talk to Carrie, Kevin's wife. She works at the bank in Merton. She can set you up with an account that has to have someone else co-sign for you. That'll keep you from blowing it all. On the other hand, you need to have some money in your pocket. Besides, it's better than stealing and we won't have Sheriff Bernard coming after you."

"Good point. If I'm going to mess up my life, I guess I shouldn't steal from others to do it."

"Kid, if you turn your life over to heroin, you are stealing from everyone who ever cared about you. Don't fool yourself. When you give in, you're hurting everyone around you."

"Good thing nobody cares about me anymore, huh?" the man said matter-of-factly.

"Yah. Tell that to CJ or Kitten."

"They don't care. You're just saying that to try to make me feel guilty."

Elton frowned, "No. First off, guilt doesn't do much but destroy people. And second, they do care. Kids don't need a resume and months of time to like someone. They go on gut instinct. I think CJ is more reticent, but he feels a bit like you are his project. When you said you'd help train Bruno, you won him over. So, you can't go back to heroin until that is done. I think you also promised to help Clarissa make some potato thing!"

"If anything will push me over the edge, that should do it!" Kid laughed. "Actually, she was pretty jazzed about it. I guess I should do that. Besides, I want to watch Pastor Ellison help!"

"How soon can you get out of bed? Did Zach say?"

"End of next week. I guess after some lab work and such. Then I have to finish detox. How am I going to do that with the kids around? I don't want them to see that."

"We have to talk to Zach about that. Okay?" Elton agreed. "The kids will be back in school this coming week. We wouldn't want them to be disrupted, if possible. However, we will manage. Zach said it'll be a lot easier than cold turkey, so maybe we're worried for nothing."

"I know, but I know how anxious I get by the time I need meds. I have no illusions."

"You are such a pessimist! Anyway, I talked to Kev while we were milking and he said that he would love a grownup partner in the rabbit business. He said to let you know, but he'll be talking to you soon. Probably not this weekend, since Keith plans to beat you in chess."

"I'm sure he will. I haven't played in years and I'm sleepy half the time."

"That's why I wanted to beat you this weekend," Keith said as he came into the kitchen and opened the fridge. "Where is Nathan's bottle? Oh, here."

Elton's oldest son put a pan of water on the stove and set the bottle in it. Then he poured himself some juice and sat down, "Burning the midnight oil?"

"Kitten came to get me when Kid crashed on the floor." Elton explained. "Got himself a shiner."

Keith looked at the bruise, "Cute! Oh, by the way, expect company. I heard Grandpa getting up when I came in."

"It's about the right time," Elton nodded and then looked up, "Hello, Lloyd. What's up?"

"I'm glad you made breakfast. We have to pick rock on that forty acres over by the fence. I see you got the boys up. Good. Hurry and eat, so we can get to work." Then octogenarian noticed they had their pajamas on and frowned, "You better get dressed. You can't pick rock like that!"

Elton answered, "We were just having a glass of juice before we take a nap. We're already done! We got all the rock picked to surprise you."

"I'll be jiggered. I didn't think you had it in you. Well, thanks boys. Good work." Then he scrutinized the situation, "You did do a good job, right?"

"Excellent and even put all the equipment away."

Lloyd sat down with a big sigh, "I figured you guys would get the hang of it eventually. Did this guy help much with that big thing on his arm?"

"Yes, Kid helped a lot."

Lloyd beamed, "Good for you. I knew you would because my relatives always do the right thing, even if it's not easy."

"Yes, they do." Elton agreed and smiled at Kid, "Yes, they do."

After they finished their juice, Keith took Nathan's bottle upstairs and Elton helped Lloyd back to bed. When Elton returned to the kitchen, Kid was trying to wipe the table. "I can do that. You'll get too tangled up."

"Did you hear what he said?"

"Who?"

"Lloyd. He really thinks we are all his family, doesn't he?"

"Yes, he does. He always wanted a big family, and he has one now." Elton put the washcloth on the counter and gave Kid a boost up, "He thinks a lot of us, even though he thinks we are pretty wobbly most days!"

"I can see why he thinks that," Kid smiled, feeling strangely proud to be thought well of by the man with Alzheimers.

Later that night, Kid woke up to the sounds of a man screaming and then heard Annie talking soothingly. Elton went down the hall and talked to Andy for a bit before he came back. On the way, he stopped in to check on Kid and Kitten. "Hope that didn't wake you."

"Is he okay?"

"Yah, He was a tunnel rat in Vietnam and was dreaming about that. That's usually what throws him into a nightmare. He is a lot better than he was though. I see my little girl is sleeping in the chair again. I'll carry her back to her bed. I wonder if I should just set up a cot in here so she has more room. She wakes up in her own bed and comes right back in here."

Kid shook his head, "Isn't that something?"

"She never wakes you, huh?"

"I rarely even see her. I see the door open, and once in a while, hear her move. I see Cotton, because the cat sleeps on my feet. If I wake up, she disappears. Did she come get you tonight when I fell out of bed?"

"Yes." Elton grinned. "Like you said, I hear the door open and then there she is, patting my cheeks to wake me up. Clarence does the same thing. CJ only rarely wakes up."

"Does Clarissa?"

"No, she never has. She sleeps like a rock. Have you heard Clancy's wolf howl yet?"

Kid grinned, "The other day while I was having breakfast. He does a good job with it. It almost sounds real."

"I better get back to bed. Good night."

"Night."

Elton picked up Kitten and carried her back to her room. Kid heard Elton go to his room. Before he fell asleep, he saw the door open to his room. Then Cotton jumped on his bed again. Kid smiled and went back to sleep, confidant that someone was watching over him.

The family alarm went off and Kid woke up. He looked over and saw the door closing, as Kitten went back to her room. He chuckled to himself. 'What a crazy kid,' he thought before he went back to sleep.

A little later, there was a knock. Keith came in carrying his little boy. "Hi, I would like you to meet Nathan."

"Hello, Nathan," Kid smiled, "How are you?"

The little toddler studied him and then smiled, "Cakes!"

"What did he say?"

"He said cakes. He loves pancakes."

"Are you going to have pancakes?" Kid asked.

"Cakes," the little dark-haired child nodded. "Bye Bye."

Kid smiled, "I think he figures he is missing his breakfast."

"Yah, worried about his belly like a true clanner. I better take him out to Darlene. I'll be back in a minute to help you get your morning started. Okay?"

"No hurry, but thanks."

A couple minutes later, Keith came back in carrying a bag. "I brought you a little something."

"Why did you do that?"

"Cause I wanted to. I saw a sale on electric razors and picked up a Norelco double head for you. I thought it'd be easier than having to use a razor with one hand, and safer than having Grandpa help you!"

"I have to say, he had me worried."

While Kid cleaned up and got ready for his day, Keith straightened up his bed and then went to bring him back to bed. "Annie stopped by while you were in the shower, and said that she'd be back in a few minutes to do your meds."

"That's good. I'm starting to feel antsy. Thanks for the razor; it was great. I didn't want to have to ask Marty again. I'll have your Dad pay you."

"No, you won't!" Keith was adamant. "It was a gift. Now, just accept it politely."

"I didn't mean to insult you."

"You didn't. Seriously, I just wanted to get it for you. Okay?"

"Thanks. I really like it."

"You're welcome. Now, which one of these fantastic outfits do you want to wear today? We have pajamas in various colors, or sweat suits in various shades of gray!"

"Yesterday, Katie fixed a sweatshirt with Velcro, so I could get it on. She did it so fast and it even looked nice."

"Don't expect that from me! You'll get it stretched out or torn. That is the extent of my abilities."

Someone laughed at the door, and they turned to see Jackson. "Kate fixed a couple more for you yesterday, so I brought them to you. Looks like just in time before Keith got to ripping and tearing!"

"She did that?" Kid was shocked when he saw four more sweatshirts in assorted colors all fixed up for him. "That's amazing."

"She's amazing. She made my shirt." Jackson said with pride as he rubbed his hand down his leather pullover with embroidery on it.

"Wow! She did that? That is fantastic. Where did she get the leather?" Kid asked.

"She uses chamois. She made it for me for Christmas!"

"That's wonderful. I heard she is really good, but I had no idea. I bet her beading is great."

"There is some beading on this, see?"

"You're a lucky devil."

"I know," Jackson grinned. "She's the best. Oh, remind me to bring you our idea for the back of your jacket today."

"Katie mentioned it. I'm pretty forgetful these days."

"Andy and I were too, when we were on so many meds. Well, I better go help earn my keep."

"Me, too," Keith laughed, "Besides, here comes Annie with her big needle!"

A while later, Kid was waiting when Grandma and Kitten brought his breakfast tray. "Looks like you're hungry, huh?"

"Yes, Keith said you were making pancakes."

"Bacon," Kitten added.

"Are we having bacon, too? That is one of my favorites," Kid said to Kitten.

Grandma got his tray set up and then said, "I see your IV has been moved. Can you handle your utensils okay with the IV in the back of your hand?"

"I think so."

"Zach said you could have half and half coffee today!"

"That's great! I can't wait."

Grandma poured his coffee, "Can you guess what day it is?"

Kid smiled, "I bet it is Kitten's birthday! Am I right?"

The little girl got shy, but nodded, "My day."

"How old are you today?"

The little Sioux girl with a pixie haircut gave Grandma a questioning look while she held up her fingers. Then she made a face and shrugged.

"Are you four?" Kid asked.

Grandma said, "Yes, she is."

"Do you know how many fingers that is?"

The little girl looked at her hand and wiggled her fingers. The man said, "Give me your hand and I'll show you."

He put his hand over hers and folded in her thumb. "There you go. Four fingers!"

Claudia studied her hand and broke into a big smile, "Four?"

"Yes," Grandma hugged her. "You are four! Do you want to go show Nora?"

"Okay."

-18-

Before eight o'clock, the phone rang. It was Sheriff Bernard asking if it was too early to come out. Nora checked with Kid, who said it'd be fine. In reality, it was a conversation he didn't want to have, but had given his word he would. So, might as well get it over with early.

It was only a few minutes later, Bernard was knocking at Kid's door. "Come in," Kid said, actually thinking it must be one of the family.

He couldn't conceal his surprise when the Sheriff came in carrying a mug of coffee for each them. Kid laughed, "You must have called from the front yard!"

"Almost," Bernard chuckled. "The wife's family is coming out, so I thought I better get my work done so I can get back home. We're going to cook out. I think that is such a dumb idea."

"Don't you like grilling?"

"Why did I install an expensive stove in a house, so I can stand outside and cook over a fire?" Bernard scrunched up his face.

Kid burst out laughing, "Never looked at it that way! You have a point."

"Then my day wasn't a total loss." Bernard leaned back. "So, you are looking pretty chipper. Carl says you're on the mend. That's great. Guess he and a crew are going up to cover that well. Sorry it can't be repaired."

"It's old. I'm not surprised. Carl and Byron both told me to get over myself and act like a regular citizen. I'm trying. I'll give you fair warning; though, it is against my grain."

"I know. Don't really see us joining a quilting bee together myself, but stranger things have happened. I sleuthed out Scab's sentence. If he doesn't get into any more trouble, which is highly unlikely, he has another ten months to serve. He'll be on parole, so shouldn't leave the state. From what I cipher about him, that won't slow him down."

"No, it won't," Kid concurred. "Sheriff, I don't think the Horde will bother with me, unless they run into me somewhere. The only thing that would bring them up this way is the bike rally in Sturgis the first week in August."

"Glad you mentioned that. I plumb forgot about it." Bernard frowned, "Do you think they would come up this way? We rarely have anyone dribble up here from that."

"I doubt it. Can I be honest with you?"

"I'd appreciate that."

"I don't like to admit it, but I'm scared to death of them. Scab has some buddies that aren't much of an improvement over him."

"If you can give me their names, I'll see what we can find out. Are they in prison?"

"Some weren't arrested when we were. I don't know if they've been since or anything. There were about four hundred in the club when I was there. Only twenty-three were arrested when I was."

"That's not encouraging. Have you made any plans so far?"

"Hoping I will leave?"

"No and I didn't say that. Just curious. I'm not so certain that you should live alone on the home place until we get this gang thing worked out. You'd make a fine target over there. I'd prefer that you're around folks."

"I don't know yet. I'm worried about going through withdrawal. The kids here don't need to see that."

"If need be, I can help you. Margie, my wife, has worked as a nurse in detox, and we have no kids. If you need a place, we can accommodate you." Then he laughed, "I even have a cell handy."

"Thanks a bunch," Kid grumped. "I'll mention it to Zach and Elton though. I should go to a treatment facility or something like that, but I know that's the first place I'd look for me."

"Good point. I never thought of that, but an AA or NA meeting would be a good hunting ground for an addict, too."

"I've been an addict hunter, so I know."

"I wondered, and you don't have to tell me, but what was your 'job' with the Horde?"

Kid grimaced, "Here it comes! I knew that was on the horizon. I should find out the statute of limitations, huh?"

"No. You don't need to tell me. I was wondering because it may make a difference on how much of a threat the Horde thinks you are."

"I doubt I'm important. Besides, it has been years since I was hands-on in the operation. I helped move product and enforce repayment policies."

"Hm. Doesn't sound like you knew where the bodies were buried."

"Actually, I might know about a few, but that was a long time ago. If I was going to flip on them, I should've done it before sentencing rather than now. I might have got a better deal."

"Did you talk to your attorney about it then?"

"I had a public defender and he said to plea it out. I really didn't care what happened; so, I did."

"We need to change that now, Kid." Bernard took a fatherly tone, "I don't want you to not care anymore. Okay?"

"What do you mean?"

"It seems to me that a guy needs to have something to care about and someone to care about him to make it in this old world. Course, you can do as you think best, but that's the way I see it."

Kid studied the man, "Like how can you make someone care about you?"

"You can't, really. You're a leg up on that already! You already have a lot of folks going to bat for you."

"Oh, I thought you meant someone who cared."

"You're really pretty vacant, aren't you?" Bernard teased. "That's caring. Not everything is as dramatic as a declaration of undying love, you know!"

"I guess I never thought about that. Just a little caring, huh?"

"Better than a little hating, right? If you respect and appreciate a little caring, a crazy thing happens. Folks start to care more. If they can count on you and you show them that you value them, it will grow."

"How do I show that I value them when they can't count on me? I don't count on me."

"Well, then you do. If you know you'll let yourself down, then you're counting on it. Man, I have to start at ground zero with you, huh?"

Kid chuckled, "Sounds like it."

"One of the first things that Carl told me about you was how you said please and thank you. You know, that isn't the first thing that folks think of when they think of bikers or drug addicts."

"Mom and Dad drilled that into us kids. Mostly, I don't even realize I say it. So, I don't know how much it means."

145

"A lot. It's a sign of respect. You were raised right." Bernard took another sip of his coffee, "You got the markings off your leathers?"

"Yes, Katie did it. She made my sweatshirts! Look at this! Isn't that something?"

"She does great work. She made my niece's wedding dress. The beading was out of this world. She's a good kid."

"Seems like it." Then Kid looked at the Sheriff in horror, "I felt like such a scuzzball when she picked up my leathers. They stunk so bad and I could tell she smelled them, but she never said a word except they'd clean them up. I could've died of embarrassment."

"Guess you don't want to do that again, huh?"

"No way. Poor kid."

The small town sheriff grinned, "Ah, being clean ain't so bad. By the way, I like your haircut and shave."

"Thanks, Marty did it for me. Grandpa was going to!"

"Lord above! That'd mean a report or two I'd have to fill out!" The Sheriff laughed. "Anyway, I have to get back and clean out that grill. I'll chat with Zach about the detox thing and oh, I need that list of Scab's friends."

The men spent the next few minutes making a list of the psychopath's friends. Then Bernard stood up, "We'll get this fixed for you. Don't lose the faith. Thanks for talking to me. I'm glad it didn't make your hair fall out."

"It didn't. I actually enjoyed it," Kid smiled. "You're as wacky as the rest of these guys."

"We might be nuts, or we might be on to something."

"Good point." Kid extended his hand.

The Sheriff smiled and shook it, "See you soon."

"Thanks, I'm looking forward to it. Really."

Kid felt good as he lay back on his bed and thought over the conversation. Maybe these guys were on to something. Annie popped her head in the door, "Guess what? I just got a phone call you might be anxious to hear about."

"Okay, what is it?"

Annie sat down on the stool. "I told Zach that you were chomping at the bit to get up and around. He got the test results back from the specimens he took yesterday. He said that your little intestinal parasites are shriveling up!"

"That's great. So, I can get up now?"

"Yes, and no. This is what the man said. You still have to return to your diet gingerly. You've read your gut the riot act, so you can't just go back to that. Hear? Your arm isn't going to allow you total freedom yet, but you know that. Now, the addiction. Here is the kicker."

"I'm not going to like this, am I?" Kid watched her face.

"Regardless, it isn't going to change. We are prepared to take you off the IV's as long as you keep your fluids up. You'll need to be zonked at least a couple hours a day and all night, because Zach wants you to sleep. We don't want you to go into major withdrawal until end of next week. First off, your gut has to improve some before then because you're working on an ulcer. Second, you'll be cranky and we don't want to deal with that right now." Annie explained, "Besides, we've been weaning you whether you realize it or not. That's why we have let you go overtime and you have gotten so agitated from time to time. Believe me, we could knock you out so that you didn't even sneeze if we wanted to."

"I wondered about that."

"If you take a good nap now, I'll give you your shots and take off the IV in a couple hours. Then you can get dressed and wander around a bit. Words of warning! You start getting on folks about getting your next shot and you'll be knocked out. You start overdoing, and you will be knocked out. You get too cantankerous, and . . ."

"I will be knocked out?" Kid asked.

"By George, I think you've got it! Kate is in the process of remaking one of Ken's old jackets to fit over your cast, so you can go outside for a bit after she brings it over. You will be tired, so don't think you'll be mountain climbing. How does that sound?"

"Great. When will Zach be back out?"

"After seven tonight, when he is off call."

"I'll go right to sleep."

Annie giggled, "You are such a little kid."

"Watch it!" Kid chuckled.

He had a terrible time getting his mind to slow down. He really was as excited as a little kid. He was thinking of all the things he wanted to do and it wasn't very long before he realized he was trying to figure a way to get to town and score some smack. When he realized what he was doing, he became half-ill. Hell, he wasn't even off it yet and he was already plotting.

He knew he was a lost cause. He was wiping his tears when he heard a knock, 'Damn,' he thought. 'Why can't they just leave me alone?' However, he did say, "Come in."

There was Byron, grinning. "Heard you had some good news, huh? That's good. Kate sent me over with this jacket. She needs you to try it on to see if she has to adjust it."

Kid didn't say anything, but slipped the jacket on. It fit very well and the Velcro allowed him to get it over his cast. "Nice," his first words were. "Tell her thanks."

Then he started to cry. Byron closed the door and helped the Kid take the jacket off. "What's the trouble?"

"I won't be able to do it! In a few minutes, I was already trying to figure out how to score some smack."

"We need to talk, huh? Let me hang up the jacket. I think I can tell Kate it's okay, right?"

"It's real good and please thank her," Kid said. "Byron, why can't I just forget that? What the hell's wrong with me? It isn't like I'm having nightmares or going through withdrawal or anything!"

"How much time do you think you have spent thinking about your next fix since Vietnam?"

"Most of my time. Why?"

"That's probably got a lot to do with it. Your brain is in the habit of thinking about that. You need to realize that it'll take about a month to form a new habit."

Kid gave the minister an exasperated frown, "What the hell do I want with another habit?"

"One that counteracts this one. We need something to keep your brain occupied, so you don't think of getting a fix. How 'bout for now—when you catch yourself thinking about that, you remind yourself you don't need one because Zach will keep you from withdrawal. Make a conscience thought of that and then put a different thought on the spindle."

"Huh?"

"Think of something else. On purpose. Don't tell me you can't because anyone can! I know that for a fact. You just need to do it. The first week is the hardest."

"You mean just think of something else?"

"Yes. Take that record off the player and play a different tune. So, what's your liking? Jazz?"

"I don't think it is that easy."

"I never said it was easy. In fact, it is very difficult. Now, what do you want to think about? What has caught your interest?"

"Nothing."

Byron grimaced, "Okay, then sit here and think of nothing. Jackass."

"Well, I guess I can—ah, I don't know. I have no idea."

"Let's first pick out what you are going to wear. Nora washed your clothes so you should have clean socks. What have you got for shoes?"

"Boots. Cycle boots."

"Got them polished?"

"I don't know. I mean, I doubt I ever did."

"Think it's time?"

"Huh?"

Byron frowned, "You should get your hearing tested. Where are they?"

"I suppose in that closet."

Byron went over and rummaged around until he retrieved them. He set them on the chair and left the room, "Be right back."

Kid looked at his scruffy boots. They looked like hell and probably smelled as bad as his leathers. He hated himself. He really had allowed himself to go to the dogs.

Byron came back in with some oil and rags. "I got yelled at by Annie. She said you were supposed to be taking a nap. What an old hen, huh?"

"We don't want to make her mad though."

"No, guess that wouldn't be wise. I told her we'd just give your boots a once over and then I have to go to Merton anyway."

Byron moved things around until they got it set up to polish the boots. Then Byron gave him a rag and a boot. Before long, they were both polishing although Kid was having problems with his IV. "Maybe you should just leave it for me," Byron suggested.

"No. I should've done this sooner. Like years ago." Kid stated, "I really went to the dogs."

"I heard that you were with a canine unit in the military, huh? Bet that was interesting work. Did you like it?"

"Yes, I did." Kid stopped and stared at Byron a minute, "You know, what you said about changing your thinking and making a habit? It is something like we did when we trained dogs! I guess you were right."

"You mean you doubted me?" Byron acted offended.

"Yah, I did. Were you surprised?"

"Not in the least." Byron laughed.

The men finished the boots and Byron put their things away. Then he got Kid settled back to take his nap. After Byron left, Kid looked over at his shiny boots. It made him feel good that they looked so nice. Before long, he was asleep.

-19-

Annie knocked at the door and came in, "Kid, did you want to sleep more or get up?"

Kid turned, "Get up. I slept for a while, but not the whole time."

"As long as you give me your word that you won't overdo it, you can get up. Let me take down the IV. Then you'll be free from this contraption,"

He watched her, "Andy is very lucky to have a sweetheart like you."

Annie smiled, "I'm very lucky to have him, too. You know, I had about given up on life when my first husband was killed. I worked and all that, but I let myself get all wrapped up in misery and loneliness. Kid, there are a lot of ways to let yourself down. With some, it's booze. With others it's drugs, sex, or whatever. Some sit in their room and cry. It's all a waste."

"I think sex would be the most fun," Kid winked.

"I don't know. I've seen what some people do with that and it isn't any prettier than the rest. I truly believe we're all meant to get out of ourselves and do something for someone else. It is amazing how much better it makes a person feel."

"Are you trying to tell me something? Who do I know that needs help?"

"Right now? Nothing too critical, but Jeff is trying to learn how to dance and the little girls are still trying to convince the boys they should sing with their band."

"Which kids are that?"

"The little boys are in the still unnamed accordion band and the girls are Clarissa and Maddie Lynn Olson. She is Pastor Marvin's daughter. When I came in here, Diane was trying to stifle the girls' tears and give the boys a lecture. It wasn't working."

"Doesn't sound like a fun problem. I never heard the boys playing their accordions." Kid frowned, "Marvin Olson, from Merton? I think I knew him. His little sister died. Wasn't her name Maddie?"

"I believe so," Annie said. "Marv is the oldest of the Olson boys. He went to seminary and is the associate pastor here at Trinity."

"I'll be damned."

Annie giggled, "Let's hope not! Anyway, he married Glenda Owens, from here too."

"I remember her brothers." Kid got a blank look on his face, "Guess everyone has made something of themselves, but me."

Annie sat down on the stool and gave him a dirty look, "It sounds like you're spewing a lot of self-pity to me. If you don't like where you are; either change your perspective or what you're doing! We'll help you, but you have to decide because we won't be much help if you give up."

Kid listened, but never answered. Finally, he asked, "Think I should wear my jeans or these sweatpants?"

"Sweats would be fine in the house and Horse gave you some bedroom-slipper moccasins. He said he'll want one back!" she giggled.

"You guys are all nuts."

"I know, and you're so jealous. You want help with the slippers?"

"When can I go outside?"

"Depends when Elton gets home to take you on the grand tour," Annie answered. "He'll be here for lunch. Anxious, huh?"

"A little."

After he got his moccasins on, Kid stepped out into the hallway. He was surprised how weak he felt. He had only been lying around a week, but as Annie pointed out, he had been sick. They entered the living room to see Jeff dancing with Nora. Clarissa was sitting by a cute, little, blonde girl, watching them.

"Hi, what are you up to?" Kid asked the girls.

"This here is Maddie Lynn. She is my most goodest friend. We were fighting, Kid," Clarissa explained.

"With each other?"

"No, those stupid boys. They are so naughty."

"Really?" Kid said as he sat down. "What's the trouble?"

"It's about our singing. They went outside now, but we're still being mad-face about it." Then she pointed, "See, Missus is teaching Mr. Jeff to dance. I let them use my phonograft. Wanna see it?"

"Okay, but maybe after they are through using it."

Jeff looked over at Kid and shrugged. Kid gave him a 'thumbs up'.

"What's that thing you did?" Clarissa asked as she made a fist.

"It is a 'thumbs up'. It means like good work." Kid explained. "Here, let me show you how to do it."

The little girls watched him and then did it. They giggled at their newfound talent and ran off to the kitchen to 'thumbs up' everyone there.

In the kitchen, Kid sat at the table and watched Grandma kneading some dough. "What are you making?"

"Rolls for the dance tonight. Nora is going to grind up some roast beef, add a little pickle, onion, and mayo for filling. You can help if you want."

"I don't think I can knead with my broken wrist. I could mix up the filling if you tell me how."

"I'd be happy to." Grandma wiped her hands.

While Kid washed his hands, she went to the pantry and brought out the meat grinder. Within minutes, she had the cold roast beef, pickle, and onion on the table. "Here you go, Champ. Grind away!"

"Any amounts, or what?"

"We want all the roast beef, but the onion and pickle to taste."

"To whose taste?" Kid chuckled.

"Ours; the cooks get to decide!" Grandma laughed. "That is why I cook!"

The two heard a little voice say, "Me taste."

They both were surprised to see Kitten had quietly sat up at the table. Kid smiled, "My little helper is here!"

"Me help," the little girl said softly.

"Since she is the birthday girl, I think she should get to taste." Grandma smiled. "Okay?"

"Okay," Kitten said and leaned back to watch.

Kid started putting the meat through the electric grinder at Grandma's direction, removing the excess fat and gristle. Before long, he had ground two huge roasts. When he was finished, Grandma Katherine asked if he wanted a cup of coffee.

"I would," Kid nodded, "Can I have real coffee?"

"Nope, orders from headquarters! Half and half."

Kid noticed Kitten still sitting there quietly, just watching. "Can Kitten have some, too?"

She smiled shyly at him. Grandma thought, "If it is mostly milk. Maybe she would like a little sugar."

Kid sat down next to her, "I can help you do that, okay?"

The tiny girl nodded watching his every move. When they had their coffees before them, Kid asked her, "Is this fun?"

"Fun."

Kid smiled and patted her head. "What is the next thing we need to do with the filling?"

"Grind up some pickle and onion. Then grind it together again, so it's mixed thoroughly. We'll add the mayonnaise before we make the sandwiches when the buns are baked."

"Looks like we have a lot of work. Don't we, Kitten?"

"Work," she nodded.

"So, what do you think, two onions?" Kid asked, looking at the pile of roast beef.

"Probably three, they're small. You need to decide which pickles and how many. I prefer dill pickles, but some folks like sweet pickles. I'll leave it up to you."

Kid turned to Kitten, "What do you think?"

She shrugged.

"Guess we need to do some tasting, huh?"

"Taste."

Kid put some ground roast beef on a half piece of bread. Then he got a dill pickle and a sweet pickle. He gave Kitten a bite of one pickle with sandwich and asked, "Do you like it?"

She nodded. Then he offered her a bite of the other pickle and sandwich. After she ate it, he asked, "Which do you like best?"

She shrugged. He studied her and then took a bite of each himself. "I agree. They are both good. Shall we make some of both?"

She nodded. He asked Grandma, "Can we do that?"

"Sure can. I'll bring you two bowls. You grind them separately. That's a good idea."

Kitten broke into a big smile and continued to quietly watch. They worked while they finished their coffees and soon had both bowls full of beef filling. Grandma smiled, "You did a good job."

Kitten patted Kid's hand with a smile, "Good."

"You look tired. Maybe you should take a rest, Kid?" Grandma asked.

"No, although I'm a little tired. I haven't done anything for a long time."

A car parked in front of the farmhouse. Marly and Gopher came in. The two little girls ran off to play with their dolls. Marly handed Kid a bag containing the gift, before she sat down to a cup of coffee. "It's all wrapped, but you can sign the card."

"Thanks for doing that." Kid said as he peeked in the bag. "I better put it away before Kitten sees it. When are you going to give her the presents?"

"At lunch today, we'll have our family celebration. Tonight, we're eating at the dance. Marly, guess who made the beef filling for the sandwiches? Kid."

"Don't forget Kitten. She sure is quiet. How can she come up and sit at the table, without anyone even hearing her?"

"She does that all the time." Grandma pointed out, "She doesn't fidget and make noise like other kids do either. I always thought Gopher was quiet until I met Kitten."

Marly giggled, "Of the two, Gopher is a real jabberbox!"

Jeff and Nora came into the kitchen for a break. Jeff smiled, "I think I managed to break most of the bones in Nora's feet this morning!"

"You're actually doing very well. Girls, I think we have another dancer in our midst."

Marly beamed, "Good, Byron and Elton's heads are way too big. What about you, Kid? Are you a dancing machine?"

"Haven't danced in years. In fact, since I was in North Dakota the last time!"

"It's like riding a bicycle, you never forget. You'll be stomping and swinging in no time when you're feeling better. Those things all come back to you."

"Speaking of which," Kid shrugged, "I should practice my chess before Keith gets a hold of me."

"I'd be happy to play with you before lunch," Jeff offered. "I need to let my feet heal up before tonight."

"That'd be great," Kid said. "Where is Keith anyway?"

"Darlene went over to her Mom's place and Keith is up with the guys covering the well. They should be home soon. Andy and Horse are working in their shop and Ken and Rodney are manning the gas station."

Jeff asked, "Who all went to cover the well? I was given a reprieve since I had dancing lessons."

"Elton, Coot, Kevin, Keith, Harrington, Matt, Clarence, and Darrell," Nora answered. "Why?"

"I should have helped, too," Kid said.

Annie came into the kitchen with a dress she was hemming and heard him. "Nope. Zach said you can go outside for a little bit, but that's it. You can't get too rambunctious."

"Yah, I heard you," Kid grumped.

"No grumping either," Annie teased.

"Let's go play chess. It'd be safer," Jeff suggested.

Nora told Jeff where to find the chessboard, but he couldn't find it. They set up the checkerboard in the dining room. The men just got started when Kitten and Gopher climbed into the chairs next to them. The guys thought the girls would tire of it quickly and go back to playing with their dolls. They didn't. They sat and watched everything closely, without saying a word. Gopher was sitting beside Jeff and Kitten was sitting next to Kid.

About twenty minutes into the game, Jeff began to move his checker and Gopher gasped. The men both looked at her. The little girl, who was just about four, made a face of horror to him and shook her head no. He studied the board and then broke into a huge grin. "You're right! That would've been a big mistake. Thank you."

Gopher gave a look of relief, "Okay."

Over the next little while, the men realized the girls had figured out a lot of the game. Kid made a suggestion, "What do you say we 'confer' with our partners" Huh, Jeff?"

Jeff turned to Gopher, "Would you like to be my partner?"

She shrugged. Kid asked Kitten to help him play and she nodded.

The four had a lot of fun, although some of the plays were likely not in any playbook. When they put it away, the girls ran off to play. Jeff turned to Kid, "I think those two are both smarter than a whip!"

Kid agreed, "I wonder how well they could play on their own. When you have time, maybe we could set up the board and let them play, with our help. Although, I think they are probably better than us."

The ladies were just getting lunch ready, when the guys came back to the kitchen to help them. "We need to set the table. Byron should be here soon, and I saw the men drive in." Nora said, "Then it is birthday party time!"

Josh, Joallyn, and Jeannie joined them for lunch. Jeannie was Darrell's wife and Joallyn was her sister that Kid remembered. She introduced him to her boyfriend, Josh Perkins, who seemed friendly.

Byron arrived and they all sat at the table. Byron led them all in grace and everyone held hands until the Amen. Kid was shocked how he felt to be a part of a group like this. It was fun and relaxed, even though he was nervous about it.

The meal was made up of Kitten's favorite things; fried chicken, mashed potatoes with gravy, and corn. She sat between Elton and Suzy. When someone asked her what she had been doing on her birthday, she pointed to Kid.

"Did you watch Kid?" Matt asked.

"Work."

"What did you do?" Matt asked Kid, "Make the little girl work?"

"We made the sandwich filling and then Jeff and I played checkers with her and Gopher."

"Who won?" Matt grinned with a tease.

"Those little gals are really good! Don't kid yourselves!"

After the meal was finished, Annie and Darlene disappeared. They returned with the presents and birthday cake. Elton lit the candles and Gopher helped Kitten blow out the candles. Then Maddie Lynn and Clarissa led everyone in singing *Happy Birthday*. Then it was time to open the presents. When they got to Kid's gift, he asked if he could help her open it. Nora nodded and told Kitten to go to Kid. He pulled her up to his lap and gave her the gift. She smiled at him and he helped her open it. When she saw the pajamas, she gave him a big smile and hugged her pajamas. "Do you like them?"

She nodded and ran to Nora to show her. Nora winked at Kid, "She likes them a lot."

Kid was pleased, but getting very tired. After a bit, he excused himself to go lie down. He was sitting on his bed, when Annie came in. "Getting jumpy?"

"Yah, and my arm hurts. I can't believe I got so tired."

"This should knock you out."

"No!" Kid snapped, "I want to go outside with Elton."

"After you rest, Hot Shot. You sleep about an hour and then you can actually enjoy being outside. Otherwise, you'll be miserable."

"Crap."

"You're so sweet when you're tired," Annie teased.

"I'd say I'm sorry, but it would be a lie."

There was a knock at the door, as Annie was finishing up. Joallyn and Josh came in, "Can we talk to you for a bit? I know you want to rest," Joallyn said. "We're taking off, so we'll only be a minute."

Annie smiled, "He's all yours. Put on your grumpy boots, because it's deep in here."

Josh laughed, "We're used to it."

The two sat down and Joallyn started, "We wanted to let you know that we have a very good idea where you are with all this, Harold. I mean Kid. Josh and I have both been through treatment."

Kid couldn't conceal his shock. "You guys?"

"Yes, I went through the last time a few months ago. Must have been through it six times. I've done better this last time than ever before." The ethereally beautiful young woman smiled, "I went through treatment in Mandan and now attend AA with Josh."

Josh was a dark-haired, extremely good-looking man about Kid's age. Kid frowned at him, "I imagine you had problems with booze. Nothing big."

Josh grinned, "Heroin and cocaine were my downfalls. And pot, of course. Never really drank that much. How 'bout you?"

"Me? Heroin and pot. Never tried anything else but LSD. That made me crazy, so I never did it again."

"That was one of my favorites." Joallyn laughed softly, "And cocaine. Where I was in San Francisco, it was a regular pharmacy. I tried it all, and wrecked my liver. I was in the ER frequently with overdoses or bad mixes. Some of that stuff didn't work well with other stuff. I didn't drink much either, because I saved my money for the good stuff."

"You must have had a good job," Kid responded unemotionally.

"Nothing to be proud of," Joallyn admitted. "You wouldn't have acknowledged me, if you saw me then."

"Hell, I didn't see much in prison—or running with the Horde. What did you do to support your habit, Josh?"

Josh was forthright, "I stole from my family, who were quite wealthy. I burned through my inheritance in less than a year and then started cleaning out my parents. Nice, huh? Sometimes I look in the mirror and wonder how in the hell I thought it was all going to end?"

"In prison or dead," Kid responded pragmatically.

Joallyn said, "I went for dead. The last go 'round, I overdosed in Darrell's chicken coop during a blizzard. Matt, Zach, and Darrell hauled me to the hospital. Zach put me in touch with his psychiatrist, who got me into treatment. I was certain it wouldn't work. So far, it has." She took Josh's hand, "And we work on it together."

Josh squeezed her hand and then turned to Kid, "We don't want to interfere with your nap, but if you ever need to talk, call either of us. We'd be more than happy to lend an ear. Being alone when I moved up here was almost my undoing. I couldn't take it. I was lucky my cousin gave me a place to stay and helped me get a job, but he works out of town. If I hadn't met up with these folks, I would've been a goner."

"What do you do for a job?" Kid was becoming interested.

"I was fired from my job in Dad's firm for embezzlement. I'd have gone to prison if he didn't give me this last chance. I teach shop at St. Johns. Getting clean is miserable, but compared to all the time that was wasted before, it doesn't take long to get on the other side. Then it's easier. Joallyn and I are pretty much home or at our AA meetings, so we are usually available.

"I won't go to meetings. That would be the first place the bikers would look. I have a mark on my back. If they find me, I'm fodder. I won't go to a treatment place or AA."

"That's okay. We can come to you, Joallyn or I. Okay? You think about it. Even if you don't like us, maybe we could help you."

"Why wouldn't I like you?"

Joallyn was serious, "We might not be your type."

"Yah, like I have some real high standards!" Kid pointed out, sarcastically.

Josh nodded, "We all do and we used to hang out at the nicest places. My favorite was a dead-end alley in Indianapolis. High class, I tell you."

"I may have been there!" Kid chuckled. "Thanks. I may take you up on it, but mind you, I'm a tough case."

"Duh," Joallyn taunted, "I know I can out-tough you."

"The question is can any of us do it straight?" Josh stood and shook Kid's hand. "Gotta go. Talk to you later."

"Yah, we'll do that. Thanks."

-20-

It felt good to sleep without the restraint of the IV. The sound of thunder awakened him. It was partly cloudy when he went to take his nap, but he hadn't expected thunder. He heard his door close and figured it was Claudia leaving to go get someone like she always did.

A knock proved him correct. Elton poked his head in and said, "Are you decent?"

Kid chuckled, "Haven't been for years!"

"Then I must be at the right place." Elton chuckled, "Ready for a tour around the yard? We better get moving before it rains."

"The thunder woke me up and I heard Kitten go out. I suppose she told you."

"Yes, but she is also terrified of thunder. I think probably because she couldn't hear it before. You'll want to put jeans on before we go outside."

A little later, they were heading down the ramp on the north side of the mudroom. Kid commented, "You guys take your patient care seriously, huh?"

"We've had so many folks in and out of here over the years that were in a wheelchair, that we just think that way now. The boys put in this ramp last summer before Carl came to stay. The interior doors had all been widened when Pepper was a kid."

"Oh, I remember that. She got tangled up with a hog, right?"

"Yes. Good memory."

"I forgot all that stuff; but since I've been here, it's coming back. Joallyn and Josh stopped to visit with me after lunch."

Elton nodded, "Josh said they were going to. I don't know about you, but I think you might want to take them up on their offer of friendship."

"I was thinking that." Kid looked back at the house, "You built on, huh?"

"Actually, the kids did. They decided they didn't want to carry folding tables and chairs up from the basement every weekend, so they built us the dining room, expanded the upstairs, and added a bathroom every ten feet!"

"I'm sure glad they added mine. I really gave it a work out."

"Yah, you're getting the bill for toilet paper!" Elton poked. "Across the road to the north is Kincaid's place. That lunatic is plowing up that whole area between the ditch and the house! He is planting some 'secret' seeds there. You and Jeff seem chummy. Maybe you could find out what it is for me? Could you be my spy?"

Kid grinned, "It might not be wise to get in the middle of that!"

"Yah, I suppose," Elton agreed. "On the other hand, you do live in my house. I think that implies some loyalty, right?"

"Jeff lives in Carl's house. So, which one of us is going to get thrown out?"

"Okay. If you happen to like—be over there and see a bag of seeds, it'd be okay for you to mention it to me. You think?"

"Okay. I'll do that," Kid laughed. "Who lives over there to the east?"

"That's Suzy and Zach's place. When you're up to snuff, we can go over and check out the airplane shop."

"I heard about that. It sounds like fun. Who lives to the west?"

"The first place is Kevin and Carrie's house and the next is Marty and Greta's place. Beyond that, Byron's house and the church."

"All in a neat little row, huh?"

"Pretty much. We get lost easily. Now, to the south of our house is the garage. The back of it is the boys' small engine shop. Wanna see it? You can visit your Harley."

An odd look came over Kid's face and he answered, "I'd like that."

Elton opened the north door and they went into the shop at the end of the enormous Quonset building. It had a couple windows and lots of shelves. There were two large worktables with lamps overhead and a radio was playing. The veterans were each working on something. They both jumped when Elton said, "Hi. Whatcha up to?"

"Scared us half to death!" Andy laughed, "We need a door bell or something!"

"Been saying that for years!" Elton laughed. "Don't see a thing stopping you dudes from putting one in!"

"Point taken," Andy grinned. "Hi, Kid. Grab a soda out of the fridge and have a seat."

"Thanks, Zach said no soda yet," Kid said, as he looked the place over. "This is really a neat set up. You have everything here! There isn't much you couldn't fix here."

"Heal up and grab a screwdriver!" Horse laughed. "Every time Elton or Kevin drive in here, they have another pile of broken appliances. I doubt there's a working one in the county!"

"I'd love to as soon as I get my wrist working." Kid walked over and watched them a bit. "It actually looks like fun."

Andy laughed, "We want to get this pile done so we can go to the dance tonight without being mobbed by angry housewives!"

Elton cracked up, "Before or after you dance with them?"

"Hey, don't say that! I'm going to try to dance with Kate tonight. I have that 'learner' foot to wear," Jackson said.

"What is a learner foot?" Kid asked.

"It isn't really called that, but it is just a plain prosthesis. It doesn't have a shoe thingie on the bottom. Just a grip dealie to stand on."

"I almost understood that!" Kid scrunched up his face, "I'll take your word for that. Hey, thanks for lending me those moccasins. I wore them in the house today. Very comfortable."

"No problem. I see Kate got that jacket for you."

"It's really nice and warm."

"Well, Kid wants to visit his bike, so I thought I'd take him to see it," Elton grinned as he opened the door to the huge garage.

Kid's mouth fell open when he gazed over the cars. "How many vehicles do you have in here?"

"Never counted them. A few. Here is Lloyd's old green Ford. It always has to be parked in front of something else, in case he ever gets out of the house. It is a '46 four-door."

"It's beautiful. Good paint job. Did someone tell me that Matt gives him a ride every day?"

"Usually, unless the weather is nasty. Lloyd loves it."

"I like this old Chevy pickup." Kid chuckled. "What year is it?"

"A '54. It is Clarence's favorite, too. I bought this brand new and was proud as a peacock. I have to admit, I'm partial to it myself. I was so mad at myself when I dinged the back over here. Big ole dent."

Kid looked it over and said, "It could be fixed easy enough. I could do it for you . . . that is as soon as my arm works. A little paint and you'd be all set."

"Anyway, your bike is over here." Elton motioned to a canvas in the front of the garage.

Kid nodded and removed the canvas. "You guys took good care of it. I should take everything out of the saddle bag."

"The Sheriff did already." Elton said seriously, "He found your little pouch of pot, if that is what you wondered about."

Kid flushed with shame and Elton put his arm on his shoulder, "I'd have checked out my booze supply, too. Bernard didn't want some kid getting it. He has it, if you want to claim it."

"Yah, that would be a terrific idea!" Kid shook his head and covered the bike again.

Elton helped him and noticed Kid's embarrassment. Elton pulled out a stool and pointed to it. "Take a load off. Look, I know it's going to eat at you like crazy. We all know that."

"I wish I could control it."

"Yah, that'd be wonderful, but no one can. That's the nature of it. It'd be like trying to control how tall you grew! It isn't something we can do. You need to get that into your head in a major way. Hear?" Elton was resolute.

"Easier said than done."

"True, but a lot of things are like that. What did Zach suggest?"

"Oh, he said talking out the crap from Vietnam and such. I doubt that would help."

"It helped both Andy and Jackson. Granted, they still have times, but nothing like before. When I quit drinking, I realized three things: One—I can't get too cocky and start thinking I can handle it. Truth is I can't. Period. Two—I stayed away from the things that triggered my binges until I got a lot stronger. And three—I'm extremely vulnerable when everything goes to hell. I know I need to talk to somebody. Otherwise, my bottle will be my confidant. Believe me; Old Jim Beam doesn't give very good advice."

Kid chuckled, "I get so sick, though."

"That's withdrawal, right? After that, you don't get physically sick."

"But it's an overpowering craving."

"It isn't any fun, but every time you feed the craving, you'll be facing another withdrawal. And let's face it; you'll never feel as good as you did the first time you took a hit."

"Yah, I've been chasing that dragon for years." Kid shrugged dejectedly. "Now I'm glad if I can just get over the feeling sick."

"Then why do it? Once you're through that mess, and know you aren't going to catch the dragon, why bother?"

Kid studied him, "It's scary; but you're making sense."

"I know, sometimes I even scare myself." Elton grinned, "Ready to walk some more?"

They went down south of the garage to a smaller, wooden building. They heard a hammer pounding inside and Elton looked in, "I hope you know what you're doing?"

"That's anyone's guess," Kevin answered. "My little buddies managed to disappear on me. The rabbits will be here in a few days. I want to get this shed ready before they arrive. Oh hi, Kid. I didn't see you there."

"Your Dad is taking me for a tour."

"I imagine it's good to get outside again. I hate being cooped up." Kevin smiled. "There's a hammer there if either of you are interested."

"I'd love to help," Kid said. "Your Dad said that he mentioned to you I'd like to help with the rabbits."

"Yes, he did. Sounds good to me." Kevin chuckled. "Those two lunkheads on my team are something else . . . a little wobbly as Grandpa would say!"

"I heard they're fighting with the little girls about them singing in a band or something!"

Elton rolled his eyes, "Yea gads, I was about ready to strangle the lot of them. I'll be glad when tonight is over! Wanna hear the latest? CJ and Charlie think they need drums!"

"Don't they have a drummer in their band?" Kevin asked. "I thought Clark was doing that so his dad would ask him to play for the choir in church! Between you and me, I don't think that Pastor Marv has that very high on his list!"

"Well, your little partners thought drums sounded like a fine idea," Elton groaned.

Kid looked the building over, "You know, Kevin, you might want to put something around the bottom of the walls, so the rabbits don't chew through."

"Yah, I was going to do that," Kevin pointed to a roll of wire mesh. "I just need to staple it on when I'm done with the insulation on the roof."

"How you feeling now?" Elton asked Kid.

"Good, why?"

"Could you hold it up for me with one hand and I can pound the staples in. What do you say? Want to try?"

Kid grinned, "Yah. I'd really like that."

Elton did most of the work, but Kid did the best he could. By the time the mesh was around the walls, Kid and Kevin had talked out their partnership. It sounded good to both of them. They all three had a good time and finished the building. Kevin went out to bring the cows up for milking while Elton walked Kid back to the house.

Kid walked back in silence until they were almost at the house, "I really enjoyed that. Thanks, Elton."

"I figured you might. It's good to do something once in a while."

"We have to find time to talk about the deal on the pasture and stuff," Kid said. "I need to pay Kevin for my share with the rabbits."

"We can do it tomorrow or the next day, okay? There is too much commotion this weekend. Okay?"

"Yes, we need to have some time to talk."

When they got to the mudroom, Elton pointed to a hook and told Kid that would be his. Kid smelled the baking of fresh bread permeating from the kitchen. He was suddenly overwhelmed with memories of his childhood home. He smiled broadly.

When they went inside, Grandma poured them coffee. Kid hadn't felt so good in a long time. Nora was helping Annie with her hair. She was going to wear it up for the dance.

"Clarissa, we can fix your hair up if you like," Nora said.

Clarissa covered her mouth while she giggled, "I would like that the most."

Kid grinned and asked, "What are you going to sing?"

165

"*Sunshine, Lollipops and Rainbows*. If you want, I can play it on my phonograft and sing it for you. It won't be the same as tonight because Maddie Lynn had to go home."

"Okay," Kid said, "Is the record player in the living room?"

"Yes, but it is a phonograft."

Elton and Kid went in the living room and the little girl belted out the song along with the record. When she was finished, she curtsied and then ran to Elton, "Mister? Do you think everybody will go 'oooooh'?"

Elton gave her a hug, "I'm sure of it. You did a great job."

Then she bounced over to Kid, "What do you think? Is it the most goodest?"

He smiled and assured her it was.

Before they were finished with their coffee, Kid was starting to ache. He decided he should go relax in the living room. Annie worried he had overdone it, but he denied it. "I wanted to. It felt good."

"You should take a nap."

"I really want to stay up for a while."

He went into the living room and sat in the empty rocking chair next to Grandpa. Lloyd looked at him and nodded, "Heard that the boys pulled out a victory on Iwo Jima?"

"Yes, I heard that."

Then Lloyd explained the Pacific theatre of WWII to him, complete with Pershing and the Otto von Bismarck! They rocked, relaxed, and before long, were both sleeping in their chairs.

-21-

It was raining when Kid woke up to the sound of a baby crying. It was little Nathan. He and Clancy were engaged in a battle over a toy. Kid was reminded of some of the fights in prison. It isn't fun to be mad at someone while caged in the same playpen!

He went out to the kitchen and poured himself a cup of coffee. "How long has it been raining?"

Grandma Katherine smiled, "About an hour."

"Have I been sleeping that long?"

"Yes, but you were tired. I have some beef barley soup ready for your dinner. Hungry?"

"Isn't everyone else going to eat?"

"Lloyd ate when he woke up. Suzy and Zach will eat before they come over."

Kid nodded, "Is everyone else milking?"

"Chores are done. They're getting cleaned up now. After you eat, I'll go wave my magic wand over myself and emerge a princess!" the tiny octogenarian laughed.

"You are pretty already," Kid winked.

"I love you," Grandma smiled as she set his soup down. "Would you like one of your sandwiches?"

Kid's eyes opened widely, "Oh no! I was going to help put in the filling!"

"You needed your sleep." She patted his shoulder, "There'll be plenty of time to help. Want a sandwich?"

Kid squinted, "Probably not. My gut isn't happy with me right now. The soup sounds good though."

About then, Matt knocked at the door and came in, "Hi! How is my favorite Grandma?"

Katherine put her hands on her hips, "Alright, what do you want?"

"I'm hurt!" He gave her a hug, "Diane said you baked cookies. I could taste one for you."

"Thoughtful," Grandma laughed. "Here you go. I'm off to get beautiful now."

Matt sat down across from Kid, "How's it going?"

"I went outside today! That felt so good. Hey, where do you live?"

"I live on Darrell Jessup's place in his cabin. He offered me a home when I came out here. He's a great guy."

Kid grinned, "He was just a little kid when I knew him. Possessed by goats!"

"Still is, but he has turned it into a profession."

"A dairy, right?"

"Right, sells the milk to Elton's brother for the Cheese Factory." Matt watched him eat. "Kid?"

"What?"

"Tomorrow after the last service, the Grey Hawk kids, Jackson, and Kevin's baby, Holly, are all getting baptized at Trinity. Diane and I go to St. Johns, but we're going to be Clarissa's sponsors, so we are going to be there. We'd be happy to stop by to take you to the baptism? What do you think? I know everyone would be pleased."

Kid was searching for an excuse, but Matt continued, "It'll be a surprise for Elton's birthday. So, please don't let it slip in front of him. Okay?"

"I won't tell him." Kid promised quietly and then added, "I don't know, Matt. I don't think I feel comfortable going to church, after all I've done?"

"Yah, guess you're right. When God said anyone can be forgiven for anything—over all the world and throughout time, He added 'except Harold'. You're really a numbskull."

Kid gave him a dirty look, "You don't understand."

"I do. Are you aware that is the most common excuse people give, except maybe that they don't believe in Him?"

Kid snapped, "No, I never did a survey, but I'm not sure I believe in Him!"

"Then why would it matter if you went to church for a baptism? Afraid it will rub off?"

"You're such a jackass."

"I know." Matt smiled and continued, "Want us to pick you up?"

"Oh, for crying out loud! Okay! Anything to shut you up!"

Matt smirked, "Works every time."

"And folks wonder why you aren't a priest anymore? Unbelievable." Kid snarled.

Annie came into the kitchen with Kitten, who was all dressed but had been crying. Annie squinted at Kid. "You're on my list in a big way!"

"What did I do?" he asked innocently.

Matt asked, "Does little Kitten have tears? It's her birthday! Annie, you shouldn't make her cry!"

"He did it," Annie pointed at Kid. "Him and his pajamas! She was bound and determined to wear them to the dance tonight!"

"You're the one that told me that's what she liked! Was I supposed to get something she didn't like? I never told her to wear them to the dance. Come here, Little One. Come sit by me." Kid patted the empty chair beside him. She sniffed and climbed up into the chair. He put his good arm around her, "You look very pretty tonight. I love that dress."

She patted the dress, while listening to him.

"You can wear that to the dance, and then tonight, wear the pajamas for sleeping. Okay?"

She pouted a little, but nodded, "Okay."

He patted her shoulder, "Are you going to eat our buns tonight?"

She nodded and then asked, "Kid dance?"

"No, I can't tonight. My arm isn't well enough yet. You go and have a good time for both of us. Can you do that for me?"

"Okay. Matt dance?"

Matt answered, "Yes, I'm going to the dance tonight. Can I dance with you?"

She shrugged and Kid smiled, "That would be fun, huh? Do you think he knows how?"

She studied Matt and asked, "Know how?"

"Yes, I do. You can tell Kid I'm a good dancer."

Kitten relayed to Kid, "Matt know."

Horse came into the kitchen dressed in his suit and without his crutches. He was walking gingerly on his 'learner foot'. "I think I'm taking my crutches along tonight. I don't know how this is going to work."

"Good idea," Matt agreed. "You look very dapper!"

"What do you think, Kitten?"

169

"Dapper," she agreed.

"You look pretty, too," Jackson agreed.

Her face fell, "No jammies."

Kid explained, "She is going to wear them tonight when she sleeps."

"That's good." Jackson assured her. "None of us can wear our pajamas to a dance."

Matt asked, "You riding up to the loft in the farmhand?"

"Yah, with Andy and Vicaro. However, they aren't likely to be falling over while they're dancing!"

"I doubt that you will either, Jackson! Kate won't let you. Now if you were dancing with me. that'd be the likely end!"

"What is with you tonight?" Kid asked in wonder.

Matt answered, "I'm no different than I ever am. Am I, Jackson?"

"Sad to say, he's usually like this," Jackson grinned.

"I hope Diane hurries, because I may be fed up with you both before she's ready," Matt frowned.

She, Annie, and Clarissa came in the kitchen then and Kid's mouth fell open. "Wow! You girls are gorgeous!"

Diane smiled, "Thank you. We think so."

Kid shook his head, "Now I know why you and Matt go together."

Darlene came in the kitchen carrying Nathan, while Nora put Clancy in a high chair. Darlene giggled, "I can't say I feel bad about leaving these two here tonight! It will be good training for Zach and Suzy."

"Oh, my," Nora handed the toddlers each a cookie, "Just think, we'll have two more babies soon! They'll outnumber us!"

The men filtered into the kitchen and helped the ladies with their coats. Matt, Diane, and Jackson left to pick up Kate. Elton went down to get the station wagon, and while he was gone, Kid told Nora that he was invited to the baptism. "That is, if you want me there."

"Of course, we do. You're family and we'd love it. Grandma and I will get something lined up for you to wear," Nora replied.

Darlene suggested the suit Keith had lent to Jackson before he got his own. Nora thought, "That would work. I know Jackson kept it in his closet after he bought his new one. I'll talk to him about it tomorrow morning and we can make whatever adjustments necessary. You might be a bit taller."

"Oh, just wear white farmer socks with it!" Keith laughed. "No one will notice if you have high-water pants!"

Nora frowned, "You guys. So, where did CJ and Clarence get off to? They were right behind us when we came downstairs."

Andy laughed, "You don't want to know, Mom."

Nora turned swiftly, "Why not? Now I'm worried. Where are they?"

"In the bathroom, having a contest about who can pee longer!" Andy was convulsing in laughter.

"Andrew Evan Grainger Schroeder! Why didn't you stop them?" Nora yelped. "I'm going to skin you!"

Elton came in then and asked what was going on. Andy told him between gales of laughter. Elton chuckled, "Nora, let me handle this. You don't want to get flustered."

It was only a couple of minutes before the boys came in the kitchen, nonchalantly. Nora was glaring at Andy, but decided to give up. It was obviously was a gender issue.

Zach and Suzy arrived as those that were going to the dance said their goodbyes. Lloyd was back in his chair in the living room while the little toddlers finished their cookies. Kid put his dishes in the sink when Kev and Carrie came in with baby Holly.

"Kid," Kev said, "I'd like you to meet our little girl, Holly."

"Hello, Carrie." Then Kid tickled the baby's cheek, "Oh, Holly is a tiny one. How old is she?"

Carrie answered, "She was born in December, about four months."

"She's a little doll."

"She cries all night, Kid," Kevin announced. "I had no idea a kid could cry non-stop like that!"

A few minutes later, Danny and Jenny Schroeder brought Baby Matthew. Kid shook his head, "Now I know what Nora meant when she said we'd soon be outnumbered!"

Danny chuckled, "Yah, I imagine they felt that way about our generation, when we showed up! Look how great we turned out!"

Kid's face darkened and he got serious, "Speak for yourself."

Dan ignored the comment, "I'm Marty's big brother. I live across the road from Harrington. Jen said you were a classmate of hers."

"You were!" Jen said as she came back into the kitchen. "Remember me? Jenny Jessup?"

Kid smiled, "I do! I remember we were both frogs in that dumb play about ponds."

Jen sat at the table and put her chin on her hands. She furrowed her brow and asked, "Just how did that happen, anyway? I'm still miffed about it. All the other kids got to be something fun."

"What's not fun about frogs?" Danny asked.

"You had to be there. We sat next to the pond and went 'ribbit, ribbit' at the end of every scene. Everybody else had real words to say!" Jenny pouted. "I think some even had songs."

Kid laughed, "Yah, but I was glad I didn't have to sing about being a tree and having a bird sleep in my branches!"

Danny chuckled, "Depends on the bird, I'd say."

Jenny rolled her eyes, "Never mind. Kid and I'll visit about this when you're someplace else."

"Did you go to school in Merton?" Kid asked Danny.

"No, I went to school in Lindel and Bismarck. My parents didn't send me to a school where they taught me to say 'ribbit'." Danny smirked, "We read Shakespeare."

"Yea gads," Jenny groaned. "When have you ever read Shakespeare?"

"There was once," Danny grinned. "I think."

Kid laughed, "Have fun you guys."

Zach came in the kitchen, "Yah, dance holes in your shoes!"

After the party-goers left, he asked Kid if he wanted some coffee. "Can I have real coffee, or tinted milk?"

"Coffee with a lot of milk," Zach raised his eyebrow. "You have to give your gizzard a chance to heal up. You're doing very well. I'm happy with your progress."

"It felt so good to get outside today."

Kid became solemn as he studied his cup.

"What is it?"

"Zach, did Elton tell you what I did?"

"Went to the shop and then helped Kevin?"

"Yah, but did he tell you about what I did at my bike?"

"Never mentioned your bike at all. I assumed you saw it at the shop." Zach studied Kid. "Were you upset about something? Was it in good condition?"

"It was perfect. They took good care of it. That's not it. When I saw it, the first thing that went through my head was to get into my saddlebag. I used to keep my dope in there. I wasn't very subtle about it. Elton watched and then told me that Bernard had my pot. I knew the smack was gone. Zach, it just came over me as soon as I saw that saddlebag! I couldn't believe it. I didn't need a fix! Why the hell did I react like that?" Then his eyes reddened with tears, "I'll never get past this, will I?"

"Yah, you will, if you hang in there. I imagine that when you saw the saddlebag, it was more like a reflex to you. You might want to get one that looks different. Then it won't trigger the reflex response."

"Seems pretty simplistic. I think addiction is deeper than that."

"It is, but changing those kinds of things can help a lot. Dieters lose more weight, if they eat in a different place than usual. All of these things develop into the pattern of the habit. If you can change the pattern, it helps to break the habit. Did you talk to anyone this week about your nightmares?"

"No, I haven't had any. I didn't want to bring them up and get myself all bent out of shape again."

"You need to do that. The way I figure it, you have another week on these meds. After that, we'll be creating more problems if you stay on them. If you talk about them now, you will still be able to sleep." Zach looked directly in his eyes, "You understand you need to put those ghosts to rest; if not all the way, at least enough so they don't drive you crazy."

"I did tell Byron that I want to get clean and be respectable again. I don't think it will work, but I'll try at least. I know I can't keep on like this. Realistically though, I also don't know if it is worth the effort with Scab's retaliation hanging over my head. It'd make more sense to just let him settle my problems for me."

"If that isn't the stupidest thing I've ever heard!" Zach frowned. "You're much more likely to get in trouble if you're using than if you're clean. That's only an excuse and not even a very good one. Unless you can tell yourself and me that you really enjoy being addicted because it is improving your life, than just accept that you don't."

"Oh."

Kid visited with Grandpa until the elderly man went to bed and the patient played chess with Zach. He went to bed early, since he'd been swindled into going to church the next day. Even though he was tired, he couldn't go to sleep. He felt almost panicky. Kid debated about calling Zach, but didn't want to bother him with it.

Later, Zach stopped by to check on him, "Need anything? All the rugrats are asleep, so I was going to wander off to my nest."

"You going home?"

"Oh, no. Suzy and I are staying here tonight." Zach answered, "Don't worry."

"I'm not worried," Kid said with bravado. His comment fell like a pat of butter on a hot floor, "That was so stupid. I'm scared to death, about everything, Zach! Everything! Today, I realized how much I wanted to be like everyone else and how slim my chances are. I can't even list the things that terrify me."

"I've been there in my life. It's horrible." Zach sat on the stool, "For me, I did the best when Elton and Byron helped me. They said break your issues into smaller pieces and solve those one at a time. The most critical things you have to do first, of course. By the time you get halfway through the list, most of the rest of the issues have taken care of themselves."

"I don't know which smaller pieces there are. I have no idea where to start."

Zach grinned, "You've already done some. You got your gut almost healed up and the bad well covered. You got your arm set. You've been getting some rest and your appetite is improving. You have made a general decision to stay and face your demons. Those are no small things and you've done it all in about a week. You've also started to set up a support system. That'll be very important to you."

"Never thought about that. But we both know my support system will evaporate as soon as I'm up and around."

"Why do you say that? I think it will improve."

"Once people get to know how I really am, they won't want to be around me. They won't stick in it for the long haul."

"Are you sure? You don't know this crew very well. We pretty much hang in as needed. If you're in, you aren't out unless you want to be; even if we want to clobber you!"

"Have you any idea how stupid that sounds?"

Zach nodded, "I do, but I've lived it. I know it for a fact. I was going to leave, move away, and change my name so many times; but they wouldn't let me go. My father was insane. He beat my mother and while she was dying, made us kids pray for her to live. When she didn't live, he decided that it was because one of us kids didn't have enough faith in God. A week later, he began 'testing' us, starting with my big brother. He made us all sit around him, recite Bible verses, and watch while he made Ezra put his hand in a gunnysack containing a rattlesnake. He told him if he had enough faith, he would live. Ezra died in front of us."

"Good grief."

"I didn't dream about it; I just didn't sleep. I threw up at the drop of a hat, hated God, and was close to losing my mind." Zach said quietly. "When the investigation started into Father's death, it got even worse. He had not only damaged our family, but many others. He left a path of destruction every place he went. The FBI moved my sister, Ruthie, from the East Coast to here for her protection. My other sister was in league with the thugs. Come to find out, she had murdered her own little boy in his crib and left Miriam in the same crib with his body for a couple days. No food and a bottle of souring milk. I was terrified it would spill over onto Suzy and these folks. I think I've an idea how you might feel, but I'd like you to realize that you can get over it. You aren't the only one who was shoveled bullshit; but sunlight will dry it and when it's dry, you can use it as fuel for a good life. I'll do anything I can to help you put this behind you. However, you can't cop out because you think you had more to face than anyone else."

"I didn't know. You don't act like you had troubles."

"Why would I want to act like that? Moaning around doesn't solve much. The whole point is to find happiness where you can. Smiling is a good medicine. Also, it's more fun for everyone else."

"I didn't expect that. You really gave me hell."

Zach broke into a big grin, "Not really. You're the one that gives you hell."

-22-

Kid slept pretty well all night, only waking when he heard Andy scream with a nightmare. He listened while Annie calmed him. Kid realized how much he missed by not having someone close to him. He had always thought it was glamorous and somehow self-sacrificing to be a loner. Now, he realized it was another of his big mistakes. He grunted, "Little I can do about it now."

He fell back to sleep and woke when the family alarm went off. Kid thought that Kitten had not come in that night, but when the alarm went off, he felt the cat jump off his bed and heard his bedroom door close. He smiled to himself. His tiny sentry had been there watching over him.

He was trying to figure out how to get out of bed when Zach came in. "Morning, I came to unhook your leash for the day. I think that we can try to dispense with it, unless you have a lot of agitation. What do you say?"

"Forever?"

"Probably not that long," Zach grinned. "I'll be home evenings and nights this week, so I can monitor it better. Annie and Marty go to work this afternoon."

"Will I still be able to sleep?"

"That's what we need to find out. You game?"

"You mean detox? I don't want to scare the kids." Kid frowned, "Sheriff Bernard said I could do my detox at his place. You told me it wouldn't be as bad as usual, huh?"

"Shouldn't be. I'm not talking detox now, just more weaning back. Your use was down during the prison years and since you were released. Besides, you've gone through a lot of it already. If you want to go to Bernard's place; that is okay, but you can come to our place. If you would prefer, we can set it up at the treatment center in Mandan or find another one. There is a good one in Canada and you could do the whole 60 day treatment there."

"I won't go to Mandan. I personally checked into a treatment place to find someone once. I have gone to about a hundred AA meetings trying to locate people. I know that's the first place Scab would look for me. Canada? What do you propose I pay for it with?"

"I will—."

"No, you won't. You're not going to pay for it out of any fund. I made this mess! Let me unmake it. Please, I think I need to," Kid said with conviction.

"Alright, I'll respect that. We'll try it your way. However, if it doesn't work, can we agree to do it mine?"

They shook hands. Zach took out his IV, "Can you get ready on your own or do you need help?"

"I'd like to try it on my own. If I'm not out in a few minutes, someone should probably come unwrap me!" Kid chuckled as he made his way to the bathroom.

Zach stayed and got out Kid's clothes, made his bed, and straightened up Kitten's chair. When Kid returned he was surprised to find him there yet. "You didn't have to wait."

"I know, just thought I'd hang around. I have to give you the meds anyway."

"I thought I wasn't going to have them."

"You still have to take some stuff for your gut and arm." Zach grinned, "You coming to the barn with us this morning?"

"I'd like to," Kid said. "Can I? I won't be much help."

"We might need another supervisor," Zach teased.

When they got to the kitchen, the milkers were about to go outside; armed with their cups and trusty thermoses. Grandma's face fell when she saw Kid was ready to go outside. "I thought you were going to help us cook!"

"I can if that is what you want!" Kid replied.

"Not this morning, I have help. Otherwise, I'd be tying your apron strings to the stove!"

"Okay," Kid nodded, quite pleased that Grandma wanted his help. "I'd be glad to help whenever."

Elton put his arm over Kid's shoulder, "I'd love to show you how we do chores, in case you ever need to help. It's my birthday, so I can get my way."

Keith rolled his eyes, "You always get your way."

"I know," Elton nodded. "Ain't I the lucky duck?"

Kevin made a face, "I can hardly stand it some days."

Kid was amazed at how little time it took the large crew to milk, separate, feed and clean the barn. In little over an hour, all the chores were done; poultry, horses, hogs, and cattle. The best part was in the middle of it; they stopped to have a break. They brought their milk stools to sit in a group and then they filled their cups from whichever thermos they wanted; hot cocoa or coffee. They took a break for a few minutes and visited.

This morning the talk was about the dance. Elton was beaming, "Did you see how well Jackson did dancing with Katie? He was so worried, but he did a good job."

Diane nodded, "And Jeff! Did you see him and Father Landers doing the Schottische with Sister Abigail? What a riot! Jeff wants to get good at dancing because he already has a date to our wedding. Matt thought he was getting the cart before the horse, since we haven't set a date yet."

"What's your hold-up, anyway?" Keith asked.

"We want to wait for Matt's niece Rain to be here. She is going to be a bridesmaid. Her school gets out in mid-May. Then you're going to Pine Ridge for Memorial Day. A little after that, Elton and Nora are going to the Caymans. When can we get married? You've filled up the summer!" Diane pointed out.

"How about before we go to Pine Ridge? What day is school out here?" Elton asked.

"Since we didn't use many storm days this winter, we'll get out on the 21st."

"I think you should get married May 22nd," Elton replied.

Keith and Kevin agreed.

"It's easy for you men to say. All you have to do is show up!" Diane laughed.

"If you set the date now, you can get to work on it right away," Kevin poked. "You have to hustle, Woman."

Diane frowned, "You know, it would be a pretty good time. Randy and Bea aren't coming to the wedding anyway. He won't be out of the service yet. We already talked about that."

Annie asked, "Have you decided on where you want to go for your honeymoon?"

"Nowhere," Diane giggled. "After our last trip, we'd have to pick out a city with a nice hospital to visit. We'll likely just stay home."

"Good, then you can still help milk," Elton laughed. "Kid, while these guys clean the barn, want to go see the horses? You can help me feed them."

"Sounds good. I don't think I'd be much help cleaning the barn anyway."

"I'm keeping track," Kev laughed. "When the cast is off, the list will come out. You'll be on barn cleaning duty for a couple months straight!"

"Okay," Kid laughed. "But then what would you do?"

The men walked over to the open shed where the horses were waiting to be fed. Kid was amazed, "I didn't realize you had so many! No wonder you need pasture."

"We have ten and will be getting more. The Grey Hawks want horses, so I relented."

"Whose horse is this?" Kid put his hand on the nose of a dark, part-Arabian. "He is beautiful."

"That's Tornado. He is Jackson's horse. He is from the same bloodline as the half-Arabs owned by Matt and Darrell. Diane's brother has one, Lightning."

A smile played across Kid's face, "Is her brother named Randy?"

"Yah, why?"

"Matt said that I could exercise his horse. So, Lightning is a brother to this one. Wow! I'd love that. I wonder how soon I can ride?"

"Better ask Zach," Elton chuckled. "I caught hell from him when he caught me trying to saw the cast off my wrist."

"You what?" Kid's head spun with surprise.

"Don't you start in! Yea gads, this whole outfit went into a tailspin," Elton grumped.

"Gee! Wonder why!"

"Don't look now, but you aren't exactly a brick in the foundation, yourself!"

"Not by a long shot!" Kid laughed, "So what kind of horses are you going to get the kids?"

"Jerald, one of our clanners, is a cattle buyer. He buys all our horses. He is a pretty good judge of what a rider can handle."

"You getting one for Clancy?"

"Heavens no!" Elton gasped, "We are hoping the little kids can inherit when the bigger kids graduate to more energetic horses. You should've seen Charlie when Jerald handed him the reins to Abner. Charlie almost croaked. He wanted a big warrior horse. Instead, he got this big old gray. He is gentle and well-mannered. Don't think it could rear on his hind legs for love nor money! Charlie's bottom lip drug in the dirt until the first time he rode him. Abner speeded up to a fast walk and Charlie was scared to death. He is now very content with Abner!"

Kid was rubbing Tornado's neck, "I remember being like that. If I get my act together, I'd be glad to help the kids learn to ride."

"What do you mean—if? You have to change that song. You say, when I get my cast off, I will be—. There's a difference. I'll be counting on it. Hey, want to get a horse of your own? You should talk to Jerald today."

"How can I do that? I don't have two dimes to rub together."

"You will when I get off my duff and pay you rent."

"Whose horse is this? He is sure friendly," Kid chuckled as the horse kept bumping his head to be petted.

"That's the horse that Kevin, Miriam, and I share. His name is Glendive."

"Why do you share him?" Kid turned to pet him.

"Because everybody else had a horse but her. She wanted to be like the other kids so much. She was so tiny, I was worried for her to have one of her own. She only weighed about 18 pounds and she was close to three years old then. She had been so abused and neglected; it was sickening."

"Zach told me some of it. Her folks must have been a piece of work."

"If there were ever two people I wanted to hurt real bad; it would've been them. I'm grateful I was never given the chance to meet them. That little Miriam would curl up in the fetal position at the drop of hat. Her body was all bruises and bones." Elton's shuddered, "Anyway, it is better now. So, Kevin and I went in on the horse with her. I'm thinking I might have to do the same thing with Kitten. She is just coming out of her shell and a bit on the fragile side."

"Think Jerald could find another horse like Glendive?"

"Likely."

"Well, I might consider being a partner with Kitten. After all, she watches over me."

"That she does. I'm sure she'd love that. We can talk to Jerald today."

"When will I pay him, ahead of time or after?"

"He takes payment when he delivers the horse."

"Elton, if I change my mind, can I back out?"

Elton nodded, "If it comes to that, I'll buy out your share. Deal?"

"Deal." Kid patted Tornado's nose, "I love this one. It is a beaut."

"You should ask Jerald if there is any more of his relatives around. I think you would love a good horse like that."

"Maybe later. I don't know if I even remember how to ride."

"Yah, right."

After walking in silence a few minutes, Kid stopped, "Elton, why? Why are you doing this? You guys are all roping me in, aren't you?"

Elton returned a knowing grin, "Oh, I think that you know your mind well enough to know what you want to be roped into. If not, you can always pull out."

"This me is the one that wants to do all this. It is the other me that doesn't."

"You need to tell the other me, you did it his way for years and it was a disaster. He can try it your way now."

Kid laughed, "I'm afraid if I hang around here much longer, I might end up thinking you make sense!"

"You could do worse!"

When they got back to the barn, CJ asked Kid if he would walk over to see the baby chicks with him. Kid nodded and the two went over to to brooder house. CJ opened the door with pride and showed Kid his babies. "You can call them, if you want," CJ suggested.

"I don't know how to do that."

"You don't? I'll show you." The little boy tapped his fingernail on the floor and all the baby chicks came running.

"How did you do that?"

"You pretend your fingernail is the hen's beak. That is how she calls her babies!"

"That is really cool. I guess I never knew how a hen called for her babies to come."

"I know, it's like when Mr. Coot gave each of us kids a whistle to wear around our necks, to blow in case we need help."

As soon as the words came out of his mouth, they both looked at each other. Silence fell over them for a minute and then Kid answered, "That's a good idea. Do all the kids have them?"

"Yes. He gave them to us after some bad boys beat up Clarence and Ginger at school."

"That is a good safety measure." Kid replied and then stood up. "I see they're going to the house. Suppose we should join them?"

CJ took Kid's hand, "I'm sorry. I didn't mean to talk about it."

Kid stopped and knelt down next to the little boy, "It's really okay, CJ. We need to talk about it. It is something that we shared, so don't ever be afraid to mention it around me. Okay?"

"Okay." CJ kept hold of his hand. "You know, after you didn't shoot me, I decided you are a pretty good guy."

"Thanks. And thank you for helping me even when I was so awful to you." Kid changed the subject, "Who are going to be your Godparents?"

"Marty and Greta." CJ said, "I might have had you, but I didn't know you then."

"That is quite okay. I wouldn't pick me to be anyone's Godfather."

"Why not? You're okay when you aren't stealing stuff or shooting people."

The biker laughed, "Think there's hope, then?

"Huh?"

"Nothing. Anyway, I talked to Kevin. I'll be a partner in the rabbits. I think that will be fun."

"Really? What kind of rabbits do you like?"

"Baby ones. I don't care about the breed. Kevin said you guys are getting three kinds; Giant Flemish, American Sable, and New Zealander. I think they're all fine."

"Some of them are going to be almost grownup and some will be babies. So, maybe you will be happy."

"I'll be happy," Kid grinned. "I'm pretty sure."

"Good!"

Kid felt different at breakfast than he had before. It was the first meal where no mention was made about his health. He felt very much a part of this family. He thought the pancakes were wonderful and he didn't even mind holding their hands when they said grace. In fact, he rather liked it.

"Kev and I have to take off right away," Carrie said. "Sunday School awaits!"

Kid turned to Kevin, "You teach Sunday School?"

"Yah, I got boondoggled into it, but I sort of like it now. We have fun. Right, Kitten?"

Kitten smiled and patted her chest, "Fun at sunny school. Kid sunny school?"

"Not this week, Kitten," Kid answered. "Maybe later."

Kid helped clear the table while everyone scurried around getting ready. Grandma patted his arm and said, "Come with me to try on your suit. I need to know if Nora needs to take it in or anything."

"I can't wear the jacket anyway, so it really doesn't matter."

Grandma shook her head, "It really does. Don't be an unruly child."

Kid chuckled and followed her.

A few hours later, Matt came to pick him up. Kid was feeling very uncomfortable in his suit. He had a white shirt with one split arm and no jacket. "Grandma said I should just wear my overcoat." He grumped, "This is stupid, Matt. I don't belong there."

"I'm not leaving you there permanently." Matt teased, "I'll bring you home. Promise. It should only take about half an hour. Are you any good at taking pictures? If I give you my Kodak, can you snap some photos for me?"

"I guess I can try, with one arm, if you show me how."

"Diane can."

Diane, Matt, and Kid came up the front steps of Trinity Lutheran Church. Kid could hardly make his feet move and hated every second of it. Matt let Diane go on ahead and fell back, "Kid, take it easy. The only person who thinks you shouldn't be here, is you. You have to make no commitment, listen to a sermon or anything. You are simply here to be a good friend to some folks who think a lot of you. Okay?"

"I guess. Matt, think we could talk later? Just you and me?"

"Sure," Matt said sincerely. "Whenever, I'll make time."

"Thanks. Where do you want me to sit?"

The service was over and Elton had just been told about his birthday surprise. He was beaming, but Clarissa was disappointed he hadn't cried yet. Nora assured her that he would have tears before it was done. Kid sat in the front pew and Pastor Byron came over and said hello. "Do you remember Marv Olson?"

Pastor Marv held out his hand and grinned, "Good to see you. I see you are the designated photographer, huh?"

"I guess. Don't know how it will work since I only have one good hand."

"If you move to this side and prop the camera on this post, you should be able to get some steady shots."

"Thanks," Kid mumbled, feeling very sick to his stomach with nerves.

To his surprise, Marv helped him adjust the camera. They chatted and then he smiled, "I'll try not to get my big mug in the way of the lens."

Kid had to smile, "I suppose they want to see their own big mugs, huh?"

Marv chuckled, "Yah, they are all vain, but us!"

It made him feel better that Marv talked to him without bringing up anything. He did relax a little, but not much. He watched the baptisms. It was quite moving. He thought he got some good shots; especially the photo of Elton wiping some tears away. He was pleased.

When they left the church, Marv came over to Kid. "Hope the photos turned out okay."

"I think there were some good ones."

"Good, I'll see you at dinner. I bet we're having chocolate birthday cake."

"Why do you think that?"

"Elton's favorite," Marv chuckled. "Maybe we'll get a chance to visit. Glad to see you up and around."

"Thanks. Good to see you."

-23-

Kid joined everyone at dinner and enjoyed the birthday party, but became extremely tired before it was over. It reminded him of past days with his family when their uncles and aunts came to visit. He used to love those times. He realized how many years he had been without that; so long that he forgot he missed it. He excused himself and went to take a nap. Zach came in behind him with some meds and asked, "How you feeling?"

"Antsy as hell and my arm hurts." He turned to Zach, "And I want to cry. What is happening to me?"

"A lot of things. You did very well and I'm especially glad that you know when to blow the whistle. That's Andy's downfall. He wants to do so much he has a heck of a time taking a rest."

"What does that mean? That I'm a baby or lazy?"

"No, I meant you know your own limitations and shut down before you got crabby." Zach raised his eyebrows, "Obviously, I made a mistake."

"I'm sorry. I hate being the center of attention."

"When were you?" Zach wrinkled his brow. "I didn't think that anyone put you on the spot."

"No, no one really did. Matt coerced me into going to church," Kid said. "I like him though. We just like to bug each other."

"He's a good sort. You take a rest and then you can play chess with Keith. I hear you guys have a match scheduled, huh?"

"What if I sleep too long?"

"They aren't going home until later. Don't worry."

He fell asleep almost immediately.

Kid heard the sound of giggling and woke to see the little girls playing with the cat. They were sitting on the floor trying to put a doll dress on the poor creature. Kid smiled, but said, "I don't know if the dress fits Cotton."

The girls looked at him in shock and ran out of the room. Cotton shook the dress off his legs and walked out behind them. Kid smiled, "Thanks to you, too."

Before there was a knock at his door, Kid was back from the bathroom and had freshened up a bit. It was Matt who knocked, "Have time to talk? I brought you some tea."

Kid sat down, "I don't want to take you away from the party."

"The men went over to the airplane hangar and the ladies are looking at patterns for wedding dresses. I wondered if you wanted to visit and then we could walk over to see the guys."

Kid sat by the window and motioned for Matt to sit down across from him. "I really don't know what I want to talk about."

"We can just visit," Matt grinned. "I heard that Elton set my wedding date this morning, huh? You probably knew before I did."

"Maybe," Kid smirked. "You might be a bit slow on the uptake! Is the date okay?"

"Wonderful." Matt looked out the window, "I love Diane completely, but she's had so many issues about commitment that I wondered if she'd ever set a date."

"Why didn't you tell her now or never!"

"Oh, I did! And we broke up so often, it was as common as hello. Meeting her mother, I can understand it better, but still not completely. After all, who wouldn't be tickled to spend their life with me?"

Kid crossed his eyes, "Me, for one."

"Seriously," Matt leaned ahead, "I was flabbergasted that anyone would even considering marrying me! You know, I made a life-long commitment to the Catholic Church and left that after nine years."

"I heard there were extenuating circumstances."

"Aren't there always? It took me awhile and more than a few lectures from Elton, Byron and Vicaro, before I realized that we just have to keep going forward. We all make turns, or step backwards from time to time; but then we have to just begin again."

"Have you ever dealt with addicts before?"

"Yes. It's a challenge, but a lot of things are. Don't build it up to be a bigger thing than it is. If you do, you'll defeat yourself. If you think of yourself as only an addict, that's what you will be. If you think of yourself as a child of God, son of your parents, member of our little clan, hero to Kitten, friend of Matt's, who happens to also be an addict, you give yourself more options."

Kid laughed, "I'm not all that stuff, though. God and I parted ways in Vietnam."

"No, you parted ways with Him. He's still there waiting for you to come back. That I know for certain."

"I can't do that in good conscience." Kid snapped in anger, "Where was He when that little kid got her head blown off?"

His expression betrayed that he had not wanted to say that. He dropped his eyes and stared at his tea cup.

Matt sat quietly a bit and then said softly, "Since it slipped out, want to talk about it? It must have been lurking just under the surface for a long time, huh? Your dreams?"

Kid nodded and then wiped his tears on the back of his hand, "It was horrible, Matt. No matter how long ago it was, it's always right there. God, I hated it. I still hate it."

Matt gave him a tissue and said compassionately, "Take you time. If it wants out that bad, let it out. Okay?"

The traumatized man stared out the window for a few minutes. "We were outside this village of 'friendlies'. It was hotter than hell and the humidity was stifling. You know, like trying to breathe steam? We were on my first tour over there. Gordie was my best friend. We'd been by this village a hundred times and often, the kids would bring us water. We never thought twice about it. There had been a firefight to the north a week or so before and after that, the fields of the village were obliterated with Agent Orange. There was talk of infiltration, but there always was. Anyway, Gordie was hot with sweat dripping from him like a wet dishrag. This sweet, little girl brought him a container of water. Several other kids brought some to other guys. She offered it to me first, but I knew Gordie was cooking, so I motioned to him. He took it and guzzled it. He thanked her and she smiled. She ran back to the group of other kids."

Then the man stopped and stared out the window, his head trembling while he bit his bottom lip. "I can't Matt. I can't talk about it. Forget it, okay?"

Matt sat quietly with him, but never moved. After a few minutes when the biker seemed to have collected himself, Matt asked softly, "What happened?"

"I don't want to. I can't," Kid pleaded.

"Okay, when you can, let me know. I can tell you right now not to beat yourself up because you gave him the water. You were being nice to him. I assume that is where you were going with it."

"I do blame myself, but not that much. He drained the whole container in a heartbeat, before a guy ahead of us dropped. The word spread that the water contained poison. Three men bled to death internally on the spot. When Gordie dropped, I held him in my arms while he died. I prayed Matt! I prayed with all my might! I tried to calm Gordie and promised him he'd be okay, but he died! Within minutes, he was gone! I was holding on to him as tight as I could, but God took him anyway. He was just gone, Matt. Gone in a couple minutes."

Matt put his arm around his friend and let him sob. He consoled him as best he could. While he was mourning, he continued between gasps of weeping and intermittent anger, "I was oblivious to what else was going on, when the Sergeant came up and asked me who gave him the water."

His tears turned to a wail, "I pointed to the little girl who was standing in a group of shocked little kids watching in horror. Matt, I knew she didn't know she'd done anything wrong! She felt bad. The Sergeant picked up his rifle and blew her head off. If I live to be a million, I'll never forget the look on her face the instant before she died. She was so afraid! I never should have said who gave him the water! It wasn't her fault. Shit, she couldn't have been over two! What the hell did she know? She thought she was being nice!"

Matt held the veteran while he wept and rubbed his back, "Life is impossible to understand. I can't tell you why it happened."

"Everyone would hate me if they knew I pointed out a little kid to be killed! All those people out there who think they want to be my friend have no idea what a worthless piece of garbage I am!"

"I know that it wasn't your fault. You were mourning. You didn't know that he was going to shoot her. You didn't point her out to be killed! It was a reflex response. It was horrible, but not your doing. Understand?"

"Matt, I should have known! I should've thought! As usual, I was just thinking about myself!"

"Hey, you were consoling your dying friend. That isn't thinking about yourself."

"I should have realized."

"I doubt anyone would have thought much at that point. Kid, you weren't responsible for what happened. Hear me?"

"Gordie is dead, that little girl is dead and that barmaid is dead. How many times can I not be responsible?"

"What would you have done differently? Drink the water while your friend was thirsty? You could have stood up to the motorcycle gang and got killed, too. When you stood on principal and didn't take part in the beating in prison, you ended up in isolation! Look, we all leave tracks on this planet—some good and some bad. Even the best in this world aren't perfect. Things don't work out, at least as often as they do!"

"And you still believe in God?"

"Yes, and you do, too. You are just mad as hell at Him. It's okay, Harold. He can live with that. It's a logical and sensible reaction. I doubt very much that He expects us to like all His plans. Our mistake is that we ask for the wrong things. We need His help to face life and accept what happens. He promises He will give us peace, not everything we want."

"That stinks."

Matt chuckled, "Yup, it really does. I'd love it if I got everything I wanted, but then it would make problems, too."

"How's that?"

"I don't know what the future will bring. It might just be the thing that I don't need. If I had stayed a priest, I wouldn't be marrying Diane. See, every cloud has a . . ."

Kid scowled, "If you say a silver lining, I'll deck you!"

"Dang, I thought it'd fit in real well. Do you think you can quit blaming yourself for her death?"

"I don't know. She was so little and died trying to do something good. I should have stood up for her."

"How long did you have to 'stand up for her'? How long between when you pointed to her and when she was shot?"

"Less than a second. Almost instantaneous."

"How about you stand up for her now? Work to help other children live better lives?"

"Oh, dear God, I knew I shouldn't talk to you! You'll have me with a collection cup and feeding starving waifs, or some damned thing," Kid groaned.

"No, I think that you should start out small. Just wherever you can, try to help someone's life be a bit better."

"I haven't got any money."

"You don't need money. You only need time and the motivation. I heard you're going to help with the rabbits, huh?"

"Yah, but what's that got to do with it?"

"You can talk to the boys, show them how to do things and listen to them. That's what folks need. Someone to listen." Then he winked at Kid, "Even if it is just you!"

"Jackass." Kid returned a slight smile, "Do you really think that matters?"

"More than you know. Listening to Grandpa is the best gift you can give him. He loves it and it makes him feel worthwhile."

Kid chuckled, "He told me about WWII the other day! He had President Woodrow Wilson holding America back from entering the war until the Battle of Verdun! I wondered if he knew what war he was talking about."

"I know, he is getting so mixed up, but he really does love us. Even dumb me and bearded you!" Matt crossed his eyes, "Then you shaved your beard and I'm still dumb."

"That might be something he is right about, after all!"

"Watch it! Wanna go with Clarence and I when we give Grandpa his ride sometime? They'd both like that."

"I guess, I don't do much else and it is a cool car." A shadow fell over his face, "Matt, I really do want to be respectable, but I don't know if I can do it. I'm worthless. Everyone is trying to find something to include me, but I know I'll let them down."

"You sure will with that attitude!" Matt agreed. "When I first came here and was on my pity-pot. I had a plan to sit and think for the six-month probation. That was a joke! These crazy people had me involved in all kinds of things and that Jessup conned me into owning every animal imaginable! By the time the sixth month came around, I had two teaching jobs, helped at St. Johns and with the dairy, had a girlfriend, and a dog, two cats, and two horses. It was nuts. But you know what? There were many days that was what kept me going. It won't hurt to get involved and you can always change how much you do later. It will keep you from thinking about yourself, which usually leads to no good."

"Amen."

"See," Matt laughed, "And you say I shouldn't have been a priest!"

"You do leave a little to be desired," Kid poked. "Matt, thanks. I still don't feel good about it, but I'd never told a living soul about what happened before. Will this help so it doesn't drive me crazy?"

"Not all by itself, but now it isn't a secret. I know that most of these folks would understand. The more daylight you give it, the less it will bother you. I wouldn't tell the kids, though."

Kid laughed and Matt frowned at him, "What's so funny?"

"Oh, CJ told me that he thought I was a pretty good guy when I wasn't stealing or shooting people!"

"God help us!" Matt held his head, "Wanna wash up and then we can get some more cake?"

The rest of the afternoon went by quickly. Keith and Kid played chess. The two little girls came and sat by them, watching every move. Kid noticed and asked Keith, "Would you mind if I got the checker board and set it up for them? We might have to help them, but they liked it when Jeff and I played."

"Sounds good," Keith smiled. "Would you girls like to play checkers?"

"Okay," Gopher said quietly and Kitten just shrugged.

They watched every move as the men set up the board for them and then said they could play. They both just sat there, not doing anything.

Kid frowned, "They liked it when they sat on our laps."

Keith thought, "I bet they could see better. I have an idea."

He went to the sofa and took off two cushions. He put one on each chair and Kid helped the girls get up on them. They both smiled and clapped their hands. Then Kid got them started. It didn't take them too long, and they were playing, but the men were helping most of the time. The chess game was ignored.

Keith asked Kid, "Did you want to finish our chess match? Or we can ask someone else to watch the girls?"

"No, I actually enjoy it," Kid said. "Besides, who wants to get beaten?"

That evening after everyone went home, Kid was watching television with Andy and Jackson when the news came on. "I think I'm going to bed. I can't stand to watch the news. I'll have a bad dream slick as a whistle," Andy announced. "Besides, it's Annie's last night at home for a few days."

"Yes," Jackson agreed. "I was worried you'd get too cold over at the hangar."

"I was warm enough, but I had a bad night last night. I tossed and turned all night. I imagine I woke up the whole house a time or two." Andy said, "I wonder sometimes if Annie doesn't like being at work. It must be quieter."

Jackson rolled his eyes, "Yah, in a fire hall with sirens going off. Must be like a tranquil evening."

Andy frowned, "I really don't like you very much. I can't see how Katie can stand you."

"She has better taste than you!" Jackson laughed, "Really she was so sweet with my clomping around on her feet at the dance. I couldn't believe it."

"How did that go?" Kid asked.

"He did pretty well," Andy said. "I was surprised."

Jackson frowned at his best friend, "Why would you be surprised? You know how good I am."

"Yea gads, I'm going to bed. Goodnight."

"Good night, Andy." Kid said, "See you in the morning."

After he was gone, Kid asked, "Do the news reports really bother him a lot?"

"Yah. Me, too, some. Do they bother you?"

"I rarely watch television, so I don't know." Kid answered honestly. "Elton says you sleep better than Andy, huh?"

"Yah, my sleep was mostly bothered by the infection in my leg. I had jungle rot before I got shot in the mud. It was a dandy. First, they thought they only had to take part of my foot, then it was up over my ankle. They were talking about taking off up to my knee before long. Thank goodness, it finally healed. I was lingering on this side of death's door for a while there. I would've missed out on a lot of good things."

Kid smiled as he listened to him, "So, you aren't bothered by war nightmares so much."

"Once in a while, but Andy was a tunnel rat. That's what gets to him; you know tar pitch darkness, bats, snakes, scorpions. All that fun stuff."

"I have enough trouble with the daytime." Kid reflected. "When did you come here?"

"In December. Andy was transferred back here after his injuries. We were shot at the same time with the same weapon, more than likely. Andy and I were dragging Chicago to a bird, when we took fire from the rear. Damn near killed Chicago. We had just pulled him out of a shallow pungy pit. One hell of a mess. He survived though."

"Where is he?"

"In Chicago, with his wife. Andy and I are going down to see him this summer. He isn't very good. Took some spikes in his liver, neck, gut, and lung and then got the calves of his legs all shot to hell. But, Old Chicago is a tough bird. Can't sing worth a damn, but he loved trying. He would start singing and empty the hooch in a heartbeat!" Jackson smiled. "I miss him. He's a great guy."

"Sounds like you were all close."

"Andy and I were like two peas but Chicago was the pod!" Jackson laughed. "I was sent back to Pine Ridge Veterans Administration center, but Mom couldn't take care of me. I'd been writing to Pastor Byron for some time, so he called to check up on me. When he found out I couldn't go home, he came down and signed papers to take me home with him. I was going to stay at their place, but since Andy was here and these guys have almost a mini-hospital here, this is now my home. Best damned thing that ever happened to me."

"You religious? Is that why you were writing to Ellison?" Kid questioned.

"Not really. I had something torturing me, and finally Andy crowbarred it out of me while we were in Cu Chi. He told me to write to Byron for advice and I did. He was great, helped me work it out, and he has never let me down."

"Something that happened in Vietnam?"

"No. Let's go to my room and I'll tell you. I don't want the kids to overhear."

They entered Jackson's room and Kid's mouth fell open. "Wow! You did all this?"

"Yah, my sketches. These guys encouraged me and between Matt, Diane, and Kate pushing me, I now sell them at a gallery in Bismarck. I still don't think they are that much, but I guess."

"These are fantastic!" Kid looked them over.

He noticed the kid's portraits on the wall and then a few he didn't recognize. "May I ask who these are?"

Jackson pointed, "Mom, my real Dad, and Uncle Bear."

"Is Uncle Bear your Mom's brother or your Dad's?"

"He is Dad's half-brother. He is half-Sioux, but my real Dad was full-blooded white."

"Are the Grey Hawk kids full?"

"Yes, their Dad is full Sioux. Confusing, huh?"

"Ever tried to figure out white man's lineage? People are part French, Polish, Dutch, and anything else on the map. Wonder how long it will be before we just say we're all American?" Kid moved over to another portrait. "Who is this beautiful girl?"

"Vienna." Horse touched the frame, "She was my problem."

"Did she leave you?"

"You could say that. Her father had some friends who were horrible characters. While her dad was at work, those old drunks gang-raped her. She and I were going together and I stood beside her through that. I knew it wasn't her fault and I loved her. Then a month or so later, she started to withdraw. One night, she and I were walking by the creek and she told me she was pregnant by one of those men! I went nuts. I screamed, hollered, and threw a major fit. Then I stomped off." Jackson touched her photo again. "After I thought about it, I realized there was nothing she could do and I was being a creep. I went back over to her place and she wasn't home yet. I got worried, so her brothers and I went down by the creek. I found her, leaning against a tree, dying. She had slit her wrists. She died a couple minutes later while I held her. One of the last things she said, was that she loved me."

"I'm sorry, Jackson."

"I let her down when she really needed me."

"What did you do?"

"I started drinking and was drunk a couple weeks straight. Uncle Bear wouldn't tolerate that, got ahold of me, and we had a fistfight. He knocked me on my ass. I quit drinking, finished school, and joined the Army. I still blamed myself for what happened, until Byron got to me. He said none of us has the right to shut down when a major disaster happens. We also have to realize that while we are all responsible for each other, no one is totally responsible for any other person's actions. It took me awhile, but I finally realized he was right. I had to put everything in perspective and realized it was an awful situation for everyone concerned. Then not long ago, after I moved here, I fell for Kate. I was worried to death I'd let her down, too. Grandma told me that I could be as reliable or as unreliable as I wanted to be. It was up to me. I decided to be reliable."

"I keep hearing the same thing, over and over. Are you guys setting me up?"

Jackson frowned, "The reason you hear the same story all the time is because most folks have a version of it to tell. You may not have been listening before."

"I've never spent a lot of time listening to other folks' problems, because I knew mine was the worst!" Kid chuckled.

"Yah, easy to think that, but it's probably not true. Your problem is the worst, only because it is yours. My missing ankle is more important to me than Andy's artificial knees, because it is my ankle!"

"Good point." Kid nodded. "I better get to bed and let you get some sleep."

Horse smiled, "Kid, it really will be okay if you give things a chance. After all, what have you got to lose?"

-24-

The busy day left Kid unsettled. He had never been one to talk about his feelings, but lately, it was all he was doing! Here he was talking to people he hardly knew, about some of his deepest, traumatic emotions and fears. He was certain it would come back to bite him. Nothing was going to change except he had lost the tiny fragments of pride that he still held.

In spite of what Jackson said, he wondered if all these people weren't making up stories to make him feel like he was one of them. Hell, he knew that when people had troubles, they almost always folded into a heap of garbage. It very rarely made them stronger. He had run with them, so he knew.

Then the image of his mother flashed in his mind. She had a rugged life. She was left at an orphanage when her father couldn't take care of her. She never knew what happened to her real mom. Then the folks that adopted her treated her badly after they had their own children. She had every reason to be grim, but she wasn't. She was always positive, optimistic, and upbeat. She had been his strength, and always had his back. When she passed away, he wasn't there, but in Vietnam. He didn't even hear that she was ill until after she was gone. He only got home for the funeral, but not to tell her goodbye. He missed her so much. She was the only one who ever made things seem sensible. He let her down, like he always did. He hated himself for that among the many other things.

Kid tossed and turned in bed. He was irritable, antsy, and wondered if they had given him anything except the antibiotic. 'They are probably just waiting for me to collapse and then . . . they will . . .' He frowned. Why would they want to do that? To watch him cry? Hell, he had already done that more than he ever had in his life. Did they want him to go crazy so they could throw him out? They could throw him out whenever they wanted. No matter how he tried, he couldn't find a motivation for these people to hurt him, or help him. Maybe they were just stupid.

He couldn't get comfortable and felt frustrated. He twisted around until he got himself tangled up in his blankets. He noticed he was starting to sweat. 'Sure,' he thought, 'They forgot to give me my meds and I'm going into withdrawal. Sure as hell! I ache all over and my stomach is churning. Damn it all. I didn't want to withdraw in front of the kids. I may be an ass, but I have some sense of decency!'

Though angry, he laughed aloud, sardonically, "Yah, right!"

That startled Kitten who had come in earlier without Kid noticing. She jumped and he heard her. He glared over at her and snapped loudly, "Go away! Get the Hell out of here!"

The little girl went out the door in a flash. After she left, he detested himself for acting that way. How could he do that? That was it! Now he knew he had to get out of there! He was getting out of bed to leave, when Elton came in. "What is it, Kid? What can I do for you?"

Kid froze and glared, "Leave me the hell alone! I don't want to be here! I want to go and now! Get out of my way. I'll get my bike and leave!"

Elton listened without expression before he said, "How are you going to start your bike with that cast on?"

"Ah, I can do it! Don't you worry, I can do it!" Then he stared at his arm and his shoulders fell. He started to weep, "I know I can do it. I'll take my cast off. Then I can. I know I can."

Elton walked over to him slowly and put his arms around him. "Want me to help you? I'd be glad to help you get dressed, packed, and walk you down to the garage. I'll have to move some cars out of the way for you. I can start your bike the first time. After that, you're on your own. Is that what you want?"

Kid was now sitting on the edge of the bed, "Son of a—! Damn it to Hell! I can't even leave, can I?"

Elton sat next to him, "I can help you leave. You can. After that, you'll have to figure it out. Do you have someplace you can go, where folks can help you?"

"No," Kid flopped back on the bed, "Nowhere. That's where I am. A nobody who is nowhere! I can't stand it. I just can't! I've been bawling around here for days and still feel like shit. I never used to talk about stuff, and now, I'm spilling my guts every time I open my mouth! This isn't me! I'm the strong, silent type."

Elton broke into a grin, "Kid. If you were the strong silent type, you'd be in the movies. You are a regular human being. Can't you just cut yourself some slack? Heal up before you leave."

"Elton," the man tried to sit up, and couldn't. Elton helped him which frustrated Kid even more, "Elton, I hate this. I think I'm starting withdrawal. I feel sick and am sweating like a butcher. I'm antsy as hell and I can't sleep. What am I going to do? I don't want to go through it in front of the kids."

"Don't have to worry about that now. I doubt Kitten will bother you anymore and the other kids will stay away if we tell them. I can find a place for you to go tomorrow. I didn't hear that they were reducing your meds tonight. I'll ask Annie."

"No! It's her last night home tonight. Don't bother her."

"I'll call Zach then."

"He has work tomorrow. Just leave me be."

"I wish it was that easy," Elton got up and went out of the room.

Kid sat there in shock, looking at the door as it closed. He hadn't expected Elton would just leave him. Suddenly, he was very afraid and felt very alone. Maybe it was the first time that he really understood his quandary. It dawned on him in cold reality, he was not able to leave and seriously had no place to go.

A few minutes later, Zach came in the bedroom. "What the hell are you trying to do?"

"Huh?" Kid mumbled, "I told Elton to not call you. You have work tomorrow."

"I know. What's going on? You're supposed to tell me or Annie, right off if something isn't right! Not going running off to the hinterland! Idiot!"

"I don't feel good. I'm sweating, have muscle cramps, and my guts are blowing up. I can't sleep and I'm antsy as hell. Am I going into withdrawal? Did you guys decide to do it and not tell me?"

"No, we didn't. I think I know what's wrong. You've been up a lot and outside, charging around for a couple days. You also have been getting in touch with some of your emotions, from what I gather. You've been stirring your lava pit and now, you got it boiling. We knew that'd happen. We talked about it, didn't we?"

"Yah, but I thought if I told someone about some of that stuff, it would go away! It didn't!"

"Mentioning it the first time is great, but you have to give it a bit to sort itself out. Hear me? It will work out. Your meds might be a little low for all the activity you've been a part of the last two days. I'll up them for you, so you can sleep. I want you to get good rest. That is very important. I do not want you to lose control and get all bent out of shape. You should have said something."

"Don't you think I get tired of saying I don't feel good? Do you think I like it?"

"You're right," Zach said mockingly, "It's better to throw a tantrum!"

Filled with chagrin, Kid sat immobile, staring at nothing. Zach gave him a shot and then said with authority, "If you don't relax soon, you let someone know. Right away! Annie will put your IV back up. Tomorrow, you're grounded. If you get some restful sleep, you can be up in the house. You start being a bastard or throwing a fit and I'll drive out to haul you back to the hospital. I mean it. I warned you before, no bullshit and no giving the ladies a bad time."

"I didn't give a lady a bad time," Kid mumbled.

"Oh, yah? Then why was Kitten crying? Elton said she came to him crying and said 'Kid mad to me.' Did she lie?"

"No, but I wasn't mad at her, I was mad at me."

"Tell her that, Jackass."

"Zach, I told you I was no good."

"I know you did. Do you want a prize for proving you can be a jerk?"

"Dammit Zach, I'm sorry! I was scared and I needed help."

"Pretty sad way of asking for help."

Kid reached out his hand, "Zach, please give me another chance."

Zach sat down, "Yah, I guess I overreacted, too. I was so pleased you were doing well. I guess I was drinking the Pollyanna juice, too. We need to be real. Sorry. Friends again?"

"I'd like that. I'll speak up before I get so bent again."

"Good. You have my word, if I'm going to change your meds, I'll let you know. You have to let me know how you're reacting. Okay?"

"I was just sweating so much and my stomach was acting up. So, I got scared."

"You ate more regular food than you have for some time, and your tummy isn't healed up yet. You got yourself all wound up, that's why you were feverish. Calm down and take a deep breath."

"Okay. Sorry I got you out of bed." Kid frowned, "Zach, what can I say to Kitten? I don't want her to think she has to sit in here, but I don't want to her to think I'm mad about it. Between you and me, I makes me kinda feel good."

"Maybe a simple 'I'm sorry I yelled' would be good." Zach patted his arm. "Elton is rocking her now. Want me to tell them to come in?"

"I guess."

Kid heard Zach say good night and a few minutes later, Elton came in carrying Kitten. "How you doing, Kid?" Elton asked.

"Better," he said sheepishly, "I'm sorry how I acted."

Elton answered, "No problem. I just hope you're feeling better now."

"I am." Kid asked softly, "Kitten, will you talk to me?"

The little girl didn't turn in Elton's arms, but shrugged.

Kid repeated, "Kitten, I'm sorry I lost my temper. I was crabby. I didn't mean to make you sad."

Kitten didn't turn around but said, "No pwoblem."

"Kitten, can we be friends again?"

She turned and studied him a minute, "Okay, you be better."

"Thank you."

Kid went to the bathroom and was beginning to feel himself calm down again. He returned to his bed and covered up. He looked over to the empty chair and wondered if the little girl would ever come back. He couldn't think of a reason on earth why she should. The man had a heck of a time relaxing enough to fall asleep. He tossed and turned for quite a while.

Then he saw the door open and a few minutes later, felt Cotton jump up on his feet. He was overwhelmed with relief. He said quietly, "Good night, Kitten."

He heard her soft, tiny voice answer, "Night, Kid."

The next morning was gray and drizzly. Kid helped Grandma with breakfast, but he was very quiet. Grandma was sweet, but seemed to sense that he was depressed. After breakfast was ready and the table set, she suggested they sneak a cup of coffee into the dining room for a chat.

Kid sat down at the table, dreading another lecture. Grandma brought them each a cup of coffee, his with a lot of cream. "I was wondering if you'd be willing to help me today."

"What do you need help with?"

"I want to do something for Matt and Diane's wedding. They are both very special people to me and I want to give them something to let them know that."

Kid was immensely relieved that it wasn't a lecture, "Like what?"

"I have no idea. Jackson is working on a portrait for them. Katie is doing Diane's dress, even though there are no beads on it. Katie will not do beads on a dress and be in the wedding, too! She did it once and almost had a nervous breakdown. Do you have any ideas?"

"I hardly know them," Kid said thoughtfully. "Matt has been real good to me, but I've hardly talked to Diane. I don't know what they would like."

"They are both so good-hearted. They appreciate everything, but I want it to be exceptional. I know they have a dog, Skipper, and each have a horse. Diane loves piano and they both like little kids."

"What kind of car do they have?" Kid asked.

"I don't know. Matt bought an old car from Kev for Diane and he drives Carl's old car. You have to ask someone else that! All I know is they have wheels!"

"Good to know." Kid chuckled, "What does Matt do for fun?"

"I have no idea. He's like Katie and does whatever someone else likes. They both seem to enjoy all sorts of things. I know they'd be happy with anything and appreciate it. That makes it even harder." Grandma turned her cup in her hand. "Any brilliant ideas?"

"Me? I've probably never had a brilliant idea in my life!"

"Then you should be due!" Grandma said. "Best be thinking fast, because we have a month. If you want, it can be from all three of us; Lloyd, you, and me. Okay?"

"That'd be great. Do you want it to be something we make, do, or buy?"

"I don't know. That's why I asked you!"

"I promise to think on it. What kind of house do they have?"

"Darrell's old sheepherder's cabin. It has one large room that is kitchen-living-dining room, a bedroom, and a room that's storage. Darrell added a bathroom and laundry room. The furniture was from Carl's old apartment and Matt's bedroom at home. Neither of them had anything."

"I thought Diane was married before. Certainly she must have had stuff."

"Not really. Some china is all. Dean died after an expensive bout with cancer. He was in business with his Dad who had dropped their health insurance. Diane had a huge debt and sold everything to pay for his care."

"That stinks. I heard her father-in-law wasn't a nice man," Kid frowned.

"He sure wasn't. He was awful. Diane had a beautiful piano there, and he got drunk one night and smashed the innards of it. That is why we got her this one."

"So, she has one now."

"Yes, and Matt replaced her sheet music. I'm at a total loss what to get them. Do you have any ideas?"

"Never even thought about it. How long do I have to think about it?"

"Five minutes," Grandma laughed. "However long it takes, I guess. They're getting married the 22nd. We need to know soon enough so we can have it done by then. Are we in business?"

Kid held out his hand, "We are. One thing though, you know I have to do detox?"

Grandma wrinkled her brow, "What's that got to do with this? Kiddo, I have to get my darned blood pressure checked, too! That's all just maintenance, my boy. Body maintenance."

"You're goofy." Kid broke out laughing, "No wonder everyone loves you!"

"Oh, something else! Matt has this begonia he drug out here from Boston. Harrington said it was dead for over a year, but he dug it up to move it. He left it in his laundry room all year and still thinks that he can plant it outside this spring and it will bloom. With him, it is a matter of faith. He rototilled a patch next to the house so he can plant it out there. Kid, I have faith; but between you and me, that thing is a goner. Maybe we should get some begonia bulbs and we could plant them in his flowerbed sometime when he's at school. Then something will come up for him."

"You mean for their wedding present?"

"No, for fun." Grandma winked.

"Does Matt really like gardening?"

"He used to spend a lot of time in his flower garden when he was a priest. He must get it from his Mom because Mo loves gardening."

"Maybe we could find something in that vein, like a greenhouse add-on or something. He has the space and the inclination. Maybe he needs a shove? I'll look around and see what I can come up with. What do you think?"

Grandma kissed his cheek, "I think I picked a great partner! I see the crew coming up from the barn. Thanks, Kid. Let me know what you discover."

Before Elton left for work, Kid spoke to him privately. "First, I want to give you my deepest apologies for last night. I had no excuse."

"It's over, let's put it behind us." Elton smiled at him, "Next time, just ask for help earlier. Okay?"

"I promise I'll do that. I wanted to ask you something?"

"What's that?"

"Do you have any seed catalogues or things like that I could look at?"

Elton's eyes narrowed, "You gonna spy on Coot for me?"

Kid shook his head and grimaced, "Do I have a choice?"

"Not much of one." Elton laughed, "I think that Doug has a pile of catalogues over at the elevator. I'll bring some home for you. Anything you're particularly interested in?"

"Greenhouses, flower beds, and such."

"You want to have a greenhouse?"

"No, I've been sent on a mission." Kid chuckled.

"Okay. Need any help with this mission, say the word. Okay?"

"Will do."

The rest of the overcast morning, Kid rested a lot, played checkers with Kitten, and visited with Grandpa. Kid was sleeping when Elton brought a fistful of gardening catalogues back when he came home for lunch. He knocked and brought them into his room, "Hey, I was thinking."

Kid grinned, "Is that good?

"Usually not, but this is a great idea! We could build a greenhouse over here. You know, we could out-Coot, Coot. I think he is going to have a small bedding greenhouse, but we'll have a real one!"

Elton's eyes were actually gleaming at the thought. Kid crossed his eyes, "You two really do compete about everything, huh?"

"Who told you that?" Elton squinted, "Don't believe it. It is just that Carl is such a braggart. He makes me crazy!"

Kid chuckled, "Oh, I see. Do you know anything about greenhouses?"

"No, but I figured you must. Huh? If we build one, you could take care of it. That would be neat, uh?"

"Elton, I love gardening, but I've never had a greenhouse. Grandma and I are trying to find something special to give Matt and Diane for their wedding. I thought maybe we could find something in these catalogues, since Matt likes flower gardens," Kid explained.

Elton slumped into the chair, "Doggone it! I thought we were really on to something. Hey, when you look these over, can you see what you think about having one? We could build it here and you could take care of it. We'd help of course. Think of it this way, then you and Matt would have something to talk about."

"We already have stuff to talk about!" Kid picked up one of the catalogues and looked at the cover photo of a greenhouse. "Wow! Look at this one! Isn't that neat how they have those racks for bedding plants on the side!"

Elton studied it, "Yah, but I don't know about that stuff. You look them over and we can talk tonight. Okay? I think it would be neat to do and besides, we have a lot of mouths to feed around here. Kids need fresh vegetables all winter, right?"

Kid chuckled, "Don't tell me, it's Nora you need to convince!"

"You'll back me up, right?"

"Elton, I owe you a lot and love you to death, but I won't take sides with you over Nora. She's been like a mother to me! I couldn't do that."

Elton nodded compassionately and patted his hand. "Afraid of not getting fed, huh? I understand, son. I understand."

As Elton pulled the door closed, Kid looked at the pile of catalogues. He thought about that crazy man and had to laugh. He really was beginning to love that guy.

-25-

Kid spent a lot of time that afternoon pouring over the catalogues. He found several things that caught his interest. He was taking a nap when Nora came to his door, "Kid, Sheriff Bernard just called. He is on his way out to see you."

"Did he say why?" Kid asked.

"Nothing, but it sounded serious. He said he'd be right out."

Kid was coming into the kitchen when the Sheriff's car drove in. Nora offered him a cup of coffee when he came to the door, but he said, "Don't have time. My niece is with me, so she won't want to wait too long in the car.'"

Nora pursed her lips, "You silly rabbit, invite her in. You can't leave her sitting out in the car! She can have some coffee, too."

"You sure?"

Nora frowned, "Do it."

Kid laughed when the Sheriff went out, "You just bossed around the sheriff!"

Nora wrinkled her brow, "So? You could do well to run a comb through your hair."

Kid shook his head and left the room to get fit for company. He hadn't thought he needed to be fancy. He was just going to talk to the sheriff! Maybe he would back Elton about the greenhouse after all.

A couple minutes later, he returned to the kitchen. The Sheriff was about to sit down with his coffee and introduced his niece to Kid. "Savannah, this is Kid. Kid, Savannah."

Kid nodded and smiled at the young lady. She was a knock-out in her blue jeans and pink blouse; slender but stacked. She had medium length, light brown hair and the darkest brown eyes he had ever seen. She was wearing no makeup, but he didn't think she needed any. She was very pretty.

He sat down quickly, suddenly feeling very underdressed in his sweats. He was wearing Horse's moccasins and, thankfully, had shaved that morning. He was glad that Nora had made him comb his hair, but he was aware he looked haggard.

"Hi," he said and then busied himself putting sugar in his half coffee.

"Hello," she smiled back, "You like sweet coffee?"

"Why do you ask?" he said, before he realized he was still pouring sugar in his coffee. "Oh, damn. What am I doing?"

Nora giggled and took the cup, "I'll dump it for you. It must be the medications, huh?"

"Yah, most likely," Kid mumbled, thankful that Nora gave him an excuse.

"How you feeling these days?" Bernard asked.

"Much better, actually." Kid answered, "Zach has let me be up the last couple days."

As Nora gave him a new cup of coffee, she said, "He overdid though. So, he has to take it cool today."

"Do you want to talk privately?" the Sheriff asked.

"Yah, I guess it might be a good idea." Kid nodded. "We can have our coffee first, huh?"

"Okay."

Nora put a plate of cookies on the table, "You must try these. These were left from the dance Saturday night. Did you make it out? I don't remember seeing you there," Nora asked Bernard.

"No, didn't make it. We had company. We have a new resident now. Savannah is going to stay with us. She got a job at Merton Retirement home like the wife, Margie."

"Oh, are you an RN, also?" Nora asked the girl in her mid-twenties.

"No, an aide," she answered modestly.

"A good aide is worth her weight in gold," Nora said. "They give the most care to the patients."

Savannah said shyly. "I try."

"That's all anyone can ask," Nora said. "Are you from around here?"

Bernard answered and Kid noticed that Savannah seemed relieved not have to talk about herself. "She is from Iowa, but lived in Milwaukee until recently. Margie and I invited her out here. I thought she should get to meet you folks. You have so many people her age around."

Kid watched her and could see she was dying a million deaths. He tried to think of something to say to her, but couldn't think of a thing.

Nora answered, "We actually do, and guess what? We have a wedding dance coming up in a month. Matt and Diane are getting married May 22nd. So, there'll be a barn dance! You have to come to that!"

Savannah returned a small, polite smile. Kid was certain that she thought it would be about as much fun as cleaning the barn with her bare hands.

"We'll be there, for sure!" Bernard chuckled. "I almost feel like one of Matt and Diane's little cupids!"

Nora giggled, "You were! I hope you can make it. They'd be pleased."

"Well, my Margie is waiting on us, so I suppose I should talk to you, Kid."

"Okay," Kid said as he got up. "Want to come to my room?"

"You be okay here with Nora?" the man asked Savannah.

"Of course," Nora laughed. "We can visit without you guys. Go."

In his room, the two men sat by the window. Kid cleared his throat, "Sounds serious."

"Could be. Got a couple calls from California. The penitentiary reported that Haskell, Scab's brother, was there to visit Scab on Friday. Had a long, cryptic talk but it was about looking for something for Scab. He told him to take Geist with him. A pencil? Does that make sense?"

"Yah," Kid's face fell. "Haskell is in the motorcycle club, but he can get in to see Scab because he has no criminal record and he's a relative. Geist follows those two around like a puppy. The pencil is me. I know what they meant."

"Scab told him to talk to Levi? This Levi would give him the cash to go get it."

"Yah, Levi holds the clean money for the Horde. At least, Haskell doesn't know where I am."

"Bad news. Your attorney called last night. Night before last, there was a break-in at his law office. Only one file was missing. Yours. We assume it was them and they now have the information about the farm. Is there any other place they'd look for you?"

"Nah," Kid barely could talk. "I'm as good as dead. I got to get out of here. I don't want to have those two come around here. I have to go."

"Where?" Sheriff Bernard asked. "You have no other place that I can see. You stay put. We'll handle this. I'll talk to Carl and Elton. I also contacted the Highway Patrol, so they are on the lookout for those two. Hopefully, we can pick them up before they get this far. Kid, are they usually 'arrestable'?"

"Huh?"

"Like if we stop them, is there something we could hold them for? Like drugs or firearms?"

"Usually." Kid shook his head, "No, I'm not going to endanger everyone. I'll go back and face the music."

Bernard took out his pistol and handed it to Kid. "Might as well do it right here. Blow your head off. It'd be faster."

Kid stared at the man, "You nuts?"

"No, but you are. I don't want any more talk like that. Hear me?"

"But . . ."

"No. You stay put. We can keep you safe. End of story. When are you scheduled for detox?"

"When will they be here? No point, if they're on their way. Hell, I should just OD."

"You're bound and determined to make me fill out paperwork, aren't you?"

"I just meant, what difference does it make?"

"Just could be a matter of life and death whether you're on the ball or not. You talk to Zach and let me know. You can stay at my place for that, if you want."

Kid's eyes flashed, "No way. It might be safe, but I won't do that. Not when you have company."

"Savannah isn't company. She's family. Don't worry about it."

"No, I'll be okay. I'll have Zach talk to you though. Okay?" Kid was definite.

"Okay. If you 'forget', I'll be calling him. You're still welcome to come to our place. Know that."

"Thanks. I do appreciate you letting me know what's going on."

"How long do you think it'll take them to get here?"

"Depends on if they are in a hurry or not."

"Yah, that's true." The Sheriff stood, "You coming back out to the kitchen?"

"No, I don't think so. Bye."

"I'll keep in touch."

He left and Kid moved over to the bed. He slumped into it and felt the world close in around him. He couldn't believe how he was sitting there actually thinking about working on a greenhouse and maybe even asking a girl to a wedding dance! What the hell was he thinking? He was nothing but an ex-con drug addict with a price on his head.

A bit later, Nora knocked and then came in when Kid didn't answer. "What did he have to say?"

Kid shrugged, "I have to leave, Nora. I won't put you guys in any danger. I won't do that."

"Kid, Bernard did tell me that he didn't have good news. I took the liberty of calling Carl. He's on his way over."

"Nora, it'll do no good. I know you mean well; but it's my mess. I have to face it now. There's no other talk about it."

"Byron is on his way over, too."

Kid had to laugh, "And where's Elton?"

"He'll be here as soon as he finishes the tire he was working on." Nora giggled, "You are beginning to know us too well! Want to come out to the kitchen, or not?"

"No." He looked at Nora in despair, "What am I going to do, Nora? What am I going to do?"

She put her arms around him and hugged him, "You're going to put up a good fight. You're not going to give in. I won't let any of my baby chicks do that!"

Byron came in just then, "I heard you had bad news, huh?"

"Yah, not unexpected though," Kid said. "I was getting too cocky. I thought I could make it all work somehow. I forgot about reality."

"Reality has more than one interpretation," Byron said as Carl and Father Vicaro came in.

"Frank was trying to beat me at chess, so I brought him along. Okay?" Carl asked, not waiting for an answer.

Nora smiled, "I'll go bring coffee. Elton's on his way."

The men all made small talk for a couple minutes and then Elton and Nora came in with the coffee pot. Elton reached down, gave Kid a hug and then said, "So, what did Bernard have to say?"

"Haskell and Geist are two of Scab's minions. Haskell is his brother and he visited him at the pen. He sent them for me."

"You sure?" Carl asked.

"Positive. Bernard said they were looking for a pencil. They're the erasers. It's code."

"Oh. And you are the pencil?"

"Yah, I know. Unless someone else in the pen disrespected him, it's me."

"Bernard said two nights ago, someone broke into my attorney's office and stole my file. It is all there about the land. They're on their way. How much time they are going to take is anyone's guess," Kid explained.

Carl squinted at him, "Did Zach say how long detox would take? Since you have been on these meds and stuff?"

"No. I thought a week or less. Why?"

"Need to get that out of the way before they show up. Huh, guys?" Carl looked at the other men.

"You guys can't handle these thugs. I need to go somewhere else," Kid protested.

"We'll work this out." Carl commanded. "Hell, they're coming here anyway! You're staying here. End of story. Are you going to Bernard's for your detox?"

"No, he has company now. I won't do that."

"Want to stay here?" Elton asked. "We can work—."

"No, I already scared these kids enough," Kid was adamant.

"My place," Father Vicaro asserted. "We got the room, and Father Landers worked in a rehab center out West for a time. You stay with us! I'm pretty sure that those cyclists won't look for you at our place. Besides, Sister Abigail would whack them into submission in no time. I have spoken! That's where you'll be."

"Good idea!" Carl slapped Vicaro on the back.

"It is a good idea," Byron concurred. "The Horde won't have any reason to look for you there, would they?"

"Not that I can think of, but I don't know. I'm not real big on religion, but I'm a Lutheran."

"So, we all have our deficiencies," Vicaro chuckled. "Maybe I can convert you!"

Kid looked at Byron in panic, but Byron laughed, "He was just kidding. Don't worry."

"Keep telling yourself that, Ellison." Vicaro smirked, "That's settled now. What else?"

"I think we need to talk to Zach and Bernard. We should have a meeting of the clanners and figure this out." Elton decided. "Right now, Kid needs some rest. I'll get everyone together tonight. Sound good?"

The other men all agreed and no one was asking Kid. After they left, he just sat on his bed and stared at the wall. A few minutes later, Nora came in with some tea. "Zach talked to Elton and Zach said to give you this pill, so you can relax. He'll see you tonight. I thought you and I could have a tea party."

"That's what we need, alright," Kid grumbled.

"Don't be a Grinch," Nora reprimanded him as she poured their tea. "Here, take this pill so I don't drop it, or something. Then we can visit."

Kid took the pill and put some sugar in his tea. Nora smiled, "She is pretty, isn't she?"

"Who?" Kid asked from out of his gloomy fog.

"Savannah."

"Oh, yah." Kid replied without much thought.

"I noticed you noticed."

Kid was taken by surprise, "What are you talking about?"

"Savannah."

"She seems shy," he responded absently.

"Yes, she is. She is quite uncomfortable around new people."

"I know that feeling."

"Then you two could be good for each other."

Kid wrinkled his brow, "Are you matchmaking, now? We just heard someone is coming to kill me, and you're matchmaking? Are you nutty?"

Nora was not swayed. "They may not succeed, you know. Then what?"

"Nora, I'm still a drug addicted ex-con. She seems like a decent person. The last thing she needs is me."

"Young man, you're a decent person, too. I'm good at this stuff, so I know. Don't try to kid me! You won't go to Bernard's because Savannah is there. I could've told you that before Elton asked."

Kid chuckled, "You're something else."

"Maybe, but I'm right, aren't I?"

"Yes, I was going to go there until I found out she was there. Now, no way in hell! It's not exactly putting your best foot forward. She seems to be a real sweetheart. Of course, I didn't talk to her much."

"I did. She is a nice gal. Her husband left her for another woman. She is trying to get her life in order again."

"How did you find all that out in such a short time?"

"We visited and I asked her." Nora smiled, "She is very nice and quite lonely. She didn't say that, I just know it. I'm not wrong that often."

"Yah, but you think I'm nicer than I am."

"I have your number, Kid. I don't have many illusions about you. You have your weaknesses. We all do. You're a decent sort—headed down the wrong trail. Now if you turn your saddle around, you'll be okay."

"You are a busy one!" Kid laughed. "I'm thinking about my demise while you are trying to hook me up with some woman."

"Savannah is not some woman!" Nora frowned. "She is a nice girl. At least, it's worth getting to know her. You both had a spark of interest."

"I know, even I could tell that. Nora, I'm not what anyone needs."

"Not yet. We have to start where we begin! I'll help you. We can always recruit Grandma."

"Do you agree that me going there for detox wouldn't be good?"

"No way. She probably already knows about it, though. But, not to worry. After she gets to know you better, she'll like you as much as the rest of us do. If she doesn't, there's something wrong with her. Oh, by the way, did I mention she is coming out tomorrow? We are making mints for the wedding and you're going to help. So, we need to find something for you to wear. Do you need that dark green sweatshirt washed? It looks good on you. Are your blue jeans clean?"

"Have you gone daft?"

"No, my boy, I have not. I'm not going to waste a day moping around when we can be thinking of something positive and happy. If it turns out to be a pipe dream; oh well." Nora got up and hugged him, "Seriously, I don't want you to sink under the weight of all this. I want you to have something fun to think about."

As she picked up the cups and started toward the door.

"Nora?" he winked, "Thanks."

-26-

Kid leaned back on his bed, still smiling about Nora. Elton was a very lucky man. Kid was certain there weren't too many like Nora around. He was beginning to get depressed again when Kitten came in. She rarely came in when he was awake. He sat up on his good arm and asked, "What's up?"

"Nuffin," She answered as she sat in her chair.

"Where's Cotton?"

"All gone."

"I'm sure she'll be back soon. Huh?"

"Okay." Kitten climbed into her chair and held the afghan from Grandma up to her chin.

Kid watched her, "You okay, Kitten?"

She shrugged. "No Gopher."

"Are you lonesome for Gopher?"

"Gone."

"Do you need someone to play with?"

"Okay," she perked up. "Kid play?"

He had only asked a question, not expecting to be part of the answer. When he noticed her smile, he relented. "Okay, let's find something to do."

She ran out of the room and he hoped to have a reprieve, but he was wrong. She came back with her doll and two dresses. She brought them over to his bed and handed them to him, "Kid do?"

"I don't know if I can with one hand."

She looked disappointed, so he said, "I can try."

The two worked together to get the dress on the doll. Kid came to the conclusion that folks who made doll clothes never tried to put them on a doll! They were struggling with it, when Nora came in. She giggled, "What are you two doing?"

"Kid try," Kitten explained.

213

"These clothes aren't made to fit over a rigid doll! It's just dumb to give these to a little kid!" Kid blabbed, "I almost broke the doll's arm off!"

Kitten's eyes were huge, "Kid broke!"

"I see you did get it on though. Good work." Nora smiled to Kitten, "Marly is bringing Gopher over to play."

"Okay?" the little girl asked the biker.

"It's okay. I have to take my nap anyway."

"Night," she said as she took her doll and ran out of the room.

Nora pulled the quilt over him, "Thanks. She was in the dumps. I thought she might just take a nap. I didn't know she'd wake you."

"I wasn't asleep. I felt sorry for her. She's a good, little kid. I still think the folks that sew those dresses should have their heads examined. They should have Velcro like Katie made for me."

"I agree." Nora pulled his shades, "Get some rest."

Later, Jeff knocked at Kid's door. "Hi, can we visit or do you need to rest?"

"No, I'd like to visit. I slept well. What are you doing today?"

"Hiding from Carl!" Jeff chuckled as he pulled up the stool. "He's a lunatic! It's raining and he still wants to dig more holes! Finally, Mo told him to dig one six foot deep, because if he didn't come in—he'd need it!"

"Do they argue alot?"

"Not at all. They get along great!" Jeff explained, "They are both full of it! They are going to plant every square inch of that place if someone doesn't shut them down!"

"I know, and don't tell Carl," Kid confided. "But it's driving Elton bugs because he doesn't know what he's planting by the road."

"No one knows, not even Mo. Carl says it's a surprise."

"What do you think it is?"

"Nothing would surprise me! I feel like I'm living with a maniac!" Jeff laughed. "I heard you had some interesting developments in your world, huh?"

"Yah. I knew it was coming, just didn't know when. Jeff, if it was you, would you waste time trying to get clean just to get beat to death?"

Jeff studied the man, "No. I wouldn't—not just to be beat to death. I would do it, though . . . for several reasons."

"What would those be?"

"First, just so I knew I did it. For myself! Also, I might be able to keep from getting beaten if I was thinking clearly, and also, I might not end up dead. Why?"

"Isn't it a waste of time?"

"Never too late to improve. Now, if I was certain I was cashing it in immediately, I'd be getting things in order with the Big Guy. I know you're not big on that, but it's a good idea to think about it anyway. You know, forever can be a very long time. When I'm facing eternity, I want to be on the winning side."

"Makes sense." Kid pursed his lips, "Honestly, what do you think the hereafter is like?"

Jeff looked him straight in the eye, "I have no idea. None, but I do trust that even if I just have to be alone with my own soul, I'd like to live with good thoughts. Spending forever mulling over the crap I've pulled, wouldn't be fun."

"No, I guess not. I doubt you have as much crap as I have."

"There are all kinds of sin, you know. Pride, lying, lack of faith. Lust." Jeff grinned.

Kid teased with a devilish grin, "Have you been lusting, young man?"

"I confess!" Jeff chuckled. "Guess what? Kathleen and I have visited on the phone a few times. She put in a request to her boss to come out for the wedding. That's so far away!"

"Nothing stopping you from going to see her before then, is there?"

"There kinda is. I start working and I need to save money to get Matt's wedding present."

"Hey, you're his best friend? What do you think he'd like for a wedding present?"

"I don't know. Matt likes all kinds of stuff, but there is very little he's crazy about except Diane, Skipper, and his stupid begonia!"

Kid laughed like crazy, "That's what Grandma and I decided. We had an idea. What do you think? We thought we might get them something like a small greenhouse. Think Matt would like that?"

Jeff thought, "Yah, he really would. I don't know about Diane."

"Oh, we forgot about her." Kid chuckled.

Jeff shook his head in despair, "No wonder you don't have a girlfriend!"

Kid beamed, "Guess what? I met someone this morning! Too bad I'm clinging on the ledge, because I think I could get interested in her. She is pretty and nice. I don't know what in hell she would want with me, but I can dream."

Jeff punched him on his good arm, "Good for you! Who is she?"

"Bernard's niece." Kid crossed his eyes, "The sheriff's niece. That should go over well!"

"I heard about her. Her name is something from down South. Georgia?"

"Savannah. How did you know about her? Have you met her? I suppose you have designs on her, huh?"

"No designs. I'm pretty well stuck on Kathleen. I heard about her because Carl and Alex are friends. They yak on the phone all the time. Want me to tell you what I know?" Jeff's eyes were gleaming with eagerness.

"Sure. Don't know why? It's just a foolish thought!"

"Better than no thought at all! She was married about four years ago. Her husband was a real jerk according to Bernard. They were in a small car accident the first year they were married and she got a head injury. She healed up, but has a slight stutter from it. He made fun of her mercilessly. The more he did it, the more trouble she had with her stutter. She wanted a family, but he told her he didn't want kids with a retard who stuttered. He cheated on her, and before long, had a girl pregnant. He divorced Savannah and married the other woman last year. Savannah was shattered and it took her a while to start rebuilding her life. Alex and Margie knew about a job here in Merton, so encouraged her to start over out here. Alex talked to Carl because he knows there are a lot of young folks her age in the clan and he'd like her to meet some new people."

"Wow! You should be a detective."

"Heaven's no! I live with one and between him, Vicaro, who thinks he's a master spy, and Bernard; they make me crazy!" Jeff laughed. "Want to go play checkers with the girls?"

"Sounds good." Kid got off his bed, "So you think I should get straight?"

Jeff frowned, "Would you be asking me so many times if you wanted to get crooked?"

Kid thought a minute, "No. I thought I might catch you in a weak moment."

A few minutes later, the men were sitting up to the table with their little checker prodigies. "I think we should teach them chess and then enter them in the world championship." Jeff suggested. "Of course, we'd have to travel with them on their world tour."

"Of course," Kid grinned. "For them."

Grandma came by and watched them a minute. Kid said, "Grandma, I asked Jeff about our mission. He thinks it would be good idea for him, but what about her?"

"Good point."

"Hey, how about a tape system for inside the place so she can listen to music?" Kid suggested.

Jeff nodded, "That's supposed to be good for growing things, too. I wish I could come up with a good idea."

"If we do this, it'll be expensive. You can be part of our mission, too; if Kid says it's okay. What do you think, Kid?"

"I think we can use another missionary!"

"Yea gads," Grandma laughed. "Better put your game away. We have to get dinner on. There's a big meeting tonight."

"Yah, I'm going to help with chores," Jeff said.

Grandma giggled, "And Kid's going to help cook."

That evening right after dinner, folks began to gather. The men all got their coffees and settled around the dining room table. The kids went off to race cars in the hallway, while the ladies met in the kitchen to talk wedding plans.

Carrie and Elton knocked on Kid's door and he called them in, "I'm ready to come out. I had to change my shirt after I spilled all over it. I'll be right out."

"We wanted to talk, first," Elton said.

Carrie was Kevin's pretty, blonde wife, "Dad told me that you wanted a checking account that has some safety features. I drew up the papers for you. If you want this, you can only sign a check for amounts of fifty dollars and under. Anything over that, and you will need either Elton or someone else to co-sign. Other than that, it's just like any other account. Since you're a single person, it's a good idea to have a co-signer anyway in case something would happen to you. We can set it so that you need two signatures on a check over fifty. I could do it for you, but since I work at the bank, it isn't a good idea."

"You mean, I could write a check for up to fifty by myself, but the other two couldn't?"

"Yes. Do you have any idea who you'd like to be the other signature?"

"Ah, not really. But that sounds great. What do I need to do?"

"Sign this card, and then Dad can sign it. As soon as you get another signature, we'll be all set," Carrie smiled as she handed him the card. "The check blanks will be here in ten days, but you can use counter checks until then."

"Don't I need money in the account?" Kid grinned.

"I have a cashier's check here for the pasture rent. I wrote it out the same as for last year? Just for this year, for now. Is that okay?" Elton asked.

"What about what I owe you?"

"I'll collect, don't worry."

Kid grimaced, "That's what I'm afraid of."

"I know I would be, if I was you!" Carrie giggled.

"Oh, hey, is Jeff still here?"

"Yes, why?"

"I should talk to him. Maybe he'll sign for me."

Elton nodded, "He'd be a good choice. I'll send him in."

Carrie took the card, "If he will, tell him I have the card. Okay?"

"Thanks Carrie."

Kid was combing his hair when Jeff came in, "Elton said you wanted to see me?"

Kid explained the situation and Jeff listened carefully. "If you're sure you want me to, I would be happy to do it. But Kid, I don't want it to be something we fight over. I mean like if you want to buy something and I say no."

"If you were unreasonable and it wasn't for dope, I'd go ask Elton."

"Okay! It sounds like you are already working a way around it! I'll go talk to Carrie."

"Jeff," Kid shook his hand, "Thanks."

"Say that after Elton and I go shopping!"

"What have I done?"

The decisions that evening included the decision that some of the guys would go up and make certain there were no tracks to Schroeder's on the home place. The gates would all be closed even though Kid was rather certain Haskell and Geist had no idea how large an area a section was.

The men were able to convince Kid that even if he left Merton now, it would not make anyone safer. Those bikers already knew he was there, so they'd show up there no matter what. They probably wouldn't leave as long as they knew he had a connection there.

They also decided that the rectory would be the best place for Kid to detox and be more difficult to locate. Bernard had already notified the State Patrol and County Sheriff's office. Everyone would keep vigilant.

Bernard also had some news. Haskell and Geist were still in California as of that afternoon. They had made a large withdrawal from a local bank that day. Kid confirmed it was the bank the Horde used for 'clean' money. They would likely be on their way by morning.

Then Bernard made a grave statement, "I'm working on a way to make this their final attempt to look for Kid. If they get deterred without thinking they've achieved their goal, they may just come back. Some of us have our heads together and we want this to be the end. Just getting rid of these two may only stand to irritate them more. Just know, I'm working on it. Any ideas would be helpful."

Zach figured it would take less than four days for Kid to detox. He had wanted to give him more time to heal, but was confident that he could begin in a day or so. He'd take some blood tests that night and let them know the results the next day. Vicaro related that a room was ready for him and Landers would be his bosom buddy for a few days. Everything was set.

That night, when Zach took his blood samples, Kid was very apprehensive, "Zach, I'm so worried. I just don't know—."

"No, you don't. None of us do. Can you just humor us for a while? This one time?"

"I have no choice, do I?"

"I love the vote of confidence you have in us." Zach put the specimens in his bag, "I'm going to zonk you good tonight, because I imagine you'll have yourself all wound up otherwise."

"Yah."

Zach sat down, "I know you're worried. We all are. Honestly, we wouldn't be doing this if we knew another way, safer or easier. You're one of us now; whether you like it or not. We're going to watch out for you and ourselves. I know you don't like to pray, but now might be a good time to give it a try. What can it hurt?"

Kid's eyes reddened, "If this all goes to hell, I want you to know that I really appreciate all you've done for me."

"I know." Zach smiled, "Thanks. Get some rest."

After everyone was asleep, Kid was still trying to get to sleep. He was a nervous wreck. He heard the door open and thought it might be Kitten. Elton said, "Hi, see you're awake yet. Want to talk?"

Kid sat up and burst out in tears, "What if this is all for nothing?"

Elton put his arms around him, "It's worthwhile, Kid. I just know it. It'll be good."

Kid sobbed for a bit and then Elton said, "Want to rest now, son?"

"Yah, I think I can."

Elton helped him get covered up and then said good night. As he went toward the door, Kid said, "Elton, you're the best."

Elton smiled back, "You aren't too bad yourself."

Kid was just falling to sleep when he saw the door open and felt Cotton jump on his feet. He said quietly, "Good night, Kitten."

The little girl answered from her chair, "Night, Kid."

-27-

He didn't sleep very well during the night, but tried to keep as calm as possible to not disturb Kitten. He would not allow himself to yell at her again. As he lay there listening to the distant thunder, he thought over the events of the day. He honestly figured he'd be dead within a week and was only doing the detox because these crazy people seemed to think it was important. What did he care? He knew it wasn't. If he did live, he wouldn't stay clean.

He was amazed by all the men besides Kevin and Matt who came to the meeting that night. Josh, Darrell, Danny, Harrington, and others. The Fathers Bart, Landers, and Vicaro showed up. It was unbelievable. The clanners from Bismarck were all there, who drove all the way out there to offer their help. They actually didn't know him from a hole in the ground. He thought about Josh, Matt, and Jeff offering to sit with him while he was going through withdrawal. They were a good bunch. A guy could do a lot worse than have friends like them.

He chuckled when he thought about how the Horde threatened their member's lives to insure their loyalty. These crazy people were simply loyal. He knew instinctively, he could trust any one of them with his life. Hell, that was exactly what he was doing!

He thought about Jeff and Zach telling him to pray. He shook his head, 'Yah, that'd make God's day. He'd think because my back was against the wall, I'd crawl back to Him and expect Him to help. Not bloody likely.'

Before long, he was crafting a prayer in his mind. He didn't say it, but he decided what he would say, if he was ever going to do it. Finally, with tears rolling down his cheeks, he prayed silently to the God he had ignored for so long.

Kid pulled his blanket over his shoulder and tried to sleep. He jumped at a loud crack of thunder followed by the bright, flash of lightning. Kitten sprang off the chair and ran out of the room, only to return in less than a second. She sat back on her chair, with her eyes wide open, shivering with fear. Still, she sat there.

"It's okay, Kitten," Kid said, realizing she was scared to death. "You can go see Elton or Jackson."

"No, watch Kid," she answered, with tears rolling down her cheeks.

"It's okay. I'll be okay. Promise."

"Kitten watch Kid," she said before she jumped at the latest bolt of lightning and clap of thunder.

Kid heard the little Grey Hawk feet patter toward Elton and Nora's room. Kitten did not move, but sat there, terrified. Kid got out of bed and went over to her, "It'll be okay, Kitten."

"Kitten watch Kid," she trembled.

"Will you sit on my lap in the rocker to watch? Come, bring your blanket. Okay?"

She nodded and walked with him to the rocker. He sat down and she climbed on his lap. "Careful of my cast. Okay? There, now relax. We'll watch over each other, okay?"

"Okay," she said trying to be brave. With the next clap of thunder, she shuddered and then patted his arm. "It be better, Kid. Okay?"

He tucked the blanket around her and started to rock, "Okay, Kitten. You're taking good care of me."

In the morning, Elton found the two sound asleep in the rocking chair. He was just pulling the door closed when they woke up. He smiled, "I see your little sentry protected you."

"Yes," Kid helped her down, "You did a good job, didn't you? You kept me safe."

"Okay," Kitten replied seriously before she ran off to get dressed for the day.

Kid shook his head, "She stayed with me, even though she was terrified."

"Thanks for watching over her. Jackson had Clarence in his room and we had the other three in ours! Those little guys are really frightened by storms. I don't suppose it helped that they were left alone so much. Their fears probably fed on each other." Elton came over to Kid, "How you doing? Did you get any sleep?"

"I was as scared as Kitten, but not of the storm. It was good for me to rock her. It helped me as much as it helped her." Kid shrugged.

He caught Elton's eye, but said nothing. Then Elton asked, "What is it?"

"I prayed last night for probably the first time in years. All I got was a thunderstorm."

"Huh?" Elton smiled, "You just told me how much it helped you."

Kid stopped cold, and then began to smile slowly, "You're right. You're saying . . . oh, I guess I did get help. I'm such an idiot. Elton, I think I'd like to talk to Byron before this all goes down."

"Sure. After breakfast? I can drop you off on my way to work. Marly can bring you back when she helps with the mints. I hear you were drafted, also?"

"Yah," Kid grinned, "I think your wife may have had ulterior motives."

"You mean Bernard's niece? She jabbered for twenty minutes last night telling me all about it. She loves that kind of stuff. I have to say though; she is usually a good judge of that sort of thing."

"I did think Savannah was nice," Kid said. "However, my situation is not exactly conducive to courting."

"Never stopped my Nora. She would introduce a guy to a gal while he was being fitted by an undertaker!" Elton chuckled. "You might as well give in, Kid. Anyway, it has to be more fun to think about than those Horders."

Kid laughed, "It is difficult to be down around you guys."

"Any damned fool can pout. Never solves a thing." Elton went to the door, "I better get out there before my coffee is all sucked up. I'll plan on giving you a ride to the church. Might want to call Preacher Man so he'll have a pot brewing for you."

"I'll do that," Kid smiled.

As nervous as he was, he spent most of his time smiling while he was getting dressed. Nora had washed his green sweatshirt and blue jeans for him, and even put a bottle of English Leather cologne out for him. She was definitely matchmaking!

He shaved and showered, taking great care to comb his hair and look nice. He dressed and then made his bed as best he could with one arm. Grandma came in as he was finishing his bed and took the other side of the blanket. "You look nice today. Do I smell English Leather?"

"Yah. Nora left it here for me."

"Savannah?" Grandma grinned. "I saw the sparks. Seems like a nice girl. You have good taste."

"I hope she doesn't."

"Stop! Nobody talks about my relative that way, even himself!" Grandma said vehemently, "You're just fine! Oh, did you think any more about the greenhouse?"

"Yes, there is this one," Kid opened a magazine and showed her the page, "It's six by eight foot and can be movable or permanent. Do you know if they want to stay in the cabin permanently?"

"No, I don't." Grandma said. "That's good thinking. How much is it?"

"It can be added on to and such. The basic kit is a hundred and fifty dollars in a kit, but three hundred all put together. Too much? I got some rent money from Elton, so I can put a good share in."

"Three hundred would be way too much, but if we each put in $50, that would be about right. Could you and Jeff put it together with the instructions? How much will it cost to put it together?"

"I don't know. If I'm around and all, I could probably do it with help. My arm you know."

Grandma took his arm, "You'll be around. Got it?"

He hugged her, "Is it okay if I say I love you, Grandma?"

"I think it's more than okay. I love you, too. Talk to Jeff and see if Elton can give us a place to do it. Okay?"

"I will." He opened the door for her, "You know what? I'm happier than I've been in a long time."

"It looks good on you."

While Kid helped Grandma make sausage, hash browns, and scrambled eggs for breakfast, Nora gathered the ingredients for the wedding mints. "Diane said her colors are pale peach and dark green. I don't suppose you could help us make little peach rosebuds, could you Kid?"

"I can show you how, but I only have one hand. I can't make them. They aren't hard to do. How many are you making?"

"About three hundred."

"What? We'll be here all day!" Kid gasped.

Nora chuckled, "Did you have some place else to be?"

"No, I guess not. I can show you, but a mold would be faster."

"They're so ordinary." Nora frowned. "We'll have lots of help. Mo is coming over, so she will help. Marly will be here. And your best candy maker, Clarissa gets out of Kindergarten at noon!"

"Oh no!" Kid groaned.

"In case you forgot, Savannah will be here. Alex is dropping her off about nine-thirty. By the way, you look nice today!" Nora winked.

Kid gave her a hug, "No, I didn't forget. Thanks for the cologne."

After breakfast, Kid walked down to the car with Elton. "It's a good rain, huh? How do you think the crops will be this year?"

Elton smiled, "Getting the farmer's itch?"

"No. We were more of a pasture type . . . not plowing. It's not right that you paid rent and then blocked off the pasture from my place. You should put something in there."

"It won't hurt it to rest for a while. We are moving the beef cattle over to Olson's tomorrow. They'll be good over there this year. After we get the Horde mess cleared up, we will use this one and yours for horses and dairy. Oh, I talked to Jerald about the horses. He has a glue factory that would be great for Kitten. I told him to buy it. He'll bring it out next week."

"What is it?"

"A gentle, old bay. He said you could play baseball under her and she wouldn't get nervous. He said he might be able to find another one of Tornado's kin. He will let me know."

"Elton, I thought a lot last night. I want to pay for Kitten's horse and my share of the greenhouse before I go to detox. I also would like you to sign a power of attorney or something; so that if I die soon, you can get my place. I want you to have it and use whatever you make on it for the Grey Hawk kids' education. I'm asking you to make me a promise, okay?"

Elton stopped walking, "You don't need to do that Kid. We aren't after your land."

"I know. I want to do this. You and Nora have treated me like family since I showed up. I wasn't exactly sweet and cuddly either. I appreciate it more than you can imagine."

"No, I do imagine. Lloyd and Katherine were there for me, more than once." Elton put his hand on the young man's shoulder, "If you're certain, we can call my attorney, Mr. Wolf, and have him draw up the papers. It sounds like you need a will."

225

"Yes, I guess I do. Sooner, rather than later." Kid helped Elton pull the huge garage door open, "Hey, can Jeff and I build Matt's greenhouse in here?"

"Matt's greenhouse? So, you guy decided to get it, huh?"

Kid explained the whole thing and Elton asked a few questions. Then he said, "Wanna take the old pickup?"

"Can we? I'd love that."

"Why not? I don't think that you should build it in the garage. Matt is in and out of here every day when he gives Lloyd his ride. He'd see it right away. I have a better idea."

"Oh, oh."

"Never you mind," Elton squinted. "I'm going to order that big one, the fourteen by sixteen on a foundation. You guys order Matt's at the same time. We can build them together, and he'll never know one is for him. Just don't tell him."

"What did Nora say?"

"She mumbled something and crossed her eyes. I think that means she's okay with it," Elton laughed.

"You must make her life hell."

"I believe you may be right."

Elton dropped Kid off at the steps of the church office and waved as he pulled out of the yard. Kid turned slowly and wondered if this was really a good idea. Then he realized he only had a few days left on this planet, so who cared! He might as well do something decent for a change. He could do anything for a few days. He chuckled at his own stupidity and went up the steps.

Byron met him in the office, "Suzy isn't here yet, so I made the coffee. She is such a shirker."

Just then she came in, "What you saying, Grinchboss? And worse, what did you do to the coffee? Yuk! How many scoops of coffee did you put in it?"

"One."

"Only one," she wrinkled her nose. "That's colored water! Don't you know how to make coffee?"

"Why do they make scoops so small then? They should be the right size to make a pot of coffee," Byron defended himself.

226

"Go away," Suzy took the coffee can. "I'll call you when the coffee's done."

Kid chuckled and Suzy kissed his cheek, "Morning, you look very nice today."

"So do you," Kid smiled.

"Oh brother!" Byron groaned. "I'm going in my office until you two are done flattering each other."

Suzy giggled, "Better go with him or he'll whine."

In the office, Byron offered Kid a chair. "I'm glad you called me this morning. I was coming over to see you but I knew it'd be a candy factory over there. How's it going?"

The two men had a long talk. Kid explained about his night, his idea for a will and how he prayed. Suzy brought them some coffee and then pulled the door closed. "Byron, I've done some awful stuff. Really bad. If I tell you all of it, you'll be sick."

"Doubt that. I never thought that outlaw motorcycle gangs were noted for their virtue. What about the war? Did you talk to anyone about your dreams?"

"Yes, I did. I talked to Matt and the veterans."

Then Kid explained about the little girl that started his nightmares. They talked it all through and Byron confirmed what Matt had told him. It wasn't his fault. He was more able to accept that now. "I think I got that now, but the stuff I did with the Horde; it was bad."

"What did you do?"

"I moved product, sold dope, and helped enforce their policies. See, I used to beat up folks who couldn't pay or somehow disrespected us. I never killed anyone, but I know I hurt some, bad. I was horrible and it wasn't a snap decision, like with the little girl. It was thought out. I knew what I was going to do and did it."

"I thought that, when you said you were an enforcer." Byron leaned back in his chair. "Kid, do you remember much about Paul of the New Testament?"

"Just that he was an apostle and he wrote most of the New Testament. Why? He wasn't an enforcer for outlaw bikers."

"Well, he kinda was. His name was Saul of Tarsus and he was one of the main persecutors of Christians! He arrested, tortured and killed them. He was good at it. He wasn't a nice guy."

"Really?"

Byron reached a New Testament behind him in the bookshelf, opened it, and read from Acts 9. It told the story of Saul who had a conversion on the road to Damascus and became a follower of Jesus. "This man became one of the greatest apostles and like you said, wrote many books of the New Testament." He handed Kid the Bible, "Here. Take this and read it when you have time. Okay?"

Kid watched Byron blankly, but held out his hand to take the Bible. "I'll do that. You mean he was as bad as me?"

"Most likely worse."

"Hm. I never thought of persecution as being like beating someone. I guess it was, huh? I'll be darned. I always thought it was nicer."

Byron chuckled, "For us reading it now, it is. For folks living back then, not a bit."

Kid turned the book over in his hands, "Pastor, I know that Lutherans don't have a confessional like the Catholics, but I wish we did."

"Come with me to the sanctuary, Harold. I'm sure God doesn't need a special place, but the sanctuary would be nice."

Kid followed Byron out of the office. On the way past Suzy's desk, Byron said, "Kid and I would like some privacy in the sanctuary now. Okay?"

"Okay."

After a very emotional time, ending with a word of prayer, the two men returned to the office. Kid felt the weight of the world had been lifted off his shoulders. He was still worried about his future and how he would do, but at least, his past was settled. He had been a bad man and hurt many people that he could never make it up to; but he knew he had a chance to do the right thing.

When they returned to the office, Suzy looked up. "Marly called. They're ready whenever you are," she smiled.

Pastor Marv and his secretary, Ruthie Harrington, Ian's wife, came out of his office. Ruthie gave Kid a hug and Marv said, "Hello Kid. Good to see you. Sorry I couldn't make it last night because I had this wedding. Please know, if there's anything I can do, I'm on board. Byron is keeping me up on the details."

"Thanks," Kid said, trying to contain his tears. "You guys have a restroom? Then I should get home to help."

Miriam, Marly, and Kid ran into the house to avoid the downpour. It was raining like crazy. "I thought you stole our flower maker!" Nora giggled. "Roads getting muddy?"

"If this keeps it up, they'll be slop," Marly said as she took Miriam's wet jacket off. "Now, you can play with Kitten. Gopher has been chomping at the bit to get over here since six this morning!"

"Kitten was getting worried since both her best buddies were gone," Nora smiled.

"Both?" Marly smiled and then winked at Kid, "Oh yah. You cut out on her, too."

"Sorry," Kid grinned. "I see you made the dough."

"Cream cheese, powdered sugar and food coloring in it. We put the peppermint in and Savannah gave her approval," Grandma giggled. "We were just about to take a break before we start the flowers."

Savannah smiled and Nora introduced Marly to her. Marly said, "Pleased to meet you. Have you met Kid?"

Savannah looked at him and nodded, her ponytail bouncing. Kid answered, "We met yesterday. We go way back, huh?"

The young lady giggled and nodded. The phone rang and Nora answered it. "It's for you, Kid."

"Me, who could that be?"

-28-

"Hello, this is Kid?"

"This is Jeff," the caller identified himself. "What did Grandma say about the greenhouse?"

"It's a go, the cheaper version; so we have to build it. Elton has a plan."

"If he's anything like Coot, I'm sure he does! Well, I have to go help that man pick up some more trees in town. Just wanted to know how much I will owe."

"Fifty each. Is that okay for you?"

"Perfect. Hey, I talked to Kathleen again last night. She got the time off! Kid, now I'm getting nervous."

"Don't be silly. She already knows you're a goon."

"How you doing with your date project?"

"Haven't even started."

"You only have a month! Get moving!"

Kid chuckled and hung up. When he did, he realized it had been a very long time since he had received a phone call like that. Just a friend, being friendly. He loved it.

The phone rang again before he got back to the table. Nora answered it and said, "Sure, he is here. It's for you."

"Me?" Kid frowned, and took the phone. "Hello."

"Hi, this is Kevin. I just heard the rabbits are on their way out from Bismarck. I'm in the middle of replacing a carburetor and can't leave. Could I ask you to turn the heat on and check the rabbit house?"

"How soon will they be here? Are they walking or hopping?"

Kevin chuckled, "They hitched a ride! They'll be delivered in little over an hour."

"Okay."

"Hey, Dad said to tell you that he talked to Wolf. He'll have the papers ready for Keith to bring out tomorrow when he helps move cattle. You helping, if Zach says you can?"

"Me? I never thought about it."

"We could use the help, since it's a work day for our usual crew."

"Sure, sounds like fun."

Kid made it all the way to the table. Marly smiled, "You are really popular."

"The rabbits will be delivered in about an hour, so Kev asked me to go check out the pen. He also asked if I was helping move cattle tomorrow, if Zach will let me."

"You can use my horse," Marly offered.

Kid turned to Savannah, "Do you ride? Have you ever been on a cattle drive?"

Savannah was shocked, "No."

"Want to try?"

She shrugged, and he smiled, "Marly, can we borrow Katie's horse for Savannah?"

"Of course, but Kid, you better show her how to ride first."

"Oh, yah. Can you wait until I find out from Zach if I can help?"

Savannah giggled, "Okay." Then her face tightened, "Who's Z-Z-Zach?"

"My doctor!" Kid laughed, "He's a pediatrician! He lives right across the fence from here."

She smiled shyly, seemingly relieved that he paid no attention to her stutter.

"Well, I better not sit here and drink coffee. I have to get ready for the rabbits."

"Show us quickly how to make the leaves and then go, okay? We want to get started." Nora said. "I can help you then, if you need help."

Kid showed them how to make a leaf and a rose bud. Nora had watched before, so she caught on right away. "Savannah, could I ask you to go out and help Kid, while I help these ladies? Only if you would like to?"

Savannah shrugged and got up to get her jacket. "Okay, I like b-b-bunnies."

The two went outside and negotiated the big puddles that were forming. When they got to the rabbit house, Kid opened the door. Inside were several hutches of various sizes and an open area with bedding. Kid could see that she was looking it all over. He began to explain, pointing out the equipment. "These are nesting boxes, pellet feeders, hay feeders, waterers, and heaters. We need to turn on the heat and fill their supplies. Okay?"

Savannah nodded. He turned on the heaters and then said, "I'll go carry some water, if you could start to fill the pellet feeders for me."

She nodded, "How?"

"Let me open the bag and here is the scoop. Can you do that?"

"Okay."

When he came back with the water, he helped her fill the hay feeders. They worked together and shared a few chuckles. But mostly, he talked. They seemed to have fun. Then he stepped back and surveyed their work. "We did a great job and finished before the rabbits got here! We are good!"

She smiled back and said, "We're g-g-g-g-."

Then she panicked and started to leave in embarrassment. He grabbed her hand, "No way. You're going to stay and help me, Savannah. I have a broken arm."

She looked at him with tear-filled eyes, "But I stutter."

He gave her a silly smile, "Big deal, I'm a drug addict."

She raised one eyebrow, "Well, I'm d-d-divorced."

He shook his head and smirked, "So, I'm an ex-con."

She took a deep breathe, "I b-b-burn the last batch of c-c-cookies."

"You win. That is the very worst!" Kid chortled. "I'll try to overlook it."

She giggled, "You'll t-t-try?"

"Now, are you going to help me?"

"Yes. D-d-do what?"

He looked around, "I forgot, we're just waiting for the rabbits. Hey, want to walk over to the pole barn and see the horses?"

She shrugged. He took her hand, "Okay, it's right over there, so we can see when the truck comes."

They looked over the horses. She was getting acquainted with Katie's Duchess by rubbing her nose, when the truck drove in. They went out to the yard and Kid waved the driver down to the rabbit house. The man helped them carry in the twelve rabbits.

After he left, Kid began taking the rabbits out of the boxes they arrived in when Kevin arrived. "Wow, you did a good job. Thanks, Kid. Hello?"

"Kevin Schroeder, this is Savannah. Sheriff Bernard's niece. She just moved to the neighborhood."

"Welcome." Kevin asked her, "What do you think of the rabbits?"

"Nice," she answered and then busied herself petting some younger bunnies in one of the boxes. "I like th-this one."

"It's an American Sable," Kid answered. "I think they are pretty, too."

"What do you think of them?" Kevin asked Kid.

"They look very healthy. Did we put them in the right hutches?"

"Looks like it to me. Have the little girls seen them yet?"

"No. They just arrived."

"Shall we go get them?" Kevin asked. "I know Gopher will love them."

"Okay. Savannah, do you want to come with us while we get the little girls, or do you want to play with the bunnies? We'll be right back."

"Stay," she smiled.

Once they were on the way to the house Kevin asked, "She's gorgeous but very shy, huh?"

"She has a stutter and is very self-conscious about it. She talks about as much as Kitten and Gopher."

"Seems friendly, though."

"I think she just needs to relax a little. She is going to help with the cattle tomorrow, if Zach says I can."

"You old devil." Kevin grinned, "You're sparking, huh?"

"What is with you people?"

Kevin chuckled, and slapped him on the back.

The little girls were delighted with the bunnies and each got to hold one. Then Kevin had to get back to work. "Bye, girls." Kev hugged them both and then said, "I hear I might see you tomorrow when we move cattle, Savannah. I'm looking forward to having a pretty cowhand."

Savannah giggled, "F-f-f-f-all off horse!"

"Maybe, but you'll be prettier in the mud than Kid!"

Savannah and Kid took the girls back to the house and helped them with their coats. They all washed up and then the girls ran to play. "How do they look?" Nora asked.

"Very nice and healthy," Kid answered. "How are you coming with the mints?"

"We have half an hour before lunch and only made a couple dozen. You guys better get to work. Kid, could you help Savannah get started and then help set the table in the dining room? I have to hurry to pick up Clarissa."

When Elton and Harrington arrived for lunch, the beef stew was ready. Elton looked over the mint project and smiled, "I take it Cyclone Clarissa hasn't arrived from school!"

"No," Marly replied. "Nora isn't back yet. Should be any minute."

"Hello, you must be Savannah," Elton smiled. "This is Ian Harrington. Have these people been working you to death?"

She smiled at Harrington and said, "No."

Kid stepped in, "She helped me with the rabbits and then I introduced her to the horses. If Zach says I can help tomorrow, she'll help, too."

"Do you ride?"

"No. K-k-kid will show me."

"That'll be nice," Elton said, "Otherwise, you and I can supervise. Deal?"

She giggled softly, "Deal."

By the time lunch was over, Kid was beginning to hurt. Nora noticed and suggested that he rest a bit after she gave him his pills. He frowned and said, "I really don't want to."

"Want to get sick?"

"No, but . . ."

Nora raised her eyebrows, "Maybe you could rest while you read to the little girls? Then they might take a nap."

"Only if you promise to not let me sleep all afternoon."

"Promise."

They were all asleep before they finished the Golden book. Nora woke him after about half an hour. "You feel like you rested enough?"

"Is Savannah still here? Does she think I'm a sap?"

Nora smiled, "She is still here and I don't know if she thinks you're a sap. She knows you still aren't well, but she knew that before. Mo is here."

He washed up and came out to find all the mints finished. "You guys really worked. They look good."

"Mister Kid," Clarissa came over to him with a small plate of her candies, "Don't eat them, but can you say if I am a spurt?"

He looked them over carefully, "They're very good. Do you know this recipe?"

Her eyes got huge, "No, I wasn't home when they cooked them. Do I have to know it?"

"Experts should know."

"What can I do?" her face fell. "I wasn't here!"

"Why don't you ask them?"

The little girl studied his face and then smiled, "Oh, that would work."

While Clarissa and Grandma had a long talk about the recipe, Mo gave Kid a hug. "How's my favorite new Laddie?"

Kid grinned, "Okay. How are you?"

"Right as rain!" Mo smiled. "Will you be having some coffee?"

"Yes, Zach said only half coffee though. Mostly milk. Nora, did he call about my test results?"

"Not yet," Nora answered. "We were telling Savannah about the wedding dances we have at Heinrich's barn. I think we have her convinced to check it out, anyway."

"Especially since she helped make the mints, huh?" Kid winked to Savannah.

"Too bad you can't come," Marly said.

Kid went pale, "Why not?"

"Because you didn't help make the mints!"

"You are as bad as your friend Nora." Kid took his coffee from Mo and sat down next to Savannah. "I don't think you should hang around these gals."

Savannah giggled, "T-t-too late."

There was a knock at the door and Nora answered it. "Jeff? Come in. We didn't hear a car, so you startled us."

"I sneaked across the road when Coot wasn't looking. I think we've planted at least seventy thousand trees this morning! He's milling around, looking for more! Mo, do something with your husband! He's out of control!"

235

"Well Noah's Ark on a go-cart! Tonight, he'll be expecting to be smothered in liniment and sympathy! Come with me, Jeffie! We need to heat a vat of dippin' lard!" the jolly lady said.

Jeff laughed, "I have to talk to Kid first. Then I'll bring the firewood!"

Jeff and Kid went into the living room and Jeff asked to see the ad for the greenhouse. "I have a check here, but need to figure out how much shipping will be."

Jeff gave Kid a check for his share. "It looks like it will be more after we start building, huh?"

"Hope not too much." Kid thought. "We can settle up anything else, later."

About an hour later, Sheriff Bernard drove in to pick up Savannah. He came in and looked over the mints. "These look nice. Did you make some, Girl?"

"Yes," Savannah nodded.

"And she helped with the rabbits. They came today," Kid put in. "We have something to ask you. If Zach says I can ride, can Savannah come out tomorrow while we move cattle?"

"Fine with me," Bernard shrugged, and asked Savannah. "Do you ride?"

"No," Savannah admitted, "K-k-kid will sh-sh-show me."

"Okay," Bernard nodded. "Let us know."

"We will."

After school, Kid went to the rabbits with the boys. They were very excited and Kid spent a lot of time explaining how to take care of them. He was getting tired and was relieved when Kevin arrived.

"You look beat, Man," Kev said. "I'll take over here."

"Yah, I'm really tired."

After dinner that evening, Kid was bone-tired and he ached. Zach stopped by on his way home from work to check him out. "Your blood levels are still a bit low. You need another day or two. As far as riding tomorrow, I don't know. Your mood is better, but I don't want you to get sick now. How much do you want to do it?"

"Very."

"Alright, if you get to bed early and sleep soundly," Zach decreed. "Take it easy. Okay?"

"I will, Zach, but I want to enjoy what time I might have left."

"I understand, but getting yourself sick won't do it! Just be careful. Did you hear any more about those bikers?"

"Nothing."

After dinner, before he went to bed, he called over to Bernard's place. A lady answered and he asked to speak to Savannah. The woman hesitated and asked who was calling, "Kid, from Elton's place."

"Okay, I'll get her."

A few minutes later, she came to the phone, "Hi."

"Zach said I can ride tomorrow. So, can you come out? Someone will come to pick you up about eight, if you can."

"Ah, wait," she said as she lay the phone down.

Kid waited nervously until she came back to the phone. "Okay."

"Eight? Is that okay?"

"Okay."

"I'm looking forward to seeing you," Kid said and then surprised himself when he added, "Thanks for helping me with the rabbits today. I had a great time.

"Me, t-t-too. Good n-n-night."

"Good night to you. See you tomorrow. Bye."

"Bye."

Kid took a hot shower and then crawled in bed. He felt very good and was genuinely tired. It felt wonderful. He was almost asleep when he heard the door open. He smiled to himself when Cotton jumped on his feet.

Kid said quietly, "Good night, Kitten."

"Night, Kid."

-29-

To everyone's relief, the weather had cleared early that night, so there was no more rain. The forecast was for a sunny day. Kid didn't even try to hide his excitement, but he couldn't hold a candle to Andy. It would be the first time that he would ride Wind, the part-Arab that Annie had bought for him while he was overseas. He had to wait for permission from the doctors at the VA. Even though he knew he'd be in pain, he was anxious to be able to ride again. Keith was going to ride Crenshaw, Annie's horse.

Father Bart was riding over from Jessup's with Darrell. Bart had become quite the rider, but this would be the first time he helped move cattle. Darrell was riding his Quarter Horse, General, a great cattle horse.

On his way out from Bismarck, Keith was going to stop and pick up Savannah. Elton had called and asked him to do it. Keith had stopped by Wolf's office and got the papers for Kid the previous afternoon on the way home from work. With Ian and Danny, there were twelve riders, even though some were novices. The men figured, since it wasn't raining, they'd have the three hundred head moved across the road to Olson's pasture by noon. Then they could close off the fence to Effan's pasture.

The livestock would be rounded up from Elton's and Effan's combined pasture. They'd divide the milk cows and horses from the range cattle. The horses and milk cows would stay in Elton's pasture. The rest would be moved across the county road. On the other side, they would follow the section line before putting them in Olson's pasture.

The Grey Hawk boys and Charlie didn't think it was at all necessary for them to go to school that day, since it was much more important for them to help move cattle. Nora and Marly put the lid on that kettle quickly. The little boys got on the bus wearing their grump-faces. As the school bus pulled away, Kid said, "I sure wouldn't want to be that bus driver today!"

"Those bean heads cause an ounce of trouble and I'll nail their hide to the wall," Nora determined without raising her voice.

Kid laughed, "You don't mess around."

"I have room for your hide right next to theirs and don't forget it!" Nora pointed out, sweetly. "How did it go with Savannah yesterday?"

Kid looked around the kitchen and noticed it was only Nora and Grandma there. "Okay. She is very self-conscious about her stutter. I wish I knew how to help her."

"I read somewhere that it's best to not pay any attention to it. Telling them to relax or finishing their sentences tends to make a stutterer more nervous. Usually, the more comfortable the stutterer is around those they are speaking too, the less of a problem it is. Generally, they can read out loud, sing, and even talk to children or animals without stuttering at all."

"Did she always stutter?" Kid asked.

"Not until the car accident. She got a head injury. In the few months it took her to get her motor skills back, her husband started making fun of her. From what Margie . . ."

"Who's Margie?" Kid interrupted.

"Margie Bernard, Alex's wife. From what she said, he loved to antagonize her and mock her when she tried to talk. She simply got so nervous, she could hardly talk at all. Margie said that she is getting better now since they are divorced and he isn't deriding her constantly."

"He must have rocks in his head. She is fun, pretty, and has a great build. I wonder what his new wife is like?" Kid frowned.

"Margie said she is teeny-bopper cute and just turned eighteen. She thinks the sun rises and sets on him. See, part of the problem was that he was showing off when he ran into the fire hydrant which caused the accident. Who can figure people?" Grandma shook her head. "Anyway, she seems to like you."

"Yah, who can figure people!" Kid laughed.

"I'm not saying you are headed to 'forever and ever' land, but you can never have too many friends."

Kid hugged the tiny grandma, "You're right. Besides, I'm in love with you."

"Yah, all the good-looking young guys say that!"

"Stop flirting with my girl!" Jackson said as he came into the kitchen.

"What about Katie?" Kid asked.

Jackson smirked, "She's not here!"

"I think I can make room for your hide on that wall, too, Jackson Fielding!" Nora threatened. "You ready to go riding today?"

"Yes, ma'am," Horse answered.

"With one foot?" Kid asked.

"Tornado doesn't care. Besides, I don't use a saddle like Pale Faces. I don't need both feet."

"How are you going to stand when you get off your horse?" Kid asked with a grimace.

"Oh, I didn't think of that. I'll have to drag my crutches along, I guess. If you have a minute, I'd like to show you what Kate and I are thinking for your jacket."

The two men went into Jackson's room and there on his desk was a wonderful sketch of a spread-winged eagle. "We made an imprint of the needle marks on the jacket and then I sketched over it. This should cover all the needle marks when it is embroidered. What do you think?"

Kid was nearly speechless, "This is beautiful! Amazing. I'd love that, but I don't know how to embroider."

"Seeing how the patches were sewn on, I'm not surprised! Kate will do it for you."

"How much?"

"How much what? I imagine she'll do all of it."

"No, how much will she charge?"

"My Kate doesn't charge for things like that! She'll just do it for you."

Kid gave Horse a hug, "That is fantastic."

Jackson beamed, "I'd say to not hug me, hug her. However, after watching you making moves on Savannah, I think I'll keep you away from my girl."

"Do you think I'm making moves on her?" Kid sat down, "I don't want to be disrespectful of her. She's too nice."

"No, not really." Jackson grinned, "You were very respectful. She does seem like a sweetheart. I'm impressed with your taste."

"I suppose you think I'd go for some doper-rag?"

"Not at all. If that's who you wanted, you wouldn't have come here after prison." Jackson put down the sketch, "Don't take everything so seriously. It has been good to see you enjoying life more these last few days. I want to thank you for rocking Claudia the other night. You know, she thinks you're the cat's meow."

"I love that little kid."

"If we don't get out to the kitchen, Elton will have scarfed up our breakfast."

A few minutes later, Keith drove in. He and Savannah came in the house and Nora offered them breakfast. "Did you kids eat already?"

"I did, Mom," Keith answered, "But I'll have another pancake or two. I ate over an hour ago! How about you, Savannah?"

"I ate. Th-th-thanks."

"Oh, you need to try a pancake," Elton said. "It's my secret recipe."

Grandpa Lloyd frowned, "No, it's mine."

"Sorry, Lloyd. I love you to death, but it is mine."

The elderly man gave Elton a dirty look, "You stole it from me."

Elton laughed, "Okay, Lloyd. Want to try one, Savannah?"

Keith was already putting a plate for her on the table, next to Kid, and Grandma was bringing her coffee, "Sit here."

Savannah giggled and sat down. She smiled at Kid and he said, "They really are good."

"Okay!" she said.

Before long, the posse was assembled at Schroeder's barn. Keith was great and helped both Savannah and Kid with their saddles. Elton adjusted Savannah's stirrups for her and helped her get in the saddle. Kid was able to do it himself, although it would have been easier with the use of both his arms. When Zach had stopped by to give him his shots, he'd also given him strict orders to keep his sling on while riding.

Elton told the boys and Savannah, "I'd like you to do something for me?"

"Sure, Dad," Andy answered. "What is it?"

"You get comfortable on your saddles and then give Savannah a few lessons, so she is comfortable. Ride around a bit, while we bring the critters in from the back pasture. Okay? Then you can come help."

"You got it, Dad. I'm already comfortable."

Elton lowered his voice, "Take some time. Hear me?"

Andy nodded, "Yah. You got my word."

"Me, too," Jackson added.

Elton turned to Kid, "I didn't hear you?"

"Promise."

"Okay," Savannah said.

"Alright then," Elton said as he took off toward the south pasture.

Andy helped Jackson get his crutches secured on Tornado, while Kid gave Savannah some basic lessons on horseback riding. She listened carefully and followed instructions well. She didn't ask questions though, so Kid asked her, "Any questions?"

Her eyes moved toward him, and he could see that she had several but was afraid to talk.

"Look Savannah, if you have a concern, you should ask now. You may not have time when you need to know." Then he rode over closer to her, "I don't care if you burn the last batch of cookies, okay? Try."

She smiled with relief and then she asked some questions. He felt much better and more secure that she was comfortable; especially since, she stuttered a lot less when asking the last questions. Kid gave her the thumbs up and then turned to the guys, "Shall we go for a short ride?"

"I think we should put a lead on Duchess until Savannah is secure," Andy suggested. "What do you think, Savannah?"

"Okay," she nodded.

They rode about a couple of miles with Jackson holding the lead. On the way back, he took it off. He was confident that Savannah could do it, and Duchess was a good horse. Then they headed out to the south pasture to help with the cattle.

Savannah was worried when they crossed the creek, but Kid stayed near Duchess until they crossed. On the other side, he could see she was more comfortable that she would be safe. At the gate, Elton introduced her to Darrell and Danny. She smiled, but stayed close to Kid. Elton posted them over by the gate to watch so no cattle would double back into Effan's pasture.

Kid loved being on horseback again, but had to admit that it did bother his arm. When Darrell brought up a rangy, wild-eyed steer who wanted no part of the herd, Kid told Savannah to stay put. He moved around with Moonbeam and returned the steer to the gate. Watching him, anyone would know that he was a skilled rider and knew cattle very well. Moonbeam was a natural cattle horse and the two made a great team.

When the steer got to the gate, he tried to charge across to Schroeder's pasture. Savannah and Duchess moved quickly to block his way. Then he reluctantly followed the rest of the herd.

Darrell came up beside her, "Good work. Sure you haven't ridden before? I think instead of Savannah, your name should be Savvy."

Bart rode up on the other side of her and explained, "Darrell renames everyone. You know, he called me Slick! Can you believe that most of the clan still calls me that?"

Savannah laughed, and Kid joined them, "I can see why, Slick."

"I really don't like you people," the young priest groaned.

"Not very priest-like," Darrell chuckled.

"I don't have to be priestly around you guys." Bart laughed, "God said."

Then he headed back to the pasture.

Savannah looked after him with worry, "Is he r-r-really upset?"

"No, he is just a Slick!" Darrell chortled. "I better follow him in case he falls into a cowpie, or something."

Savannah turned to Kid, "Are they g-g-good friends?"

"Yes, very good." Then he gave her the thumbs up, "I was proud of your riding, Savvy."

She laughed softly, "Thanks."

They had little trouble moving the herd and were back home by twelve-thirty. When they got to the barn, Nora waved to them from the house. "I have little girls here that want to go 'horses'. Once Miriam saw Glendive, that's all she talked about."

"I can't make my arthritic bones go one more foot, but Kevin, will you give Miriam a ride?" Elton asked. "Darrell, can you take Clarissa?"

"I'd be glad to, but what about Kitten?"

"Kid, go give your sentry a ride. I'll help Savannah with her horse." Elton answered.

"Okay?" Kid asked Savannah.

"Okay," she nodded.

On his way to the house, Kid wondered why he did that. She had no commitment or tie on him, but everyone was treating them like they were a couple. He was delighted, but didn't know if it was being fair to her. She might not like that.

Marly had the girls ready for their ride and helped them on the horses with the guys. Clarissa and Miriam had ridden before, so it was old hat for them. Kitten, however, had never been on a horse before. She liked being with Kid, and doing like the other girls, but was uncertain about the horse.

Kid got her adjusted on the saddle and then said, "Our horse is named Moonbeam. It is Marly's horse. She said we can borrow it. Isn't that nice?"

She looked at the tall animal with doubt if nice would be how she would describe it. Kid continued, "Can you say Moonbeam?"

"Moonbee?"

"Good. Let's go."

The six rode about half a mile and then went back to the barn. Kitten enjoyed the ride after she realized that she wasn't going to fall off. After unsaddling the horses, they all walked to the house.

Waiting for them was a big lunch of homemade chicken noodle soup, buns, and summer sausage. There were brownies for dessert. Everyone was excited the morning went so well. Then folks started disappearing to go back to work.

Keith told Kid, "I have those papers from Wolf's office. He said to get them signed and back to him when you can. Are you ready to go, Savvy?"

She stopped helping clear the table, "Okay."

"Oh, I forgot to mention it." Nora interrupted. "Savannah, your uncle called and said that he'd be out about three. He wanted to talk to Elton and Kid. He can take you home then, if you want. That way, you can help with dishes!"

Savannah giggled, "L-l-l-lucky me. I'll stay. Thanks K-k-keith."

"The pleasure was mine," he said. "Anytime."

She looked at Grandma, "Nice g-guy."

Grandma gave her a quick hug, "Yes, he is."

While waiting for the Sheriff, Elton and Kid looked over the papers in Kid's room, "Is that what you were thinking?"

"Yes, they look good. Elton, I've been feeling so different lately."

"Different? How?"

"Like this is the end. I really think I'll be dead soon." Kid answered straightforwardly. "I've been having such a good time these last couple days. I really appreciate all these folks for being so good to me. I want you to know that if I die, I'll be happy because of your kindness."

Elton leaned back in the rocker, "Maybe you feel like it's the end, but maybe you're not going to die. Maybe it is the end of your other life. You have been a delight to be around and I'm very glad for that. I know you're facing a big challenge, but please don't give up. We all like this new Kid."

"Thanks, but realistically . . ."

Elton put his hand on his shoulder, "Rest assured, Kid. If something tragic does happen, I'll let everyone know."

"That makes me feel better, knowing that."

"All we need is a notary and we can sign it. Carrie can do that for us."

"She is a nice gal. I really like Kevin and Carrie. I wouldn't mind having a life like theirs."

"They make a good couple. You could have that, you just have to find someone that is a friend, besides being a lover. Sounds easier than it is. Then, you need to treat them like they are valuable. That's why I treat Nora so well!" Elton chuckled.

"That, and the fact that she can be brutal. I see that," Kid laughed.

-30-

Grandma Katherine opened the door for Bernard and took Kitten to the other room for a nap. Nora brought him a cup of coffee and refilled the others' coffee. Bernard looked very serious and Kid felt the blood begin to pool at his feet.

"May I speak freely?" Bernard asked Kid.

"Go ahead," he barely could talk.

"Heard from the Reno police department. Guess who got themselves arrested for disorderly conduct? Haskell and Geist! They're now guests of the correctional department there, but will be out in about forty-eight hours. That gives us a little window here. We know now, they're on their way. With any luck at all, they'll get arrested at every pit stop between here and there."

"No firearm or drug charges?" Elton asked. "Maybe they'll get thrown in the slammer and not show up ever."

"No, they were on foot, in a bar, breaking chairs. So, it wasn't much, but it'll slow them down." Then Bernard turned to Kid, "Besides, if they get stopped, Scab will send someone else. It does give you a reprieve of sorts. When did Zach think you could detox?"

"When my blood tests are okay. I guess it has something to do with the intestinal infection. He took more blood this morning," Kid answered weakly.

He felt sick and almost dizzy. Kid knew Savannah was watching him and could have died. He thought that maybe he should have asked to speak privately, but what the hell difference did it make at this point. "I'll go as soon as Zach says, but I don't know what it will accomplish. When those two show up, I'm as good as dead."

He couldn't bring himself to look at Savannah. Then he took a drink from his coffee, "I just need to get some papers signed first."

"Papers? What do you need?" Bernard asked.

"A Notary," Elton answered. "Carrie can do it for us when she gets home. Then he can do his detox."

"I'm a Notary," Bernard offered. "I can handle it for you, right now; if you want."

Kid shrugged, "I'll go get the papers."

He returned with his will and power of attorney. He signed them and pushed them over to the Sheriff. "I'd like to go for a walk. Okay? You guys do what you have to do."

"Sure, Kid." Elton said with worry. "I understand."

Kid put on his jacket and numbly walked down the steps. He had no idea where he was headed, but felt like the world was a blur. 'I sure screwed up my life, big time. Well, Mom and Dad, you were right. I'm reaping what I planted.'

He walked aimlessly until he got to the pole barn fence. There, he leaned against the fence and wept into his hands. A few minutes later, he climbed onto the top rail of the fence and got lost in his gaze over the prairies. The horses came over and nuzzled him. Without thinking, he rubbed their necks.

He heard a voice, "They l-l-like you."

He shrugged, "I like them."

"Want to b-b-be alone?"

"Not really."

She climbed up on the top rail and sat next to him. The horses were delighted to get pats from another admirer. "I don't want to p-p-pry. I don't underst-st-stand all this."

"Oh, Savannah, I made a horrible mess and now have to face the music."

She didn't react for a bit and then said, "I'm a g-g-good listen-n-ner and I l-l-love your deep voice."

"Thanks, but I don't want you to think any worse of me than you must already," he answered without looking at her. "I'm just being a big baby."

She studied his face, "Is someone tr-tr-trying to k-k-kill you?"

He climbed down from the fence and helped her down, "I guess you should know. Feel like walking while we talk?"

"Okay."

They walked out to the pasture and found a huge rock to sit on. On the way, he told her the whole sordid story. He started with Vietnam and continued to the present. When he finished, he put his head in his hands on his knees, "I made so many mistakes."

Savannah patted his back, "Th-thanks for telling me. I want t-t-to say something, b-b-but it takes me so l-l-long."

That was the first time he looked at her, "I have time. No rush. I'd really like to hear your honest opinion."

"N-n-not many p-p-people tell the tr-truth. Thanks. I'm proud of the ch-changes you've made. You aren't st-st-stubborn. You're a g-g-good person. Be brave."

"I didn't think I'd get this scared. I guess I'm a chicken."

"No, no one wants t-t-to be beat up."

"You are sweet to say that," Kid smiled.

"It's only the tr-tr-truth." Savannah smiled at him, "You'll be okay. I'll pr-pr-pray."

He put his arm around her, "I'd like that."

"G-g-go back?"

"Yes, I guess we better. The kids will be home soon. Thanks for coming out to talk to me." Kid stood and reached out his hand to her, "Savannah, if I get through this, will you go with me to Matt's wedding dance?"

She shrugged, "Even if I b-b-burn cooki-kies?"

"I'll try to overlook that."

"Nice," she smiled.

They arrived at the house as the little boys got off the bus and ran over to them. "Did you miss us when you rode horse?" CJ asked.

"Only a little," Kid teased. "Boys, do you know Sheriff's Bernard's niece? Her name is Savannah."

"I'm CJ. Hi, Sasavananah. What sort of name is that?" CJ scrunched up his face.

"It is a pretty name," Kid said.

"Call me Savvy," the young woman offered.

CJ was relieved, "Hi Savvy. You're pretty. Do you know Kid? He's an okay guy. He knows about boats. Do you?"

"Not much."

"Too bad. We're going to read books about them. You could too, and then you might know about them."

"Okay."

The other boy held out his hand to shake hers, "My name is Clarence Grey Hawk. I'm going to read the whole library so I know about stuff. Have you read most of it?"

"Not yet," Savannah admitted.

"Maybe you can come with me and Matt sometime when we get books."

"Okay."

"I bet you can't wait to meet me," a little tow-headed boy said. "I'm Charlie. I'm Uncle Elton's turkey man, but I ride horse, too. Were you ever a turkey man?"

"No."

"Neither was Kid, but he can ride horse."

"I know," Savannah grinned.

"We like him. Do you like him?" Charlie asked.

"I do," Savannah smiled.

"Cool," he said as he ran off with the other guys.

When they came back into the house, Bernard said, "Ready Savannah? We have to get home. Margie will be waiting on us."

"Okay."

Bernard patted Kid on the arm, "Let me know when you're done with the detox. Okay? Things should be all settled, soon."

Zach came over after dinner and talked to them. "The blood tests were good. We can do the detox whenever you're ready. Landers said anytime."

Kid cleared his throat, "Now's as good a time as any."

"Look, it'll be a piece of cake this time. You've been through the worst of it already. We just need to get you off the last of the prescriptions that have been keeping you calm now. It won't be like before."

Kid shrugged. "I'll get my things. What do I need to take?"

"Just a couple changes of clothes. I'll help you, if Elton will call Landers."

"I'll do that," Elton said.

Zach carried Kid's bag to the kitchen. Andy, Horse, and Diane wished him the best. Then Grandma gave him a big hug, "You take care now."

All the while, Kitten was watching wide-eyed until Nora told him goodbye. Kitten frowned and started to cry. She ran to him and grabbed his leg, "Kitten watch!"

He bent down to the little girl, "I have to go away for a couple days, but I promise I'll be back."

She cried harder, "Kitten watch. Kid no bye-bye!"

He sat down and pulled her onto his lap, "I have to go to the doctor for a couple days. I will be back when I'm all better. Okay?"

"For long time?"

He held up her four fingers, "This many days. Maybe I can be home sooner, if I'm better. Can you be brave and watch over my room for me?"

"Okay," she nodded, with her bottom lip quivering. "Come back, Kid."

"I'll be back soon."

"Promise?"

"A big promise."

"Zach make you better?"

"Yes, he will."

"Okay," she said as Elton picked her up.

She put her arms around Elton's neck and cried. Kid patted her back, "I'll be home as soon I'm better. Will you be good for me?"

"Be good," she nodded.

Elton patted Kid's arm, "Be strong, son, and we'll keep in touch. I'll let Bernard and Byron know. You're doing the right thing."

"I know," he said quietly as he patted Kitten's back. "Take care of Kitten."

In the car, Kid couldn't hold the tears back, "Kitten really got to me."

"She really thinks a lot of you."

"Damn, I feel like I'm falling off a cliff."

"I'm sure. You'll be surprised, it won't be so bad. You should be home by the weekend. I'll stop to see you every day. You know you have no real good choice, don't you?"

"Yah, I know. Zach, how will this detox be different? You keep saying I've been through the worst of it."

"You'll get a stomach ache, but nothing like that water stuff. Severe muscle cramps, profuse sweating, and pain from your arm. Because you'll be off the medications that kept you calm, you will be antsy and nervous. You'll be fighting that urge to get a fix, but you know that isn't an answer for any of your situation. It shouldn't take more than three days, on the outside. Of course, the urge to relapse is real."

"Yah, I know. I'm not so worried about the detox as what comes after."

"You have to make a conscious decision to not fall back into it. You've been making good progress in building a new life. I've been impressed."

"Yah, but . . ."

"Will you stop with the 'yah buts'? Aren't things better already than you thought they could be?"

"They are. I just don't want to mess up again!"

"You'll be tempted often, but we all are. Each step you take forward will be less difficult the next time. We all have to learn to lean on each other when we're weak. I think it says something in the Bible about not worrying about tomorrow, because today has enough trouble of its own."

Sister Abigail answered the door. Bart was right behind her, "I'd offer you dinner, but I imagine you already ate. What did you have?"

"Swiss steak and mashed potatoes. It was good," Kid answered.

Landers met them in the hallway, "Sister put us all on a diet! We had broiled chicken and salad for dinner."

Sister gave him a dirty look and he quickly added, "And it was delightful."

"Yes, it was. I know you had cookies this afternoon at the meeting, so no whining!" Sister pointed out.

"Only a few!"

Sister nodded, "More like a few handfuls."

Landers grinned to Kid, "She's a tough one. Come, I'll show you your digs for the next few days."

They went downstairs into the recreation room and then a small bedroom. It contained a twin bed, a chair, and a small bathroom off to the side with a little closet. There was only a small window near the ceiling on one side. The room was stripped of most other things, but it was warm and nice.

"You can put your things in the closet and then come up to join us in the den."

Landers left the men alone and Zach put his bag in the closet. Kid looked around and slightly grinned, "Nothing here to hurt myself with, I see."

"Landers knows his stuff. You think you'll be okay? Landers will call me if things get out of hand. Try not to worry."

"That is all I do."

"I know. You should really stop that."

"I feel like such a freak."

"Remember, every one of us is a freak in some ways. You aren't any freakier than the rest of us."

"Yea gads."

"Ready to go upstairs?"

Kid sat on the edge of the bed and tears rolled down his cheeks. "I had a pretty good day, you know? I really did."

Zach put his arm around him, "It will be good. Really."

Kid shook his head, wiped his tears and said, "Let's get on with this."

"Yah," Zach said. "I want to talk to Landers. Wash your face and let's go upstairs."

Bart and Kid sat in the kitchen and talked over the cattle drive while Landers and Zach went into the den and talked about Kid's condition. "His meds were due about an hour ago, so he should be starting to get antsy in another hour. I've been having him rest as much as possible and keep up his nutrition. Here are some pills to relax him if he gets too wild. He's been doing pretty well."

"Has he been verbalizing some of his demons?"

"Yah, this last week he has talked a lot about Vietnam and some of the gang things. He is really worried about those bikers that are looking for him. He is more worried about them bothering Schroeders, than his own welfare. He is beginning to look outside himself and bonding with some of the clanners. He is especially close to the little girl, Kitten."

"Oh, the one that 'watches' over him?" Landers smiled. "I heard about that. That is very encouraging. Once an addict starts to look outside himself, it's a very good sign."

"He told me when he was very down, that he just wanted to come home. I think he wants to return to his life before the war. Being at Schroeders was good, because it was similar to his home here. Elton told him he could build a life like that and he seemed to respond to that."

"That's good to know. He has a sense of purpose we can build on." Landers nodded, "I think we're over halfway there with him. I'll keep you in the loop."

"Well, I better get moving. Call me anytime. I don't have any surgeries scheduled this week, so I'll be available by phone. Here are all my numbers."

"Let's go see if Bart found any cookies, and you can tell Kid goodbye."

Zach popped his head in the kitchen and told him goodnight. "See you tomorrow morning."

Kid got up and gave him a quick hug. "Thanks, Zach."

Vicaro came into the kitchen, "Can we play cards for a while? Maybe Sister will make us some popcorn."

"Bye," Zach laughed. "Good luck, Sister."

"These guys! Wanna take them home with you?"

"No way!"

She returned to the kitchen after walking Zach to the door, "Okay, I'll pop some corn, but no butter."

Vicaro rolled his eyes, "You go read a book or something and I'll pop the corn."

"Not on your life! You keep eating like you do, and I'll have to let out your robe!"

The men played whist while they stuffed themselves with unbuttered popcorn. Kid passed, since it seemed like popcorn would not be a good thing to eat when he was going to be sick.

Vicaro grumped. "You aren't missing anything, This is like eating wallpaper without the paste!"

Everyone laughed except Sister, who warned, "You'll be lucky if you get paste tomorrow!"

After a couple hands, it was time for bed. Kid was nervous, but he didn't think it was because of his meds. He was more nervous about the situation. He and Landers walked down the stairs. "I'll be sleeping here in the den on the hide-a-bed."

"You don't need to do that."

"Yes, my room is way upstairs. This is more convenient. You need anything, just yell."

"Don't worry. My nightmares usually wake the dead."

"Do a lot of work with resurrections, do you?" Landers smiled broadly. "I might want to keep your number handy for future reference."

"Father, I need a plastic bag to take my shower." Kid said, and then noticed the grimace on the priest's face. "To cover my cast. It can't get wet."

"Okay," Landers chuckled. "You had me going there a minute. I'll get one."

After his shower, Kid returned to his bedroom. The door to his room was ajar and he noticed the priest saying his prayers. Kid thought that might be a good idea. He crawled in bed and said his own prayers.

It was about an hour later, when he started tossing and turning. He missed the cat and Kitten. He couldn't get over how the little girl cried when he left. It broke his heart. He had to do a good job so he could get home to her. He wanted very much to be someone she could be proud of and depend on.

He hated this and wondered if any of it made a bit of sense. He tried to get comfortable, but couldn't. Before long, he had been up and down about ten times. He started pacing the floor. He finally convinced himself to go back to bed. He was able to get relaxed enough to doze off. It was a restless sleep, with many disjointed dreams.

By two in the morning, he was sweating like crazy and his leg muscles were beginning to cramp. He tried to convince himself it was from riding horse, but he knew better. Soon, he was nauseous. His arm was bothering him, but not much worse than his legs.

He managed to stay in bed and by thinking about the greenhouse, managed to fall back to sleep. At three-thirty, he woke up with a scream. Landers came right in to try to calm him. He stayed with him the rest of the night. Kid went back and forth with tormented nightmares, punctuated with piercing screams.

In the morning, Father Bart came in and talked to him, while Landers went to shower and change clothes. Then he brought breakfast down for Kid. He and Bart convinced him to drink some juice and then Bart had to go to work.

Kid was in a horrible mood and no longer pretending to be nice to anyone by the time Zach arrived at six-thirty. "What the hell am I supposed to do with my friggin' arm, anyway? Never thought of that, did you? That's what I get having a baby doctor instead of a real one! You are all a bunch of morons. I should sue the whole damned bunch for malpractice."

Zach nodded. "Other than that, how are things?"

"You jackass."

The rest of the conversation was mostly profanity or sullen glares. After Zach checked him out, he and Landers went upstairs to talk and left Kid in his room. When they were gone, Kid decided to get dressed and get out of there.

He fell while trying to get his jeans on, and Sister Abigail came in to help him. "Come on, there's no place you need to be. I can help you get dressed if you like, but you might be more comfortable in your sweats."

"Dammit. Sister, I'll be okay, really. I just have to get out the hell out of here."

"I know. I feel that way myself sometimes," the little nun agreed.

He stopped and stared at her, "I'm sorry."

"What do you say? Want to go with the sweats?"

"I guess."

Sister was helping him with his sweatpants when Landers came back. "I'll help him. Thank you, Sister."

Kid sat on the edge of his bed, "What the hell am I doing?"

Landers sat down next to him, "Relax a little and we can talk. Maybe Sister can bring us some dry toast."

"I will do that," She said as she left the room.

"I'll just throw it up."

"Better than the bile of an empty stomach," Landers responded.

Kid flopped back on the bed, "I have no idea why in hell I ever got myself into this blanking mess. I'm such a stupid bastard."

-31-

The rest of Wednesday degenerated from that point. Harold Effan was miserable, sick, and extremely unpleasant. Jeff came in to relieve Landers for a couple hours so the man could get a rest. When Jeff left, he needed a rest. Everyone was worn out but Kid. He paced constantly, when he wasn't throwing up or contorted into the fetal position groaning in pain.

When Zach knocked on the door on his way home from work, Sister answered. "If you thought this wouldn't be bad; I wonder what it was like when he withdrew before. He is having a terrible time."

"Prescription meds are a problem of their own. How is his broken arm?"

"Giving him a great deal of pain. Isn't there something we can give him for that?"

"Not really. Has his language been offensive to you?"

"I worked in a lumber camp! Let's just say, I didn't learn any new words!" she laughed. "My respect for Landers has grown. He worked in a detox center for about five years! I couldn't last. He has the patience of Job."

"Yah, that wouldn't be for me, either." Zach agreed, "Well, I better go see how they are doing."

When he came in, Kid was throwing up again and Landers was straightening his bed. "How's it going?"

The middle-aged priest smiled, "Not too bad. I think it is calming down a little. He had a real tough time for a bit there, mostly his stomach. I thought he had some blood-tinted vomit, but he wouldn't let me see it. He was being crabby."

"He can do crabby very well." Zach frowned, "I'm worried about his stomach. That water really messed him up and he's nursing an ulcer. I hope this doesn't throw him into a bigger problem."

"I asked him about it the next time he upchucked and he snarled that he wasn't going to die, so I shouldn't get too excited." Landers grinned. "You know, that stuff must really make a person feel good when they take it; because they sure pay when they get off it!"

"I know, huh? Sister said you worked in a detox center for five years?"

"Yah. It's like anything else, you get used to it. At least, he hasn't tried to choke me or knock me out. Looks like our boy needs some help," Landers went to help him.

After Zach checked him out, Kid decided he'd try to get some sleep. He sat on his bed, but they all three knew he wasn't about to sleep a wink. Zach and Landers went upstairs. "How's he doing?" Landers asked.

"Good. It should be subsiding in about eight or nine hours. He said he could really go for a milkshake."

"He has been only eating dry crackers or toast. It only stays down minutes," Landers explained. "Sister, do we have some ice cream?"

"Yes, vanilla." She replied. "I can make him a shake. You may have to lock Vicaro in his room, so he doesn't swipe it. I think that'd be good, if he can keep it down. You said we should try to keep his blood sugar up, but he hasn't kept anything down, even juice."

"I'll bring some ice cream tomorrow morning for you. If he can keep it down, maybe you could try adding some juice or a banana to it. That would help him," Byron said.

"Okay. I'll do that."

Landers suggested that she make a couple and keep them in the fridge so he could have some later. "I think he'd feel better if he got some nutrition. I know how I feel when I get hungry."

Sister giggled, "They haven't built a cage that would constrain you and Vicaro after five minutes of fasting!"

Landers became defensive, "What about Bart?"

"He isn't in the slightest overweight," Sister replied. "And he is the only one who isn't complaining."

"I'm starting a collection to send you on an extended world-wide cruise!" Landers threatened.

Later, Landers brought a milkshake for Kid. He was pacing in his room again. He looked up, "I thought maybe you just cut out on me. I wouldn't blame you."

"No, I brought you a treat from Sister. I hope it stays down."

He managed to keep it down for about an hour and then didn't lose it all. He felt a bit better, but the night was still very long and contentious.

About four in the morning, Kid started to calm down. He was getting depressed, but not as angry. He had tremors more than agitation and while his stomach was still very painful, he was no longer vomiting. Landers asked him if he'd like more milkshake. He said he would.

Landers brought it down to him and smiled, "Want to sit out in the rec room while you drink it? Maybe a change of scenery will do you some good."

Kid's eyes darted back and forth with suspicion, "Why?"

"I'm tired of this room and I thought you might be, too."

"Trust me?"

"Yah. Do you trust me?"

Kid looked a bit foolish and shrugged, "Yah. I would like to sit in the other room."

They sat in the rec room and discussed why hunters stuffed animal heads to put on their walls, while Kid slowly drank his shake. This time he was able to keep the milkshake down. He was becoming weepy and remorseful, apologizing for everything imaginable. Landers just smiled, "You need a nap. Maybe that milkshake will allow you to rest some. Then we can talk."

"I'd like to try to sleep now, if I can. Thanks for the shake," Kid said as he crawled into bed. "I'm sorry to be such a bother."

Landers helped him cover up and smiled, "I'll take the rest of your shake upstairs. If you want more, there is more in the fridge. Don't be afraid to ask. I'll be out here reading."

As Landers moved toward the door, Kid said, "I'm sorry I was so awful."

"You weren't so bad. Good night."

Kid wasn't able to sleep, but kept tossing and turning. He was very restless until Landers came back in to see him about an hour later. "Not resting much, are you? Want to try more milkshake?"

"No, I'm freezing!" Kid shivered.

"I have a shawl you can borrow. Let me get it."

Landers returned in a few seconds with a dark blue, knitted shawl. Kid wrapped it around himself and smiled, "It feels good."

"My mother made it for me." Landers nodded, "You must be feeling better. I actually saw you smile."

"My gut hasn't cramped at all for a while. It must have liked the milkshake."

"Poor Father Frank. He was devastated that he couldn't have one."

Kid smiled weakly, "Sister said no?"

"You got it," Landers chuckled. "When you want more, I'll go get it for you. Zach said in the morning you can have some with fruit in it. That should help your system."

Kid nodded, "I haven't had a Charlie horse in a while, now. These chills are a fright, but I think I might be settling down."

"Would you like to visit some? I'd like to talk to you about some things that I've learned working in the addiction center. Or not?"

"I'm real tired of my own company. I'd promise not to yell at you, but I couldn't begin to live up to it."

"No problem. It keeps me from getting a big head."

The men visited throughout the night until Zach arrived, bearing ice cream, bananas, and strawberries. Father Vicaro looked the groceries over and pouted, "If it didn't seem like such a struggle, I might consider withdrawal myself."

Zach checked Kid out. "I think you've turned the corner. You should be feeling a lot better by this afternoon. Oh, I brought some letters from the kids for you."

Kid eagerly took the scribbled, colored notes. There was a drawing of a goat from Clarence and a boat from CJ. Charlie had sent a colored picture of "Engelmann" Lake, while Ginger drew a picture of two kinds of dirt. Miriam, who rarely touched crayons, drew him a pencil picture of a horse. Clarissa drew him six pictures of all kinds of things from candies to dancers. He had to chuckle, "She draws as much as she chatters!"

Then there was a nice card, which included a drawing of a kitty, from Grandma. It was from Claudia. He could tell that Kitten had help drawing what was supposed to be Cotton. Then Grandma wrote what Kitten dictated, "Dear Kid, I'm watching your room. Jackson helped me draw Cotton, by holding my hand in his. She is watching your bed when she takes her nap. I miss you. I only have to wait three more finger-days. Love, Kitten."

Tears rolled down Kid's cheeks, as he mumbled to himself, "I miss you, too."

"Others wanted to stop by, but were waiting for word you could have company," Zach said.

"I don't want anyone to see me."

"Byron or Elton?"

"They'd be okay," Kid broke down in more tears.

"I think you're feeling rather weepy."

"Hell, I'm a babbling idiot! Shit, I never felt like this when I detoxed before. My hands quiver steady."

"It's from the pills in your prescriptions. They'll do that." Zach answered, without emotion. "I think you're over the worst of the rest, though. How's the arm?"

"Still hurts, but not as bad. Have you ever had a Charlie horse in a cast? I didn't think that was possible. I found out it is." He looked Zach, "Ever talked to Landers much?"

"Some. He seems like a great guy."

"He's the real deal. I like him. He is unflappable."

Zach grinned with a tease, "You know because you tried to flap him?"

Kid raised his eyebrows, "And he doesn't tell lame jokes!"

"I'm deeply hurt. Have I been replaced?"

"You should be so lucky."

Landers and Kid talked about Vietnam until about ten when Byron came by. Landers went to take a nap and as Byron teased, "I have to make sure you guys didn't brain wash my parishioner!"

"Working on it," Landers chuckled. "He and I are going to do resurrections! Eat your heart out!"

Byron and Kid had a good talk about Kid's future plans and things that he could do in that direction. That was seriously hampered by Kid's concern about the bikers. "You guys don't believe me, I know. It isn't the Horde that's after me. It's Scab! He won't give up until I'm dead. He and Haskell are a pair. Geist is a wanna-be and worships both of them. He is a psychophant."

Byron leaned back, "I've noticed before you have quite a vocabulary for a biker. Do you read a lot?"

"Always have. I like words, although I only use a few, mostly profanity."

"Only when you are out of it. Have you ever thought about writing?"

"Yah, like when?"

"You were sitting in isolation for almost a year!"

"Oh yah, huh?" Kid shook his head, "I'm not so bright, huh?"

"Your bulb needs a little more polish. I need to go. Any messages you want me to give the kids?"

"Tell them thanks for the pictures and stuff. Give Kitten a hug for me." Then he teared up again, "I really do miss her."

"I know," Byron gave him a hug, "Harold, we are taking the threat against you seriously. Please, give things a chance. God knows what He's doing."

By eleven-thirty, Kid's throat was becoming very hoarse and he could barely talk. Kid croaked, "Must have been my screaming, huh? Was I really awful? Is this Friday?"

"No, Thursday. Screaming, crying, upchucking, all that breeds a sore throat. You'll have bad pipes for a while. Now, you have to listen while I talk!" Landers grinned. "You get ready for a nap. Why don't you take a shower and get ready for bed? I'll get your lunch and we can visit. Then, you should try to get some sleep."

"I bet you'll be glad when I do, huh? Have you been up all the time?"

"No. Josh, Jeff, and Bart gave me some breaks so I could nap. Matt will be in this evening. Vicaro was going to, but Sister won't let him near the milkshakes!"

Kid did sleep after his lunch of cream of wheat, dry toast, and a banana milkshake. He still had the chills and his hands trembled, but he was able to sleep. About three, Elton stopped by to see Kid. He knocked at his door and Kid invited him in. "Hi there," Elton grinned as he looked around, "Nice digs."

"Yah," Kid got out of bed and hugged the sixty-five year old man. "I missed you. I'm so homesick. I mean, for your home."

"It's yours, too. Everyone misses you. How's it going?"

"Yesterday was a bearcat, but I'm a lot better. Really shaky yet, but—hey, come in."

Elton sat on the edge of his bed, "Here is some more mail for you. Clarissa has about six papers for you and wants you to know that she hasn't forgotten her recipes."

He smiled, "That's good. Tell her I'm glad. How's my little one?"

"She is pretty lonesome for you and spends most of her time in your room in her chair. She's watching your stuff."

He looked at Elton, "Isn't that something?"

"It is. Oh, Bernard asked me to stop by. He said to tell you that Haskell slipped in jail and got a black eye. He thought you might enjoy that. He gave me this card from Savannah for you." Elton winked, "You're a real mover!"

"She's a sweetheart. Did she start work yet?"

"Today, that's why he gave me the card."

The two men visited for about half an hour before Elton had to go. "Anything you want me to do for you?"

"Nothing, I guess." Kid obviously didn't want him to leave. "How are the rabbits?"

"Good. The boys named the big black one Buck Fifty for you. Then they named the sable one, Savanananahannah." He chuckled, "Now they just have to learn how to say it! Oh, Jeff and Grandma mailed in your order with mine. I ordered the big greenhouse. We are going to have lettuce year round."

"We're growing lettuce?" Kid wrinkled his brow quizzically. "We're building a whole green house for lettuce?"

"Oh, we'll grow some other stuff. While you're sitting here, you can make out a list."

"I better not. Sister has Vicaro on a diet, so he's planning a visit to see Coot. Since he and Carl are good buddies; he'll let it slip that you have a greenhouse. Think about it."

Elton furrowed his brow, and then nodded slowly, "Good thinking. Best keep it under wraps. You didn't hear what that goof ball is putting in that field by the road, did you?"

"No, Elton, I didn't. I'll keep my ear to the ground though." Kid stood and said, "Tell everyone I miss them. I'll be home soon."

As Elton went to the door, Kid grabbed him in an embrace before he left.

Kid sat on his bed and carefully opened the envelope from Savannah. It had a picture of a bunny in a carrot patch on front. He smiled and opened the card. Inside was a printed comment, 'You are in my thoughts'. Below she wrote, "Try. Thinking of you, Savannah."

He lay down with the card on his chest and fell asleep.

After a dinner of poached eggs and boiled potatoes, Kid took a shower. He and Landers had a long visit about his time with the bikers. Kid was relieved to know that Landers knew a lot about outlaw motorcycle clubs and their memberships, so he could speak frankly.

"How did you know about them?"

"I was in San Diego when I worked in the addiction center." Landers explained, "It was an interesting experience. Kid, you need to understand something. Humans are social creatures. We need to belong. Where we get that feeling has a lot to do with how we live our lives. You fell into a bad crowd, but they did offer you a sense of belonging and security. You lost that after Vietnam. Then during your time in prison, you lost it again. Now, you're in another crowd, the Engelmann clan. I think it's a better place to be, but that's your decision in the final analysis. You can depend on us and we're rather certain, we can depend on you. We don't have the strict rules that the biker club does. I'm sure you know that, but we have your back. I hope you can rely on that. I know you haven't been around us very long, but I can testify that this group is sincere."

"I know," Kid agreed. "It is something else. Does the clan ever kick someone out?"

"No, but they don't pull any punches if you are messing your life up," Landers grinned. "That you can count on."

"Good grief, sweet Grandma Katherine can have your shorts starched in a heartbeat!"

"I imagine that's as bad as a biker beating!" Landers chuckled.

Matt came by about eight and they visited for a long time. Kid really enjoyed his company and Matt was very friendly and helpful. When he left about ten-thirty, Kid was still trembling and felt very chilled, but he was able to get to sleep.

Friday morning, Zach gave him the word, "If your tremors are better, I can take you home today after I get back from town. What do you say?"

"Really? That would be fantastic! Then I'm okay?"

"No, you're not okay, but you're a lot better. Are you having a lot of cravings?"

"No. I'd love a beer, but Landers told me that is a no-no. Guess it weakens my resolve or something. Besides, it will mess up my gut!"

"Yes, and it is a trigger. I'd like you to talk to Josh and Joallyn. Keep talking about your feelings, or you'll backslide. We don't want to have to do this again."

"No, I can't do that to Kitten."

"Or yourself. Kid, you've given your liver the business and your stomach is constructing an ulcer. Neurologically, you're a mess. Your hands have a tremor. You can't keep this up. You'll kill yourself," Zach's look penetrated him, "This is no longer a game. You're playing for keeps. Understand?"

"Yah, but I don't smoke!" Kid proclaimed proudly.

"That's good!" Zach shook his head. "But you are still playing with fire."

"Oh. How long am I going to shake like this?"

"It should dissipate, but I can tell you—a few more go-rounds with the dope and pills, it will be permanent."

"Damn. Really?"

"No, Sap, I made that up."

"I know you didn't. I didn't mean it that way. It'll go away now though, huh?"

"It is better than it was, so I think this was just a warning. Heed it."

"I will."

-32-

Kid was showered, shaved, and dressed, waiting for Zach to pick him up. He liked everyone at St. John's, but was anxious to get back to the farm. He couldn't believe how excited he was when Zach pulled into Schroeder's yard. The huge, two-story farmhouse looked warm and welcoming in the early evening light. Kid almost ran to the house. Even Zach had to grin as he followed with Kid's forgotten bag.

The lanky, dark-haired former biker knocked and opened the door in one movement. He entered the kitchen and immediately gave Grandma a huge embrace. "I missed you so much."

"He's not lying," Zach chuckled as he followed him in. "I think he'd have walked home if I hadn't gotten there when I did!"

All the residents except Lloyd and Kitten welcomed him home and he hugged every one of them. He asked, "Where's Lloyd?"

"He's sleeping. He has a cough and didn't feel up to snuff," Grandma answered. "Kitten is sleeping in your room."

Kid's eyes crinkled in a smile, "In her chair? I have to see her."

He entered his room and there was his little sentry, curled up in the barrel chair by the door. She was wearing the pajamas with feet in them that he got her for her birthday and cuddling her afghan from Grandma. Cotton was sound asleep on his bed.

He knelt down and tickled her cheek, "Kitten, I'm home."

She turned a little and he did it again. Her eyes opened widely with surprise and she threw her arms around his neck. She tightly embraced him and with tears of joy exclaimed, "Kid! My Kid!"

"I'm home. I got home early! It's so good to see you!"

He hugged her and then carried her to the kitchen, both beaming from ear to ear. Kitten turned to Elton, "Kid home! No more finger-days!"

"That's right," Kid smiled. "No more finger-days!"

265

The little Indian girl with the pixie haircut sat on her idol's lap and shared his milkshake. Every so often, she would turn to him and pat his arm, "Kid better."

Zach went over his diet with the ladies and talked about what he needed to do to get his strength back. "I'd like him to take it easy tomorrow, but after that, he can do as much as he feels he can handle. Kid, I'm counting on you to use your head. You mess this up, and you could be in a world of hurt."

"You have my word."

Kitten nodded to Zach gravely, "Kitten word."

Zach laughed, "Somehow I think your little sentry will keep you in line."

She smiled and patted his hand, "Line."

That night, Kid set all his cards and letters up on the dresser, except the ones from Savannah and Kitten. He put them on his bedside table and crawled into his bed. He said his prayers and scrunched into his pillow to go to sleep. He heard the door open and felt Cotton jump on his feet. Harold August Effan felt like a king. He said quietly, "Good night, Kitten."

A little voice answered, "Night, Kid."

The next day was dreary and overcast, but the kitchen smelled great. Grandma was baking and that was always a good day. Jeff stopped over and brought Miriam with him. He and Kid played checkers with their little prodigies and tasted Grandma's culinary products. Then the men talked over the greenhouse project.

After lunch, Kid visited with Grandpa for a bit and went to take a nap. Byron stopped by later and the two talked more about Kid's future. He was beginning to get a vague idea of a goal. He knew he wanted to move to his place, but also recognized that he had to rebuild it from the ground up. None of the buildings could be salvaged and were standing simply because the wind hadn't bothered to blow them down.

Kate showed him the work she had done on his jacket. It was fantastic! Kid was very impressed with it and praised her work. "That is beautiful! I'll be proud to wear it!"

He helped Grandma set the table for dinner, and then ate his bland diet. Zach had promised him that in a few more days he could start to get back to eating regular food.

After the dinner dishes were finished and Elton was patrolling the kitchen for his bedtime snack, a car pulled up by the kitchen door. It was Alex Bernard and his niece Savannah. Elton welcomed them in and grinned, "Now we can have a treat. Grandma cooked all day and all I got was a few cookies and blueberry pie for dessert. Whatcha got for company?"

Bernard shook his head, "If I ate like you, I'd weigh a ton."

Elton chuckled as he offered them coffee. "You look exceptionally pretty tonight, Savannah."

"I p-p-put makeup on. Went to w-w-work."

"Do you think you will like your job?" Nora asked.

Savannah nodded with a smile. Then she looked around, "K-k-kid?"

"He's in his room, reading to CJ about building boats." Nora said, "You can go see him. First door to the right, across the hall. I know he'd love to see you."

"Okay," Savannah said as she got up from the table.

"Come, I'll show you the way," Grandma grinned. "I want to get CJ in the bathtub anyway."

They knocked at the door and Kid said, "Come in."

He and CJ were sprawled on his bed, holding the book between them. Grandma said, "Say goodnight, CJ. Bath time."

CJ gave Kid a hug and then climbed off the bed with his book. On his way past Savannah, he reached up to hug her. "Did you know we named a bunny for you? The one you liked. Good night."

"Thank you, CJ. I never had a b-bunny named after me before. That is very n-n-nice."

"I know," he smiled as he took Grandma's hand and went out the door.

Kid sat up and held out his hand to the young lady, "This is a pleasant surprise. I loved your card."

She looked over and saw it. She seemed pleased it was on his bedside table. She took his hand and they both froze. For an eternal moment, it was as if they were lost in each other's soul. They both realized the other felt the same way. Neither spoke a word; but the electricity in the room was palpable. Kid was so entranced all he could think of was pulling her onto his bed and making wonderful, passionate love to her, forever.

Reality came pattering down the hall, in the form of Clarissa in her nightgown, bathrobe, and slippers. "Missus said to tell you goodnight, Mr. Kid."

He gave her a hug and kiss on her cheek, "Sleep tight, Clarissa."

"Okay. I hope you don't scream tonight. Think about lollipops! That's what I do!" She stated bluntly. After giving Savannah a hug, she bounced out of the room, "Good night!"

"What a kid!" Kid shook his head, "Come, sit over here by the windows with me."

"Thanks." She sat down and then asked, "How's your th-th-throat?"

"Much better."

"I love your v-v-oice, even if it's hoarse."

"How do you like your job?"

"Okay, n-n-nervous."

"First days always make a person nervous. Do you think you'll like it?" She nodded.

Kid leaned back, "Savannah, I've had to do a lot of thinking lately. I know we just met, but I think a lot of you. I need to get my act together."

She smiled, "No burnt c-c-cookies?"

He chuckled, "Something like that. I'd love to spend more time with you. Do you think you can be patient with me?"

She gave him a serious look, "I have a lot of t-t-time."

Without thinking, he blurted out, "I really like you."

Savannah blushed, "Me, too."

Kid wanted to embrace her, but thought he'd better diffuse things a bit, "Do you work tomorrow?"

"Morning."

"Maybe we can do something tomorrow night? Okay?"

She nodded as the bedroom door opened. Alex Bernard and Elton came in, "Sorry to interrupt, but we need to talk to you."

"Come in. I'll bring a chair," Kid offered.

When everyone was settled, Sheriff Bernard said, "Those creeps got out of Reno this morning. They held them as long as they could justify it. I give them a couple days to get here. Have any ideas how to handle things?"

Kid's countenance fell, "Not a thing, except to leave."

"That's not an idea! That's stupidity!" Bernard retorted, "Besides, do you even have a driver's license?"

Kid chuckled, "Not a valid one."

"Then you don't have one. You can only drive on private land. I'll arrest your ass the minute I see you on the road, so don't even think about it," Bernard said forcefully.

"Got it," Kid grimaced. "I imagine they'll hit a local bar and see what they can find out. Then they'll bludgeon me to death with a tire iron. That's their favorite MO."

Savannah gasped and Kid was shocked, "I'm so sorry. I forgot. I shouldn't have said anything in front of you, Savannah."

"The truth can be ugly, but we need to have it out there," Elton said as he patted her shoulder. "We aren't going to let that happen. You can be assured of that, Savannah. Kid has too much work to do and promises to keep. We aren't letting him squirm out of that very easily."

"I wor-rr-r-y."

"I know, we all do." Elton assured her. "We'll give Grandpa Lloyd a gun before we let them have Kid."

"Heaven help us!" Kid rolled his eyes.

"We have folks to keep an eye out for the bikers and notify us as soon as they see them. I'm deputizing citizens to help out as of Monday. The county sheriff will have two extra guys up this way, and the State Patrol of course, is watching their every move. We may have to put you in hiding, but you'll be safe. If I had my way, I'd just shoot them both on sight, but I imagine that would mean a lot of paperwork."

Kid laughed, "For real! And besides, it'd just piss Scab off even more."

"Good point. We're trying to plot some devious scheme to get them out of our hair permanently. There's no way I want any of them hanging around here. Besides, I don't have my suit back from the cleaners, so I won't be going to any funerals," Bernard blustered. "You need to keep a low profile and do as you're told."

Kid scowled, "I should leave. That would solve all of this."

Savannah turned to him directly and stated, "No."

He dropped his head, "Okay, but I probably won't do as I'm told."

"Figured as much," Bernard grumped. "I just knew you were trouble. I might have to decide which offense to arrest you on: driving without a license, possession of marijuana, or an illegal weapon."

Kid's eyes snapped, "Jackass."

"I know," Bernard smirked, "Doesn't it just bug you? Anyway, we have to go pretty soon, but I'm going to have another piece of pie."

The men left and Savannah observed Kid for a few minutes without a word, "I want to t-t-talk, but it's s-s-so hard."

Kid moved over in front of her chair and took her hands into his, "Savannah, your uncle is right. I'm just trouble. I'm so sorry I didn't meet you before all this. I don't want you to be involved with this. I like you too much."

Savannah gave him a dirty look, "No, you don't. If you d-d-did, you wouldn't th-th-think about leav-ving."

She became so frustrated that tears started to roll down her cheeks. Without a thought, he put his arm around her, "I'm so sorry."

"Say you will t-t-try."

He stopped and looked her square in eye, "You have my word. I will try. Cross my heart."

Then he kissed her gently on the lips. She pulled back and smiled, "G-g-good."

Then she kissed him back. He got up and smiled, "I think I've been conned."

She giggled, "Tomorr-r-r-ow?"

"I'll see you tomorrow. Can you call me after you get home from work? I can pick—."

"No, no l-l-license."

"I can see that dating the Sheriff's niece has definite drawbacks," he laughed.

She teased, "I can r-r-ride out in the pol-l-lice car with the s-s-sirens on!"

"Good grief," he muttered as they walked to the kitchen.

That night, Kid was torn. He was delighted with his budding relationship with Savannah. It was the first time in his life he ever felt that way. Of course, he had crushes in high school, but this was different. He knew that it was only a beginning step, but one that he wanted to take. He was at a point in his life where he was ready to put down roots and make a real home.

On the other hand, it was the worst possible time. He would likely not even survive the next few weeks. He was bringing a hideous wrath on his new family and friends. He didn't have a job, or even an inkling of one, and he had no home. He covered his head with his trembling hands, "Yea gads, I can't even hold my hands still! What the hell am I thinking?"

After Cotton and Kitten came in to take their posts, Kid relaxed somewhat. He tried to think of how he felt when he took Savannah's hand and when they shared a gentle kiss. He finally was able to fall asleep.

During the night, he woke up with a terrorizing scream and Kitten ran to get Elton. Elton came in and comforted the man, who was thrashing wildly, sweating, and mumbling. Elton was able to get him awake enough to realize where he was. He put his arms around Elton and cried like a baby.

"What am I going to do? I'm scared to death. I tell you, if I had half a chance, I'd get higher than a kite and never come back down. I can't take this! I'm not like you guys. I'm no good and a chicken shit besides!"

Elton held him tight, "You crazy kid, you're just like us. Don't you realize that all of us are scared half the time? Why do you think we're not? You may not see it, or even understand it, but it's there. I can make you two promises. One—the good Lord will always have your back and Two—the more times you face uncertainty, the easier it becomes. Can you just trust me on this?"

Kid stared at his quivering hands, "I guess. God, look at my hands! I can't even hold them still."

"Didn't Zach say it will get better? But even if it doesn't, look at Harrington. His arm is a decoration. Part of Eddie's arm is missing. Consider yourself lucky," Elton pointed out sternly. "I'm going to make us some tea. Want to join me?"

Kid nodded numbly, "Okay. A beer would be better."

"Don't tell me that. My favorite was whiskey. It was wonderful. Especially the time that Byron and Jerald had to carry my sorry ass out of a dirty bar bathroom. I was passed out on the floor by a leaky toilet. Know what I did? I tried to fight them off! Drunk on my ass, and I was going to fight both of them off! One quick punch from Jerald and I was out like a light. Byron carried me over his shoulder like a pack of dirty laundry. It was very impressive!"

By the time Elton finished relating his story, Kid was laughing. Over their tea, Elton brought up Savannah. "I see she's sweet on you, too. Good choice, son."

Kid perked up, "You think she's nice?"

"I do. She seems a decent, kind person and easy on the eyes. I like the way she talks to the kids and Lloyd. I wonder if she goes to church?"

"Don't know. Does Bernard?"

"Yah, he and Margie go to Trinity, first service. Savannah might be Lutheran, huh? That would be handy."

Kid looked at Elton in surprise, "Do you think that really matters? I mean, going to church?"

"It isn't a deal breaker, but it can be something that a couple can share. For a long, good relationship, you need a lot of help. A common faith is very helpful. Good friends, family, and shared interests are very important. You have to love someone, but not want to control them. Nora and I are very different, but we value each other's qualities. I couldn't make it without her, and I like to think that she prefers having me around. We argue, of course—because she is wrong sometimes." He chuckled, "About the real core things, we're together."

"How can you be different and yet the same?"

"Look at your hand. Well, look at your good hand. And then look at your foot. They are different and each have things that they can do better than the other. You need both of them, and when they work together, it is like they are one."

Kid considered what the man said, "I think I understand. I've always heard how wonderful it is when couples do everything together and even wear matching clothes every day. I heard if you love someone, you never fight."

"I love Nora more than anything, but she wouldn't look very good in my coveralls. If I had to go spend time in a fabric store, I'd pull my hair out. We disagree all the time. She has one take on something and I have another. It isn't a matter of being right or wrong; it's just that we both have thinking minds. Folks rarely think exactly like someone else. I don't think those things you mentioned are true love. Loving someone is allowing them to be themselves and appreciating that."

"You know, I've been here too long. You make sense."

"I know. Now, let's get down to the serious stuff. How do you plan on finding out what that lunkhead Kincaid is planting out front of his house?"

"Maybe nothing. Did you ever wonder if he just had it plowed to bug you?"

Elton shrunk into his chair at the thought, "Now why did you go say that? He wouldn't have done that, would he? Is he really that low down?"

Kid got up to clear the table, "I don't know, Elton. I honestly don't."

-33-

When the morning alarm went off, Kid dressed and headed to the kitchen. Kitten and Cotton were already gone. When he got his coffee cup, Kitten patted his leg. "No, no. Milkshake."

He gazed at his cup yearningly and put it back, "You're right, I'll put it back. Want some of my milkshake?"

The little girl shrugged, "Okay."

He tousled her hair, "I think you have ulterior motives!"

CJ sat at the table with his milk, "Kid, can you be my helper today? Charlie has to work for his dad."

"Sure. What's he doing?"

"It's a real stinky job."

Elton put his cup on the table and sat down, "What job would that be?"

"Polishing pews." The little boy related, wrinkling up his nose. "I don't like pew stuff."

Elton chuckled, "That's the name of the benches we sit on in church. It doesn't mean they stink."

CJ frowned, "Then why are they called pews?"

"Pew means bench." Kid answered, "I thought Byron was just joking when he said he wanted me to help polish pews. I should call him and see if he needs my help?"

CJ grumped, "I thought you were going to help me?"

"How about we hurry and do your work, then we both go help Charlie polish pews? Wouldn't that be fun?"

"Not fun, but it'd be good to help Charlie," CJ shrugged, "Only if it doesn't stink!"

"Cross my heart," Kid promised. "If it stinks, we'll leave."

"Okay. We have to do the ducks, chickens, turkeys, and rabbits. You have to see how big Buck Fifty is now! He is going to be a monster rabbit!

Kevin says that boy rabbits are bucks and girl rabbits are does. Did you know that?"

"I did."

"Clarence said that goat boys are called billy and girls are called nanny. And their babies are kids, like people! It's pretty confusing, huh?" CJ related. "When I get married, I'm going to name my wife Nanny."

Jackson shook his head, "You knothead, the girl will have a name before you marry her!"

"Then I'm not going to ever get married. I'll live with Charlie and eat over here."

Kid called over to Ellison's and talked to Byron. Charlie was very relieved he had help with the pews. Byron chuckled, "He's been trying to convince me that we should sell the pews. We can use the help, but he isn't going to do the work alone. He's just having a fit. He keeps it up, he'll be cleaning with a paddled behind!"

"You can tell him to lighten up; we'll be over after we get our chores done."

Kid loved helping with chores and being outside. He and CJ went to the rabbits. CJ took great pride in showing off Buck Fifty, the huge Flemish Giant buck. He was a black rabbit with a few pale spots. He wouldn't have been good for showing, but no one intended to do that. CJ had befriended him and played with the giant oaf a lot. Flemish Giants are known for being docile, but Buck Fifty was downright lazy and ate like a horse. He was an adult and weighed about nineteen pounds. CJ loved that stupid rabbit.

The little boy would sit on the floor of the pen, Buck Fifty would come over and flop on his lap, squashing him to the floor. It was a delightful game to both of them but held little interest to anyone else.

Kid liked the Sable doe that the kids had named after Savannah. It was still a little skittish, but was so very soft. The coloring was that of a dark Siamese cat and once picked up, it liked being held.

CJ said that Charlie liked one of the New Zealand bucks. It was about eleven pounds and pure white. Kevin said he liked them all, but the nearly black sable buck was his favorite. "Mr. Kevin said that we will breed the grownups in a couple weeks and then have babies in only four weeks after that! Won't that be cool? When it gets nicer outside, Kevin wants us to take out the sod, put down wire and finish building the outdoor rabbit pen, so they can get some sunshine."

"I know. They'll like that; especially when we put the sod back down over the wire and seed it, so they'll have greens to eat," Kid explained. "Before fall, we can start selling them."

"Do you eat rabbits?" CJ asked, watching for Kid's reaction.

"No. I hear it's good, but I don't. Are you anxious to eat one?"

"I couldn't eat Buck Fifty. He is my friend. Who eats their friends? That's plain weird."

After finishing their chores, they went over to Marty's to take care of the Great Dane, Bruno. He was still a clumsy pup, a slate gray male. Kid loved him and they played with him for a while before going over to Kincaid's to take care of the ducks. Kid had to admit, the little boy did have plenty of chores to do.

They were about finished feeding the ducks when Jeff came out of the house. "Mo said to come in for a treat when you're done."

"What you doing today?" Kid asked.

"I imagine digging more holes with Johnny Appleseed," Jeff made a face.

"Is he a new friend?" CJ asked sincerely.

"No, it's a nickname for Carl. It is someone who plants trees all over the place," Jeff answered unenthusiastically. "What are you guys going to do today?"

"We're off the help polish pews at Trinity when we're done here," Kid answered.

"I was wondering if I can hide Carl's shovel this afternoon, can we go horseback riding? What do you think?"

Kid thought, "I'd like that. I'll have to check and see if we can borrow some horses. That would be fun. I'll call you."

After they went home and cleaned up, Kid and CJ walked the mile over to the church. When they got there, CJ knew the way in the side entrance to the sanctuary. "How did you know about this door?" Kid asked.

"Jackson and Andy go in this door. It's for guys who don't have all their legs and stuff," CJ answered practically.

They were met by Byron, Pastor Marv, their wives, and all their kids except Ken, who had to work. Ruthie Harrington was also there. "Hi," Kid said with surprise, "They drafted you, too?"

"Since Suzy isn't much into polishing these days, I won the drawing," the pixie-like, dark haired girl answered.

Byron came over, "Let me introduce you to your polish rags. You'll become great friends."

By twelve-thirty, the project was finished. The pews glistened under a polished sheen and looked great. Kid was partnered with eight-year old Ginger Ellison, the dirt expert. By the time they had worked the two and a half hours, Kid was up to date on several different kinds of soil. She became quiet after he drew her into his confidence and asked her to research the best kind of soil for greenhouses.

"I'll look in my books. Would it be okay if I talk to Jeannie about it? She is my teacher and good at keeping secrets. She is my Godmother and she is married to my uncle Darrell. He keeps secrets good, too."

"You can tell her, but don't let the cat out of the bag. Okay?"

"We can't have a cat. Katie sneezes from them," Ginger answered factually. "I'll tell you as soon as I find out. Okay?"

"Thanks, Ginger."

They all had beef barley soup when they finished with their work. Kid asked if they could ride the horses that afternoon, and Marly happily agreed. "Can I ask you a favor?"

"Sure," Kid nodded. "What is it?"

"Can you take Ginger and Charlie out on their horses at the same time?"

Kate piped in, "I can come along. Maybe Jackson would like to ride, too!"

"That sounds good to me."

When CJ and Kid arrived back at the farmhouse, Kid asked if Savannah had called. Nora pulled him aside, "Kid, Margie called a bit ago. Savannah probably won't call. Seems some of the gals at work started making fun of her stutter. She was devastated. She came home and cried. She has been soaking in a bubble bath ever since. She asked Margie to call you and say she can't make it."

"SOB! Those miserable bastards! I have half a mind to go to that nursing home and start cracking some heads!" Kid bellowed as he clenched his fist.

Nora glared at him, "You! Me! Your room, now!"

The little girls put their hands over their mouths and CJ eye's became huge. They looked at each other as Kid followed Nora to his room.

She closed the door and turned on him, "Don't you ever pull a stunt like that again in front of those kids! Where is your head?"

"I'm sorry I said it in front of the kids, but those friggin' people will hear from me! Savannah doesn't deserve to be treated like that! I'll straighten them out!"

"All you'll do is get yourself arrested and embarrass Savannah. You have to quit thinking like that. What outcome do you want?" Nora stood her ground.

"What do you mean? What outcome? I want them to leave her alone and treat her right!"

"Do you really imagine that beating them will make that happen? They will resent it and avoid her. Sit down, now, and think!"

Kid did, but he wasn't backing down from his position, "I suppose you think I should just pray and everything will be better. Real life isn't like that!"

Nora stared back at him, "You might want to do something that will truly help."

"Like what?" Kid snapped sarcastically. "Ask them to stop?"

"You can't do anything about them. Get that through your stupid head. You can't follow her around beating up everyone who does something offensive to her. That's impossible."

"So, what should I do? Let her suffer? Someone should pay for this!"

"When you quit acting like you're in cell block ten, we can talk this out," Nora retorted.

"Boy, you cut right to the quick, don't you?"

"I don't want to waste time sugar-coating anything. Unless you can get your attitude straightened out, you'll be setting yourself up for more trouble. Haven't you had enough?"

"What has that got to do with Savannah?"

"When a situation arose, you immediately reverted to bad behavior! You need to think. Use your head! Now, honestly, what do you think Savannah needs?"

"Hell, I'm not a shrink. I don't know. She should pulverize those creeps."

"Okay, we both know that won't work, but I think you're on to something. She got into her problem because her husband antagonized her to the point she couldn't talk. The average person would have told him off, but she backed down. She needs to find the strength to stand up to those people at work. Until she does that, it'll keep happening."

Kid thought, still trying to defend his position, "I know. I said she should just deck them."

"I think that if they knew it didn't get to her and she had self-confidence, they wouldn't do it anymore. She might even become friends with them. What do you think you could do to help her do that?"

"Me? Hell, I think a tire iron would be quicker."

"Yah, that's what she needs. A jailbird for a boyfriend! Men! When a woman needs a man's strength, they don't need someone to go fight a duel! They need someone to lean on." Nora stood straight and tall, "Now, hear this. You're going to clean up and go apologize to Grandma and the kids. Then bring the car up. I'll change my shirt and meet you in the kitchen. I'm driving you to Merton. I'll drop you off at Bernard's house while I run to the grocery store. You'll go in there and talk to her. Listen to her and let her cry, if she wants. You will not suggest beating anyone, just help her be strong! Hear? I'll wait in the car. You ask her to come horseback riding this afternoon. No back talk."

"Ah—,"

"Now!"

"Yes, ma'am."

Kid cleaned up and went to the kitchen where the kids were waiting anxiously. "Did you get a big spanking?" Clarissa asked anxiously.

"I bet he got his mouth washed out with soap," CJ said with authority.

"No. I didn't, but I was wrong, kids. I shouldn't have talked like that or acted that way. It was very bad. I'm sorry and please, don't you guys do it. Okay?"

Kitten ran to him and hugged his knee, "Kid better?"

He stooped down and put his arm around her, "I'm a lot better."

Then he kissed her cheek and stood up. He apologized to Grandma and she nodded, "Nora called Margie to say you're on your way. CJ and I will call the other riders and get the posse together."

On the way to Bernard's house, the two said nothing. Just as they turned on their street, Kid said, "You're right, Nora. I really have to work on thinking straight. Thanks for slapping me upside the head."

"No problem. It will take a while, but you'll get there. It might take longer for Savannah. From what Margie said, the head injury precipitated the stuttering, but her husband really exacerbated it. Until she can regain her confidence, it'll be there. Now she is so self-conscious of that, it makes her feel even more inferior. Marge said that her doctors said she will always have a tendency to stutter when she is tired, intimidated, or weak. However, with work and time, she should overcome most of it."

"Maybe I'm not good for her then. She needs someone respectable."

"I've met respectable people that were awful, and vice versa. You guys like each other. It may not be lifelong; but right now, you're good for each other. Just don't go off half-cocked and give her any more worries than she has now."

Kid was nervous when he knocked at the door. Margie answered. She was a middle-aged lady about five-five, with brown curly hair, glasses, and a big smile. She motioned him in and then held out her hand, "I take it you're Kid? Alex would have my neck if he knew I just let someone in before I knew who he was. So, we won't tell, okay?"

He nodded, "Okay. Is Savannah ready?"

"Oh no, Sonny. She got out of the tub a bit ago. Good thing, because she'd be as wrinkled as a prune. She is holed up in her room, vowing to never see the light of day again. I'd be mighty appreciative if you'd go talk to her."

Kid pursed his lips and followed her directions up the stairs to her room. On his way, he was thinking that maybe this girlfriend stuff was very overrated. When he got to her door, he knocked.

"G-g-g-go away, Aunt Margg-g-gie," she said through her tears.

"I'm not your Aunt Margie," Kid answered. "Can I speak to you?"

The crying stopped and there was dead silence. He thought about leaving, but instead knocked again. He heard some scurrying and then the door opened a crack.

"May I come in?"

"No."

Her hair was wrapped in a towel and her eyes were swollen from tears. She was wearing a white robe. Her feet were in enormous, pink, fuzzy slippers that looked like piglets.

He looked down at her feet and started to laugh. She frowned at him and then opened the door. "I l-l-like them."

"I'm glad. I'd hate to think you were wearing them if you didn't."

She swatted his good arm and looked at her feet, "C-c-c-come in."

He went inside the door and closed it. "I heard you had a bad day, huh? I'm very sorry about that. How soon will you be ready to come out to the farm?"

"I'm n-n-not c-c-coming."

"Yes, you are. You said you'd see me today."

"I c-c-c-an't."

"Did I hurt your feelings? If I did, I'm sorry."

"You kn-kn-know you didn't. I don't belong out there."

"Yes, you do. Wear you riding clothes, unless you want to wear your piggy slippers. Will they fit in stirrups?"

She sighed, "I c-c-can't do anymore tod-d-d-ay."

"This isn't work," Kid said. "This is for fun. You'll be with friends."

She didn't move, "I d-d-don't know."

"Please try," he said as he put out his hand. "Please."

She put her hands up to her face and started to cry. He embraced her gently, "Don't let this happen to you. Don't let those boneheads ruin your whole day, and mine, too. Please. You tell me to try, now you have to, also."

Before they knew it, they were kissing. He could feel himself being overtaken by passion and pulled back, "Now, you get dressed and I'll wait downstairs. Nora was going to the grocery store and she'll be back any minute. Hurry."

He went out the door and closed it. There he took a deep breath and seriously considered going back into her room. Then he snickered and thought, 'Yah, broad daylight in the sheriff's house with Nora waiting out front! Good thinking, Kid.'

A little over an hour later, a group of riders headed out across the pasture. It was a fun afternoon of fresh air and relaxation. When they returned to the house a couple hours later, dinner was on the table. Nora told Savannah that her aunt and uncle would be out to pick her up about nine, unless she wanted a ride home earlier. Kid looked at her, and she smiled, "Stay."

That evening after chores, Kid asked her to go for a walk, before Bernards came. As they left the house, Elton informed them that hot fudge sundaes would be ready about a quarter to nine.

The couple held hands and walked out to the pasture without a word. Kid was rather tired. He didn't want to let the day end though, because it had been wonderful. When they got over the first ridge, he put his arm around Savannah's shoulder and gave her a squeeze. She smiled and they walked a ways before she said, "Th-th-thank you."

"For what?"

"Mak-k-king me come out today."

"Did you have a good time?"

"Everyone's n-n-nice. Th-th-they make me f-f-feel norm-m-mal."

"You are normal, you dingbat!" Kid laughed, "Except for those slippers! What's the story with them anyway?"

She raised her head defiantly, "I like th-them."

Kid chuckled, "Okay, then."

They sat on the rock and visited. Kid extracted a promise from her that she wouldn't hide anymore if those morons at work gave her the business. They saw a car pull into the yard and thought they had better go back to the house. On the way back, she turned to him and asked, "Th-th-think the bik-k-ers will be here to-to-morrow?"

"Probably Monday. Don't worry about it, Savvy," Kid stopped walking. "I told you I'll try to be careful. I have a reason to now."

She gave him a questioning expression and he kissed her. It was a passionate kiss and they both knew they wanted each other. As he held her close, she shook her head no. He stopped, "I'm sorry. I didn't mean to come on too strong. I know we don't know each other very well yet, but I hope we can try to build a life for ourselves."

"I'd like to tr-tr-try, but it is too s-s-soon."

He hugged her, "I know. I should've thought of you. I'm not used to thinking of other people first. This all new to me."

"I don't belie-lieve that." She put her hand on his cheek, "Will I s-s-see you tomor-r-rrow?"

"I'd like that. Can I call you? Do you work?"

"Not til Tu-Tuesday."

"I'll call you."

-34-

Sunday began a warming trend. It was bright, sunny, and at least ten degrees warmer than it had been. Even the livestock seemed to enjoy the weather. Kid helped with chores that morning. When he and CJ fed the rabbits, Buck Fifty tried to follow CJ out of the cage. He would have made it out of captivity, if he had moved a little faster.

"You'll have to keep an eye on him. He'll follow you because he likes you and knows you feed him treats," Kid warned. "You wouldn't want him to get lost or run over."

"I'll try to be careful."

After breakfast, Kid visited with Grandpa Lloyd while everyone else scurried around getting ready for church. Kev stopped to pick up the kids for Sunday School and while waiting for them to get their coats on, asked, "You coming to church today?"

"Hadn't thought about it," Kid answered.

"I think he will," Nora answered. "We're watching Little Matt during the 9 o'clock service, so Danny and Jen are going to keep an eye on dinner and Lloyd while we go at eleven. Right, Kid?"

Kid shrugged, "Sounds like it."

The phone rang and it was Jeff for Kid. "Hey Dude, I'm heading off to Merton in about half an hour to pick up Sister Abigail's casserole. I can bring Savannah out with me, if you want to go to Trinity with her."

"I don't know if she's going."

"Duh, call her and find out. How many filaments are burnt out of that light bulb of yours, anyway?"

"I'll call you right back."

Kid called and when she came to the phone, he asked, "Savannah, I don't know what church you go to, but Jeff said he'll pick you up. We can meet at Trinity for the eleven o'clock service, if you want, and have dinner here with us afterward."

"Oh, Marg-g-gie and Alex go to Tr-tr-trinity at n-n-nine. Wait."

He heard her talking to Margie and then she came back to the phone, "Okay. What time will J-j-j-, he pick me up?"

"About ten-thirty. I'll ride over with Schroeders and meet you there. Savvy, I haven't been to church in years, so I'm kinda rusty."

"I'm sure God doesn't m-m-mind."

He turned and Nora was beaming, "What you smiling about?"

"Nothing," she winked. "Dinner, huh? What are you bringing? Do you have a clean shirt?"

"What do you want me to bring to dinner? I imagine I could bring rabbit stew!"

"Never mind, just help set the table. I'm giving you the business."

Kid was uneasy as he waited on the front steps of Trinity for Jeff and Savannah. They all walked in together and then sat with Nora and Elton. It was a nice service and Kid was amazed how many folks he knew, although they were mostly clanners. He was also surprised how much of the liturgy he remembered. He noticed that Savannah had a beautiful voice. He loved singing some of the old hymns that he knew. That is the comforting thing about tradition. It is always the same and that is very reassuring.

After service, Kid rode back to the farm with Jeff and Savannah. At the farmhouse, the number of clanners left her intimidated. She had met many of them, but didn't do well in crowds. Kid noticed that she had withdrawn into the living room playing with Clancy. He touched her arm, "Want to go for a short walk before we have dinner. The St. John's contingent isn't here yet, so we have a few minutes."

"S-s-something wrong?"

"No, I thought you might want a breather. We can go see the rabbits?"

They walked down toward the rabbits and he said, "Savvy, you don't need to feel uneasy around any of these folks."

Her eyes searched his face, "I'm not."

"I thought you were getting antsy?"

"L-l-l-ook! I'll n-n-never be the b-b-bell of the ball."

He took her hand, "I don't expect you to be. I just don't want you to feel nervous."

"I'll st-st-stutter and embar-r-r-ass you."

He grinned, "No, you couldn't embarrass me. I do very well in that department all by myself. I just want you to be comfortable."

"Sure? Co-o-ody said I acted like a m-m-moron."

"I'm completely positive that Cody must be an idiot. I love the way you are." He stopped and pointed, "Look, there's Buck Fifty. That little rat got out. Good thing we checked. Where did he get out?"

The couple looked around and found a piece of wire pushed out with tell-tale bits of black fur on it. "You're going to have to be in a nesting box until after dinner! Then we'll fix this so you can't get out. You're in big trouble."

After Kid put the rabbit in a more secure area and closed the door across the pushed wire, they went back to the house. "We left the door open, so they could get some fresh air and sunshine. We can fix it after lunch. We could have rabbits all over creation."

"Will it tak-k-ke long?"

"No, why?"

"I pr-pr-promised Marg-g-gie I'd help s-sew today."

"Whatcha making?"

"A dr-dr-dress." She stomped her foot, "I h-h-ate this. I can't s-s-ay a thing."

"You have a beautiful voice. I noticed at church."

"You do, too. Did you ever sing in a ch-choir?"

"Oh yah, in prison!"

The smile left Savannah's face, "That wasn't nice."

"I know. I'm really sorry. Will you forgive me?"

She answered seriously, "Try not to do that."

"I promise." Kid kissed her cheek and then turned to her, "Tell me the truth now. I have to know. If you could talk easier, would you jabber like Clarissa?"

She giggled, "No!"

"What a relief."

After dinner, Kev, Kid, and Jeff went down to fix the rabbit cage. Katie and Savannah got into a conversation about beading and sewing.

Kid was delighted that she seemed very comfortable. When the cage was finished, Jeff offered to give her a ride home and Kid rode along.

On the way back to the farm, Jeff said, "I think she is becoming more at ease, huh?"

"I was pleased how her visit with Katie went."

"Unless you are Charlie or CJ, there's no reason for anyone to be nervous around Katie. She and Jackson make such a good couple."

"They do, and it is amazing because they are so young, but old souls."

"They are, aren't they?"

"Jeff, can you promise me that if something happens to me, you'll help Savannah overcome her insecurities?"

"I promise, but you can do it." Jeff became somber, "Hear anything about the bikers?"

"No, they'll probably be here tomorrow. Could have made it tonight." Kid stared out the window, "Isn't that just it? About the time things start getting better, it all goes to hell?"

"What an asinine thing to say! It is all together! None of this wouldn't have been without the trouble with Scab. It all works together."

"I guess I can see that. Do you think they'll bury me in the Trinity Cemetery?"

"Yah, after you die, when you are old. You idiot! Don't be so sure you are done for. Things may just be okay."

"I wish I believed that."

"What is stopping you? You can believe it, if you want to. Just do it."

"If you say so," Kid sighed. "So, tell about the latest with Kathleen."

"She says she's looking forward to coming out. Goll, she is going to be here for a week, and I have no idea what to do with her!"

Kid frowned, "Do with her? Put her on the mantel and dust her daily! Now who is a dumb head? You visit with her. You can go horseback riding, the wedding stuff will take time and you can just be with her. What's so hard about that?"

"You've done it before," Jeff pointed out. "I never did. I only took a date to the movies or for a hamburger in my whole life."

"You can do that. I never dated much either," Kid pointed out. "I take Savvy out to the pasture or down to the rabbit cages! Big deal!"

"Are you sure she likes it?"

Kid slumped back in the seat, "Do you think she hates it?"

"No," Jeff laughed. "I don't. I love getting to you. It's so easy! Maybe we can double-date when Kathleen is here?"

"If I'm around. Or you can go with Matt and Diane. You know, two ex-priests and their girls."

"I really don't like you. You're a jerk."

"Think so?" Kid laughed.

That evening when the house was becoming quiet, the phone rang. It was Bernard for Kid. "Got a call. Your biker buddies are at a campsite west of Mandan. They raised hell at a convenience store because they couldn't get beer on Sunday, but they left before the cops showed up. Thought I should let you know. Things are in play. Promise me you'll keep secluded. Got your word?"

"It would be . . ."

"Have I got your word? Or do I have to put you in protective custody?"

"You have my word, but I hate it."

"We all know that. We've heard it enough. Get some rest. I'll be out to see you tomorrow early."

"Good night."

Kid would have given his eyeteeth for a fix, joint, drink, or even an IV. He was wound up and scared. He knew he had to talk to someone before he went out of his mind. He asked Elton if they could talk.

"I'll fix the tea, and if you want, we can sit on the patio. I might need a cigarette or two."

"I could use a joint."

"Yah, I suppose you could, but don't count on getting one."

"I know."

A bit later, they were sitting on the patio with their tea. Elton shivered, "It seemed like a better idea than it is. I thought it was warmer when I was looking out the window."

"What is this called? Brisk?"

"I always thought that was a stupid thing to call the temperature. I could see calling the wind that, or a walk; but not the temperature."

Kid looked at the older man in amazement, "Has your mind always worked like that?"

"Yah, it is improving over the years! Jealous?"

"Not quite. Elton, when I was in Vietnam, I never got this freaked about an impending battle. What's wrong with me?"

"You are older, heal slower, and realize your mortality. Happens to all of us."

"You know, I feel really bad. When I was after some of those guys for the Horde, I imagine they felt like this. I never thought about that before. I guess I deserve this."

"No one deserves this. Your life has a different purpose now. When you just have yourself to think about, it's easier to be cavalier. When you think of Kitten and Savannah . . . that's different. Sure, they'll all survive without you, but they'd be effected if something happened to you. Honestly, between us, do you think that you could win in a battle with those two bikers?"

"Before, I could've handled myself alright in a fight, but now I got this bum arm. One, yah. Both, no." Kid stated flatly, "If they get to me, I'm dead. I hope they make a direct hit with the tire iron, so I'm unconscious."

"I hope it doesn't get that far. Did you know that half the clan has been deputized? Carl and Harrington, of course, but others, too. Darlene's mom who lives down the road from your home place is on alert, as are the Swensons. The bartenders in all three Merton bars are on board to let Bernard know what they hear."

"Knowing isn't going to stop them. Watching isn't going to change anything," Kid pointed out.

"Are they armed?"

"Oh, yah. Maybe not on them, but on their bikes."

"Besides beating someone, what do they usually do? I mean, they don't poison or that kind of thing."

"Stabbing, burning, or shooting."

Elton was surprised, "Burning? Like how?"

"Oh, locking someone in a car and setting it on fire, in a shed, or something. Geist gets a kick out of that. I think Geist is a firebug. He loves that. He says it burns up a lot of evidence."

"Has he ever been arrested?"

"Oh yah, since he was a kid. He used to brag he spent more time inside than out. Haskell has only been in jail for misdemeanors. He sets others up to take the fall. I know a man who's serving a life sentence for something he did. I have to say, he always lands on his feet, no matter how far the drop. His odds are good."

Elton raised his eyebrows, "Or running out. My prayer is that we can get this resolved. We need to think of what to do to get them to leave and carry the word back to Scab that you're history. Then he'd be done with it. How much do you think it'd take to convince him to leave you alone?"

"If he thought I was dead, or a vegetable. That's the way he is. Diablo said he was like a crocodile with a critter in his jaws. He won't let go."

"Is he very intelligent?"

"Not really. Devious, but not smart."

"So, what is Haskell like?"

"He got where he is by lying, cheating, and extorting. He is more of a conniver. And like I said, Geist is a kiss-up wannabe. He'll do anything for approval from Haskell. He is the dumbass that takes a bullet to show those guys he's tough. He'll dive into a fight, take a beating, or be the most vicious for an atta-boy from those other two. And if they get caught, he will take the fall."

"He is the pyromaniac?" Elton lit his cigarette and looked to across the dark prairie. "It is sure peaceful, isn't it?"

Kid looked around, "It would be great to have a place out here and be a quiet farmer."

"Decided what to do about your well?"

"I don't know. I'd like to live there, but the well is shot and there isn't a building worth saving. I'd have to tear the whole place down and start over. Might be better to move to a different location on the land."

"You'd have new power lines to run. How is the tree row?"

"Not very good. Most of trees are dead or overgrown. The lilacs are thriving though. You know, a guy should probably just tear the joint down and start over."

Elton listened and nodded quietly, "Would the lumber be any good to use over?"

"Most of what I saw is rotten. The roof has a gaping hole in it and rotted most of the house. The only room that is vaguely standing is the kitchen. There's no bathroom. I went down to the cellar and the old tin bathtub was still hanging on the nail, rusted through."

Elton got an odd look on his face, "Is there a root cellar?"

"Yah, but it's in the yard, not attached to the house. It was a storm shelter-root cellar."

"How far from the house?"

"It is down by the garden, probably hundred-fifty feet. Off the front yard."

"Oh, so visible from the front?"

"Yah, between the house and the barn. The garage is to the right of the house and the root cellar on the other side. Why?"

"No reason. What is in the basement or cellar?"

"Half caved-in rock walls and the coal chute."

Elton perked up, "Where does that open to?"

"Out the back of the house. What you thinking?" Kid studied Elton.

"I think I'm growing an idea."

"Should I boil water before we deliver it?" Kid smiled.

"Smarty pants."

-35-

The next morning while Kid helped with chores, Elton asked him to help at the pigpen. When they got out of earshot from the barn, Elton looked over the horizon, "Looks like we might have a thunderstorm this afternoon, judging by the cloud bank to the west. You think more about last night?"

Kid nodded, and held up his trembling hand, "Think I can do it?"

"Do you think you can? That's the question. If you make up your mind, you can face this mess. I have every confidence. If you're unsure, then probably not. Only you know that."

"I don't want to keep this sword over my head. I'd rather have it just be over. It was weird this morning when I got dressed, wondering if this was what I was going to wear when I died."

"Yah, I imagine. But look how many times it could've been, and wasn't. Life is a mystery. We have to trust the good Lord with that and carry on." Then he put his arm over his shoulder, "I don't mean to make light. This is risky business and I don't relish the thought of losing you. Keep strong, clear-minded, and remember, we all care a lot about you."

Kid hugged Elton briefly, "I hope you know what you and Nora have meant to me."

"Okay, grab that pail. Everything in place?" Elton looked at Kid. "You got this? I need to run my errand. Let Kevin know I'll be back in a few minutes."

When the milkers were taking off their jackets in the mudroom, the phone rang. It was Sheriff Bernard. He talked to Kid to tell him he was going to make a run by the home place and then he would stop by Schroeders. Kid said okay, he'd be waiting. Then Bernard said, "Got a minute to talk to Savannah?"

"Of course."

"Hello," she said sweetly. "I was think-k-ing about you all night. Be c-c-careful and keep calm. Promise to tr-try."

"You have my word. Thanks. Savannah, you mean a lot to me."

"You, too. Take c-care."

Kid hung up and went immediately to his bedroom. No one could have understood how much he hated the mess he had created. He threw himself across his bed and wept. He lost track of his surroundings until there was a gentle pat on his arm. He froze and turned to see CJ.

"Mister Kid, Nora said to tell you the waffles are ready. You coming?"

Kid sat up, "Yah. I'm just . . . just . . ."

CJ sat next to him and said very seriously, "You know, sometimes I do that, too. A guy just doesn't know if he should run away or eat a cookie."

"That's so true," Kid chuckled. "What do you do?"

"I figure I can't run fast enough and we didn't used to have a cookie jar. So, I would just mess around. Before long, I'd forget about it."

Kid squeezed the boy's shoulder, "I'm so glad I got to meet you. You're a great guy."

"You think so?" CJ asked, "You aren't too bad either. But you know who is bad? Buck Fifty! He sneaked out of the rabbit house two times this morning! I didn't know rabbits were sneaky, but he is. I don't know how he got past me."

"He wants out, huh? When we get the outside pen fixed, he won't be able to get out. We'll have to keep a good eye on him, huh?"

CJ grinned, "I know. I'll tell Kitten to watch him. She is a good watcher and isn't so busy now that you're well."

"That might be a good idea."

They went out to breakfast.

Elton opened the door for the Sheriff and Nora gave him some coffee. "How's it going today?"

"S'posed to get a heck of a storm tonight, couple inches of rain." Bernard said, "Hey, what is Carl planting between his house and the road?"

"Who knows what that knucklehead dreamt up? I've been trying to figure it out." Elton shook his head.

"Well Kid, heard your buddies were still sacked out when I left the house. I checked on the home place. Quiet and secure. I imagine they'll be out later today. Keep your cool and lay low. Hear?"

Kid's eyes met Elton's, and Elton replied, "Kid and I had a long talk. He's good. As soon as I get a few things cleared up at work, I'll be home. I think before noon."

"Okay, then. Everyone's on top of this," then he shook Kid's hand. "God speed, Harold."

Kid mumbled a thank-you. Then the Sheriff asked, "What you doing today?"

"I'm going to help the boys at the appliance shop or fix the rabbit cage."

"Good idea. Keep busy. I'll let you know when I hear anything."

Kid was a basket case, but decided to go check on the rabbits. CJ did talk to Kitten, so she wanted to go along with him to check on Buck Fifty. Nora gave her approval but told him to be sure to get her back up to the house shortly. She reminded him that Marty would be over before long, so he would be in the house with Grandpa and Grandma. He was going to be around all morning, and Nora thought that Kid should get outside for a time to blow off some steam.

At the pen, Kitten played with Buck Fifty while Kid fiddled around with the door. He wanted to be able to let the rabbits get some of the fresh air. After putting the big rabbit back in a couple times, he and Kitten finally waved good bye to the bunnies and went back to the house.

When they got to the house, Nora said that Bernard had called. The bikers were on the move. Kid tried not to think of it, but it was driving him crazy. Grandma took him by the arm, "Kid, go down and help the boys. It'll get your mind off this. You'll drive yourself bonkers if you don't. We can call down there as soon as we hear anything. Promise."

Kid shrugged, "I guess I might as well."

He felt better after Andy gave him a seat and Jackson put a toaster oven in front of him. "The lady said it doesn't work."

"You don't say? The switch is twisted completely off!" Kid chuckled. "How strong was this lady?"

"I think she wrestled with Gorgeous George."

The young men worked over an hour when the phone rang and it was Nora. "Bernard called to say the bikers are at a local bar asking a lot of questions. They're still there."

Kid said thanks and then went to the bathroom to throw up. Somehow, he hadn't figured this is how his last day would be. He didn't know how it should be, but putting together a toaster oven didn't seem like the thing he'd be doing. The young men understood how he might be feeling, and when he came out of the restroom, they had moved the appliances back. They had some coffee and a cup of hot water with a teabag in it for Kid. He looked at them, "I bet you think I deserve every minute of this, huh?"

Andy patted his back, "Nope."

The men visited about their time in Vietnam and their mutual disdain for high humidity and slithery reptiles. Of course, Andy had to rant about mosquitoes, the bane of his existence. The phone rang again, and Andy answered it. "I'll tell him, Mom."

Andy hung up and relayed the information, "Mom has to go pick up Clarissa from school. Grandpa, Grandma, and Kitten are at the house, but Marty is with them. Bernard called. The bikers just left the bar. Some drunk gave them the directions to the home place and this place. Seems the drunk told them that Dad had rented the farm for years and was known for taking in 'strays', as he put it. The sheriff will be heading out of town in a few minutes. He called Dad and Carl."

The men heard Nora's car pull out of the yard and watched from the window in the side door of the garage as she turned onto the road. Without a word, Andy went to the cupboard and took down a couple hunting rifles and put them on the workbench. Then he handed a couple boxes of shells to Jackson. Without a word, the three men loaded the rifles.

They thought they heard a large thump by the rabbit cage, but then heard the dogs barking. They decided it was the just the dogs antagonizing the rabbits.

Time was dragging and Kid's head was about to explode. It reminded Kid of right before a battle in Vietnam. That dreaded lull before all hell broke loose. He kept exercising his trembling hands to make certain his free one worked.

"Maybe one of you should go to the house." Kid suggested. "I don't like them being up there without protection."

"Marty's there and he is a good shot. He has a rifle. Don't worry." Andy looked out the window, "Let me see what I can see down the road."

Just as he said that, the silence was shattered by the sounds of the loud pipes of two Harleys. The choppers barreled into the yard. Kid's heart stopped and he said, "I'm just going out there. To hell with this."

"I was sworn to keep you here until Elton says different," Jackson glared. "And I will."

The bikers tore around the farmyard in circles, revving their engines, and spraying gravel all over the yard. After a few laps, the biggest brute, with a reddish beard and ruddy complexion, yelled at the house, "Harold Effan? Geraldo, you chicken-shit bastard! Get your ass out here before we burn this place to the ground! It's your day of reckoning!"

Kid shook his head no and reached for the door, "I'm going out."

"I'll knock you on your ass," Andy snapped. "Stand back!"

Then they saw it. The big black rabbit hopped obliviously out into the middle of the yard. The bikers laughed and Geist charged at it with his bike, just barely missing it. They were playing a rodeo of sorts, torturing the poor creature.

While the guys in the shop were all worried about Buck Fifty, none of the them were prepared for what they saw next. Kitten ran down the ramp from the house toward the rabbit. Jackson's face hardened as he trained his rifle on the bikers. Andy warned, "Don't! Jackson, Bernard said only if it is life threatening!"

"Easy for him to say. She's my sister!"

Andy stood in front of the side door to block Kid's exit and called the house. The line was busy, so he figured that Grandma had called the sheriff. Kid said, "I'm going out there!"

"We already have one too many out there!"

Though Geist had been tormenting the rabbit, Kitten seemed a more lucrative target. He got off his bike and grabbed the little girl around her waist with one arm. He took out his switchblade and held the knife to her neck. Haskell bellowed, "Gonna let a little kid die for you, Geraldo? Come out like a man. Take your whipping and we might let her go! If you don't, she's dead and this farm is ashes!"

Kid's brain was inflamed. He pushed Andy aside and walked out into the yard, "Let her go, Geist. Put the girl down! She has no part of this fight. Let her go!"

Geist still held the girl, but Haskell laughed, "You dipshit! Look Geist, he just came from the barber! You look like a real citizen, ready to meet the undertaker! Too bad you are going to get all messed up!"

"Let her go!" Kid slowed his walk. "Now!"

"What you going to do about it?" Haskell taunted as Geist laughed.

Just then, the two veterans from the shop came out with their rifles aimed, as three cars pulled in from Kevin's place. There were other cars coming from across the road at Carl's and the sound of police sirens coming down the gravel road.

The bikers recoiled and looked at each other, evaluating the situation. "Should I do her?" Geist asked as he shook the girl.

"Not now, you crazy bastard! Drop her and let's get the hell out of here." Haskell shouted as he charged toward Kid on his bike, with his tire iron raised.

Jackson shot the tire iron out of his hand, but Haskell still charged Kid, knocking him to the dirt. He ran over the side of his foot and took off out of the yard. He screamed his threat, "This isn't over. Next time, you're dead!"

Geist threw Kitten as hard as he could on the gravel and tore out after him. The cars and the Sheriff let them pass through the ditch and onto the road heading east, without giving chase.

Kid tried to stand, but couldn't so he pulled himself over to Kitten. She was terrified and crying but only had skinned knees and arms. Grandma came out of the house, in tears, "Marty was trying to control Grandpa and I tried to stop her! She saw the rabbit while I was on the phone to the sheriff!"

"It wasn't your fault, Grandma," Jackson hugged her. "How is she?"

Kid answered, "I think my girl is okay, huh? Will you be okay, Kitten?"

She clung to Kid, "Bad man make Kitten cry. Bunny?"

Andy brought the big old rabbit up to her, "He's okay, Kitten. He is scared and dirty, but he's okay. I'll hold him until he calms down and then put him back in his pen. Want to pet him?"

She nodded, and Andy held the traumatized rabbit so the little girl could hug him. "Be good, bunny."

By then, Kevin had arrived and carried the little girl to the house. Kid got up with the help of Carl and Elton and followed into the house. Nora and Clarissa arrived home, luckily having missed the fiasco. Marty checked Kid's bruised ankle, and wrapped it. He assured him it wasn't broken, but would give him trouble for a day or so.

After a few minutes, some of the men went back to work. Bernard, of course, had some of his precious paperwork to fill out. Kid answered questions and then went to see Kitten, after the ladies had finished cleaning her scratches and Marty put bandages on them.

He went into her room and she was on her little bed, whimpering. "Hi, Kitten," Kid said as he sat down beside her. "How's my girl?"

"I scared, Kid. Can you make the bad men go?" She pleaded as she crawled into his lap.

"Yes, I promise you. They won't bother you ever again. Would you like me to rock you for a little bit?"

"Okay," Kitten said as she crawled his lap and took his hand.

Together, they went to his room and she stood by his rocker, waiting for him to sit down. When he sat down, he helped her on his lap, and they rocked. It was a short while later, when Nora peeked in and whispered, "She's almost asleep."

He nodded and continued to rock. After she was asleep, he carried her back to her room and put her on her bed. The rough enforcer of an outlaw biker club gently covered the little girl with her favorite afghan and kissed her cheek. "I promise. They won't bother you anymore."

He went quietly down the hall and out the back door of the house. It was easy to do because everyone was talking in the kitchen. He sneaked around the back to the outhouse and down behind the workshop. He grabbed one of the hunting rifles and a handful of shells. Then he went to the pole barn. There, he pulled himself on Andy's horse, Wind. He took the back way to the creek and then to the far end of the pasture. When he got up by the big rock, he looked back at the place he now called home. No matter how things ended, those bastards would not bother his new family anymore.

As he came over the final rise from the pasture to the old home place, he saw the two bikers. They were parked on the edge of the gravel road, on top of a hill to the south, watching the old place and having a cigarette or joint; licking their wounds. He knew they saw him, and he didn't care.

They would return to the home place. This time, it wouldn't be vacant. He rode Wind to the edge of the pasture before he sent him back home. He climbed the fence and limped over to the old house, from the back. He went into the house and looked around the kitchen. There he made his preparations.

He didn't have a long wait, but wished he had brought something to drink. He would've loved to have a beer, but even tea sounded good. He thought about his terrified little sentry. Those vicious, despicable swine! How could they be so cruel to a little kid? For once in his pathetic life, he was going to take a stand. He really didn't care how it ended for him! The only ending he wanted was for them to be gone.

While he was waiting there, to shoot someone, he was praying. He stopped and had to laugh. "What the hell business is this anyway? Why do people pray before they think they are going to kill someone? I bet you are a heavy drinker, huh, God? I know I'd be if I had to deal with all us idiots!"

He spent the rest of his time mumbling to himself, until he heard the motorcycles come up toward the house. Kid stood up and braced his rifle against the window frame. Everything else was quiet. Dead silence, except the beat of his heart and the rumble of the biker's hogs.

The bikers got off their bikes. Kid aimed carefully and took the first shot. The bullet went high, but the bikers both took cover. They got their handguns and started shooting back.

The volley of fire went back and forth for a couple minutes. No one was shot. Kid reloaded and couldn't help himself but to take one last aimed shot at Geist. He said aloud, "This is for Kitten."

He shot Geist in the arm, which invited a flurry of fire in return.

The bikers heard Kid scream and gunfire from the house ceased. Geist unloaded his firearm at the propane tank on the side of the house. A couple seconds or so later, it exploded. The bikers saw the flames burst rapidly in the kitchen area. Haskell looked up from where he was tying off Geist's bleeding arm and said, "We got the piece of shit and you got your fire. Now, let's get the hell out of here!"

The old shack was quickly consumed in flames and the dilapidated roof fell in within minutes. There was no sound or movement from the house. The bikers knew there was no back door, since they had been by it earlier. They had gone there from the bar and finding no one, went back to Schroeders.

As the house was engulfed and the fire was spreading over the dead grasses around the building, Haskell let out a war hoop of victory. The two outlaws headed down the road to the south. There, they stopped on top of a hill to see if there was a slim chance Kid had gotten out of the house. There was no movement. The two were overjoyed as they saw the Sheriff escorting the Rural Fire Department toward the place from the other direction. "Damned fool hicks," Haskell proclaimed. "Let's get out of here before they start looking for us!"

By this time at the Schroeder farm, everyone realized that Kid was gone. No one was surprised when Bernard's radio went off and said there was trouble at the old Effan place. Then, there was a report of a fire. Elton and the other men went to help fight the fire, so it wouldn't spread into a prairie fire.

Margie brought Savannah out to Schroeder's so she could take turns wringing her hands with the rest of them. Everyone was worried and fear hung over them. The kids got home from school, and were very anxious. They were worried about the fire and Kid. The little boys were also disappointed they had missed all the excitement.

Savannah and Diane went with the little boys to check out Buck Fifty. They petted him while he was 'resting'. CJ scolded him, "You were a naughty rabbit. You should never sneak out again. Mr. Kid had to save you."

Then he started to cry, and Savannah took him in her arms. "Be strong, CJ. K-kid wants that."

"Do you think he's okay, Savvy?"

"I don't know, CJ. He wants us all s-safe."

It was still out and the sky to the east was blue with a few fluffy, white clouds. To the south, the beautiful sky was marred by a huge plume of ugly, acrid smoke. Everyone kept an eye on it. The little boys thought that they should go fight the fire, but Marly and Nora put the kibosh on that. "We don't know what those bikers are up to, so you're not going over there. The men don't need to have to watch out for you. They're busy enough. If you want to help, just settle down. I brought some soup, so sit down and eat," Marly ordered. "We'll hear, soon enough."

After eating, they all went out and sat on the patio, waiting for the men to return. While the smoke was dissipating, the black clouds were beginning to roll in from the west. There was lightning and thunder off in the distance. Sheets of rain were following behind the dark clouds. The rain was about half an hour off.

It was late afternoon, when Bernard drove in and some of the men came back from the fire. They were all covered in soot and ash, but safe. Everyone was in the front yard to hear the news. "The house is gone, and most of the outbuildings, but the fire is out."

Nora told them to come inside and have some soup.

CJ took Diane's hand and whispered to her, "I didn't see Kid. Did you?"

"No, but I haven't s-seen Elton, either."

"Did you get the bikers?" Margie asked, as she put the buns on the table.

"No. They're gone." Bernard said, "They evaporated before we got there, probably half way to Montana by now."

"How's Kid?" Grandma asked.

"You got some coffee?"

"Sure," Nora answered, "A fresh pot. Is Elton coming?"

"He'll be along."

-36-

Nora and Savannah were both watching the turnoff into the yard anxiously. The sky was darkening and the stillness had given way to a chilly breeze. Finally, the old blue pickup turned into the farmyard. Nora and Savannah led the pack of folks to the yard. The pickup doors opened and Elton helped the passenger from the seat. Barely recognizable because of his cover of coal dust, Harold Effan limped along beside him.

Savannah took one look and ran to him. He looked up at her and broke into a huge grin. Then they embraced. She put her arms around his neck as he buried his head in her shoulder. She whispered, "I was so worried."

"It's over now, Savannah. The good Lord has given me a second chance. Now, we can try to build that life."

"Okay. Are you safe?"

"I'm fine." Then he stood tall and teased, "You have soot on your face."

She giggled, "Think so?"

Nora came over as Kitten ran over to the young man. "Kid, Kid! You okay?"

He knelt down to her, "I'm fine, Sweetheart. I'm just fine."

She narrowed her eyes, "Grandma say you doirty."

He laughed, "I am. Think I should wash up?"

"Okay, be better." Kitten giggled, "Savvy doirty, too."

"Do you want to give me a hug, Kitten?"

She studied him, "No. Doirty."

He laughed, "Very wise."

"I'm so relieved to see you," Nora said as she hugged him. "Elton said the worry is past. Thank God."

It started to sprinkle, so everyone went inside. When they had moved halfway up the steps, the sky opened to drench the earth. Once in the door, after several greetings, Kid went to wash up and change clothes. When he came out to the kitchen, some of the men had left for their homes to do their evening chores. The young folks at Schroeder's went out to do chores, while Elton and Kid sat down to eat. Carl poured Bernard another cup of coffee and sat across from them. Byron looked at the two and said, "We know you two are hiding something. So, what do you have to tell us?"

"We came on the idea last night while having tea." Elton explained, "Kid said that Geist was a pyromaniac. We wanted to get rid of those guys and have them quit looking for Kid, so we thought we'd give them what they wanted. I went over to the home place early this morning, and drenched the inside walls with gasoline. Our plan was that I'd take Kid over there after I got home about noon. We didn't think they'd be out here that early or come to this place."

"When were you planning on sharing this tidy bit of information with me?" Bernard blustered. "I'd have told you it was too dangerous."

Elton looked at him and said flatly, "That's why we didn't tell you."

"Who in hell thought it would be a good idea to have a gunfight in a room soaked with gasoline?" Carl roared. "That is the most totally embecilic, asinine, moronic idea ever concocted!"

"All that, huh?" Elton chuckled. "And what was your grand idea to get them off our back? You never said anything more than hiding and giving them the runaround. That wouldn't have lasted more than a day before someone was dead or someplace was burned to the ground!"

Kid started to explain the plan, "The idea was that they'd come to the yard over there and I'd let them know I was in the house. I needed to start shooting before they came inside. I knew how much Geist loved fires, so I thought if he thought I was shot and burned in the fire, he'd leave us alone."

"How did you get out of there?"

"I crawled down into the cellar and out the coal chute. Ran into problems there though, because I forgot about my cast and hadn't planned on hurting my foot. I got stuck in the chute and had to tear part of the cast apart to get through. I really thought I was a goner there for a bit. I also hadn't planned on Geist shooting at the propane tank. That explosion cut my escape time by half. Heat is a hell of an incentive for crawling out through a hole, though!"

"Do you have any idea how many things could have gone wrong? That plan was shaky at best. Very risky." Bernard groaned, "I would've never approved it."

"Me, either," Carl concurred.

"We knew that," Elton responded matter-of-factly.

"Look, I've never stood up for anything in my life, but I wasn't about to let those slimes mess up this family! I wouldn't let that happen," Kid said defiantly. "I couldn't have allowed myself to live if something happened to one of these guys because of me. I'd rather be dead."

"You almost were. I could just wring your neck for taking such a chance," Bernard glared back. "Let's just hope it worked. I hope they get back and tell Scab it's over."

"I think they got away, uh?" Kid asked. "I was a bit occupied and couldn't tell when they left. I hoped they'd think I died in the flames. Hell, I almost did!

"I tell you, I was sick when I got to the farm and couldn't find you out back. I was afraid you were overcome with smoke," Elton shook his head. "I was never so glad to hear someone cough as I was when I found you stuck in the end of that chute behind the house."

"You sure took your sweet time getting to me. I was unconscious for a while, I think."

"Well, they were gone when we got there. I imagine they're on their way back to California. I'll call that warden and have him start monitoring calls to Scab. They will want to let him know they succeeded." Bernard groaned.

"Did you plan on having a gunfight with them?" Carl asked pointedly.

"Yes, but I wanted them to get away, so they could report back to Scab. I aimed over their heads."

Bernard eyes penetrated Kid, "Like hell. You winged one of them. There was blood on the ground. I suppose you missed, huh? My guess is you missed the one that held the knife to Kitten's throat. Am I right?"

Kid dropped his eyes and thought a minute. Then he replied, "Yah, I couldn't aim very well with this cast, you know. Are you going to arrest me?"

Bernard snorted, "Don't know why I would. Stupidity is not a crime. They were trespassing and you probably yelled to tell them to leave. Right? You were protecting yourself. That's well within your rights."

Kid sighed in relief, and Bernard groaned, "I really hope this is the end of your bucking every rule and regulation. Now that it looks like you'll be lurking around my niece, I don't want to have to explain anything to my brother. I told him how she needed to come out here where it was safe and peaceful. Maybe she could meet some fine, young men, like these guys out here. If he knew what these last couple weeks were like, he'd skin me alive! Harold, I just want to grow old living a peaceful, contented life without having to do too much paperwork. Got that?"

"I understand," Kid put his hand on Bernard's shoulder. "You may not believe this, but that's what I want, too. More than anything."

Byron smiled, "And he has me and Elton to keep him on the right track."

"You might be helpful," Carl burst, "But Magpie here, needs his own keeper! I never thought you were very bright Schroeder, but this was one of the dumbest things you ever did!"

"No it wasn't. I've done a lot—ah! Never mind," Elton blustered.

"Poor Nora," Bernard chuckled.

"I used to feel sorry for her, until I lived here. She's as bad as he is." Carl grumbled.

That night the house was quiet with only the sound of rain and an occasional rumble of thunder. Everyone slept peacefully, and they all needed it. The next morning, the sun came out between the rain clouds about ten. By afternoon, the warmth of the sun was drying off the yard.

The next few days were good. Tuesday, Zach had Elton bring Kid in to replace his cast. Not only was it filthy, but it was smashed and crumbled. Zach shook his head, "I have never seen a cast look so bad in such a short time! But good news, we can shorten it and you need only wear a brace on your wrist."

Darrell gave Carl some directions on seeding, but then Carl insisted on seeding the patch in front of his house himself. Neither Jeff nor Darrell was able to discover what his secret crop was, even though they helped him cover the patch with yards of clear plastic. Maureen was even recruited, but she said he wouldn't even tell her what the crop was!

Wednesday, Jeff drove Grandma and Kid over to plant a begonia in the small patch beside Matt's front door, while Matt was teaching. No one saw them do it. The lumber store in Bismarck delivered the greenhouse kits to the farm in the afternoon. Elton and Kevin made plans to pour the foundation for the greenhouse over by the garden. Jeff, Kid, and the veterans looked over the kit and tried to figure out the instructions.

Thursday evening, Josh and Joallyn picked up Kid and took him to an AA meeting in Bismarck. He didn't think he should go, but Josh pointed out the threat was lifted now. Kid wasn't thrilled, but did feel better after the meeting. He was especially glad when Josh said he'd be his sponsor. He had to admit, he was beginning to think more and more about not so much getting high as getting drunk. Even though he really wanted a beer, he was relieved when Zach said he could start drinking more coffee in his milk and promised that in a couple weeks, he could have cola from time to time.

Friday, Jeff asked Kid and Savannah to a James Bond movie in Bismarck with him. Jeff drove and the three had a good time. They followed Elton's recommendation and ate at the Log House before they went home. Jeff was getting anxious for his girlfriend to come out for Matt's wedding, now only a few weeks away.

Saturday morning, Bernard came out while they were at the barn. "Hi, thought I would drive out and tell you the news. The warden called. They listened in on a call from Haskell to Scab. He said the pencil was erased. Then he laughed about this huge fire they saw while an old farm burned. Scab was delighted. So, you bonehead's pulled it off. I imagine those boys will sleep soundly every night knowing they completed their assignments. Even though it was more luck than brains, I'm so glad it worked out. Well, I gotta run. I guess Margie thinks I wanted to take her and Savannah shopping in Bismarck today. I don't remember saying that, but I must talk in my sleep. See yah."

Kid and Elton stood outside the barn and watched Bernard pull out of the yard. Then Elton put his arm over Kid's shoulder, "Well, now all that's left is living the rest of your life!"

Kid gave him a hug, "I don't care what the rest of them say, it still was a darned good idea."

"I agree, it was at that."